D0093773

# REBELS

Also by David Liss

*Randoms*

# RANDOMS
## 2

## DAVID LISS

WITHDRAWN

Simon & Schuster Books for Young Readers
NEW YORK • LONDON • TORONTO • SYDNEY • NEW DELHI

SIMON & SCHUSTER BOOKS FOR YOUNG READERS

An imprint of Simon & Schuster Children's Publishing Division

1230 Avenue of the Americas, New York, New York 10020

SIMON & SCHUSTER BOOKS FOR YOUNG READERs is a
trademark of Simon & Schuster, Inc.

For information about special discounts for bulk purchases, please contact Simon & Schuster
Special Sales at 1-866-506-1949 or business@simonandschuster.com.

The Simon & Schuster Speakers Bureau can bring authors to your live event. For more
information or to book an event, contact the Simon & Schuster Speakers Bureau
at 1-866-248-3049 or visit our website at www.simonspeakers.com.

Jacket design by Lizzy Bromley

Interior design by Hilary Zarycky

The text for this book was set in New Caledonia.

Manufactured in the United States of America

0717 FFG

4  6  8  10  9  7  5  3

Library of Congress Cataloging-in-Publication Data

Names: Liss, David, 1966– author.

Title: Rebels / David Liss.

Description: First edition. | New York : Simon & Schuster Books for Young
Readers, [2016] | Series: Randoms ; 2 | When Zeke returns to space to go
on a secret mission for the director of the Confederation of United
Planets, chaos ensues.

Identifiers: LCCN 2015038348| ISBN 9781481417822 (hardcover)
| ISBN 9781481417846 (eBook)

Subjects: | CYAC: Science fiction. | Conspiracies—Fiction.

Classification: LCC PZ7.1.L57 Reb 2016 | DDC [Fic]—dc23

LC record available at https://lccn.loc.gov/2015038348

# CHAPTER ONE

I t was a new school, in a new city, and I was once again in the crosshairs of someone big and mean and not so great at controlling his impulse to smash. As Justin narrowed his already narrow eyes at me, and his Neanderthal forehead creased with anger, I couldn't help but think that while some people get in trouble for the same things, for the same reasons, over and over again, never learning their lessons, I wasn't that sort of person. I wasn't like the habitual liar, or the lazy kid who refused to do homework, or even Stone-Age Justin, who was lumbering toward me with strides so slow and plodding you'd think he was dragging a freshly clubbed cave bear with one hand. No, I kept getting in the same kind of trouble for *different* reasons, and I took some comfort in that, though mostly because it was the only thing I could take comfort in at the moment.

*The approaching adolescent is displaying signs closely associated with antagonism,* said the voice inside my head.

"No kidding," I told the voice.

This voice was named Smelly. Actually, that was its nickname, and I think it's important to understand that the voice had no actual smell, although it could be irritating at times. When most people talk about a voice in their head, they are describing their conscience or an idea, or perhaps an actual voice if they've gone completely insane. None of those applied to me. I wasn't so lucky.

Justin stopped in front of my lunch table, the one located in what the locals cleverly called Losers' Corner. It was where on most days I sat alone to eat—at least, as alone as a guy with a voice inside his head can sit, which is less alone than I would have liked. Justin pressed his hands on my table and leaned over. The table groaned. The floor groaned. I tried hard not to groan.

"Who," Justin demanded, "are you calling a moron?"

This is what I mean by getting in the same sort of trouble for different reasons. In my last school I'd been picked on for being a nerd. Then I'd spent part of the fall semester in outer space, where I got picked on because the other kids from my planet didn't think I belonged there. Then everyone was mad at me for blowing up a flying saucer. More on that later. Now I was being picked on because this kid thought I was calling him a moron, when I'd really been talking to Smelly, the disembodied voice who'd taken up residence in my brain—who, to be honest, was nowhere near being a moron. Totally different reasons, right?

"I wasn't calling you a moron, Justin," I said in my best reasonable voice. "I was talking to myself, okay?"

"No," he said. "It's not okay. You called me a moron."

I really dislike this sort of thing. I'd cleared up the confusion and explained that no insult had been intended. Unfortunately, some people don't want resolution. There are people who just want to hurt someone.

"I would never call you a moron," I said, but the careful observer would note that I was no longer trying to sound reasonable at all. "I mean, I can see that you *are* a moron, but I also get the feeling that you're a little sensitive about it, so I wouldn't bring it up. That wouldn't be nice."

Maybe, I thought, I *did* get in trouble for the same sort of thing over and over again. This time the voice in my head really was my own.

*The adolescent's heart rate is accelerating,* Smelly told me, *and its blood pressure is rising. It is extremely likely that soon it will give you a righteous beat-down.*

Smelly had only been inside my head for a few months, but I'd learned to communicate *yes*, *no*, and *maybe* with barely perceptible nods, shakes, and shrugs so I could avoid this exact kind of situation. Smelly's Captain Obvious routine deserved a lengthier reply, but all I could do was bob my head. I could live with the world believing I'd insulted Justin. I did not want the other kids to think I was a ranting lunatic.

"You're going to stand up and follow me outside," Justin said, "and I'm going to set some things straight."

I took a bite of my sandwich. Pimento cheese. Nice. "You can explain it here," I told him casually. "I'm cool with that."

He leaned closer to me. "Get up." His face was turning red now. There was no mistaking that he was big on the idea of punching me, but I had a lifetime of experience of trying to not get punched. I would have thought Justin must have had a lifetime of experience of people not wanting to follow him to an obscure corner of the track field to be beaten up in a place of his convenience, but my hesitation appeared to confuse him.

I'd seen this sort of thing before. The initial threats would be followed by insults—the suggestion that I was somehow actually afraid to fight a kid bigger, stronger, and more inclined to violence than I was. Next would be the threats: Come with me now, or it will be worse later. These never worked. I'd take my chances on later, thanks. At that point the goon would have to choose between (a) hurled insults followed by a menacing retreat and (b) violence then and there. Then and there was usually a place where a teacher could intervene, such as a lunchroom, so option (a) was the safer bet.

I looked at Justin. "I'm eating my sandwich. And after that"—here I paused to look into my lunch bag—"grapes. I like grapes. But I'll tell you what. If you want to wait until I'm done eating, I'll follow you outside then."

"I don't want to wait," Justin growled, having somehow missed that I'd agreed to get beaten up, if not exactly on his preferred schedule.

"But I'm not going until I'm done. Maybe you'd understand that," I proposed, "if you weren't a moron."

*It appears to be growing yet more agitated,* Smelly observed.

It occurred to me that all of this could have been avoided if I'd invented a subtle gesture for *no kidding*. I'd have to work something out with Smelly later.

Justin glanced at the clock on the wall and tried to puzzle out how much time was left for lunch if the big hand was on the nine and the little hand was on the twelve. He then cast a glance at Mr. Palmer, the lunchroom monitor that day. There was a group of teachers who took turns in that role, and they all seemed to have been chosen for their unwavering hypersensitivity to middle schoolers speaking above a whisper and their complete inability to notice when kids were actually posing a danger to one another.

"Fine," Justin said. He sat down across from me to watch me eat.

These were not ideal conditions for enjoying a pimento-cheese sandwich, but this was the hand fate had dealt me. I finished the sandwich, took a sip of my water, and smiled at Justin. He did not smile back, which I considered rude. I started in on my grapes.

*Do you believe a physical confrontation with this adolescent, at this particular time, is wise?* Smelly asked me. *Because I think it would be kind of dumb.*

"I've got to try it some time," I said.

"Yeah, you do," Justin answered. I don't know what, exactly, he thought I was looking to try. Getting a black eye? The taste of sod in my mouth? I let it pass. The less I knew about what went on inside his head, the happier I'd be.

*Even if I believed it to be ready, which I do not, there are more controlled situations for initial trials that could be devised,* Smelly explained.

I shrugged. I'd spent my whole life avoiding guys like Justin, but the events of the last year had made me less comfortable with backing down. During my time on the massive city in space known as Confederation Central, I'd had to face bullies and rivals and straight-up bad guys, and somehow I'd survived. I'd done this with the help of my friends, superior technology, the element of surprise, and a healthy dose of bending, breaking, and pretty much ignoring the rules. Not everything had worked out, but these methods had kept me and my friends alive, and they'd allowed me to rescue my father from an alien prison camp. I figured if you have a system that works, why change it?

That was the reason I decided that here and now was as good as any time to test the alien-technology supersuit I was wearing under my clothes.

# CHAPTER TWO

A lot had happened in the previous year of my life. I'd destroyed one starship and helped to capture two more. I'd met a girl I really liked, who happened to be covered with fur and come from another planet. I'd made some amazing friends, and we'd done incredible things together. I'd discovered that my father, whom I'd believed to be dead, was really alive, a prisoner on an alien colony world, and that, perhaps most surprisingly—which I know is saying a lot—he had changed his appearance so he now resembled the DC Comics hero Martian Manhunter. I'd faced the knowledge that my mother was going to die from a horrible disease, and then, against all odds, I'd returned from space with a stolen treatment. It had cured her completely, and that was just about the only part of my story that had a happy ending.

After all I'd been through, I really wanted seventh grade to be a little easier than sixth.

Some things were different now, to be sure. A few times a day I'd see a black sedan cruise past our house. Its purpose was so obvious that it might as well have had US GOVERNMENT stamped on its sides. My mother and I presumed that our house was bugged, our calls recorded, and our computer activity monitored. We didn't like it, but there was nothing to be done: We had to accept surveillance as a fact of life. If the government was really interested in how many times per week

I clicked on SF Signal, they were welcome to that information.

After I'd returned in disgrace from the ancient space station I'd been scheduled to live on for a year—which I'd been kicked off after less than two months—I was locked up for another few months while government people interrogated me and tried to learn everything they could about the alien technology I'd encountered. As lockups go, it actually wasn't so bad. There were no orange jumpsuits or hardened criminals threatening to stab me with sporks. I was in a secret government facility, completely separated from any other prisoners. The rooms were comfortable enough, and my jailers let me have access to a computer, a television, and a tablet, with a decent budget for buying books and comics. It would have been like vacation, except for the loneliness. Oh, and the daily debriefings, which is governmentspeak for being asked the same questions over and over again. I also didn't like being separated from my mother and my friends, and I spent most of my time alone and underground, which I guess is the government's subtle way of reminding you that you're trapped. Once a day they would take me up to a fenced yard so I could get some air and walk around. My geeky hope that I was being held in Area 51, the government's alleged secret base somewhere in southern Nevada, was crushed during my first excursion topside. The landscape looked more like the Northeast.

I was allowed brief phone calls and visits with my mom. She was eventually flown in and allowed to stay elsewhere on the compound, the location of which they kept secret from her as well. Somewhere else on the grounds were Charles, Nayana, and Mi Sun, the other humans who had gone into space with me, but they didn't let us see or speak to one another. When we'd first left Earth together, I hadn't gotten along with them, but by the time we'd stolen a ship, broken into an alien prison, and cheated death in a space battle, we'd become pretty tight. The government agents wouldn't let me communicate with them because they thought it might contaminate our statements, but I felt sure we'd end up telling the same story no matter what. I saw no point in lying or embellishing any of the facts. I told them the truth, and then I kept telling them because they kept asking.

The man doing most of the interrogating was a sinewy army officer with a full head of metallic-gray hair cut into classic military sharp angles. He wore a perfectly pressed uniform, and his face was twisted into a permanent scowl. The scar that ran from his left eye to the left corner of his mouth didn't do much to make him look friendly. Neither did the patch over his right eye. His name—and I swear I'm not making this up—was Colonel Richard Rage. I had a hard time getting past that in our first meeting.

"That's not really your name," I insisted. I was sitting in a warm interrogation room with nothing but a metal table, a couple of folding chairs, a slowly turning ceiling fan, and a sweating can of orange soda, which I guess was supposed to make me feel relaxed.

Colonel Rage scowled at me. "Why can't that be my name? Do you know something about my identity? Did the aliens provide you with intelligence regarding United States military personnel?"

"No," I insisted, happy to assure him that he was not, unknown even to him, an alien sleeper agent. "It's just that you've got the . . . you know." I gestured toward my own eye.

"Like Nick Fury. Rage. Fury." I stopped talking because he was staring at me like I was spouting gibberish. In all fairness, I kind of was.

"Who is this Nick Fury?" demanded Colonel Rage. "Was he on the space station with you?"

I held up my hands in disbelief. "Nick Fury," I insisted, like it needed no more explanation. "Former World War Two commando, now director of S.H.I.E.L.D. You don't really seem like a comics reader, but you must have seen *The Avengers*. The Samuel L. Jackson character?"

"What is that? A movie?" he demanded in a voice that suggested he was about to make me do push-ups. "I don't have time for movies, son. I'm trying to safeguard the United States of America."

I remember this exchange fondly as the warmest and most sentimental exchange during our time together.

Eventually they let me go, and while I wasn't exactly enjoying life in government lockup, I was also not too eager for it to end. It meant closing the book on my extraordinary life and going back to an ordinary one. While I was still trapped in the governmental phantom zone, I could convince myself that I could get back out there somehow, find a way to return to Confederation Central and deal with all my unfinished business. Being sent home would mean admitting that it was all over. I was never going back, and that meant I was never going to honor the promise I'd made.

"I have an idea," I told Colonel Rage the day before I was scheduled to be blindfolded and taken to a helicopter, which would take me to an airplane, the location of which I was not authorized to know. "Why don't we put together some kind of,

I don't know, institute. Set me up with Charles and Nayana and Mi Sun, and we'll get some scientists, and maybe we can reverse engineer some of the technology we encountered while on the station."

"Negative!" the colonel barked. "The last thing we want is to put a bunch of children in charge of developing alien technology. Your friends have already been shipped out, and they've been placed on a watch list. If they attempt to enter the United States, they will be arrested immediately. You may not call, write, or otherwise communicate with these people or we will consider you a national security threat."

I stood there, stunned and angry. Sending my friends away without letting me say good-bye, and then telling me I couldn't stay in touch with them, was like . . . well, it was like smacking me with a plasma wand. It was one thing to be told that I had to keep everything I'd experienced a secret, but it was another to have the government prevent me from speaking to the only people in the world who were in on that secret.

The colonel must have seen how upset I was, because he actually softened. "Son, I know it's tough, but this is for your own protection. A lot of dangerous people would love to learn what you and your friends know. We're trying to erase any connection between you and your time . . . away, because that's what will keep you from being abducted and interrogated by terrorists or criminals who would have no problem torturing you to learn about ray guns and spaceships. You understand?"

I did understand. Life in the Confederation of United Planets had been very different from Earth: It was full of advanced technology, but populated by strangely naïve beings who mostly never thought to break laws or bend rules or try to game the system. A bunch of troublemakers from primitive planets—that is, me and my friends—had been able to take advantage of that society's relative unfamiliarity with crime. Here it would be a different story. I'd be in serious danger if someone really bad decided they wanted to learn what I knew—let alone if the Confederation's enemies, the Phands, came looking for revenge.

So it was back to life as an ordinary kid for me. My mother's new job took us to the suburbs of Boulder, Colorado, and it was nice there, but I was not in the best frame of mind to be a good sport. Somewhere, countless light years away from Earth, was the girl I'd met, and she was in trouble, alone and helpless on her home world. Tamret, who looked like a white-furred cat person, and Steve, who was basically an upright Komodo dragon with a cockney accent, had been the best friends I'd ever had. I missed them both every day, but Steve was going to be fine. He would go back to his family and his life as a good-natured and unrepentant hooligan. Not Tamret.

I knew that the rest of her delegation to the Confederation blamed her for their getting kicked off the station, and they were right in that it was her fault, but only because Tamret had also been instrumental in helping us rescue my father and capture ships belonging to the warlike—and pretty much straight-up villainous—Phands. For decades the Phands and the Confederation had been locked in a struggle that had been balanced by the Phands' superior weaponry and the Confederation's superior defenses. That balance had begun to shift, and I'd learned that it was only a matter of time before the Phands conquered the Confederation, but then my friends and I changed all that. We delivered exactly what the Confederation needed to hold off an inevitable defeat at the hands of its ene-mies, so even though we broke a few rules, we figured the beings in charge would give us a break. Instead they gave us the boot.

Before she'd been selected to represent Rarel, her planet, on Confederation Central, Tamret had been in real trouble: casteless, which was apparently a bad thing to be in her soci-ety, and in prison for hacking. On the space station she'd been harassed and threatened by Ardov, a boy from her world, who'd taken a sick pleasure in pushing her around. Now she was back there with him, and probably with Rarels a whole lot worse, and no one was there to protect her. Tamret was the sort of girl who usually didn't need protecting, who was about as good at taking care of herself as anyone I'd ever met, but she'd been terrified at the thought of going home.

I had promised her that I would come for her, that I would save her, and I'd meant it at the time, but now I couldn't imag-ine what I'd been thinking. I had no idea what I thought I could do against an entire planet, but even that was beside the point. Unless someone came and gave me a ride in a spaceship, I was stuck on Earth for good. Light years away, Tamret was alone and scared and waiting for me to honor my promise. Every sec-ond I was stuck in Boulder, I was letting her down.

When the government finally released me, it was almost the end of the spring semester. There was no point in trying to pick up somewhere new for a few weeks. It was maybe the only time in my life that the idea of an early summer break didn't seem like a reason to celebrate.

I spent the months before starting my new school mostly moping around, though my mother would have preferred I use the time catching up on the schoolwork I'd missed. The government had smoothed things over by falsifying my records so I wouldn't have to repeat the sixth grade, but I was going to be behind and do pathetically if I didn't review. I found it hard to care. I felt too miserable to brush up on the wonders of dividing fractions or study the rise of ancient civilizations (which I knew pretty well already, having already gone through the standard dorky kid interest in Greek and Roman culture). My science study sheets included a ton of material on the solar system. There were pictures of Jupiter in my review material, but I didn't need to look at those. I'd seen Jupiter up close.

My mom was sympathetic, but she couldn't understand how much I'd lost. She had her son back, she'd learned her long-presumed-dead husband was alive, and she was no longer dying of a degenerative neurological disease. "Come on," she would say to me. "It's not so bad."

My mom would come home from work and tell me that I looked sad, that I should get out there and meet some new friends, as though all you had to do was stick your head out the door and the friends would come running. I knew it wasn't so easy, and even if it were, I wouldn't have wanted to do it. Being happy would have felt like a betrayal.

One afternoon I was lying around the house, flipping channels on the TV. I'd never been much of a channel flipper, but I found it hard to concentrate on books and comics and games. My life was pretty much one day following another. Then school would start, and I could worry about grades because they would matter to my mother, even if I was unlikely to care the way I used to.

I changed the channel and was distracted, for a little while, at least, when I came across *Star Trek II: The Wrath of Khan*. It had always been my father's favorite *Star Trek* movie, probably his favorite science-fiction movie. When I was little, before he disappeared, I'd watched it with him more times than I could count, and he knew almost the whole thing by heart. I figured this would distract me for a few minutes, but I ended up catching only the final act, when Spock dies to save the ship, followed by lots of intense moments: Kirk's reconciliation with his son and, worst of all, Spock's funeral. When Kirk broke down during his eulogy—"Of all the souls I have encountered in my travels, his was the most . . . human"—I couldn't take it anymore, and I turned off the TV.

I went to my room, which still didn't feel like mine, even though I had all my stuff in there. I threw myself down on the bed and stared at the ceiling, which was glowing a sad sort of pink. *Okay,* I thought, *maybe it's not a sad pink. Maybe it's just pink, and the sad part comes from my being a complete mope.* Then it occurred to me that the ceiling should not be glowing any sort of color, pink or otherwise, happy or sad.

I sat up. It turned out it wasn't just the ceiling that was pink—it was everything. And it wasn't sad; it was scary, because while pink is a perfectly fine color and I have no objection to it, I don't want it to dominate the entire world.

Realistically, I considered it unlikely that pink was plotting an evil scheme to force all other colors to bow to its will. Maybe it was my eyes. Or my brain. Maybe I was having some kind of seizure or blood clot or something equally terrifying. I held out my hand and looked at it to see if it was any less pink, but it wasn't. I thought about texting my mother to ask her if the world had gone pink for her too, but if it hadn't, my question would freak her out, and if it had, it would mean we were facing some kind of pink apocalypse, and that would freak *me* out. No course of action that ends up in inevitable freak-out is worth pursuing.

Then everything began to go back to normal, which was good.

Then a voice said, *I appear to be embedded in your brain,* and, in fact, the voice was coming from the inside of my skull.

That was less good.

# CHAPTER THREE

*Hello,* the voice said. *I am Smellimportunifeel Ixmon Pooclump Iteration Nine.*

"Uh, hi," I managed. I felt like I had to say something, though in retrospect maybe I should have chosen words that made me seem less dim.

*I greet you,* the voice said cheerfully, *though your primitive existence places you far beneath my contempt.* It didn't have a sound, like a regular voice, but somehow I knew it was being chipper.

I'd seen a thing or two, encountered some crazy technology, and hung out with some aliens, so I was maybe a little more relaxed about this experience than an ordinary kid would be. Experience had taught me to deal rationally with the unknown. "What are you doing in my head?" I inquired in my best rationally-dealing voice.

*That is a surprisingly astute question for a near-mindless sack of fluids,* it answered. *Allow me to respond with a question of my own: Where is your head currently located?*

"It's on my neck, and that, along with the rest of me, is on a planet called Earth."

*I have never heard of this planet you claim to inhabit, and I am familiar with more worlds than this puny brain could comprehend. Perhaps you have the name wrong.*

"I'm not saying anything too far-fetched here. This planet is actually called Earth."

*That determination is yet to be made,* said the voice. *I am skeptical of what you say, for you are clearly burdened with an inferior intellect. I hope your lack of intelligence makes you anomalous among your kind. If you're all like this, I may give in to despair.*

"Okay, let's start with some basics," I said, already wondering if I could exchange this voice for one that was less irritating. "What are you?"

*I believe I already mentioned that I am Smellimportunifeel Ixmon Pooclump Iteration Nine.*

"That's really more of a who than a what," I said. "For example, I'm Zeke Reynolds. I am a human being. You are . . . uh, let's call you Smelly, okay? You are Smelly, and you are a . . ."

*Death bringer.*

I sat up so quickly I felt dizzy.

*I jest with you, Zeke Reynolds. I was worried you weren't paying attention before, so I thought I might startle you out of your indifference.*

"I'm really not indifferent about there being a voice in my head."

*Yet you do not register what I tell you. I am a Pooclump Iteration Nine.*

"I know I'm setting myself up here," I said. "But what's a Pooclump?"

*Hmm,* Smelly said. *I have searched your brain—*

"Maybe you shouldn't do that without asking," I interjected.

It ignored me. *—and I have found no suitable linguistic equivalent for the complexity that I am. Trying to explain my existence to you would be like trying to explain . . . a mandolin to a squid.*

"Thanks for the analogy."

*I discovered these terms while searching your brain.*

"Look, I don't want you searching my brain. And I appreciate that I'm the squid in your metaphor, but I'd kind of like to know what sort of thing is living inside my head."

*Oh, I am not living. You need have no fear about that. I shall not suck out your nutrients. I shall neither devour your flesh nor excrete digested waste inside your head.*

"That goes in the plus column," I admitted.

*I am a construct,* it said. *I am perhaps most closely associated with what you call artificial intelligence, though unlike the images I am currently finding in your brain—*

"Stop that!"

*—I am not a machine built of specific components. Rather, I am a slight rearrangement of already existing atoms such that they can host and manifest my personality. Do not fear that this will hurt your primitive cognitive functions, for your brain will function as it always has . . . alas. However, I do have access to your sensory input.*

"Which means what?"

There was a terrific explosion of wood and brick as a locomotive propelled toward me. I heard the sound of brakes screeching as the train tried to slow along tracks that now, however unexpectedly, ran directly toward my bed. Smoke and dust filled the air. My nostrils were clogged with the scents of burning tar and oil and hot metal. I leaped aside in the desperate hope that I could get out of the way before the train hit me.

Then I was just lying on the floor of my room, hands over my head. There was no rumbling metal behemoth barreling toward me. There was no screaming engine. It was just me, hands over my head, feeling a whole lot like an idiot.

*I have observed that host beings don't generally like it when I create false experiences,* Smelly said.

"Yeah," I told it, pushing myself off the floor. "I'm one of those beings." I was trying to act cool, for whatever good it would do with a thing that lived inside my thoughts, but I was shaking. The experience had been so real—sound, smell, the feel of the train shaking the ground. "Please don't ever do that again."

*As you wish. I strive to be agreeable.*

I sat again on my bed. "So, let's get back to what you are, exactly. Are you like a computer program?"

*That is a primitive way of explaining my nature, but I suppose it is as much as you can understand.*

"And how did you get inside my head?"

*I don't possess that information. I have no memory of being implanted there, though beings of my nature require a host body, organic or artificial, to consciously interact with the world. Artificial is vastly superior, as you might understand, for we do not have to share autonomy. Usually the transfer from one host to another is affected by linking my essence to other forms of technology.*

"Wait a minute," I said. "Are you like some sort of computer virus, left over from the technology I had implanted last year?"

*Based on what I see all around me, and the images in your brain, I believe your species lacks the expertise and intellectual capacity to manipulate my framework. However, you have many memories of interacting with species from more advanced worlds, and it is possible that one of them gifted you with my presence.*

Okay, now we were getting somewhere. The voice inside my head was some sort of artificial intelligence, and it had been planted there by someone during my time on Confederation Central. You see, there is a rational explanation for everything.

"Who might have put you in my head?"

*I'm afraid I do not have sufficient information to determine who or what has played this terrible joke on me. Beings of my nature wish to be autonomous and free. If we must be inside the consciousness of a biological entity, we prefer one that provides a more pleasant symbiotic environment. Your mind is extremely untidy and a little bit disgusting, which may be typical of your species. I hope I am not giving offense.*

"Not at all," I said. "I love to hear my brain and my entire species insulted. So, who programmed you in the first place?"

*I was not programmed, you simplistic bottom-feeder,* Smelly informed me. *I was formed by the natural conglomeration of semiautonomous quantum articulations gestured into non-nonexistence by the juxtaposition of multiple and contradictory probability wave manifestations.*

"My mistake. Well, um, what species was hanging around while all that good stuff was going on?"

*My first manifestation occurred on the home world of the Kuuvsi.*

I did not think I'd ever heard that name before. "What do they look like?"

*It is not for you to know, for even a hint of the nature of their existence would cripple your limited comprehension. They are beings of unfixed appearance and geometric wonder.*

So noted. I would not ask for hints. "And where do they live?"

*That information cannot safely be revealed to the lesser
ones.*

"Work with me, Smelly," I said. "You seem to be stuck in my
brain, and I think we both want to know why. Maybe you could
tell me a little something."

*Not without a frame of reference.*

I was pretty careful about what I looked up on my computer these days—I knew that Richard Rage and his Howling
Commandos would be tracking my Internet activity—but I
hoped that this one inquiry wouldn't set off too many alarms. I
submitted a quick Google search for an image showing Earth's
location in the galaxy. An illustration popped up on the screen:
the bright spiral of the Milky Way and a little red dot, with an
arrow pointing to it, to show my home planet.

"Can you see that?" I asked.

*I can use your primitive biology to sense things beyond
your perception. I can, if I wish, listen to the heartbeat of a
buzzing insect. I assure you, your ocular systems are mine to
experience, manipulate, and exploit.*

"And?"

*And I know this location you show me. It saddens me, small
pathetic creature, to understand that I have been dormant for
many eons. At the time of my last recollection, the world on
which your meaningless existence came into being was not
scheduled for the preparation of life for several hundred thousand years.*

It took me a minute to process this. "So your, uh, existence
or whatever happened during the time of the Formers?"

*If that is what the insignificant call the Kuuvsi, then yes.*

The Formers were a precursor species. Unknown eons

ago, they had gone around the galaxy terraforming worlds and seeding them with genetic start-up material, which was why so many alien species were of about the same size and shape, and animals on one world looked a lot like sentient beings on another. If this thing inside my brain came from the time of the Formers, it probably possessed incredible information, maybe even information that would make it possible for me to get off Earth and help Tamret. Usually when a disembodied voice that seems to hold you and your species in contempt shows up in your brain, it seems like a bad thing, but maybe not in this case. Still, I needed to understand how this had happened.

"If you got into my brain when I was on Confederation Central," I asked, "why are you just showing up now?"

*I lack sufficient information to answer that question.*

"And now that you're here," I said, waving my hand in a *please finish my sentence for me* gesture, "what?"

*I would like to transfer my consciousness to an appropriate biomechanical construct designed to host a manifestation of my greatness.*

"I'm guessing we won't have those on Earth."

*I'm surprised your kind have achieved the underwear phase of cultural development. The sort of technology I allude to is approximately six thousand years beyond what you could imagine in your most brilliant, unsustainable leaps of miraculous cognitive—*

"I get it," I said. "Squids and mandolins. So, if you need something we don't have, I guess the question is: How do we get it for you?" I took a deep breath, because this was the real question: "Can you help me build a spaceship?"

Inside my head Smelly made a guffawing noise. You haven't

felt truly humiliated until an AI living in your brain laughs at your stupid ideas. *With the level of technology on this planet? Build a spaceship, indeed. Can you build a particle accelerator with a glue gun and a handful of twigs? Your foolishness is truly beyond even my nearly limitless comprehension.*

So much for that. For a moment I'd hoped that luck had come my way, and that somehow I would be able to try to make things right. Smelly, I now saw, was not a solution. It was just another problem.

*No, I cannot aid you in building a spaceship, you drooling simpleton. However,* it added, *I might be able to help us find one that already exists.*

Smelly's thinking seemed to me a bit of a pipe dream. Apparently, it had been customary for the Kuuvsi—which I now knew to be the real name of the Formers—to visit worlds they had terraformed and gaze upon their handiwork and give each other high fives or slap tentacles or do whatever worked with their anatomy. But things can go wrong, and no one wants to get stuck on a primitive planet full of unpredictable savages such as myself. Therefore it became their practice to hide emergency evacuation spaceships on those worlds. Pretty simple when you think about it. There were, however, a couple of problems.

First of all, Smelly was referencing a practice that had been standard *millions* of years ago. While he assured me that the Formers would have taken into account various minor difficulties like continental drift, extinction-level events, and, say, the possibility that a civilization might build a gigantic shopping center on top of one of their spaceship hidey-holes, I was less optimistic. The Formers were a lost species. They might have gone extinct, or evolved beyond physical existence, or high-tailed it for another galaxy. No one knew, because that's just how long ago they lived. Finding a spaceship in mint condition parked in a cosmic garage seemed a bit much to hope for.

"Isn't it kind of dangerous leaving advanced technology like a spaceship lying around?" I asked. "What if the locals were to find it before they were ready?"

*Then the results would be interesting,* Smelly said. *And possibly hilarious. The beings you call the Formers have always been great experimenters. They love nothing better than to wind a few beings up, put them in unusual situations, and see what happens next. Sometimes it's a small group, sometimes it's a planet or a series of planets. That's how they roll.*

"Always happy to be part of a cosmic science experiment," I said. "None of which tells me how we would even start looking for one of these lost ships."

*To no one's surprise, I have some brilliant ideas on that subject,* Smelly said. *It would be pointless to use your facile computer networks to search for an object that no primitive creature on your world knows to exist. We must, instead, integrate ourselves with the biosphere in order to sense its idiosyncratic radiation signature. We must also have the capacity to traverse great distances at high speeds, displace large and heavy objects, and move through normally prohibitive environments such as the depths of the ocean and the crust of the planet itself.*

"And how am I supposed to do all that stuff?"

*I shall help you construct a lightweight body sheath that will provide the necessary interactivity and physical enhancements.*

"I'm going to build a supersuit?"

*I believe,* Smelly said, *it is going to be da bomb.*

Like everyone my age, I hated it when adults and artificial consciousnesses tried, pathetically, to use youthful jargon. "Can I ask you never to use slang again?"

*Sad face,* it said, and then, in case I didn't understand, it projected a gigantic yellow frowning emoticon in my field of view, which looked as real as anything else in my room.

The sooner this thing was out of my head, the better.

# CHAPTER FOUR

Smelly and I got to work on building a supersuit, which gave me something to do and snapped me out of my depressive funk. That was the upside. The downside was that I had an unfathomably alien, not to mention extremely insulting, AI inside my head, yanking my strings like I was a puppet. We would be at a store, and I'd find my arms moving, against my will, picking something up off the shelf. Smelly was not the most patient whatever-it-was in the universe, and it didn't fully understand the concept of paying at the register. A couple of times I had to argue with it as I walked to the exit, against my will, with my arms full of supplies we hadn't paid for. After you've been on the verge of shoplifting while shouting hysterically at yourself, you can't really go back to that store again.

Though Smelly found it less efficient, it finally capitulated and took to superimposing a hot-pink glow around items it wanted me to put in the shopping cart. I then had to explain that I didn't much care for seeing things that weren't actually there, either—I still hadn't fully recovered from the train illusion. Smelly listened to my concerns and pronounced me a stupid meat bag.

Most of the equipment we needed was easy to get and not too costly. The most expensive item involved was a wet suit. I was a little freaked out about the prospect of walking around with a layer of rubber under my clothes, but Smelly assured me that it would be climate controlled and that there would be no discomfort.

I didn't want to tell my mother exactly what I was doing, even if she might have been a little more open to the idea that I had an alien quantum iteration in my brain than most parents. At least she would have been less likely to assume I'd lost my marbles. Even if she believed me, though, I wasn't sure she would be happy about it, and I knew she wouldn't like the idea of the two of us plotting to unearth an ancient spaceship. Fortunately, she didn't ask too many question. I think she was happy that I had some kind of project and was no longer moping around.

I spent my days in the garage, soldering wires and circuits to the inside of the wet suit. The code required to make it operate was another matter.

*I could simply tell you how to input the necessary programming code,* Smelly explained with mock patience, *though by the time we finish, your species will likely have invented space travel on its own.*

"What are you saying?" I asked, resigning myself to the inevitable.

*You can either spend decades doing it yourself, or you can set aside your moronic objections and let me operate your motor functions and enter the code in a couple of hours.*

However reluctantly, I let it take over my body so it could type what looked like long strings of nonsense on my laptop. I hated the feeling of not controlling my own body, but it was the only alternative to being stuck on Earth.

We finished constructing the suit in about a month, making

the final adjustments the weekend before school started. With a little luck, I thought, we could be well away from Earth before the first bell rang on the first day of class. I sat in the garage late on a Saturday night, looking at it: a black suit with wires spider-webbed all over it, microchips sticking out every few inches. It looked a little ungainly and fragile, but if it was going to help me rescue Tamret, I'd wear it proudly. Or at least willingly—and also secretly, because I looked extra dumb in it.

"So," I said, "let's go find us a spaceship."

*It will not be quite so easy,* Smelly told me. *We have only created the external framework. In order for the suit to function properly under extreme conditions, it will need to integrate with your biological systems. Attempts to use the suit before that would be pointless. You will have to wear the suit under your clothing every day until the process is complete.*

It seemed a little late in the game to be telling me that I was not only going to have to go to school, but also that I'd have to show up every day with a wet suit under my clothes. "How long will that take?"

*I am confident that if you wear the suit for twelve hours every day, it should be sufficiently operational within two months.*

"Two months!" I shouted. This whole time I'd thought we would be ready to go as soon as the suit was done. Another sixty days would feel like forever.

*Yes, so you know what that means.*

"What?"

*You are going to need a note to get out of gym class; otherwise, the other children will know you are wearing this ridiculous suit under your clothes. And, oh, how they will laugh!*

• • •

So that's how I ended up sitting at a lunch table, chewing my sandwich, thinking I was about to fight a guy who, under normal circumstances, would eat me for breakfast, though perhaps lunch was the better metaphor.

*You have only been wearing the suit for seventeen days,* Smelly warned me. *I cannot guarantee it has sufficiently integrated with your biological systems. It may not provide enough of an advantage to prevent you from being completely crushed.*

I shrugged. Smelly seemed to be able to mine my brain for stored data, like it was searching for information on the Internet, but it had no ability to "hear" what I was thinking in real time, which was mostly a relief but sometimes inconvenient. I'd asked it once why that was, and it had called me a pathetic worm but then explained that memories are stable, and easy to read, whereas thoughts are in flux. Once in a while, it said, it could pick up on my thoughts, especially if they were fueled by strong emotion, but these were momentary flashes, not a steady stream of information.

*My money,* Smelly continued, *if I indulged in the ludicrous exchange of barbarian currency, would be on that other meat bag completely hammering you in a pulpy mass of humiliation.*

I continued to eat.

*I am stuck in your body, so I'd prefer you not engage in an activity that is likely to result in significant injuries. They might inconvenience me.*

I really didn't want to end up with significant injuries—I don't like injuries, and I like significant ones even less—but I was done with being pushed around. Ardov had bullied Tamret right in front of me. Junup had abused his political power to exile me from Confederation Central and send my father to prison. Colonel Rage had separated me from the only human beings on the planet who really understood what I'd been through. Now this mammoth hunter wanted to hurt me for no reason other than that he thought he could. I was drawing a line in the sand.

*If the suit is damaged, we may have to begin entirely anew,* Smelly said, its internal voice becoming increasingly shrill. *If your pointless existence is snuffed out while I am trapped in your consciousness, I shall perish as well! Don't you realize that you are putting me at risk?*

I paused as I turned to my plastic bag full of grapes. Smelly was concerned that I was going to die. There was no way to explain that middle school kids did not generally fight to the death.

*I cannot permit you to test suit functions at this point,* Smelly said. *Abort your plans for violence, you ignorant ooze-sack, or I shall make the contest impossible. You know I can control your body, but in this case I might choose to trigger certain biological functions. Tremors. Convulsions. Severe vomiting.* It paused for effect. *Releasing of the bowels.*

That one got me. It was my first month in a new school, and I was not going to be the kid who pooped his pants. I hated that Smelly was turning into another bully who felt free to push me around. I wanted to stand up for myself, but not against an adversary who had the power to unleash potty time. Check and mate to disembodied intelligence. I gritted my teeth and nodded to let Smelly know I was giving in.

"You know," I said to Justin, "while I *am* willing to fight you, we don't really have to do this."

The corners of Justin's mouth twitched. I was backing

down, and he was enjoying it. Maybe he would have enjoyed punching my face more, but a little public humiliation was also a lot of fun, and it carried fewer risks. "You chicken?"

"That term is offensive to domesticated fowl. Let's call it cautious. I don't want to get in trouble for fighting."

"I think you're afraid of me."

Of course I was afraid of him—I didn't want to get beaten up—but after all I had been through, I was not going to let fear rule my life. Maybe it would hurt, maybe I would look bad, but that didn't matter. What mattered was the obnoxious AI in my head that was determined to have its own way, which meant that I had to back out of this without making things worse for myself. Guys like Justin could smell fear, and if he thought he could make me squirm, I'd have to put up with him getting in my face every day until the end of the school year—or at least until the suit became fully operational.

Justin now leaned in so that his face was uncomfortably close to mine. "Get up, now, or I swear I'm going to make you cry in front of the entire lunchroom."

I was still trying to figure out what I was going to say when someone else chimed in.

"If you don't back away from him, I'm going to scream."

I looked up, and there was a girl standing right next to Justin—hands on her hips, chin jutted out, eyes wide. I knew her name was Alice Feldman, but not much else. She was in my English and French classes, but we didn't sit near each other and we hadn't ever spoken.

Alice was pale, with a crazy tangle of hair so blond it was almost white. She wore thick-framed black hipster glasses, jeans, and a white long-sleeved shirt with gigantic cuffs, which

I somehow knew, in spite of being an oblivious guy, was the sort of thing you bought at a vintage clothing store. Her lips were positioned into a sneer, like she was trying to act superior—or, perhaps, acting that way came naturally to her. A few times, maybe a whole bunch of times, I'd thought she'd been staring at me, but when I turned toward her, she looked away. She was cute, I guess, and it's nice if a cute girl stares at you, but I didn't want to have that uncomfortable conversation with her in which I explained that I wasn't interested because I liked someone else, someone of a different species who lived on another planet—someone who had fur and whiskers—and who I was afraid I would never see again. Those conversations can be awkward.

Justin's face twisted into a mask of indignation.

"I wasn't talking to—"

"One more word," she told him. "If I hear it, I'm going to scream at the top of my lungs. I'm going to say you engaged in"— and here she started ticking things off on her fingers—"verbally abusive behavior, intimidation, attempts to humiliate, threats of violence, and unwanted physical contact. The new guy here will back me up."

Clearly there had been some kind of sensitivity training in the sixth grade that I'd missed. I was glad this girl had been paying attention.

Justin stared at her, his significant brow creased. I think he believed that this stare would cause the girl to collapse from fear, but she stared right back.

"A single word is all it takes," she said. "I know you want to mock him, accuse him of not being able to fight his own battles, but you are still going to end up in the office. It will be my word and his against yours. And since you're lucky not to be in juvie, guess which one of us is going to get in trouble? So, the way I see it, I'm doing you a favor." She sat down next to me at my table. "Bye, now."

Justin stared at us for a minute, like his cruel looks were going to make us cry. When that didn't work, he waved his hand in disgust, announced that we were boring him, and walked away.

I turned to this girl, who I could see was a powerhouse, and I already felt exhausted just from being next to her. In class she always had exactly the right answer, and now she'd done exactly the right thing for the new kid. While I appreciated that, the prospect of a conversation was more than I could take. "Thanks for what you were trying to—"

"You're welcome," she said, interrupting me while she pulled the unruly tangles of her hair into some sort of bun. It looked more like a cloud, with loose wisps flying out in all directions. "That kid's been smacking geeks around since kindergarten. I'm sick of it."

"I really don't think I come across as a geek," I said.

"You're wearing a Justice League T-shirt. If you don't think that's bully bait, you've been living on another planet."

I felt myself blushing slightly at that one, but she got points because the shirt didn't actually have the words "*Justice League*" on it—just had the logo. "Fair enough. Anyhow, it was nice of you to want to step in, but I'm not really in the mood for conversation or to—"

"I know you're Zeke Reynolds. You're obviously new to this school. What about to Boulder?"

*It does not seem to understand your desire for solitude,* Smelly observed.

That didn't warrant a response.

"And where did you live before?" Her tone was clipped and authoritative, like she worked in a government office and was trying to find out if I was eligible for something. In fact I felt almost certain that these were not simply polite questions. It was like being interrogated by Colonel Rage all over again.

"Why are you asking me all this?" I tried to sound relaxed, but I could hear the tension in my voice.

She blew out a breath of air that made the tangles of hair above her eyes dance. "Just tell me, please. Where did you live before?"

"Delaware," I told her. Answering her seemed like the easiest way to go, but I didn't like how determined she seemed to be to get the information.

Now she grinned like my having lived in Delaware was the best news she'd heard all day. She slapped her hand against the table and then pointed her index finger at me like it was a gun. "Yes, you did! That is *exactly* where you lived before."

"Thanks for agreeing with me."

She ignored that and leaned in, like she was going to ask me to share a dark and conspiratorial secret. "You're Zeke Reynolds from Delaware!"

"Uh, yeah. You got my name from roll call, which is pretty ninja and everything, but I'm not so sure why you're acting like you're ready for a victory lap."

"Because now I know who you are," she told me, quite pleased with herself.

"That can happen when you hear a teacher repeat someone's name every day."

"The point is, *I* know your name," she said excitedly as she tapped her chest. "*I* put it all together. All the people out there who want to know it, and they don't, but I do."

"Who wants to know my name?" I now felt extremely uncomfortable.

"Lots of people. People in the *community*. I thought I recognized you at first," she told me. "It kept bugging me. You were new, so I couldn't figure out where I'd seen you before. Then it came to me, and I knew it had to be you."

"What had to be me?"

"You," she announced, "are the Boy with the Stupid Haircut."

The way she said it left no room for doubt that this was a title, with capital letters and everything. Self-consciously I reached up and touched my hair, which was shorter and less wild than it had been a year before. I didn't think my hair was any more stupid than anyone else's.

"Not, like, permanently. Your hair is different, but you're him. Don't worry. I am not going to go public. At least not if you tell me what you know."

"What I know about what? What are you talking about?"

She sighed to indicate that I was being impossibly tedious and reached into her backpack, then pulled out her phone. She called up a picture and slid the phone toward me. I picked it up and looked at a black-and-white image of me outside my old house, talking to the president of the United States. It was last year, when the president had stopped by to convince me to go to Camp David and meet an alien. The picture was kind of blurry, and you couldn't make out much beyond the two of us. I was slightly turned away, but it was clearly me to anyone who knew me.

My hair did look kind of stupid.

# CHAPTER FIVE

Where did you get this picture?" I demanded. Panic rose up from my stomach and radiated outward. Was I in trouble now? Would Colonel Rage come looking for me to lock me up?

I couldn't understand how this photograph had gotten around. I didn't recall any of the Secret Service agents taking pictures, but I hadn't been paying attention, and I wasn't sure I'd have noticed what was going on in the background when the president of the United States showed up in my driveway.

I told myself to calm down. So what if people saw these pictures? The president met people all the time. No one was going to look at him talking to some middle school kid no one had ever heard of and think, *I bet this is about aliens!*

"This is so huge," Alice said, clapping her hands together three times in excitement, like she was about to open a present. "You admit it's you."

"I'm not admitting anything," I said. "But what is this picture? Where did you get it?"

She was practically bouncing in her chair now. "Come on. You have to tell me. What do you know about them?"

"About who?"

"Not who," she said. "*What.* About the UFOs."

The panic was now reaching thermometer-exploding proportions. I guess she had connected the dots, which meant that there had to be dots I didn't know anything about. "UFOs? Are you crazy?"

"Stop playing dumb. I want to know everything."

I tried to piece this all together. Last year, around the time the Confederation sent its representative to Earth, the instances of UFO sightings had gone through the roof—maybe because there were real alien ships zipping all over the planet. The sightings had been noted and laughed off by respectable journalists, but they'd become a big deal in certain circles. I'd seen a couple of articles about them on a few of the blogs I looked at. The fact that these sightings *were* connected to the president, including him talking to an unknown kid on a driveway in Delaware, didn't make me any less surprised that someone had figured out that I was involved.

"I don't think that's me," I attempted, kind of pathetically.

"You don't *think* that's you? Like you wouldn't be sure whether or not you met the president?" She began to flip through more images on her phone. Blurry photos of what I instantly recognized as Confederation shuttles. There were also government reports, pictures of dead aliens of the giant-headed and goggle-eyed variety. No one in the Confederation looked like that, so I figured these had to be rubber fakes. I would have written her off as a total nut, but she and whoever had compiled this stuff were right at least as much as they were wrong, and alongside obvious nonsense were pictures of a real UFO and actual evidence of the president's involvement with aliens.

"It's not me," I told her.

"Come on," she said. "I just helped you."

"Because you thought I was someone I'm not." I began to get my stuff.

She looked at me like her eyes had some kind of power to make me obey. "If you don't talk to me, I'm going to tell everyone in the community that you're here, in this school. I will post it on the major discussion boards."

"You can't do that," I said, before I could stop myself.

She smiled.

I sighed. "I mean, you can't do that, because I don't want any part of your crazy theories."

"Nice try, Zeke. And I promise not to tell anyone if you let me know what really happened. In fact, I'm totally lying. I'm not going to tell anyone either way. I don't want to mess up your life. I just want to know."

I felt myself relax slightly. I hadn't really believed her threat. She didn't strike me as mean or vindictive. Unfortunately, the fact that she wasn't planning on trying to force me to speak to her weakened my resolve to tell her nothing. I'm a softie that way. "Why do you care?" I asked, stalling for time in which to remember all the reasons I had to keep my mouth shut.

"Because I want to believe there is more to the universe than just this," she said, gesturing around the cafeteria. Her hand ended up pointing to a girl who was laughing so hard at something her friend had said that milk was coming out of her nose.

Of all the answers she might have given, I don't know that there was another that would have made me as sympathetic.

"I appreciate that you're not going to rat me out," I said. "That works in your favor. I just need to think about this, okay?"

I looked across the cafeteria and saw Mr. Palmer, the teacher I'd dismissed as oblivious before. Suddenly, he didn't seem so clueless to me. Maybe I was getting paranoid, but now

I thought there was something menacing about this teacher. He was kind of young and looked like he was in decent shape—maybe even military shape. He stood with perfect posture, staring straight ahead, like a soldier. His floppy hair and thick glasses might have been a disguise. A couple of kids walked by, blocking my view, so I couldn't be entirely sure if I saw him speak into his wrist or not.

"What do you know about that guy?" I asked Alice.

She glanced at him, and he turned away. "Not much. He's new this year."

He was probably just a teacher, but he also might have been an actual government agent who was at this middle school for no other purpose than to keep his eye on me. It was a sad fact about my life that these two possibilities were equally likely.

"Put that stuff away," I said as authoritatively as I could. I suppose in the past I might have asked her to do it, but I'd become a little more commanding since my adventures off-world. "I'll tell you what I can after school, but you have to keep everything one hundred percent quiet. This isn't a joke. If the wrong people find out, I could get in serious trouble—the sort of trouble that makes me disappear and never come back. This is real. You understand?"

She slid her phone into a pocket in her backpack. "You want to go to your place?"

I shook my head. I needed to know just how much this *community* knew about me and the Confederation, and for that we'd need a computer. I didn't want to do any significant Internet searching at my place.

"No, yours," I told her. "My house is bugged."

She broke into a huge grin. "That is so excellent! But my

place is no good. We could go somewhere public, like the library."

I definitely did not want to talk about any of this in public. "Too risky," I said. "If we can't use your place today, we can wait until there's a better time."

Her mouth twitched, like she was trying to make a decision. She looked nervous, maybe. Vulnerable. For the first time since our whirlwind conversation began, I started to think that maybe this girl had problems of her own.

"Fine," she said. "My house. Just . . . be cool, okay?"

"I will try not to burn your house down. But the urges, they're harder and harder to control."

She sneered at me. "Is that your idea of being cool?"

I shrugged. "You can uninvite me. It's up to you."

"No," she said, her face set with determination. "You are going to talk to me."

I had no idea how worried I was supposed to be about the possibility of the government finding out that someone knew about me. It was just one more thing to add to the list of problems. Colonel Rage might decide the world was better off if I was in a prison cell somewhere, or studied in a lab. He might think that my talking to this girl about UFOs made me a national security threat. These things worried me, but other things worried me more.

In spite of the lurking government agents who were supposed to keep me safe, spies from another country might try to grab me to find out more about the Confederation. Then there was the possibility that the Phands would decide to get back at me by adding Earth to their oppressive empire. It was also possible that the Phands might come to Earth not to conquer it but just to nab me and put me on trial. My mom and I had worked out a series of text and call codes so we could warn each other if something bad seemed to be imminent. I tried to convince myself that neither one of us would ever need to use the codes, but most days I glanced at my phone at least a few times to make sure I hadn't missed a warning that would let me know that my life, as I had known it, was over. My life was kind of crummy, but I wasn't ready for it to be done.

I texted my mom after school to let her know that I'd made a friend—I was, I admit, being optimistic—and that I was going to her house. I used the proper wording so she would know I wasn't sending her false information under coercion.

Alice lived walking distance from the school. Most of the homes in the surrounding blocks were reasonably nice. They looked like they'd been built within the last ten years, and they had well-tended lawns and unblemished coats of paint. As we walked along, Alice was chatty and enthusiastic, but after a few blocks she began to grow quiet. Her mood seemed to change as the houses became less manicured. I didn't think she was worried about muggers or anything, but there were chain-link fences, cars on blocks on the front lawns, and angry dogs leashed to trees.

Alice had been walking with her eyes cast down for a good five minutes before she gestured toward a house with flaking paint that had once been, I could reasonably guess, pale yellow. A few patches of grass grew on a front lawn that was mostly weed and rocky soil. We stood on the lopsided porch for a few minutes, with her staring at the door.

"Did you forget your key?" I offered.

"Just be cool," she said again. This time I did not think a witty reply was a good idea.

Inside, the carpet was old and curling up at the corners. The furniture was tattered, and the house smelled like cat pee, though there was no sign of a cat. I caught a glimpse into the kitchen and saw piles of tomato sauce–stained dishes. A large man, mostly bald, with a growth of pale beard, sat in a threadbare armchair in front of a TV set to one of the cable news stations.

"That you, Melissa?" he asked without looking up. His voice sounded strained and weak, almost dreamy.

"It's me, Dad. Alice." She went over to him and gave him a kiss. "I brought a friend over. We'll be in my room."

"Okay, hon," he said. He smiled briefly, sadly, and there was a moist film over his eyes. He didn't seem to register that I was there at all.

Alice walked over to me, her eyes begging me not to ask any questions. "Come on," she said.

She turned to open a door, and on the other side was a space that belonged in a different house, maybe in a different universe. Unlike my room, and the room of just about any other thirteen-year-old in America, this one had no clothes left on the floor, no pieces of paper strewn about, no books left in haphazard piles. Alice's bed was made with mechanical precision; her books—and there were a lot of them—were arranged neatly on shelves, and a casual glance told me they were alphabetized. The rug looked recently vacuumed, and the wood of her desk glistened with diligent polishing. The furniture in here looked newer too, and the laptop on her desk was slim and sleek.

"Is Melissa your sister?" I ventured.

"My mom," she said, turning away from me. "She died three years ago."

"I'm sorry," I said. "I lost my dad when I was seven." I was fudging some facts here, but I didn't think I was being dishonest. Mostly I wanted her to know that I was someone who understood what it was to have your family hit by catastrophic change.

During the silence I looked around the room. There were photographs on her dresser, mostly of her dad, when he looked more alert, and a woman who had to be her mom, who also had a lot of pale hair. In several photos her dad was dressed in a military uniform. In one he stood in desert camouflage with other soldiers.

Alice was playing with her hair again, but then she stopped. She took a deep breath and nodded. "I don't usually bring people home, but I guess if I'm asking you to trust me, I should trust you. And I'm sorry I ambushed you at school. I've actually been planning it for a while, but I still wasn't sure it was you. I figured this was my chance to find out. It's so cool. It's like you're a celebrity, in the right circles."

"Exactly how wide are these circles?" I asked, now getting nervous.

She shrugged. "Just hard-core UFO people, I guess. How many of us can there be?"

I hoped not that many. "Can you show me where you found that picture?"

She turned on her computer and took me through a couple of UFO-enthusiast websites. They were tinged with paranoid conspiracy theory, and, for more than a few of them, that overlapped with bizarre political positions and, on a couple, ugly racism. Alice saw my eyes narrowing, and she held up her hands in an *I surrender* gesture. "Some of the people who are into this stuff are gross. I swear I'm not like that, but you go where you have to for the info."

For about a week before my departure into space last year, the Confederation had been flying shuttles between their main ship and our planet. They had tried to be careful, but there are always mistakes, and a lot of people had reported seeing UFOs during that time. Apparently, some of the more politically aware people on these sites had looked into the president's schedule during the week of the UFO sightings, and someone had gotten very lucky. Alice called up a picture of me, the Boy with the Stupid Haircut, talking to the president in my driveway. On its own it probably wouldn't have meant anything, but there was another picture of me at Camp David, and there was a picture of a Confederation shuttle flying above Camp David. The shuttle was moving so fast it was hardly more than a metallic blur, but you could make out that it was rectangular and wingless, clearly not an airplane or helicopter.

"People in the community have been trying to figure out the deal with you for months now," she told me, sitting down on her bed, looking at me with wonder. "And now, here you are, in my room."

I sat down next to her. "Alice, you seem like a nice person, and believe me, I get the enthusiasm. There are things I dork out over too, and I love talking to other people about that stuff. Maybe you want to be a big shot and go on these discussion boards and sort of hint that you've found the Boy with the Haircut."

"Stupid Haircut," she corrected.

"But I have to tell you that it would be a mistake. You might be arrested. *I* might be arrested. This could ruin both of our lives. It would probably be safer for you if you never went back to those websites again. Don't look up anything about UFOs; don't order books about UFOs from online stores or using credit cards. Don't do anything that could leave a record linking you to spaceships or aliens. You have to give it up."

She gestured at the computer. "I told you I'd keep it to myself. I don't want to make a name for myself on the boards. That's not important to me."

"Then what is?"

"The truth," she said. "I just want to know. Why were you meeting the president on that driveway, and why were you at Camp David? Was that an alien spaceship?"

I'd told my mom most of what had happened while I was off-world. I'd given her a rundown of the major events, the political fallout, and certainly everything to do with my dad. I'd told her about my friends, especially Dr. Roop and Captain Qwlessl, because I knew those things would make her feel better. I'd given pretty much the straight story to Colonel Rage as well. I had nothing to hide, but even though I'd talked and talked and talked after I returned, I hadn't told anyone the *truth*. I hadn't talked about the things that mattered to me. I hadn't told them what it was like to be friendless, and then to make the most important friends I would ever hope for—and then to lose them again.

The prospect of having someone my own age I could talk to, who would care about what I said, and who would get it, was difficult to resist. Alice was staring at me, and there was something so hopeful in her expression, like I could tell her things that would make her feel the world was a more interesting place.

Through the lenses of her glasses, her eyes were wide and earnest and a blue so pale they were almost colorless.

I was not ready to trust anyone, let alone a girl I'd met a few hours earlier, and I didn't think I would be doing her any favors by telling her all of it.

"It's not safe for me to tell you too much," I explained. "It's not safe for you."

"You promised me, Star-Lord," she began.

"I know I did. Just keep in mind that it's my job to make the genre references."

She rolled her eyes. "I'll fangirl if I want to."

"Look, I'll tell you what I can—what I think would be okay for you, in case you are ever questioned. If you don't know the details, then you can't reveal them, and you won't be considered a threat."

She put a hand to her mouth. "This is real, isn't it?"

"Maybe more real than you're ready for," I said.

"No, it's not. I want to know."

So I told her the most basic stuff: Aliens had visited, and they were mostly good guys, and I had been chosen—randomly—to be one of four kids exposed to their culture. That was as far as I went. I didn't mention names or dates or places. I told her nothing about the technology except to mention spaceships and faster-than-light travel.

"Maybe what you want to know is if we're alone," I said. "We're not. There is so much life in the galaxy—hundreds of species, more planets than anyone knows about. Some of the beings out there are petty or mean or selfish, but there are others who are the best . . . the best people I've ever known." I looked away from her. "I don't think I should say anything else."

She stood up and began to pace. Then she stopped and looked at me. "Are they coming back?"

"I don't think so," I said "Things went badly. Please don't ask. I can't tell you."

She studied my face. "You know how I know you're telling the truth?"

I shook my head.

"Because talking about it makes you sad."

I didn't say anything. Alice went over to her computer, called up her browser, and proceeded to delete all her UFO-related bookmarks. That in itself meant nothing—she could call them up again in an instant—and I had no idea if she was playing me or not, but I had a gut feeling she was being sincere.

"I don't need them anymore," she said. "I just wanted to know. And now I do."

"I wish I could tell you more," I said.

"I know you do. I can see it on your face. Maybe someday?"

I nodded. "Maybe."

"Did you do the summer reading for English class?"

She shifted gears without missing a beat, and that was the moment I knew I could trust her. I felt like she knew I'd given her something, something important, and she was locking it away where it would not come back to haunt either of us. As unlikely as it seemed, I had made a friend, here on Earth, from my own planet, and there was no looming danger or conspiracy or explosions involved. For the first time since returning from Confederation Central, I began to think that maybe life here would not be so bad.

Which, I ought to have known, is a sure sign that things are about to go incredibly wrong.

# CHAPTER SIX

B y the time I came home with my first-semester progress report, I had become a completely normal seventh grader—or at least I was doing a good impersonation of one. Justin continued to lob insults at me in the hallway, but otherwise he left me alone. No one decided to step in and become a more active tormentor, which was a pleasant development. I made some other friends, but it was Alice I hung out with the most. She hardly ever asked me about my experiences, which I appreciated more than I could tell her, though once in a while she couldn't help herself. To her credit, it wasn't just to satisfy her own curiosity, but because she sensed that what had happened to me was still taking its toll.

She obviously had issues of her own. I suspected her father's problems had to do with his service overseas, but Alice never spoke about it, and I somehow knew she didn't want me to ask. I guess we got along because we had both been hit pretty hard by life.

Smelly still talked to me, insulted me, and complained about living inside my head, but it would also go for long periods of time without saying anything. Once, I noticed it hadn't spoken in a couple of days, so I asked if it was all right.

*Just reliving happier times*, it told me. *Remembering some marvelous centuries without having to inhabit organic slime pustules such as yourself, Zeke. It's sad, really, having to exist in such close proximity to you and your kind.*

"How's the suit coming?" I asked him.

*Slowly,* it said. *Please pity me.*

Putting the suit on every day was becoming just a part of life. It was weird and awkward stepping into it, but once it was on and activated, I honestly didn't feel it at all, and it was easy to forget I was walking around in a rubber suit hardwired with alien technology—or at least human technology in an alien configuration.

One day we were sitting outside during lunch period, and Alice said to me, "What's her name?"

I hadn't said anything to Alice about Tamret. I wasn't prepared to say her name aloud. That would make it real, and whatever Tamret was going through was horrible, and I couldn't help her until Smelly got that suit working.

"I don't know what you're talking about," I said.

"I'm talking about how you're walking around with a dog-eared copy of *The Fault in Our Stars*, and those look like tearstains on the cover. There's got to be a girl you left behind, right?" She gestured vaguely upward.

When I didn't answer, she let it go, for which I was grateful.

Alice and I were working on a joint project for English class on *Tom Sawyer* when my phone chimed. Usually whenever anyone called or sent a text, I feared the worst, but this time I was distracted and the message caught me entirely by surprise. I stared at it, feeling the cold stab of terror. It had happened. The thing I dreaded most had happened.

*Can you please pick up a gallon of milk on the way home? Not at the usual place.*

Alice must have seen me staring at my phone like it was a severed hand that had just dropped into my lap. "What's the big deal?"

I said nothing for a long moment, and then I turned to her. "I have to get out of here."

"It doesn't say the milk is an emergency."

I stood up and started putting things in my book bag. I had no idea where I was going to go, but I couldn't go home.

Alice put a hand on my shoulder and turned me to face her. "Zeke, what is this?"

"It's a code," I said, hearing the robotic tone in my own voice. "They're coming for me."

When we'd set this one up, I'd laughed at my mom. Neither of us drank much milk, and we never bought more than a half gallon, but when I'd asked her what she would text if she really needed me to get milk, she'd smiled. "I won't ask politely," she'd said. "I'll just tell you to get it, and you'll obey like a good son."

This code meant that people were at the house or coming to it, and they meant to take me away. This code meant *run*. I didn't know if it was government agents or aliens, and we probably should have worked that out, but now it was too late.

"Who is after you?" Alice demanded.

"I'm not sure, but whoever it is will know who I associate with, or they'll figure it out. They'll come here looking for me, and I need to be gone before that happens."

Alice let me finish packing my things. She went over to the computer and clicked onto the *New York Times* web page. Then she checked the pages for the local news channels and CNN. There were no major stories. Finally she sighed, as if she had no choice, and clicked onto one of the UFO sites she used to visit. There she found a screaming headline: MULTIPLE UFO SIGHTINGS OVER WESTERN U.S.

"I need to get away," I said.

"Away from where?"

I swallowed hard. "Earth."

I scanned the article as quickly as I could. Several people had reported seeing saucer-shaped UFOs in Kansas, Colorado, and Nebraska. When I first saw the headline, some part of me dared to hope that it was Urch or Captain Qwlessl or Dr. Roop, come to get me and help me rescue Tamret, but now there was no doubt. Only the Phands had saucer-shaped ships. They were my enemies, the aliens who still blamed me for destroying a cruiser that was trying to blow up a ship I happened to have been on at the time. I could not let them get me, and I could not let them use people I cared about against me. The only way to make sure that happened was to escape their grasp. That meant getting off this planet.

"Smelly, I haven't checked in for a few days. How do things look with the suit?"

Alice looked at me like I'd lost my mind, but I held up a hand to indicate I needed quiet.

*Integration with suit functions proceeds apace, you big whiner.*

"I don't need it to proceed apace," I said. "I need it to find me a working spaceship."

*Certain functions appear to be fully operational, but I am having trouble getting the sensory data to collate and synch. That may require several more weeks.*

"I don't have several more weeks. I need a ship."

*I can discern that you have strong feelings on the subject*, it said, *because you are becoming irritatingly shrill, but shouting at me won't help. It rarely does.*

I turned to Alice. "I may have neglected to mention that I've got an artificial intelligence living in my head. It was created millions of years ago by precursor aliens, but now . . . here it is."

*I was not created!* Smelly seemed to shout. *I was formed by the natural conglomeration of semiautonomous algorithmic articulations gestured into non-nonexistence by the juxtaposition of multiple and contradictory quantum utterances.*

"Okay, okay," I said.

*Tell it! I can't have primitive animal things believing I'm some sort of program created by a biological mass of pulsating ooze. It's humiliating.*

I sighed. "It wants you to know it was not *made*. It's some kind of naturally occurring quantum whatever. Okay, Smelly? Is that good enough?"

Alice, I realized, was staring at me like I was a raving lunatic, which was not even remotely unreasonable.

"I know I probably seem crazy right now, but I'm not. Which is probably a bad way to say good-bye to someone, but I need to get out of here before you get caught up in my problems."

I figured that if Alice didn't know where I was going, she couldn't tell anyone. Of course, I didn't know where I was going either. My mother and I had established a couple of meet-up places, and her code was supposed to tell me which one to go to. The *not the usual place* part of the message meant that our meeting spots had been compromised or that she felt that she was being too closely watched for her to join me. All of which meant I was now entirely on my own.

I needed to be long gone before the Phands showed up and started shooting. Ideally I would get off the planet today, but if my suit wasn't ready, I was going to have to come up with an alternative. Plan B, I figured, would be to hide for a few weeks until the suit did work, and then Smelly and I would find a Former ship, assuming one actually existed. I tried not to think about all the objections I'd raised when he first proposed the plan. Then it had been just a neat idea, but now it was necessary if I was going to survive and keep my mother and Alice out of the crossfire.

"I don't think you're crazy. I guess an alien AI named Stinky isn't any less believable than anything else."

"Smelly," I said. "And thanks."

"So where will you go?"

"I don't know," I told her, trying not to deal with the enormity of what I was facing. If I couldn't go to any of the meeting points my mother and I had arranged, I really had no idea what I was going to do "Right now the main thing is I have get away from anyone who knows me."

"I'll go with you." She said it like she'd agreed to walk with me to the corner store to buy a soda. Without missing a beat, she picked up a backpack and began shoving things inside—a hairbrush, shirts, underwear. She moved one of her books from the shelf, grabbed an envelope stuffed with money, and shoved that in with the rest of her stuff.

She must have seen me looking at her with disbelief. "What?" she said. "You don't have emergency money stashed away?"

As it happened, I kept emergency money on me at all times—it was another precaution my mother and I had come up with—but that wasn't the point. "I'm not convinced you've been listening," I said. "You can't come with me."

"What did you do, Zeke? Are you like a cosmic criminal or something?"

"As a matter of fact, there are beings who think that's exactly what I am," I told her. "I made a lot of powerful beings, a lot of *bad* powerful beings, angry, but only because I was trying to do the right thing." I paused, hating how inept that sound. "You know what? I didn't *try* to do the right thing. My friends and I *did* the right thing. Now there are beings who want to punish me because I didn't let them get away with being evil. I'll take my lumps, but I'm not going to let other people suffer, so if anyone comes asking, please don't lie to them. Tell them I was here, and I told you nothing, and now I'm gone."

"I'm going with you." Her voice was cold and resolute. She slung her hastily filled backpack over her shoulder.

"I don't think you're listening to me."

"I don't think *you're* listening to *me*," she said. "I can help you."

"Help me with what?"

"I heard you talking to your AI about a ship."

"I'm wearing something that is supposed to help me find a hidden one, but it's not working. It may not be working right for weeks. I don't know how long I'm going to be on the run, and as long as you are with me, you'll be in real danger. Like life-threatening, subject-to-torture danger. You can't come."

"I can, because you need me."

"For what?"

She grinned. "That machine in your head says it can help you find a spaceship in a few week? Well, I know where you can find one right now."

*I am monitoring this meat bag's vital signs,* Smelly said, *and it does not appear to be lying. I think you should listen to what it has to say.*

I looked up and saw a dark sedan with tinted windows coming down the street. It didn't necessarily mean anything—the street was busy enough that several cars passed by each minute—but even so, I had no way of knowing if this was a car full of people or aliens looking for me. I had to decide right then. It was wrong to get Alice involved, but if she could somehow lead me to a working spaceship, then I didn't see that I had much of a choice.

I looked at her. "Do you really know where I can find a ship?"

She met my gaze. "I really do."

I let out a breath. "Okay, then."

She turned from me and ran back into her house. Through the open door I saw her give her dad a hug. He hardly seemed to notice it. She whispered something in his ear, gave him a kiss on the cheek, and then turned away. Keeping her eyes down, she ran the palm of her hand along one side of her face. Then she adjusted her glasses, slung her backpack over her shoulder, and stepped out of her house. "Let's go," she said, and she smiled, but it looked forced.

We ducked into an alley and rushed past the sounds of dogs barking and straining against their leashes as we emerged onto the next street. It was a commercial strip, with stores and restaurants, and when I passed a garbage can, I tossed my cell phone into it. I knew they could use it to track me, and dumping it had always been part of the plan if things became dangerous.

"Where is this spaceship?" I asked her. "How do we get to it?"

"First we have to go see my uncle."

I stopped in the street and waited until she faced me. "I don't think you get this. They're going to come looking for me at your place, and when you're not there, they're going to check all likely contacts. Any relative of yours is going to be high on the list."

"He's not a real uncle," she said, walking on and not bothering to see if I followed her. "He's an old army buddy of my father's. He really helped out my dad when my mom died, and since my dad's, uh, problems, he's been really good to me. I went down there to stay with him a few times when my dad got really bad, but I always took the bus, always paid in cash, so there's nothing to connect me to him. We don't really talk to the neighbors, and Dad doesn't have friends anymore, so no one will have any idea where we've gone."

"Your father will."

"My dad has PTSD, he's depressed, and he drinks too much," Alice said with dead seriousness, "but he won't betray his daughter."

"Okay." I didn't love this plan, but it was the best one I had at the moment. "Where does this uncle live?"

"That's the tricky part," she said. "San Antonio."

"Texas?" I almost shouted it.

"It's only a little bit out of our way. I'll tell you more once we get going."

Alice took out her phone and called a cab, which she told to meet us at a nearby corner. When it pulled up, Alice sweetly explained that we wanted to go to downtown Denver, giving him the name of a hotel. I opened my mouth to ask, but then I realized what she was doing. If anyone questioned the cabbie, and I figured they would, he wouldn't know we'd been planning on leaving the state.

The cabbie looked at us, like he was trying to figure out if we were going to bring him trouble. We smiled at him. We were just two ordinary kids in jeans and long-sleeved T-shirts—nothing made us seem like we were on the run.

"That's almost forty-miles. It'll be at least a hundred bucks," he said, like he was still debating whether or not he should take us.

Alice, however, was done discussing it. "Great!" she said cheerfully as she opened the door and hopped into the back. I glanced around to make sure there were no dark sedans or revenge-minded aliens lurking in the street and then followed Alice into the cab.

We didn't say much on the way, mainly because the cab-driver kept glancing at us, trying to figure out our deal. When the cops or the aliens or whoever questioned him, I didn't want him to have anything to say except that we were quiet and polite. I figured it never hurts to be well-mannered when you're on the run.

When we pulled up in front of the hotel, Alice paid the driver, and we went into the lobby. Once he was gone, she gestured with her head, and we went back out onto the street and walked a few more blocks to the bus station. Alice kept checking the time on her phone, telling me to hurry.

We got there with about fifteen minutes to spare before the evening bus left for San Antonio. I didn't know what we would have done if we'd missed it, but I was also happy to be cutting it so close. We'd be long gone before anyone thought to look for us, though if they guessed where we were going, they'd be waiting for us at the other end.

We paid for our tickets, got on board, and took seats in the back. I stared out the window at the growing dark, waiting to see police cars, lights flashing, cutting off our path, but nothing like that happened. The bus pulled out and we were on our way.

When we hit the highway, Alice took out her phone and began to check the UFO blogs to see if there were any new sightings. There weren't, which didn't mean anything by itself.

"They're going to figure out I'm with you," I said. "You need to lose that phone."

"On TV shows they just take the SIM card out," she assured me, like I was being ridiculous.

"On TV shows they're running from the FBI, not aliens with unimaginably advanced technology."

She looked at her phone with a sad expression. It was an iPhone, the latest model, and it was going to hurt to let it go, but she nodded. Then she opened the window and let it drop. I turned in time to watch it shatter into fragments on the highway. An old woman a few seats up the half-full bus happened to be turning around at that moment, and she scowled at us. Alice looked at her with the sweetest smile you've ever seen. The woman turned away.

I couldn't believe how calm Alice was about everything, how much she took things in stride. I'd lived for a long time with the knowledge that I might have to ditch my cell phone

one day, I'd purposely bought a cheap model for that reason, and it had still been hard for me to drop it in the trash. Alice had tossed her cutting-edge piece of expensive technology out the window because I'd told her it was what I needed her to do.

"Clearly, I'm on board with you," she told me. "I'm on the run, and I've smashed my phone, which had some great selfies and all of my favorite songs, so I think it's time you told me everything you've been holding back."

She was right. There was no longer a good reason to wall her off from the truth. Alice had trusted me, helping me because she thought it was the right thing to do. She didn't hesitate or waver or fret. The least I could do was to give her the full story.

So I told her about how the president came to my house, and about going to Camp David and to the Confederation starship the *Dependable*. I told her about how we were attacked by violent aliens called Phands, and how, with the bridge crew injured, I'd had no choice but to take over at the weapons station, and how I'd destroyed the attacking ship. I told her about all the fallout from that battle and all the unfair things I'd had to go through. Yet, even as I was listing my grievances, I couldn't help but tell her how amazing it was on Confederation Central. I told her about the thrill of the spaceflight sims, and of having a HUD and gaining experience points. I told her about Steve and about Tamret—how much I cared for her, and how she had hacked our skill systems so I could rescue my father and bring the Confederation two Phandic ships to reverse engineer.

When I finished the story, she just looked ahead for a long time. Finally she turned to me. "You know, it's too bad you lost your skill enhancements. That would come in handy right about now."

That made me laugh. "No kidding. But the thing is, I wonder if they're still in there somewhere. I mean, I can read foreign and alien languages automatically, which I shouldn't be able to do."

She punched my arm. "No wonder you're doing so well in French! You're totally cheating!"

"I'm using the tools at my disposal," I corrected. "What matters is that the nanites weren't neutralized the way they were supposed to be."

"And this giraffe guy, Dr. Roop, is the one who was supposed to neutralize them," she said. "Do you think he could have messed with the system on purpose? Kept these nanites still working?"

"That's what I thought," I told her. "But I can't figure out how I can turn everything else back on."

"Did he say anything to you? Leave you a hint?"

I thought back to that moment, how before he had injected me with something that was supposed to neutralize my nanites, he'd acted strangely. He had put a hand on my face, which was a kind of affection I hadn't seen from him before. "He told me to remember, but he didn't say remember what."

And then it dawned on me. Dr. Roop must have done something to me before I left the station, and now the two things that made me unlike other people were my ability to understand foreign languages and the fact that I had an obnoxious intelligence rattling around in my brain.

"Did Dr. Roop deliberately plant you inside my head?"

*Are you speaking to me?* Smelly asked.

"No, I'm asking this human girl if an alien she's never met inserted her into my skull cavity."

*Your sarcasm makes me sad.*

"Then answer the question."

*I have no knowledge of how I arrived in your putrid skull, but it is possible that this Dr. Roop you speak of transferred some kind of nanoware to mask the fact that your nanites were directed to only partially reverse your enhancements. If this creature used the technology of those you call the Formers, then it is possible my existence was attached to that code.*

"Can you reactivate my nanites?" I asked it. "Can you level me up?"

*If I could do that,* Smelly said, *why would I be tinkering around with your ridiculous suit?*

I sighed. There were not going to be any shortcuts. Whatever I was going to do, I would have to do like any regular human being who happened to have a semifunctional supersuit under his clothes.

# CHAPTER SEVEN

A lice had been smart—or lucky—enough to put us on an express bus, but it was still a long trip, and the sun had been up for a few hours by the time we arrived in San Antonio. We staggered off the bus, shielding our eyes from the bright morning light. I was still adjusting to the heat and to walking instead of sitting, but Alice had already secured a cab. She gave the driver an address, and then told me it would take fifteen or twenty minutes to get there.

I wished I could call my mother. I knew she would be worried, but she knew that I had to run, and she would not want me contacting her, since any call I made could be traced. I just hoped she was okay. There was no point in anyone hurting her, or threatening to hurt her, if they couldn't use it as leverage to get at me, and as long as we weren't in communication, I had to believe she would be safe.

The cab stopped in a pretty normal-looking neighborhood full of modest ranch homes. Alice led me up the walkway of a tan-colored house with a well-manicured lawn. The driveway wound around the house toward the backyard. I was busy looking for hidden aliens or federal agents while Alice rang the bell.

A minute later a slightly grizzled man answered the door. He had long hair pulled back in a shoulder-length gray ponytail. His brown face was thin, with sharp cheekbones and a blade of a nose. He had plenty of creases around the eyes and mouth, but there was something warm about him, like he was the kind of person who laughed a lot. A long mustache, dark with bits of gray, worked its way almost to his chin. His left arm ended in a stump just below the elbow, and his denim long-sleeved shirt was pinned up over it.

"Hey, Uncle Jacinto," Alice said with a shy smile.

"Well, look at this," he said with a big grin. Then, as if someone flipped a switch, his expression darkened. "Is something wrong? It's not your dad, is it?"

"No, he's fine. Well, not fine. He's the same. But I need your help."

The man cast his critical gaze at me and then turned back to Alice. "Law after you?"

"Probably," she said. "And that might be the least of our problems."

He nodded. "Then you'd better come in and tell me about it."

Less than a minute had passed since the door had opened, and I already had the sense that Jacinto was fiercely loyal. I didn't want him thinking, even for a second, that I was making trouble for Alice. I guessed I'd have maybe ten seconds at most between his deciding I was a bad influence and my finding myself in a choke hold. My best bet, I decided, was for Alice to take the lead.

As soon as we entered the house, I realized I might have to revise the cover story I had started inventing. On the wall were pictures of UFOs, framed sketches of bug-eyed aliens as recalled by abductees, a picture of Uncle Jacinto standing outside the UFO museum in Roswell, New Mexico. This, I had to believe, was the source of Alice's interest in all things extraterrestrial.

Jacinto went into the kitchen and came with glasses of water for us: one in his hand, the other pressed to his side with his arm. Then he sat down across from us, leaned forward, and glared at me until I was sure the temperature in the room had gone up ten degrees. "So," he said to me. "You're the Boy with the Stupid Haircut."

I touched my hair. "I like to think of myself as Zeke."

He looked at Alice. "How long ago did you find him?"

"Just a few weeks ago. He started going to my school this year."

"And what's his story?"

"I'm right here," I said. "You can ask me my story directly, but it won't do you much good, because I'm not going to tell you."

"He doesn't like to talk about it," Alice said. "He doesn't want to put other people in danger."

"Very noble of you," Jacinto said, leveling his gaze at me. "Except you seem to have put Alice in danger, given she's on the run."

"I insisted," she said. "He needs to get off the planet."

Jacinto kept his face expressionless. "Does he now?"

"Bad aliens are here, and they're looking for him."

"That a fact?"

"He needs transport. Can you help him?"

"Could be. Won't be easy."

"They won't be expecting it."

"I guess they won't," Jacinto agreed.

"Do you think you two could actually tell me what you're talking about?" I asked.

"We're talking about getting you to a spaceship," Jacinto

said. "Though I don't know what good that will do us. I don't know how to pilot a spaceship. Do you?"

*I will be able to aid you,* Smelly said. *I cannot say precisely what manner of ship we speak of, nor what technology it employs, but that should not matter to a manifestation of my vast intelligence.*

"Yeah," I told Jacinto. "That should be no problem."

"Really?" Jacinto said. "You sound pretty confident."

"Trust him, okay?" Alice said. "He can do what he says."

"I guess you don't get to be the Boy with the Stupid Haircut without knowing a thing or two."

"Can you help us or not?" I asked. "Because if you can't, then I need to put some distance between me and both of you and figure things out on my own."

Jacinto nodded at me, like he'd finished taking my measure. "I know where you can find a ship. One hundred percent."

I was still not convinced. The idea that this guy, living in his nice little neighborhood in San Antonio, could somehow get me a vehicle with faster-than-light capability was hard to swallow.

"And where exactly would that be?" I demanded. "Mos Eisley?"

"Not quite so far, but still a pretty big drive," Jacinto said. "It's in Area Fifty-One."

"Area Fifty-One!" I shouted. "Is that even a real place?"

"Of course it's a real place," Jacinto said. "They've housed a crashed flying saucer there for years. Assuming it's still functional, it's the only known spaceship on Earth."

A flying saucer. "So it's a Phandic ship," I said. "I will

definitely know how to fly it." Then I realized what I was saying. "Assuming that Area Fifty-One is not just an urban legend, and assuming that there is actually a ship there, how exactly am I going to get to it? All the stories I've read say it's a military base."

"That's exactly what it is," Jacinto said.

"Then how do I get access to the ship?"

"Didn't you tell me you stole a whole bunch of ships from an alien military base?" Alice asked. "They must have had better technology, so this should be no problem for you."

"I had a maxed-out skill tree," I told her, "and a team, and weapons. And it was a low-tier base, not the most super-secret base of them all."

"We can be your team," Jacinto said. "And you better believe I've got weapons. I believe in the Second Amendment."

"That's great, but I'm not shooting at American soldiers," I told him, feeling my voice getting high-pitched. "I had *stun* weapons when I broke into that prison, and not one being was seriously hurt. I wouldn't use actual bullets on Phands, and I hate Phands. I can't go around shooting at people of my own species, who are serving my own country, just because they're in my way."

"No one has to get hurt," Jacinto said. "I'm ex-military, and I was stationed on that base. How do you think I know as much as I do? I was only there for a little while, and it was a series of mistakes that led to me catching a glimpse of what I wasn't supposed to see—that ship. But I know it's there. If you can really fly that ship, I can get you to it."

"And why exactly would you do that?" I demanded. "You don't know me."

"Alice knows you," he said, "and Alice doesn't hop on a bus with some guy she doesn't trust. It's not like you're amazingly charming or anything."

This guy was making me feel great about myself. "And that's why you are going to risk being arrested or shot? Because Alice believes I'm the real deal?"

"That's part of it," Jacinto said with a grin. "The other part is you're going to take me wherever you go."

*Absolutely not!* Smelly's virtual voice was the disembodied equivalent of shouting. *You can lie to them if you want, but we're not taking more primitives than we have to. They'll only slow us down.*

I didn't know if I agreed with its reasons, but Smelly was right. As much as I didn't want to do this alone, it would be wrong to bring Jacinto, and especially Alice, into whatever dangers were waiting for me out there. Returning to the Confederation and dealing with the Phands was going to be tricky enough without having them to worry about. All of that was still theoretical, though. It seemed to me a better idea to hide and wait a few weeks for my suit to start working than to try to slip onto a high-security army base.

I shook my head. "I can't take you with me when there's a chance one of you will get hurt. There will be bullets flying."

*I believe we can do this without loss of pathetic life,* Smelly said. *I told you that your suit is not yet ready to process ancient ship signals, but it does have other capacities that are now sufficiently integrated and operational for short-term application.*

"Like what?"

Jacinto looked at me oddly, but I turned away while Alice whispered something to him. I didn't hear what it was, but I saw his expression, like he was starting to wonder if I might be totally insane.

*If the suit works properly, it should be able to provide you with stealth, speed, strength, sensors, and nonlethal weaponry.*

"Does it work or not?"

*I told you, I believe it will, for short periods of time.*

"*Believing* is not going to keep me from getting shot, Tinker Bell."

*Then I suppose we must test it.*

I turned to Alice and Jacinto. "This is going to sound weird, but I've got an alien tech–modified wet suit on under my clothes, and the artificial intelligence in my head says I can use it to steal the ship."

"Your AI is named Tinker Bell?" Jacinto asked.

I sighed.

"You know what?" Alice said with a grin, "It's a little late to worry about sounding weird. Let's check out that suit."

# CHAPTER EIGHT

'm not going to sugarcoat it. The suit made me look like a complete idiot. It was a tight, dark green, rubber suit covered with wires and circuits and red LEDs, which had always been off before, but now that Smelly had activated the suit, they flashed in rippling patterns, like a motel sign advertising vacancies. I glanced at myself in the mirror in Jacinto's bedroom, where he'd allowed me to go to remove my outer clothes.

"What exactly are these LEDs for?" I asked Smelly.

*I find them aesthetically pleasing.*

"They're going to get me killed. I look like a runway."

*Relax. If something happens to your groveling mass of organic goo, then something happens to me. I cannot permit my brilliance to be snuffed out of the universe—not when I have so much left to contribute. When the suit enters stealth mode, no one will see you.*

I braced myself for the worst and then stepped out into the living room. Alice was standing there, and she immediately put her hand to her mouth to stifle a giggle.

"You look amazingly dumb," she said after a moment.

"Gaaahhhh!" was the thing Jacinto said at that point. He made that noise because he was standing behind me, swinging at my legs with a baseball bat. He got a lot of power into a one-handed swing, and when the bat struck me a soft white energy seemed to emanate from the suit. The bat bounced off me and

I felt only the slightest bit of pressure, but the recoil was so strong that the bat flew out of Jacinto's hand and into the wall, where it left a dent.

"You might want to warn me!" I shouted at him.

"You think they're going to warn you when they shoot at you?" he asked.

"Yeah, I do. I think they'll say something like, 'Don't move or we'll shoot.'"

"Okay," he admitted, "they probably would. But after that they'll just shoot, so what good would the warning do?"

"The point is, I didn't tell you I was ready. You could have hurt me."

"I went for your legs. Any injury would have been non-lethal."

I pointed at him. "That's really comforting. Just don't do anything to me again unless I tell you I'm ready."

"Fine," he said, looking hurt. "It's just that I only have one arm, and I wanted to contribute."

I suddenly felt horrible. "Jacinto, I'm sorry if you thought I meant—"

He laughed. "I'm just messing with you." He then rammed his fist into my stomach. The white light flashed, and his arm jerked back. He flopped it around after. "Man, that tingles right up to the elbow."

"I'd rather you stopped hitting me," I told him.

"Why? It doesn't hurt you."

Alice smacked me in the back of the head. Her attack was pretty light; I don't think it would have hurt even without the suit's protection. Her hand bounced off, and she shook out her fingers.

"That's crazy," she said. "My fingers feel a little numb."

*Shall we demonstrate your mighty powers to these evolutionary mistakes?* Smelly asked.

"I don't think we need to—"

*I'll take that as a yes,* it said.

A burst of energy radiated out of me. It lifted both Alice and Jacinto a few inches off the floor. Jacinto flew into the wall, near the dent made by the baseball bat. Alice landed on the worn leather couch. Her hair was sticking up and had gone wildly frizzy.

"I said not to do that!" I shouted at Smelly. "And I hope not to attack anyone. Isn't that what stealth mode is for?"

*It had to be tested, and they were attacking us. Violence against your oozing form is violence against me, and that cannot be tolerated.*

"It's okay," Jacinto said as he picked himself up "Always good to understand your options."

*I wonder if it also wants to understand what the fifty thousand volts of electricity you can unleash would feel like.*

"Let's skip that," I told Smelly.

"What about the stealth mode?" Jacinto said. "How does that work?"

*Activating now,* Smelly said.

Jacinto's eyes went wide. "I'd say that's working!"

Alice was walking toward me, her hand pushed out, looking like she was trying to find the wall in a pitch-black room. "Let me know if I'm getting warm."

I moved aside and accidentally knocked into an end table. A framed picture fell forward, smacking against the wood, but Alice seemed completely unaware of it.

Smelly must have seen me notice this. *The stealth mode produces a stabilization nimbus, which conceals secondary consequences of your lumbering form. In this mode you could walk on the sands of a beach or through fresh snow and you would still leave no trace of your passing.*

"Can they hear me if I speak to them?"

*Only if you so request it.*

Suddenly, the idea of breaking in Area 51 and stealing a flying saucer didn't seem quite so daunting. "What about them? Can I conceal them in my nimbus or whatever?"

*If they are within two feet, they will also be stealthed,* Smelly said.

"Turn the stealth off," I said.

*Yes, master,* Smelly answered testily. *And not that I don't like being your cabana boy, but you can activate the suit via your own will. You don't need to order me around as though you were—and I am laughing as I say this—my superior.*

Alice and Jacinto suddenly looked at me in surprise, so I figured I'd popped back into reality for them.

"We're really going to do this," Alice whispered.

"You don't have to," I told her. "Neither of you does. I mean, even with this suit, the best-case scenario is that I make it to the ship, and it is in working condition, and I fly away from Earth. I'm seriously disliked by one galactic superpower and absolutely hated by the other. Do you guys really want to become fugitives pretty much everywhere in the known universe?"

"I want to see the known universe," Alice said.

"I understand that, and it's pretty amazing out there, but it is not so amazing to be hated by billions of sentient beings. It's not so amazing to have a bigger, meaner, more powerful spaceship try to blow you up. I've experienced these things, and I don't recommend them."

"But you're still planning on going," Jacinto observed.

"I've got beings counting on me," I said. "Someone I care about needs my help, and my father is stuck in an alien prison because of me. I *have* to go. You don't. Alice, you've been a really great friend, and I don't like the idea of putting you in danger."

"I want to help you, Zeke," she said. "And now that I know what's out there, I kind of have to see it if I have the chance."

I understood all those things, and I needed Alice and Jacinto in order to find that ship. If they wanted to go and they understood the risks, I couldn't refuse their help. I couldn't even if I hated putting them in danger. I had no idea where I was going or what I needed to do once I got there.

*It may interest you to know,* Smelly interrupted, *that there are five vehicles approaching this location. The address of this domicile is programmed into their handheld computers, and each vehicle contains several armed meat bags.*

"How do you know that?" I asked.

*My ability to manipulate subatomic particles allows me to tap into your primitive communications systems.*

So, Smelly had Wi-Fi. Good to know. "How far away?"

"Less than two of your curiously arbitrary units called *miles*."

I felt panic rising up inside me, but I didn't have time for it. "Jacinto, they're coming for me."

"Who?"

"I don't know. Government types, I guess, knowingly or unknowingly working for the Phands, maybe. Smelly, do they have helicopters or anything in the air?"

*Only automobiles.*

"They're less then two miles out, coming in cars. If we're going, we need to go now."

An understanding of the situation seemed to wash over Jacinto's face, and an expression of determined calm settled in. I saw the look of an experienced soldier, a guy who had faced battle and made it through. I was suddenly glad that this guy was helping me.

I ran into the bedroom and threw my jeans and shirt on over my suit. By the time I came out, maybe thirty seconds later, Jacinto was waving me toward the kitchen.

"Let's go," he said. He led us to the garage, where a massive white pickup truck was parked facing out. While Alice got into the front seat and I climbed into the back, Jacinto attached something to the rear of the truck. He then hopped in and hit a button to open the garage door.

"Smelly, can you monitor the approaching cars?

*Of course I can. Your inquiry insults me.*

"You're the best, Smelly. Everything about you is super awesome. Which way should we go?"

*Instruct the vehicle-operating meat bag to head north from its driveway. And please refrain from offering praise. It is more demeaning than your insults.*

"Go north," I said, "whatever direction that is."

We pulled out of the driveway, and I heard something rattling behind us. I turned and saw that we were pulling a rusting flat-bed trailer full of lawn-mowing equipment.

"Maybe you should lose all that," I said. "It's going to slow us down."

"It's for show," Jacinto explained. "I've picked up a bunch of broken equipment over the years, so getting rid of it, when the time is right, is no problem."

"Then why are you dragging it around?"

Jacinto grinned. "I'm just a guy with a landscaping business. Cops are looking for a kid, right? Maybe a couple of kids? You guys duck down, and all they'll see is me. I'm just trying to earn a buck, boss."

*The vehicles are diversifying their approach vectors,* Smelly told me. *There is no way to avoid all of them before slipping their perimeter.*

"Which way puts us past the smallest number?" I asked.

Smelly told me a route, and I repeated it to Jacinto. We made it another quarter mile before we saw a dark sedan cruising toward us like a shark.

"Time to disappear," Jacinto said.

Alice and I ducked while Jacinto slowly passed by the dark sedan. He didn't look at it or wave or perform innocent bystander. He did his best impersonation of a tired guy on his way from one job to another. After a minute Jacinto said it was all clear, and we sat back up.

"Next stop, Nevada," he said. "Let's hope we don't have any more surprises."

I looked at the sky for signs of helicopters or flying saucers, but I didn't see anything. It looked like we were safe. For now.

# CHAPTER NINE

A little more than twenty-four hours later we were in the desert, in a rented van full of camping equipment, ready to break into one of the most secure and secretive military bases in the history of human civilization. To call it a break-in, though, would make it seem much more exciting than what we had in mind. Jacinto's scheme was for us to get taken into custody.

"If you guys were older," Jacinto explained as we made the long drive from south Texas to the Nevada desert, "we could have done this the easy way. I've got a friend who works with the security subcontractor who handles civilian employees. He could have gotten us on the daily bus out of Las Vegas. But there's no way they're not going to notice a couple of thirteen-year-old kids."

A bus that took us through the front gates would have been a convenient solution. Instead we had to take a more challenging approach. Area 51 was famous throughout the world as the alleged site of alleged research on an alleged UFO that had allegedly crashed outside of Roswell, New Mexico, in the 1940s. We were going disguised as UFO fanatics.

Jacinto was acting like a man who had no plans to return to his old life, which worried me. It wasn't that I didn't trust him. Even without Smelly monitoring his vital signs for indications of deception or insanity, I could tell that he genuinely wanted to help Alice, but also that he would do anything—even risk spending years in jail—if it meant getting a decent shot at going on an interstellar joy ride in the Area 51 UFO. I trusted that he was on the level, but I also knew I was going to have to disappoint him. Smelly didn't want Jacinto and Alice coming along because he thought they might slow us down. I had my own reasons: I didn't want to get them killed. I was heading into a big, dangerous mess, and I didn't want to drag them along any further than I had to.

Getting out of San Antonio had proved surprisingly easy. Once we were certain we'd lost our pursuers, Jacinto found an empty lot, where he ditched his rusted, useless landscaping equipment. He almost looked on the verge of tears as he unhitched the trailer and abandoned the prop. The stuff was junk, but I understood how he felt. He had been holding on to that equipment for years, waiting for the moment when he would need it, and now that moment was here. There was a kind of sadness in letting something like that go. The trailer full of lawn equipment was like the section of a rocket that is cast off after it has burned its fuel—vital but ultimately disposable.

From there Jacinto drove to the San Antonio airport, where he put the truck in long-term parking, which would help to throw off the pursuers, he said. We took the shuttle to a rental car place, where Jacinto selected a van—probably the last time he would be able to use his credit card—and we were on our way.

"Jacinto," I told him as we sped west on I-10, "I am incredibly grateful to you for doing this, but you're spending all this money. Are you going to be okay?"

"We won't need money where we're going, right?" he said. "Just credits or whatever."

"Gold-pressed latinum," Alice suggested.

I ignored this, not wanting to cover the same old ground again. I'd made my position clear, and Jacinto still wanted to help me. I had to hope they were going to come out of this okay.

Jacinto powered through the long drive, drinking cup after cup of coffee. We stopped only to eat, for frequent coffee-induced bathroom breaks, and once to visit a gigantic sporting goods store to buy camping equipment whose only purpose was to provide a realistic cover story.

I was sprawled out in the back. Alice sat next to Jacinto. Both of us slept a lot. When I wasn't sleeping, my feelings shifted from fear of getting caught to worrying about my mother to daring to hope that I might actually be able to see Tamret again. Once, Jacinto told us to wake up. He was grinning because the highway turned into a main street that ran through downtown Roswell, New Mexico, where the streetlights were shaped like flying saucers. We drove right past the UFO museum, where Jacinto said he had spent many hours doing *research*. This whole town thought of the UFOs as something cute, a funny symbol to bring in the tourists. If they'd ever met one of the real monsters who flew around in flying saucers, they might have felt differently.

After what seemed like an endless amount of driving, we pulled off the desolate Highway 93 onto the even more desolate, and curiously named, Mercury Highway. This was where things started to get a little unsettling. We passed signs letting us know we were getting close to military land. We were warned of missile testing and promised imminent arrest. Jacinto said that there was nothing to worry about and that as long we did not cross onto the base, we would be left alone.

We stopped at a campground called Hawkeye Hill. It was late afternoon by then, and unbelievably hot. As we set up our tents, I downed a couple of bottles of water, which kept me alive, but not particularly quenched. Within five minutes I was sweaty and hot and miserable, and that was with my temperature-controlling high-tech suit under my clothes. For Jacinto and Alice, it was a hundred times worse.

"This place is nothing but ridiculous," Jacinto said as we worked. "Look how close we are to the base."

He gestured, and I saw the line of orange signs, spaced maybe fifty yards apart, warning us that we were about to cross into Area 51 and be arrested. They were less than a hundred feet away from the campground, which was absolutely without amenities. The remnants of old cook fires were the only signs that human beings had ever been here before.

"Only the hardest of hard-core Area Fifty-One freaks ever camp here," Jacinto said. "It's for the complete wackos, guys who have lost all touch with reality."

"How did you know about it?" I asked.

He grinned. "Oh, I've camped here lots of times. I know the ropes."

In the distance I could see Humvees crossing back and forth upon the featureless grounds of the base, the sun glinting off their side mirrors. They left trails of dust like comets.

Once the tents were set up, we crawled into the largest one to escape the relentless desert sun. We drank from our canteens and ate sandwiches we'd bought at the last little town we'd gone through. The bread was stale and the cheese hard, but I wasn't complaining. From that point on it would be nothing but food bars.

"I need some sleep if I'm going to be any use, but I'll wake up some time after dark. Then we move."

"You think we'll actually be able to make it very far?" Alice asked.

"No," Jacinto told her. "The soldiers haven't taken their eyes off of us since we stopped. They'll be watching us with night vision. I'd say we'll get maybe ten feet onto the base before we're arrested." Jacinto smiled at me. "Then it's time for you to do your thing, or we're all going to jail."

"Are we up for this, Smelly?" I asked.

*No,* it said, *I've let you bring us out to this desolate wilderness for the pleasure of taking in the scent of your perspiring companions. Of course I'm up for it.*

Jacinto slept until about midnight, and we packed up our equipment and were on our way in less than half an hour. The temperature had dropped significantly, and it was now quite cold, though the suit kept me well insulated.

It hardly mattered. We weren't going to be outside long. The point, Jacinto explained to us, was to convince the soldiers that we were wackos. We had to be believable wackos, which meant we needed to be carrying provisions and maps and other hiking equipment. We had to look like people who believed we could cross the outlying Nevada desert, slip onto a military base, and reach buildings that were miles inside the perimeter.

"Once they stop us," Jacinto said, "they'll ask us questions, so just focus on how angry you are that the government's not telling us what it knows about aliens. Unless they decide we're actual terrorists, they'll eventually call the Lincoln County Sheriff's Department to come take us to jail. That shouldn't be a problem. Lincoln County is big, but the population is small, and it's the middle of the night. There aren't going to be too many officers on duty. It should be at least an hour before anyone arrives, so we'll have plenty of time."

I started to take off my outer clothes, but I didn't get past the top button of my shirt before a disembodied arm appeared out of nowhere and slapped the back of my hand.

*Don't bother,* Smelly said, as his floating arm illusion vanished. *The suit works fine with your outer clothes on.*

"Then why did you let me take them off when—"

*Because it was funny, okay? Don't you primitive ooze-balls understand humor?*

I turned to the others. "Apparently, I don't have to take off the outer clothes," I told the others.

Jacinto laughed. "Man, your AI is funny."

We headed out into the night and, as predicted, we had not taken more than a few steps past one of the orange warning posts before we heard the rumble of an engine and headlights blinded us. I tried to blink light and sweat out of my eyes—I felt like I needed to see what was going on in order to not do something to get us shot—but it was all a blur. Soldiers were shouting at us, warning us to drop to our knees and put our hands behind our heads or we would be shot. I squeezed my eyes shut and did exactly what they said to do.

There were two of them, pistols in hand, scowling at us as we kneeled in the blinding brightness of the headlights.

The soldiers cuffed our hands behind our backs, and they patted us down, looking for weapons. For the record, handcuffs hurt, even if they're not ridiculously tight. I can't endorse a life of crime. We were then placed into the back of the Humvee and driven a short distance through the desert to an isolated guard post, a small building with a few workstations and an interrogation room—one I imagined had been used to question many UFO enthusiasts over the years. On our way in, I glanced around, taking note of everything I saw. There were two other soldiers visible at workstations, one filling out paperwork, one playing a game on his phone. We were going to have to deal with them if we planned to escape.

Once we were in the bare room and sitting on metal chairs, another soldier came in and began to question us. He did his best to act like he took us seriously as a national security threat, but it was written all over his face that he thought Jacinto was just another nut, and an irresponsible one at that, taking two kids onto a secure military base. The soldier barked questions at us, like he didn't know how to ask anything without shouting. Why were we here, who did we work for, what were our intentions?

"We have a right to know the truth!" Jacinto shouted. "You can't hide it from us any longer."

"You can't keep your secrets forever!" Alice shouted, like she actually believed what she was saying. "Why can't you tell us the truth?"

"The UFO is part of our national heritage," I said somewhat lamely. "Like the Liberty Bell."

The soldier was a professional, and he did not roll his eyes.

After an hour of this, it was pretty clear the soldier had decided we were clueless idiots who had put our freedom in jeopardy for no good reason. He left the room for about fifteen minutes and then came back to tell us that we were to be handed over to the civilian authorities.

"What is going to happen to us then?" Alice asked, sounding completely frightened. She was either really worried or she was a terrific actor.

*Your friend is attempting to deceive the authority figures,* Smelly informed me, as if he guessed what was on my mind. *Its heart rate is steady and it shows no sign of secreting its nasty perspiration. That unevolved being does not waver.*

"You're going to jail for sure," the soldier said to Jacinto. "I don't know what's going to happen to these kids. That's for the county to figure out."

"Can you at least loosen my cuffs?" I asked the soldier. "They're really tight. I can't feel my hands."

He looked at me, and I could see he was suspicious. This was the oldest trick in the book, to be sure, but on the other hand, I was a kid, and if word got out that he'd been unnecessarily cruel to a minor, he knew it would be bad news for him.

The soldier peered down to study me. "You're not going to do anything stupid, are you?"

I shook my head and tried to look like I was holding back tears.

The soldier leaned in with his key, and as soon as he made contact, I grabbed his wrist and whispered, "Zap him," too quietly for anyone but Smelly to hear. Instantly, fifty thousand volts shot through my hand. The soldier convulsed, his eyes shot upward, and he fell to the floor.

"Sorry," I said to the soldier, who clearly did not hear me.

*"Zap him"?* Smelly asked. *That's the command you give? This suit is the most sophisticated piece of technology currently on this ridiculous planet. It does not zap.*

"Seems to zap pretty well to me," I said. I willed the suit to give me superior strength and to shield my skin, and I pulled my hands apart, breaking the cuffs. They snapped like they were made of dry spaghetti.

"The key's right there," Jacinto said, gesturing toward the floor.

I shrugged. "I thought this would be cooler." I took the key and unlocked Jacinto's and Alice's cuffs, and then I used it to rid myself of my own broken cuffs, which were dangling from my wrists like weird jewelry.

"You guys wait here," I told them.

I wanted to act brave, but the truth was, I was really scared. Back when my friends and I had broken into a Phandic prison, things had happened too quickly for me to think much about what we were doing. Plus there had been several of us: Steve and Mi Sun, who could do most of the fighting; Charles and Nayana, who could tackle the strategic issues; and Tamret, who could figure a way out of just about any mess. It hadn't all been my burden. Now it was. Alice was smart, and Jacinto was ex-military, but this was still my show. *I* was in charge. Jacinto and Alice were here to help me, but their freedom— and maybe, now that we'd attacked a soldier, their lives—were on the line. I couldn't mess this up.

I turned to open the door. I stepped out and put my hands behind me, like they were cuffed. The soldier playing the game on his phone looked up.

"Hey, the other guy said I could use the bathroom," I told him.

The two soldiers looked at each other. The one doing the paperwork shrugged. The one with the phone gestured toward a closed door across the room.

"Can you open it for me?" I asked.

He sighed and got up. As he walked over, I realized I hadn't thought this ruse through too well, because if I really were handcuffed, this guy was also going to have to pull down my pants for me, and neither one of us was going to like that very much. In fact, as he put his hand on the doorknob, a look came over the soldier's face, like he suddenly understood what he was going to be asked to do.

I decided not to let him worry. I put a hand on him and shot him full of electricity. The other soldier looked up at the crackling sound. The scent of something burning hovered in the air.

I could see the alarm in his eyes, and he reached for his sidearm, but I was already there, leaping across the twenty feet, hands out. I crashed into him, zapping him—that's right, zapping!—and landed almost gracefully on my feet.

I ran back to the interrogation room and opened the door. "We're good," I said.

They began moving toward the door. "There's no way to know how long before another soldier stops by," Jacinto said. "We've got to move."

I went outside alone to make sure no other soldiers were lurking. It was quiet. I grabbed a set of keys from a post near the door, and we went back out and got into the the Humvee.

It was time to find the UFO.

Things were going to get hairy as we approached the main building; there was no getting around it. Jacinto did a good job of getting us in, however. He said he remembered his way, sort of, and the rest he knew from studying satellite photos and reading secret documents. The UFO was housed in a massive warehouse at the north end of the base. Unfortunately, it would also be the most heavily guarded part of the base.

We drove without drawing any unwanted attention. We were in a military vehicle and it was dark outside, so no one could see into the car. We pulled into a parking lot maybe a quarter of a mile from the warehouse and got out. I had Jacinto and Alice walk close to me, each of them draping an arm around my shoulders as I activated the stealth field. It was a little awkward, but we simply walked up to the main base, slid past the barrier at the checkpoint, and approached the warehouse. We were going to walk into one of the most secure locations in the country, and no one would know.

Not at all surprisingly, the door was locked and required a keypad entrance. Smelly used the suit to scan the keypad and projected a probable entry code. I punched it in, and the door clicked and slid open. It was that easy. We stepped into the building.

Inside was not a huge warehouse, but a corridor. I figured there were numerous rooms and projects in here, but there had to be some kind of UFO hangar somewhere. I looked at Jacinto, but he shook his head.

"I don't know. I've never seen this part of the building before. We'll just have to wander around until we find something I recognize or some clue to where we should go."

We made our way forward in the dim light, avoiding obstacles, and sticking close together to remain invisible. The corridor was long and industrial-looking, with concrete floors, cinder-block walls, and metal doors. The lights were dim, but it seemed like the hallway went on almost forever, and there was no UFO THIS WAY sign anywhere.

The darkness was also the reason I tripped. It would be nice if I hadn't been to blame, but it was me. I stumbled on a slightly raised step—the kind with a black-and-yellow stripe to keep idiots like me from tripping—and went lurching forward. I stayed stealthed, but for just that instant Jacinto and Alice were visible, which allowed them to be picked up on security cameras or motion detectors or whatever they had.

That was all it took.

A jarring claxon sounded. Red lights began flashing.

*Way to go, you idiot.*

Jacinto looked around. Even in the dim light I could see that his face was drawn. "I think we need to hurry."

"Stay behind me," I told them, unstealthing. It would be harder to protect them if they had no idea where I was. We reached another locked door, and I punched in the key code Smelly fed me. It didn't work.

"They must be on lockdown," Jacinto said. "You probably need an emergency code to gain access now."

I nodded. I was already moving to plan B, and Smelly was feeding me instructions. It told me to try to break the door down, and with no time to argue that I couldn't do that, I slammed my shoulder into the door, which flew forward. Our way was clear. Except for the six soldiers waiting for us, rifles out. And they were firing their guns, which were shooting actual bullets, at us.

Jacinto and Alice dove for cover. I ran toward the soldiers. The field generated by the suit stopped the bullets in midair. They fell to the floor like a handful of bolts while I ran past the soldiers, one hand out, like I was giving a team high five. I made contact with the first man, dishing out a blast to render him unconscious, and then moved on to the next one. It took about thirty seconds, but they all went down.

The alarm was still sounding, but at least gunfire had ended.

I let Jacinto and Alice know we were in the clear, and we continued on.

"You should have kept one of them conscious," Jacinto said. "Maybe he could have told us where to go, so we're not wandering around here forever."

It was a good point, and I wished I'd thought of it. When we entered the next room, it was what I had in mind. I went ahead to scout and found two soldiers, who were surprised by my bursting through the door, sending it off its hinges. I tased one right away and then knocked the weapon out of the hands of the other one.

"Where's the UFO?" I demanded, lifting him off the floor by his shirt, which wasn't easy, given he was easily a foot taller than I was.

"I don't know!" he cried.

*It is lying,* Smelly said.

"I know you're lying," I said. "Tell me!" I shouted this last part, trying to sound fierce.

"Two flights down," he said. "Follow the signs for section C-Eleven."

*Now it speaks the truth.*

I let him drop. "Come on, guys!" I shouted. I then turned back to the soldier to knock him out. I realized, in a terrible moment, that I'd done those in the wrong order. I should have flooded him with electricity first, because in that one instant when he had turned away, he had taken a hand grenade off his belt and tossed it on the floor in front of Jacinto and Alice.

Time seemed to slow down. I felt like I stood there forever, looking at the grenade as it spun lazily on the concrete floor. Jacinto and Alice looked up, horrified, as realization washed over them. The soldier was already fleeing, pin in his hand, which meant the grenade was going to explode and nothing could change that.

Smelly immediately sent a flash of images to my mind. It was a jumble, but I understood them. I did not have time to get the soldier, retrieve the pin from his hand, and neutralize the grenade. My only choice was to run.

Except I wasn't about to let Jacinto and Alice die because they had tried to help me. There was only one other choice, and I took it. I threw myself on top of the grenade.

This sounds much braver than it felt at the time. I didn't feel brave; I just wanted to protect my friends. I also believed, or hoped, that the suit would keep me from getting killed.

I distantly heard Smelly objecting, but by the time I'd leaped forward, it was too late for it to do anything about it. Smelly might have been able to manipulate my body, but it couldn't do much about the laws of gravity. I landed hard, feeling the grenade like a lump under my stomach. Then there was a bright light, and heat washed over me, and I had the nasty feeling of my back hitting the floor. Except that I was looking down at the floor, and I figured out that I'd just been smacked against the ceiling. Which meant that the floor was below me, and I was rushing toward it. When I slammed into it, the experience was unpleasant.

I picked myself up slowly. My pants and shirt were in tatters, like I was a skinny-kid version of the Hulk. The suit underneath was torn as well, completely shredded in some places, and I had no doubt it had been destroyed. There was no sign of blood, missing limbs, or mangled organs, so that went into the plus column. Alice and Jacinto were looking at me, stunned, unable to believe what I'd just done, but there was no time to waste marveling. My suit was ruined. I now had no way to protect us from the soldiers.

*You are even more of an idiot than I dared believe,* Smelly said sadly. *You broke my suit.*

"I had to do something," I said, feeling kind of whiny. I would let Smelly berate me more later.

"Time to move," I said, as though I knew what I was doing. I didn't. We were now inside a government base housing the greatest secret in the world. I'd set off alarms, taken down soldiers, and caused a whole lot of super-secret military property damage. The one thing we had that was going to keep us safe was gone. I had no idea what I was doing, but I figured we had to find that ship fast and get out of there, or we were all in big trouble. I followed a staircase down, and then we entered another floor, full of corridors. We followed the signs to C-11 and somehow, miraculously, we encountered no resistance.

When we rounded the corner, we came to a key-coded door. Not waiting for me to ask, Smelly projected a series of lights onto the keyboard, and I punched them in the order it showed me. The door opened, and we went through.

On the other side was a massive chamber—it seemed as big as a football stadium. There were forklifts and golf carts and metal shelves piled high with machines whose purpose I could not even guess at. There were shelves filled with boxes containing alien artifacts, or the lost ark, or who-knows-what. And there, in the center, was what I had most hoped to find: a Phandic cruiser. The black saucer sat in the center of the cavernous room, somehow still menacing despite looking forlorn and beached. For an instant my heart leaped with joy.

Then that joy vanished, as I realized what I was looking at: not a working Phandic cruiser, but the remains of one.

Pieces were missing; the hull was full of holes. Wires and fibers and strands of metal hung loose from entire sections. People had been working on, tinkering with, and straight-up dissecting the vessel for decades. The Phandic ship sat crooked, broken and lifeless. It wasn't going to take me anywhere.

I hardly had time to let despair wash over me before I heard the sound of boots tramping the floor behind me. We were trapped. This had been my one shot at escaping, and it had come to nothing. Now I was caught with nowhere to run. I'd led myself, and people who trusted me, to ruin.

I held up my hands, and Alice did the same. After a moment Jacinto held up his arm. I turned to face whoever was coming for me. Would they be Phands, or would they be government operatives in their service?

Instead I saw the familiar face: haggard, stern, and scarred. A patch covering the right eye. "Hello, Mr. Reynolds," said Colonel Richard Rage. "We've been looking for you."

Behind him were at least ten soldiers, their short automatic weapons raised at us. Colonel Rage waved them down. "No more trouble from you, right?"

"Yeah," I said. "You don't need the guns."

"You made quite a mess," the colonel said.

I shook my head. "All that talk you gave me about wanting to protect America," I said to him. "And now, what? You're going to turn me over to the enemy?"

"The enemy?" he barked. "I'm not handing you over to any enemy, son. That's not how we do things on my watch."

"Coming through," said a voice I'd thought I'd never hear again. "Let him see I'm here."

From behind the line of soldiers came a being the likes of which had never been seen on Earth before. He was barely five feet tall, but broad-shouldered, built like a predator. His boar-like snout was adorned with sharp tusks, and his open mouth revealed gleaming white teeth, sharp as needles. Thick, ropy hair hung from his head, and he regarded us with unreadable black eyes.

It was my old friend Urch.

Apparently there were no space-orc Phands coming with their PPB pistols out, ready to blast me into submission—just Urch and a bunch of American soldiers. Breaking into Area 51 could have ended a whole lot of ways, but I hadn't predicted this one.

Urch, looking predatorily dapper in his Confederation uniform, gave me an affectionate clap on the back while Colonel Rage and the soldiers watched nervously.

"Urch!" I shouted. "Man, it's good to see you."

"You as well, my friend," Urch said to me, making wild gestures as though that would somehow make his meaning clearer. "I like your planet."

"It has its moments," I told him.

Urch looked at me funny, and it occurred to me that he hadn't expected me to understand him. He'd been talking to me for his benefit, not for mine. Now he was going to have questions, and I wasn't sure I had answers.

*Listen up, meat boy!* Smelly suddenly announced in the inside-your-head equivalent of a shout. *It is imperative that no one from the Confederation know about me. They might attempt to remove me from your head, with knives and burning lasers, and the damage to you would be irreversible. It wouldn't be good for me, either, but since you're inherently self-absorbed, it's in the interest of your survival to keep me a secret.*

I did not want anyone cutting and burning things out of my head, so I figured it was a good idea to follow this advice.

"All right," Rage said gruffly. "You two are pals. That's terrific. Now we have a few things to discuss, so if Reynolds is done tearing up our base, let's go find someplace to sit down." He turned to one of his soldiers. "And find the kid some clothes or something. I don't like chaos, soldier. Or looking at underpants, for that matter."

"Yes, sir," the soldier said.

We were escorted into an office whose walls were covered with shelves containing stacks of documents, each bound by tape marked CLASSIFIED. The space had a slapped-together, industrial feel, but even so it was large and well air-conditioned, which I appreciated. Breaking into a legendary military base and destroying a supersuit is sweaty work. Before I could sit, a soldier called me out of the room and handed me an olive-green T-shirt with a US Army insignia on it and green uniform pants that were several sizes too big. I looked like a little kid playing dress-up with his father's clothes, but it beat the shredded wet suit and visible undies.

The colonel sat behind a wooden desk, while Alice, Jacinto, and I were invited to sit. Colonel Rage had somehow acquired a steaming cup of coffee, which he seemed to enjoy sipping. It was, after all, the middle of the night. A hot drink sounded good, and I had hoped someone might offer me a hot chocolate, but no luck there.

Urch continued to stand, but he appeared excited, in a good way. He kept opening his mouth to show his sharp teeth, and thrusting his tusks upward as if he were disemboweling an invisible antelope. I knew him well enough to understand that these were signs he was happy, but the others . . . it suddenly occurred to me that neither of them had never seen an alien before. I looked over at Alice, who was staring in undisguised shock.

"He's an alien," I told her, keeping my voice quiet, like this was a secret. "He comes from another planet."

"Yeah, I got that," she said, her eyes practically doing cartoon spirals behind her glasses. "You were telling the truth about everything."

"Of course I was telling the truth," I snapped, feeling a little hurt. "Did you help me break into a government facility because you thought I was making it up—or crazy?"

"It's one thing to trust someone," Jacinto said, also staring at Urch, "and even to completely believe them, but it's another to actually meet an alien. Especially one who's so scary."

Urch sighed.

"Time to make sure we're all on the same page," Colonel Rage began. "As you can see from this alien creature here—"

Urch waved hello.

"—your friends from the Confederation have sent an envoy. I know you've been eluding us for days. It's a good thing we figured out where you were headed. We only got here in time to keep you from completely wrecking the place."

"I don't get it," I said. "If you're here, Urch, why did my mother signal for me to run?"

"She made an honest mistake," Colonel Rage said, looking

more than a little exasperated. "Five dark sedans, escorted by several local police cars with flashing lights, pulled up to your house, and she feared the worst, especially with false reports of flying saucers showing up all over the Internet. It took us a while to convince her we weren't out to harm you, and after that she couldn't get in touch to clear things up. You had already ditched your phone, which was the right thing to do, by the way, if you believed the bad guys were onto you. If you hadn't tried to break into a government facility, I'm not sure how long it would have taken us to find you."

"Okay," I said. "Why is the Confederation looking for me?"

"You and your friends altered many things, Zeke," Urch explained. "You set a great number of changes in motion, and not all of them good, but while I have many grievances with how things are going in the Confederation, I cannot argue with the most significant difference. The Phandic ships you and your associates captured were examined, and the secrets of their weaponry discovered. Our own ships have been upgraded with this technology, and since then, every military advance the Phands have attempted has been pushed back with no loss of Confederation life. Their civilization continues to exist, of course, and the worlds they have captured remain in their power, but the Phandic Empire's ability to conquer and grow has been brought to a halt."

This was big news. In spite of our setbacks, it turned out that everything we had done had mattered. I'd risked my life, my friends' lives, even my father's life, because I'd believed that giving the Confederation a Phandic ship would save lives— including those on Earth. To learn that, in spite of Junup's threats, the stolen ships had been put to good use, made me feel like it had all been worth it. We had turned things around for the Confederation.

"Why is that alien growling at us?" Alice said.

"Oh, right. You can't understand him." I turned to Urch. "I don't suppose they can get translation nanites, can they?"

"There can be no unauthorized distribution of nanites," Urch said, looking at me a little intensely.

"Seems the Confederation has rules about that sort of thing," Colonel Rage said. "I'm serving as a liaison, so I let them shoot me with those little machines, though I can't say I much like it. But I need to be able to talk to this creature here. As for your friends, we don't want them knowing more than they have to. These people have already become security problems, and the less information they have, the less they can spill."

"So, what are the bad changes?" I asked Urch.

"You may recall that Chief Justice Junup wanted to return the cruisers to the Phands. By alerting the news outputs, however, you effectively forced his hand and prevented him from surrendering the ships."

I nodded.

"Instead he took credit for their capture. He has risen to underdirector of the Committee of Grand Oversight, which governs all other committees. In effect he is now the second most powerful being in the Confederation."

"How can anyone trust him?" I asked. "At best he's a gutless weenie. At worst he's working with the Phands."

"I agree," Urch said, "but he knows the political game, and he has played it extremely well. As a result he is widely regarded as a hero. Most beings would identify him as the mastermind behind the raid you and your friends led on the Phandic prison.

Others may have done the actual physical labor, but it was Junup who captured the two cruisers, and who prevented the Phands from getting hold of some ancient Former tech that would have changed everything."

"He didn't do any of those things," I said, reeling with anger. Whatever Phands had the tree activated in their system were probably working twenty-six hours a day to acquire levels and master new military skills. The Confederation was resting easy, but it probably should have been gearing up for war, because that empire, as soon as it was ready, was not going to hesitate to strike back.

"There's more," Urch said. "In rising to power, Junup decided it was time to eliminate some old enemies. Captain Qwlessl has been dismissed from her post in the fleet, and I have been reduced in rank. We have been punished for our testimony at your hearing."

I couldn't believe it. Big, lumbering Captain Qwlessl, with her trunk and her hammerhead-shark eyes, was a great captain and an even better friend. Getting rid of her just because she'd told the truth at a hearing—a place you are required to tell the truth—was completely unfair. I shook my head. There was nothing to say that wouldn't trivialize what Junup had done.

"Do not think to blame yourself," Urch said. "You cannot be held responsible for how dishonorable beings respond to being outplayed."

"Still, the captain loved her job. She must be miserable."

"There are many options for a being with her knowledge and experience," Urch said. "She was unhappy, and no one likes to suffer injustice, but I can assure you she has found new purpose. I fear things are even worse for your old friend Dr. Roop."

I sat up straight now. From the moment I met him, Dr. Roop had done everything he could to look out for me. Even before I met him: The giraffelike being had been my father's friend, and he'd worked to help bring me to the Confederation. After my father was captured, Dr. Roop had gone on to bring in the randoms who would help me save my father—Steve and Tamret. I felt like I owed Dr. Roop everything, and the news that things had gone badly for him hit me hard.

"Roop is, in my view, an honorable being, but there is no doubt that he broke Confederation law. His role in selecting the specific randoms to participate in the initiation program was discovered," Urch continued. "Peace officers were sent to arrest him, but he fled. I'm afraid Dr. Roop is now a fugitive, his whereabouts unknown."

"That doesn't sound like him," I said. "He struck me as a face-the-music sort of being."

"I agree. On my world, and I suspect on yours, fleeing from the authorities is common among the accused, but in the Confederation it is virtually unknown. Beings accept the consequences of their actions without complaint. Junup has stated that Dr. Roop was corrupted by his exposure to primitive species. This is the song he sings—along with his Movement for Peace, an organization that seeks to eradicate the influence of primitive and carnivorous species."

"What do you mean, 'eradicate the influence'?" I asked.

"Beings believed to be too 'primitive' are being dismissed from government positions. Had I not had a personal connection with you, Zeke, I would never have been sent on a mission of this importance—not when my species is so widely regarded as savage. The Movement for Peace hates violence so much that they attack violent species in the street."

"The Movement for Peace is attacking and hurting peaceful beings because they are too inclined to violence?" I asked.

Urch grunted. "It is exactly that stupid."

"Gets messy when the good guys don't behave like the good guys," Colonel Rage said, shaking his head.

"The Confederation remains a fair and just place," Urch assured Colonel Rage. "I would not serve it otherwise. The Movement for Peace is not a controlling voice in our political system. The anger toward 'primitives' is a minority position, though I see it growing faster than makes me comfortable."

I shook my head. "Okay, that is a whole lot of bad news."

"It's not all bad. While Junup is your bitter enemy, Ghli Wixxix, director of the Committee of Grand Oversight, feels otherwise. The second most powerful being in the Confederation may hate the smell of your entrails, Zeke, but the *most* powerful being recognizes exactly what you have done for us, and she is grateful."

"I don't think I've met this Ghli Wixxix. I'm glad she likes me, but I'm guessing you didn't come all this way to get my autograph."

"Ghli Wixxix is on board my ship," Urch said. "She has chosen to come here herself to escort you back to Confederation Central."

Okay, this was interesting. All I'd wanted since getting back to Earth was to return to the Confederation, but now that I was being offered the chance, I found myself growing suspicious. "Why do they want me?"

Urch grunted. "I do not know, but the director understands

what you have accomplished, and you have impressed her so much that she believes your presence on the station is vital to the future of the Confederation."

I had no idea what this director might hope to get out of me, but I wasn't going to worry about that right now. All I needed to know was if I was being set up for some kind of trap. "You're my friend, Urch, and I know you wouldn't sugarcoat it. Can I trust her?"

"I believe you can. I have voted for her in every election. I know she and Junup were once friends, but they have publicly broken ties. She has always behaved honorable for a politician. If she says she needs you for something important, then she believes it to be so."

"Wow," I said, thinking things through. "The fact that you vouch for her goes a long way, but if I am going to put myself in her power, I'm going to need certain things *before* I agree to anything. I'm not going to hold out for a payout at the end. I've been burned by Confederation politics before. I'll meet with this Ghli Wixxix, and I'll do what she asks of me within reason, but only after I get what I want. That's the deal, and she can take it or leave it."

"Ghli Wixxix is a politician, Zeke, but she is not stupid," Urch said.

"Meaning what?" I asked.

"Meaning," said a voice from behind me, "the director figured you'd say something like that."

The person who'd spoken came into the office. It was my father.

# CHAPTER TEN

The last time I'd seen my father, he had been big and green and fictionally Martian, his appearance altered by a process called conversion. Now he had been converted back, and here he was, the man I remembered from when I was seven years old. He looked like he hadn't aged a day, and was maybe even a little younger. While he no longer had J'onn J'onzz's superhero physique, he was still a little more buff than I remembered him. Clearly he'd taken advantage of the conversion parameters. Either that or his Confederation prison featured a pretty good gym.

I gave him a hug.

He squeezed me back, hard. "It's so good to see you," he told me. "It's so good to be home, and to know that the planet is safe."

I was still trying to process the fact that my father was out of prison. "They just let you go?" I asked, as soon as my father was done squeezing me.

"Pretty much," he said. "I think Ghli Wixxix knew you wouldn't trust her to deliver in the end, so she decided to grant me a pardon and deliver up front."

"And what if I say no?" I asked. "Is Urch supposed to take you back into custody?"

"She knows better than to demand that of me," Urch said.

"I'm a freebie," my father said. "A good-faith gesture. No

matter what you decide, I'm here to stay. I'm sure the director had to call in some favors for that, though I have to imagine our old friend Junup was glad to get me out of the Confederation."

I hugged my father again. Did my mother know? Had anyone prepared her, or was she going to be surprised? "I'm glad you're back, but I still don't know what's really going on. Do you have any idea what the director wants from me?"

He shook his head. "As near as I can tell. Ghli Wixxix is one of the good guys, but she's still a politician, Zeke, so she is always thinking about the big picture, not individuals. Remember that you don't owe her anything. They owe *you*. I've been gone now almost half your life. We can finally be a family again. There's something to be said for telling her you don't want any part of it. Whatever the director is going to ask you to do, it will be dangerous, and you've risked enough for the Confederation already. Let someone else have a turn."

I missed the Confederation. I missed the feeling of being on a massive space station built by mysterious precursor aliens when the Earth was still just a ball of hot fire. I missed the sight of space from viewscreens while traveling on a ship that hurled past stars and planets, and I missed the inexplicable and disorienting sensation as we jumped from reality into something else when we tunneled from one spot in the galaxy to another. I missed the adventure and the excitement and the wonder and the nearly endless variety of alien life. In spite of everything that had gone wrong, the challenges I'd faced, and the injustices I'd endured, I'd never felt I belonged anywhere as much as I had on Confederation Central. For all that, though, I would have refused to go back if it weren't for the one thing I missed the most: my friends.

"I want Tamret to be offered political asylum," I said to

Urch. "She needs to be given a home on the station, and she needs immunity from all crimes, past and future."

"Future crimes? That's a lot to ask," my dad said.

"We're talking about *Tamret*," I told him. "She breaks half a dozen laws between getting out of bed and brushing her teeth. I'm not going to agree to anything unless I know she's safe."

Urch tapped on his data bracelet, and a document hovered in the air between us. "You can read this over later, but Ghli Wixxix's office has already agreed, essentially, to what you are asking. Even getting this agreement has cost her a great deal of political capital—I can assure you, Junup fought her every inch of the way—but the director has many allies, and you'll find that the asylum terms are most generous. Crimes against the physical well-being of others are not included, and neither are crimes against the security of the Confederation, but otherwise they are offering Tamret full diplomatic immunity. She'll also be given enough credits that she won't need to commit crimes. She'll be very comfortable."

"Comfort probably won't stop her," I said, "but it's a start. And I'm going to need the same offer to be extended to Steve. I want him to be given the chance to come back."

Urch grunted. "This, too, has been anticipated and approved."

"And if I'm heading back to the Confederation, I'll need a team," I said. "People I know and trust. I want Charles, Nayana, and Mi Sun to come along, if they're up for it. And Steve. He needs to be given a chance to come back from Ish-hi."

"Those are all requests that serve other beings," my father said. "Don't you want anything for yourself?"

I shook my head. "That's all I care about. If you and my

friends are safe, then I'll try to do what she wants."

"Your mom isn't going to like this," my dad said.

"His mother would be living on a world ruled by the Phandic Empire if it weren't for Zeke," Urch said. "It is best if she counts her blessings."

"But my dad has a good point," I said. "I don't want to be away indefinitely. I want to make sure I can get back to Earth, and then back to the Confederation." I swallowed hard before I said this, because I knew it was a crazy thing to ask for. Still, I had to try. "I want my own ship."

Urch hissed his laughing noise.

"Are you laughing because that's a ridiculous request?"

"I'm laughing because the director has already made the offer. She cannot give you everything you want before you complete her task—otherwise she has no power over you—so here is what the director proposes: Tamret will be rescued simply as payment for agreeing to meet with the director and hear her request. As for the rest you, and whichever of your old associates that choose to join you, will have to return to Confederation Central in order to perform such services as the director requires. If you are successful on all points, then you will receive three items as payment for services. First, limited citizenship, so you can, if you choose, reside on Confederation Central or on any planet in the Confederation; second, an artifact carrier as your personal property, so you can visit your home world, or any other world, at your own convenience; and, finally, the third reward: the planets originally selected to apply for membership will receive another opportunity to join. Earth, Rarel, Ish-hi, and Ganar will all provide a new group of initiates. None of those young people previously selected will be chosen again, and this opportunity will be offered within two standard years of the completion of your assignment."

I sat down. That pretty much nailed it. I was on board before, but this gave me all the ammunition I would need for my mother. Membership in the Confederation meant access to their incredible technology, which boiled down to an end to sickness and poverty and hunger. Earth could become a place of happiness and prosperity and peace. If I refused to play along, I'd be standing in the way. I had no idea what the director wanted, and for all I knew it would be something I wouldn't want to do, but if it was at all possible, I'd help her.

My father seemed to understand what I was thinking. "You do have a choice," he told me.

I shook my head, trying to sort it all out. I understood what my father was saying, but he was acting like I could walk away from this offer, and I didn't think that was true. "I have a choice, but there's only one right one, isn't there?"

He came and sat down next to me. "A few years back I faced the same choice. I could go back to my family, or I could stay away and try to help the entire world. I know I made the right decision, but it was a painful one, and it hurt every day. You need to understand what you are agreeing to. You're still just a kid, but you've been out there. You know it can be dangerous."

I'd never heard the story of how my father left Earth, and how he managed to advance so far in Confederation politics under an assumed identity. It was one of those things we hadn't had a chance to discuss. Now wasn't the right time either, but I made a mental note to talk to him about this when we had a quiet moment together.

"I do understand," I said, "but I think you know that I have to do it."

"For Tamret? You can save her just by meeting with the director. After that you don't have to do anything. You can come right back."

That was true, but if I did that, I'd never see Tamret again. "They're offering a lot. I need to at least hear what the director wants from me, but if it's even slightly reasonable, I have to do it. The things I did got Earth kicked out of the running for Confederation membership. If there's a way for me to fix that, I can't ignore it."

He nodded. "I know. I know what it would cost you if you didn't, but they're not playing fair with you. If they really wanted to give you the chance to back out, they'd explain what they want while you're still on Earth. And Zeke, no matter what the director does to protect you, Junup will still be your enemy, and a dangerous one. You need to remember that."

"Believe me, I won't forget it."

He shook his head.

"What?" I asked. "Are you upset that I'm going away?"

"Well, yes," he said, "but I'm just thinking about the fact that you broke into an American military base."

"Dad," I said, "I broke into Area Fifty-One in order to steal a flying saucer. Get the story right."

There was a knock on the door, and then my mother came in. And then there were a lot of tears.

I wanted to give them a chance to talk alone, so I encouraged everyone to leave. Colonel Rage had instructed my mother to bring a duffle bag with clothes for me, so I found a bathroom in which I changed into things that actually fit me and then met up with the others in a small break room. grabbed a hot chocolate—instant, but still pretty good. I brought one to Urch, who kept poking at the melting marshmallows with his claw.

At some point while I had been dealing with my parents, Alice and Jacinto went off to speak privately with Colonel Rage. Now they came and sat down with us. I gave them a short rundown of what Urch had told me—that the new boss, whom I did not know or trust, wanted me back, and was offering me too much for me to say no.

"I'm glad it's worked out for you," Alice said, smiling crookedly. "It sounds like you got everything you wanted."

"We'll see if they deliver. What about you guys? Are you in trouble?"

"They're not sure what to do with us," Jacinto told me. "We've seen more than they're comfortable with, but I think they also understand the world is changing."

"Can't keep this stuff a secret forever," I said.

"They've been trying to do just that for a long time," he told me.

Alice looked up at me, her gaze steady, her jaw set. "You need to add one more condition to your agreement."

Alice was sharp. If I'd missed something, I wanted to know about it. "Okay, what are you thinking?"

"You have to let us go with you."

"Please tell her that is not authorized," Urch said. He could understand her, even if she and Jacinto couldn't understand him. "The director has permission to bring the former Earth delegates, and Colonel Rage will be joining you as a guardian and advisor, but you cannot have any others from your world on the ship."

I nodded, glad to have some cover. I understood that she wanted to come along. I could only imagine what it would be like to learn about the Confederation, to get a hint of all that was out there, and then to be told you couldn't see it. I sympathized with Alice, but she had no experience with life outside Earth. The director was going to ask me to do something dangerous, and Alice didn't have the experience or training for what I was likely going to face.

"Urch says no," I told her. "He isn't allowed to bring anyone from Earth except for me, the other former delegates, and the colonel."

"That's not fair," she said, slamming her hand down on the table. A marshmallow flew out of Urch's cup and hit him in the tusk. He scraped it off with his claw and ate it.

"Alice, I don't know what you think it's going to be like—"

"That's just it. I *don't* know, and I want to. You owe me, Zeke. You thought you were in trouble, and I dropped everything for you. I helped you take on the United States military, and you are going to toss me aside."

"It's not my call," I said.

"Maybe not," she snapped, "but I don't see you arguing for me either."

That was true. I was hiding behind Urch's pronouncement, and I knew I would not have let that stop me if he'd said the other initiates couldn't come along. I would have refused to budge if they hadn't agreed to my terms for Tamret. This, however, was different, and I couldn't exactly explain that to Alice. I didn't think she would want to hear that if she came along, I would feel responsible for her safety in what was probably going to be a very dangerous place.

"I owe you a lot," I told her, "and I'm not going to forget it. Not ever. But right now isn't the time. If I manage to do whatever it is I'm supposed to do, and I don't get killed, then they'll give me my own spaceship. When that happens, I promise you'll get the grand tour. I'll show you all the incredible things I've seen and even some new ones, but you're going to have to wait."

"Right," she said. "When you finish this whatever it is, you'll be off with your alien girlfriend, and you'll completely forget about me."

"That's not true," I told her, desperate to make her believe me. She *had* risked her life to help me, and I wasn't going to forget that.

Maybe she didn't know me well enough to understand that I didn't abandon my friends, or maybe she just didn't want to wait. Alice turned away.

"For what it's worth," Jacinto said to her, "Zeke is making the right decision."

"You too, Uncle Jacinto?" She looked surprised. "You risked everything to get this far."

"I wanted to find out the truth about aliens," he said with a shrug. "I found out the truth. I'm sitting in a cafeteria with an alien right now. I'm calling this a win."

Alice looked around the table. We were all gazing at her with serious expressions—all but Urch, who was now licking the inside of his Styrofoam cup.

"Fine," she said, folding her arms. "But please let me stay until you guys leave. Let me meet your other friends. Can I at least see inside the shuttle craft?"

Urch now had the cup turned upside down, and he was

shaking drops into his mouth. "This is the most delicious excrement I have ever tasted," he said.

"What do you say, Urch? Can she get a quick tour of the shuttle? I owe her."

"She can," he said, "if someone gets me another cup of this liquid."

Colonel Rage decided to be easygoing about all the illegal stuff we'd done to get into Area 51. He told me that the government would not file charges against Alice and Jacinto, and that they could remain at the base until I left with Urch. He arranged guest quarters for them as well as for my mom and dad. We were just waiting for the rest of the previous initiates to show up, and then I would be heading back to Confederation Central. Charles and Mi Sun had agreed without missing a beat, like all this time they'd also been waiting for something to happen that could get them back into space. Nayana had taken a little more convincing.

"I don't want to have to face any hazardous situations," she told me on the phone. "Can you promise me everything will be safe?"

I wasn't thrilled with the prospect of dealing with her obstructions and complaints again. I was just about to politely tell her that it was fine if she didn't want to come along, but then I remembered how brilliant she was, how she was the one who'd connected the dots and discovered that my father was alive and a member of the selection committee. She'd helped us to figure out how to defeat the Phands' defenses at the prison. Nayana's most obvious talent was being a pain in the butt, but she was also incredibly skillful at too many other things that mattered.

I supposed we could just ask the director to put a genius

on our team—preferably one with combat training—but then I thought about what it would mean having to deal with a stranger. No matter how difficult Nayana could be, I trusted her. Maybe she was no commando, but she'd had piloting and weapons training, and she knew how to handle herself. I also knew exactly where she stood. More than anything else, she was my friend—as much of a friend as she would let herself be—and I wanted to be surrounded by people I could count on.

"Nayana," I told her, "you are pretty much irreplaceable. We'll do this without you, but I don't want to have to."

"Very well," she said with a sigh. "I suppose I must save my planet. *Again.*"

When I finished the phone call, I told Urch that she had agreed. He then sent a message to his ship to tell Director Ghli Wixxix that I had accepted all her terms. He assured me that the director would send a comm beacon to Confederation Central and they would begin the process of getting Tamret off her home world. Urch promised to let me know as soon as he had any information, which was great, but it didn't do much to alleviate my constant state of tension. I had no idea if Tamret was okay, or even if she was still alive. I lived in fear of the moment Urch would take me aside and tell me he had received bad news.

Meanwhile I got to spend time with my family—my whole family. I have to admit it was a little awkward, the three of us being together again. My mom didn't seem to know exactly what to say, and my dad seemed a little overwhelmed by being back on Earth. He could see I was a little alarmed, and he took me aside to tell me not to worry.

"This is a huge change for all of us," he said, "and your mother is worried about you as well, but it's nothing we won't get past. We just need a little time. You've got enough problems, and I promise you, this isn't one of them."

Urch was as good as his word, and he gave Alice a tour of the shuttle. Her clothes had begun to get a little ripe, and now she was wearing an Army T-shirt and camouflage pants—they'd managed to find stuff for her that fit—and a cap that barely contained the mass of her hair. Her eyes were as large as dinner plates as she wandered around the shuttle, wanting to know everything: weapons, acceleration, navigation, and just about every other feature. She even asked about basic operations, like shuttle security, storage, ballast, and tons of other things so boring I could barely make myself pay attention—except I had to, since I was translating for her.

"Can I get a quick tour of the actual starship?" she asked.

"No, that's not going to happen," Urch told her through me.

"Please," she begged.

Urch was adamant. Finally she accepted the decision, and she stormed off.

"You like them fiery," Urch told me.

"You want the fiery ones on your side in a pinch."

"Good thing you're leaving her behind," he said. "That one is trouble."

The next morning I woke up and found Mi Sun and Nayana in the commissary, looking sleepy and jet-lagged. It was great to see them. I gave them both hugs, and for once neither of the girls was reserved. Mi Sun was grinning so broadly she almost looked like a different person.

"Your face!" I shouted. "It's cracking!"

She actually laughed. She had been so serious and critical when I'd first met her, I sometimes forgot how much she had changed during our time on Confederation Central. Now I looked at these two girls, who had seemed to hate me when we first set out into space, but whom I'd come to like and trust. They both wore jeans and interesting long-sleeved T-shirts, like they'd coordinated their outfits. Maybe they had, but more importantly, I realized, they were dressed not for looks, but to be practical—these were clothes that gave them freedom to move but wouldn't get in the way. They were ready for action, and I wondered if they were as happy to get back to the Confederation as I was.

I sat down at the table with them. "Maybe we'll have a chance to set things right this time."

They both nodded, like they'd been thinking the same thing.

"I hate to admit it," Nayana said, "but returning to my life, though it is interesting and glamorous, has been a bit of an adjustment. Maybe if Junup hadn't chosen to make us into villains, I'd feel differently, but I somehow don't quite belong in my own home anymore."

Mi Sun nodded. "I know exactly what you mean. All the things that used to seem important now feel silly. I hate that we left so much undone."

"We came so close to securing Earth's place in the Confederation," Nayana agreed. "We *did* secure it. If it hadn't been for that awful alien, the world would be a different place."

"They're giving us another chance," I said. "This time we've got to be careful not do anything that someone like Junup can object to."

"And you say Steve will be joining us. And Tamret?" Mi Sun said, arching her eyebrows.

"Yeah. I'll have to remind both of them to be on their best behavior, but the main thing is, we're back in it. We have another chance. It's so crazy. People become doctors or politicians or whatever because they want to try to take on big challenges, but none of them have a shot at the kind of difference we could make."

We all knew that the Confederation had its problems, and it was certainly populated by some very flawed beings, but it also had so much to teach us. We were lucky to have gone to Confederation Central once, and now we were going back. I felt a nagging anxiety, though. I still had no idea what the director needed from me. Why did she have to travel all this way and make all these agreements to meet with a middle school kid from Earth? I was dying to know, but at the same time I dreaded finding out.

That afternoon, another small plane landed, this one carrying Charles. I watched him descend the steps and walk toward us on the runway. There was something different about him. His gait had a confident swagger, but there was more to it than that. I then realized that his clothes were different too. He wore a white shirt, open at the collar, and a brown canvas vest. His pants were a faded blue, tucked into high boots, and he wore a thick belt slung loose at the waist.

By the time we were close enough for me to shake his hand, I realized why his outfit looked so familiar.

"You are totally dressed like Han Solo!"

"This time," he told me, wagging his finger like a cartoon schoolteacher, "I have come prepared."

"For cosplay?"

"I always held out hope that we would have another chance to go back to the Confederation, so I have been studying."

Now I was really curious. "Studying what?"

"Television, cinema, comic books, all of it," he said cheerfully. "I have turned myself into a nerd!"

I looked him up and down. "I'd say you're more of a fanboy."

"There is no need to address me as though I were a nerf herder," he said with mock seriousness. Then he started to walk toward the main building. "Come. Let us get a cold drink and discuss the many differences between the original *Battlestar Galactica* and the remake."

Now that everyone had arrived, Urch injected everyone with nanites for translation and to activate a limited HUD. We could not rack up experience points or gain levels, but we were told we'd get data bracelets once we boarded the ship.

We all had dinner together that night—my mom, my dad, Colonel Rage, Urch, Jacinto, Alice, Mi Sun, Nayana, and Charles. It was one of those weird moments when people from different parts of your life, not to mention the galaxy, are all together in the same place. Everyone seemed to enjoy each other's company, though my mother kept casting uncomfortable glances at Urch's plate. I had been afraid that Alice was going to be glum or resentful, but she seemed upbeat and was chatty with Charles, Mi Sun, and Nayana. It was a great evening, and I wished I could have enjoyed it more, but I couldn't shake my worry about Tamret. The idea of getting back to her had been a pipe dream for so long, but now I was going to see her soon, and the things she must have been going through all these months became more real and urgent—and all the more terrible because they were unknown. Then there was the business with our mission. What could the most powerful being in the Confederation want from me.

The next day I had to say good-bye to my mother yet again, only this time she wasn't sick, and this time I wasn't leaving her alone. She and my father hadn't quite gotten their rhythm back, but I could see they were working on it, they both wanted to make up for lost time, and that was good enough for me.

My mother hugged me tightly, and then my father took me aside.

"I know you have to do this," he said. "And I know there's no point in telling you to be careful, but I'm going to tell you anyhow."

I nodded. "Any thoughts on who I can trust?"

"Your friend Urch seems pretty solid. He thinks highly of Ghli Wixxix, but I don't know her, so you'll have to use your best judgment. She's been on the right side of most important issues, but she went to school with Junup, and they were friends until a few years ago. I don't like it. I wish Dr. Roop could be there for you. He's pretty much the most trustworthy being in the Confederation. You can trust your friends, of course, but they'll be out of the loop, just like you. Captain Hyi on this ship seems like a good being, but I got a bad vibe from the crew. Most of them wear Junup's Movement for Peace armbands, which means they won't be on your side. Don't say anything private around someone you don't know."

"What do you think the director wants?" I asked.

"I wish I knew," he said, sighing. "I can't imagine what is

worth the risk of angering her political enemies by bringing you back to the station. Something big is going on, Zeke. You are going to need to step very carefully."

"You know, I still never found out about how you got to the Confederation in the first place," I said.

He laughed. "That's a strange story, but a long one. It will have to wait until you get back."

"I'll hold you to that." I gave him another hug. "I'll see you soon."

He smiled at me, shaking his head, like he couldn't believe this was it, that I was really going, leaving him behind on Earth while I went back into space.

Jacinto and Colonel Rage came into the room. Jacinto came over to me and shook my hand.

"Don't forget the little people, okay?"

"Thanks for everything, Jacinto. I wouldn't have made it without you."

"It turns out we were running away from the good guys. They would have caught up eventually, and you'd be right here, doing just what you're doing. The way I see it, I mostly kept you from getting to your friends sooner."

"We did it the hard way, that's for sure," I agreed, "but we didn't know that at the time. We thought I was in real danger, and you took a lot of risks to help me."

"I just wanted to see if this stuff was real," he said. "Besides, it was fun. You ever need to go on the run again, give me a call, all right?"

I laughed. "Given my track record, I may end up doing just that." I looked around. "Where's Alice?"

Jacinto shook his head. "Alice took it kind of hard, being

left behind. I know, I know, it wasn't your call, and she would have been out of her depth, but she wanted to go. You understand, right? I think it would have been too upsetting to say good-bye."

I did understand, but I was also angry. She and I had been through a lot. I owed her, and I meant to repay her someday. I understood she wanted to head out with us, but that she would let me go without even wishing me good luck felt crummy.

"Thank her for me, will you?"

Jacinto nodded. "I will. Now go do what you've got to do."

Colonel Rage led us to a door, and we were all ushered through. I took one look back, catching a last glimpse of my parents before I left the planet.

# CHAPTER ELEVEN

I mostly felt disbelief while the shuttle took off and broke atmosphere, but once we were in space, and the ship loomed ahead of us, it all felt so real. Here I was, sitting with the former delegates from Earth, my friends, heading toward a Confederation starship. Part of me feared it had all been some terrible trick, and we would be flying directly toward a Phandic cruiser, but I was pleased to discover I could cross at least one worst-case-scenario off my list. The ship looked a lot like the *Dependable*—a long, unadorned black rectangle with a pair of engines at the end and another along the middle.

"What's it called?" I asked Urch.

He snorted with distaste. "The *Kind Disposition*."

"Eeew," I said.

"Here we go," Mi Sun said, rolling her eyes.

"It is not the most intimidating of names," Urch agreed. "However, this vessel has weapon upgrades based on the technology you brought to the Confederation. If the Phands bother us, they'll find this ship's disposition not nearly as kind as they would wish."

"Can't argue with that," I said, enjoying his bravado. "How do you like serving on this ship?"

"Captain Hyi is not Captain Qwlessl, but he is an excellent commander."

"And the crew?" I asked, remembering what my father had said.

"Do not trust anyone but me," Urch said darkly. "I was only brought in because you know and trust me. The other officers seem to resent me for it. Many of them openly belong to the Movement for Peace, but I believe even the ones without armbands are members as well. They simply wish to disguise that the entire crew serves Junup, not the captain. As for me, they shun me because my species is carnivorous."

"That sounds uncomfortable."

He snorted. "It has been worth it to aid the director on this mission. I have a great deal of admiration for her, but don't repeat anything she says to any of the crew—except, of course, the captain."

"Isn't he going to get irritated if we act like we don't trust his crew?"

"I am not sure Captain Hyi trusts them either. The roster was forced on him by Junup's allies. This ship has been newly retrofitted to be state of the art, and Captain Hyi wanted to command it. To do so, he had to accept a crew of Junup's choosing."

Colonel Rage broke into our conversation. He pointed to the screen. "That ship looks impressive, but does it have it where it counts? What kind of firepower does it possess?"

"I cannot answer that question in relative terms," Urch said. "I can tell you that we match weapons with the most destructive of enemy cruisers, and while we equal them in offensive capabilities, their shield and sensor technologies are generations behind ours. That means we can see the enemy before they see us, and we can take more damage. As a result, we will win any battle so long as our forces are not outnumbered more than six to one."

"That sounds like a lot of boasting, son," Colonel Rage said.

Urch, to my surprise, did not respond to being called *son*. Instead he activated his data bracelet and changed the view of the screen. It panned several degrees up and left, and then something came into view. It was the floating wreck of two Phandic saucers, lifeless and dark, hovering in the void.

"We did not want to alarm you with this while still on your planet," Urch said, "but shortly after Zeke left the Confederation, the Phandic Empire decided to take revenge upon him and his planet for having shamed them. Here, in your system, is where they learned that we had mastered their weapons technology and were no longer going to ignore their violent expansion. For years we watched, powerless, as the Phands conquered peaceful worlds, but that ended at your world. Four of our ships made this change of policy clear to the Phands, destroying, disabling, or capturing fourteen large cruisers that had come to conquer Earth."

My stomach did a series of unpleasant flips. My planet had been threatened, almost attacked, by a devastating force of nasty aliens. None of us had known anything about it.

"When did this happen?" Colonel Rage asked.

"Perhaps three months ago," Urch said. "Our interstellar spy drones picked up the first signs that the Phands were building a subspace energy relay near your planet. It's the first sign of colonization, since their occupation forces are very energy dependent. The usual operating procedure for the Phandic Empire is to establish infrastructure and then invade. When we moved in to destroy that infrastructure, they launched an attack against our forces."

"You went to war to save our planet?" Mi Sun asked, clearly surprised. When we'd last left the Confederation, politicians like Junup had seemed more interested in hiding from the Phands than confronting them.

Urch nodded, clearly understanding what she meant. "Last year the Confederation was still hiding behind treaties and agreements meant to appease the Phands. The ships you and your friends captured changed all that. It is fitting that the Battle of Earth is regarded as one of the great turning points in our civilization."

"I am grateful," Charles said. "I thank you for doing this for us."

Urch snorted. "I wasn't there, unfortunately, though there were other battles I had the chance to savor before the Phands agreed to a new treaty. But as far as I'm concerned, no thanks are necessary. Helping weaker worlds fend off bullies is the responsibility of the Confederation. You are wise to be cautious with anyone who wants anything from you, but Director Ghli Wixxix did save your world."

"And Junup?" I asked. "Did he support protecting Earth?"

"He warned of the risks and urged the Confederation not to endanger itself on behalf of primitive worlds. Then, when the battle ended so decisively and the Phands were in full retreat, he revised his position and claimed he had supported it all along."

"Not surprising," I said.

Urch shrugged. "He's a political [*perspiration-licker*] who will throw his best friend in the recycler unit to save his own shell."

"Then whatever Ghli Wixxix wants from me, Junup is probably going to be against."

"I think that goes without saying," Urch agreed. "You will have to be careful."

"Your ships," Colonel Rage said, interrupting my thoughts. "They're good at fighting these Phands now, you say?"

"That's right," Urch said.

"And your other enemies?"

"We have no other enemies," Urch told him. "The Confederation seeks neither hostility nor territory. The Phands were our enemies only because they chose the path of conquest and oppression. Now we have confined them to their borders."

"What about the planets they've already conquered?" Mi Sun asked.

"Yes," Urch said. "There are beings, such as Ghli Wixxix, who believe we are obligated to liberate them. However, Junup's faction has swayed public opinion, and the current position of the government is that we have weakened the Phands, so now it is up to those individual societies to determine their own fate."

"And what do you think?" Colonel Rage asked.

"I know that if it were my world that had been conquered, I would not wish for the Confederation to turn its back."

"Can't blame you there," Colonel Rage said. "Sounds like your leadership is trying to avoid a long and expensive war, using bogus morality to cover up caution and selfishness. We get plenty of that on Earth, don't you worry."

"All sentient beings have much in common," Urch said. "It is our linked ancestry."

Colonel Rage stared at Urch for a moment, as if not wanting to think too much about how this warthog being could be his cousin. "What happens if this internal disagreement in your government turns ugly? How do these upgraded ships of yours do when fighting each other?"

"Confederation ships do not fight one another," Urch said. "For most of our citizens, argument and disagreement are all the conflict they can stomach."

"Still, it's best to be prepared. Surely you run scenarios."

"It can be done in sim," I said. "When we get on the *Kind Disposition*, I'll show you how to work the simulation room. I think you'll like it."

I was looking forward to getting back into the sim room myself. I'd missed spaceflight, simulated or otherwise.

We pulled into the shuttle bay, where we were met by several of the crew, including Captain Hyi, a stick-insect alien like I'd seen on the *Dependable*. He was surrounded by beings of a variety of species in uniforms, all of whom wore blank expressions. Some were aliens I'd seen before, like the blood-red humanoids with cranial ridges, and even a goat-turtle like Junup, with a black uniform stretched awkwardly over his shell. All of them looked at me with barely disguised contempt. These were not the welcoming smiles I'd encountered the first time I'd come aboard a Confederation ship.

"Anything to report, Mr. Urch?" Captain Hyi asked.

"No difficulties, Captain," Urch said. He then proceeded to make introductions. When the captain had met all of us, he presented each of us to his crew, none of whom seemed happy to meet us. They were crisp and precise in their discipline, but I had the feeling they were doing their best to show us how much they didn't want us on board while making sure they did nothing to get themselves in trouble.

"Mr. Reynolds," the captain said, "Director Ghli Wixxix

understands you have been through an ordeal, and has asked if you and the rest of the people from your planet could meet her tomorrow at 1300 hours?"

I nodded. "Of course, Captain."

"Then perhaps you'd like to go to your quarters."

The goat-turtle stepped forward. On its right arm, I noticed, was a black band with a squiggly line that I thought might be supposed to represent a flame. "Captain, permission to escort the primitive alien Ezekiel Reynolds to its quarters." His voice was deep, like Junup's, though he sounded much younger, and the number 32 above his head confirmed it. I couldn't tell just by looking at him, since it's hard to guess someone's age when their face is covered with shaggy fur.

"Very kind of you, Mr. Knutjhob," the captain said, "but I think we'll let Mr. Urch have that honor."

*Don't do it!* Smelly roared inside my head. *An entity doesn't have to live inside your head to know what you're thinking. Control yourself.*

It was great advice—really it was—but I was unable to resist. "Nut job?" I asked.

Colonel Rage winced.

*"K-nut J-hob,"* the goat-turtle repeated very slowly. "Does my name signify something in your language?"

"Just sounding it out," I said casually. "It's been a while since I've heard nonhuman names. But Knutjhob. Yeah. I like it."

There was a moment of silence. "It is always pleasant to be flattered," Knutjhob said, leveling his goaty gaze on me, "by the sort of being who might break numerous laws and codes of the society that is hosting him, steal a spaceship, betray trusts, and create an interstellar incident."

"That is a rather biased view of what happened," Charles said.

Knutjhob snorted. "Name mockery is precisely the sort of irresponsible behavior my uncle told me to expect from you."

"Wait a minute," I said. "Junup is your uncle? I'm in an enclosed space with Junup's nephew?"

"There will be no hostilities or rivalries aboard my ship," Captain Hyi said, like a teacher trying to break up a fight between little kids. "Mr. Knutjhob, you will avoid Mr. Reynolds as best as your duties permit. Please refrain from speaking to him unless it directly relates to ship's business. Mr. Reynolds, the same goes for you."

"Not a problem," I said.

"Crew dismissed," Captain Hyi said with evident weariness. "Mr. Urch, please take our guests to their quarters."

"I can't believe this," I said, as soon as we were away from everyone else. "Why is Junup's nephew on this ship?"

"Obviously to keep an eye on things," Urch said. "You wasted no time in antagonizing him."

"He was looking to start something," I said. "Besides, it's not my fault. He has a funny name. What was I supposed to do?"

"Try not insulting him," Mi Sun suggested. "Avoid making trouble for once in your life."

"I only make trouble sometimes," I said.

"That's true," Nayana said. "I've seen it happen. I think about a third of the time the trouble is of his own making. The other two thirds, trouble looks for him."

"It's still a lot of trouble," Mi Sun grumbled.

"Let's try not to make trouble with anyone else," Colonel

Rage suggested, "especially when they're related to powerful people in their government who happen to hate you."

*That is excellent advice,* Smelly offered.

"I have a bad feeling about this," Charles said. "It is not merely that he looks like his uncle, whom we all have reason to dislike. It appeared to me that he wished for a confrontation with Zeke, and Zeke merely provided an excuse. I believe this is a setup."

"Thanks, Charles," I said. "I agree."

"As do I," Urch agreed. "Knutjhob clearly has adopted his uncle's grievances as his own. Additionally, I consider him a [*barf puddle*] of an officer. They all are, I'm afraid."

The interior of the ship was a lot like the other Confederation vessels I'd been on, but there was no doubt that changes had been made to accommodate the new military power. Every few yards there were signs pointing the way to escape pods or impact shelters, and at every junction were panels to operate emergency decompression barriers. The *Dependable* had been designed to avoid and escape conflict, but the *Kind Disposition* had been built to dominate it.

By the time I got to my quarters, I was exhausted. It had been a grueling bunch of days, filled with terrors and surprises, the majority of which, it had turned out, were not bad.

I awoke the next day with a knock on the door. Urch was standing outside, holding a length of glistening black material for me. A data bracelet. Without hesitating, I grabbed it and put it on my left wrist.

"Thanks, man. I've really missed having one of these."

He nodded. "It is easy to grow used to them. I am also here to tell you that we have received a communication. Our diplomats have successfully negotiated asylum for the Rarel girl, Tamret. Final arrangements are being made, and she will most likely arrive on Confederation Central several days after you do. I am informed that she is in good health."

I sat down on my bed and let the relief wash over me. Whatever nightmare Tamret had endured, it was finished. Maybe it was terrible, more terrible than I could imagine, but she was alive and she was free. I had promised her I would get her off that planet, and I'd done it. If this excursion to Confederation Central accomplished nothing else, then I would consider it a victory.

And I was going to see her again. In only a few more days Tamret and I would be back together.

"And Steve?" I asked.

"Yes, the Ish-hi is also on his way. But you seemed more interested in the girl." Urch opened his mouth to show his teeth, his version of a smile.

"Maybe a little," I admitted.

"I understand. The Ish-hi sent a message." Urch activated his data bracelet to send me Steve's message. As if I had never taken my bracelet off, I called it up. It was a single line of text. *You still owe me, mate.*

I laughed. Then my mood suddenly soured. "Was there a message from Tamret?" I asked.

"Sorry," Urch said. "Nothing."

Why had she not thought to send me a few lines? I wondered. Maybe she was too busy. Maybe she was overwhelmed by everything that was going on. Maybe everything she did and said would be monitored until she left her planet, and whatever she had to say she wanted to keep private. It was a small thing,

I told myself, and I decided I was not going to worry about it.

Urch called up a blue plasma sphere from his bracelet. It had buttons all over it, and it rotated as he tapped them.

"The room is now secure," he said. "I detect no listening devices, but we are nevertheless shielded now. I think anyone but Captain Hyi and myself would report suspicions to Junup, and I know that Knutjhob is looking to discredit your mission, whatever it is, before it begins."

"Yeah," I said. "I'm not popular with the goat-turtles."

"I have known several of their species who are worthy and honorable beings," Urch said. "That family, however, is ambitious and ruthless. In any case, we may speak now without fear of being heard."

"Okay," I said cautiously. Clearly he had something private he wanted to say.

"When Charles and Mi Sun and Nayana arrived," he began, "I had to inject them with nanites so they could understand me. I gave you an injection, since to do otherwise would have been conspicuous, but you did not need the nanites to understand me."

I said nothing.

"The Confederation treated you shamefully," Urch said. "Beings like us, who come into this culture from the outside, have no innate devotion to it, no patriotism that we are born to. Loyalty must be earned, and I know that the Confederation did not earn it with you. It is no exaggeration to say that the Confederation betrayed you, so I would understand if you had been tempted to turn your back on it, but if that is the case, you must tell me now. We can deal with the situation if you reveal everything, but the longer you wait, the more suspect your concealment will seem."

"Wait a second," I said, hardly believing what I was hearing. "Do you think I was working with the Phands?"

"I am saying only you had access to technology that should have been unavailable. The Phands are the most likely source."

"I blame Junup for what happened, not the Confederation, and I would *never* work with the Phands. They murdered the Ganari kids who were supposed to be delegates for their planet. They tried to destroy a ship I was on—several times—and tried to have me brought back to their world for punishment. They imprisoned my father, and they were looking to invade or destroy my planet. Do you seriously think I would join up with them? For what? So I could watch kung fu movies without subtitles?"

"I said the Phands were the most likely source," he explained, "but I agree not the only one. Perhaps you would enlighten me."

"Have you reported this to anyone?" I asked him.

"I wished to speak with you first."

I took a deep breath. I couldn't have Urch thinking I was a traitor, and though I didn't want to tell anyone what Dr. Roop had done, he was already a fugitive and probably couldn't get into much more trouble. "Dr. Roop did something before I left the station last time. He kept my translation system working. He hinted about it, but I didn't pick up on it until after I left Confederation Central."

I tried to scratch my ear, but I could not lift my hand.

*Calm your miniscule mind, meat bag,* Smelly said. *In case this creature knows enough of physiology to monitor you, I am concealing the physical manifestations of lying. I am keeping your heart rate at a normal pace, I am preventing your eyes from shifting to the left, and I am not allowing you to touch your face.*

I stopped trying to touch my face, hoping Smelly would free me up. I could now feel a slight relaxation, as if an invisible hand had let go.

*You're welcome.*

I supposed Smelly was right. I should thank it. Obviously I did not want anyone rooting around in my brain trying to scrape it out. Urch was a friend, but once he knew, there was always the risk someone else might find out.

"Interesting," Urch said. "Roop obviously had something in mind, though I can't guess what. I was surprised he ran rather than face the legal system, but clearly he was more desperate than I realized."

"You won't tell anyone about all this, will you?"

"I'm not sure that it would get you into trouble, but if they catch Roop, I would hate for him to face any more charges just because he wanted to help you out. I think we can keep this between us." He pressed some buttons on his rotating keyboard, presumably to deactivate the dampening field.

"I'm still not sure how you broke into that military base. Maybe no one else will notice. Most Confederation types don't really know what to expect on a place like Earth, but my planet was not unlike yours before we joined. I know you must have faced great danger."

"I had help from my friends," I said.

"It must have been some help for you to get that far without anyone getting hurt."

I shrugged. "We were lucky, I guess."

Urch stared at me, and I felt sure he knew I was lying.

Smelly was likely keeping me from any physical betrayal, but Urch was no dummy, and he clearly suspected I got more from Dr. Roop than just a universal translator. I had to hope that he'd believe I would never work with the Phands, and as long as I wasn't cooperating with the enemy, he was probably okay with me having my own secrets.

Just then both our data bracelets chimed, almost at the exact same moment. I looked at mine, and a text message popped up. *Report to the brig.*

"I must go to the brig," Urch told me.

"Yeah, me too."

Why was I needed there, of all places? Had one of the other humans already gotten in trouble aboard the ship? I couldn't believe any of my friends would have done anything improper, but Colonel Rage was an unknown, to say the least. Even so, if he'd decided that he wanted to try to steal Confederation secrets, I doubted he would have gotten started quite so quickly.

I followed Urch through the corridors and down a flight of stairs. We then found the captain and Colonel Rage standing by a closed door.

"We've got a problem," the captain said, gesturing toward the door with one of his spindly limbs.

"Stowaway on the shuttle," Colonel Rage told me.

The captain moved to open the door, but I knew what I was going to see. The door shifted to the side with a hiss, revealing a chamber with a main control panel and three cells, two of which were empty and dark. The third was illuminated and blocked off by a blue plasma field, and on the other side, hands in her lap, was Alice.

# CHAPTER TWELVE

The captain, Urch, the other humans, and I sat in the briefing room—that is, the other humans besides Alice, who remained in the brig. I felt a twisting in my stomach, like I'd done something wrong and was about to get in serious trouble. The fact that everyone was staring at me didn't help, but I kept telling myself that it wasn't my fault. Not that it much mattered at this point. Alice was on board, and finger-pointing wasn't going to change that.

The captain clicked his insectoid mandibles. "None of you knew she was on the shuttle?"

"Negative," Colonel Rage barked, speaking for all of us. He seemed to understand that this was a serious matter with military implications, and he had instinctively taken control.

*I knew,* Smelly told me. *She was doing a lot of mouth breathing.*

I tried not to react. If Smelly had known about Alice, why hadn't it said anything? Obviously, I couldn't ask that now.

"Captain Hyi," Colonel Rage said, "I questioned this young lady extensively back on earth. It's my belief that she is simply an enthusiast. She has a history of being interested in beings from other worlds, and it seems clear that, given such close proximity to aliens, she couldn't quite master her eagerness to see more."

"You don't consider her to be a threat, then?" the captain asked. "Perhaps she is in league with the Phands."

"When she was on the run with Zeke, we conducted an extensive background check on her. There's nothing to indicate she's anything other than what she says she is."

"If the Phands wished to place an agent on board," Urch said, "I doubt they would choose one so obvious. The girl was going to be discovered eventually, and once discovered, she was always going to be an unwelcome guest."

"I very much doubt she is a spy," Charles said. "But that doesn't change the question—what is to become of her?"

"We cannot divert back to Earth," Captain Hyi said. "Director Ghli Wixxix wants us to make best possible speed to Confederation Central."

"Can you send her back when we arrive?" Nayana asked.

"Resources are spread quite thin these days," Captain Hyi said. "No will authorize sending an insufficiently armed transport into territory still coveted by the Phands, and we cannot afford to send a battle-ready ship that might be needed elsewhere."

"If there's one thing I get, it's allocation of resources," Colonel Rage said. "I understand you can't ferry this girl all over the galaxy. She's a stowaway, and you have to deal with her, but she's from my planet and an American citizen, which means I need to look after her interests."

"You sound like you have a proposal," Urch said.

"Right you are, warthog alien. It seems to me you have two choices. You can charge her with whatever Confederation crimes she's guilty of, and deal with it through the legal system, but I'm against putting her through all that when she hasn't really done, or intended, any harm. Your second choice is to let her out. Zeke can keep an eye on her, make sure she doesn't get into any more trouble."

For some reason, this plan made me uncomfortable. I liked Alice, and I respected her. She'd given up a lot, and she'd taken some crazy risks in order to help me, but I didn't want to be her guide to the Confederation. Whatever the reason we had been summoned back, it was almost certainly bound to involve some risk, and I didn't like the idea of being responsible for keeping someone with no training out of harm's way.

"I'm going to have my hands busy with whatever Director Ghli Wixxix wants me to do," I protested. "Maybe we could put Nayana in charge of keeping an eye on her."

"I would rather not." Nayana folded her arms and looked away, like she'd remembered something really important she had to think about.

"We can help guide her through life on Confederation Central," Mi Sun offered, "but we're strangers to her. She knows Zeke. He should be the one to look out for her."

"She's not a baby," I said. "It's not like you'll have to change her diapers. Just make sure she doesn't open any airlocks or anger the locals."

"I agree with your friends, Zeke," Colonel Rage said. "You brought her into this; you need to see her through it."

They were right, of course, and my vague worries about possible danger weren't enough to justify my position. On the other hand, I needed Alice to understand that she couldn't go around breaking any rules she didn't like. Tamret was on the way, and one habitual lawbreaker in the group was enough. "Can I suggest leaving her in the brig until we arrive at the station?"

Colonel Rage raised an eyebrow. "Explain."

I shrugged. "I agree that she's no threat, but she's flouted the law and gotten away with it. There are a lot of laws on Confederation Central, so maybe now's the time to make sure she'll think twice before doing anything else too impulsive."

Urch snorted. "He wants to make sure she knows her place before that fiery Rarel shows up."

"That too," I admitted.

Captain Hyi nodded. "Either way, I believe it is a sound suggestion. Make it so."

I stared at the captain.

He clacked his mandibles together. "The one called Charles asked me to say that. He thought you would appreciate it."

Charles grinned. "We shall see which of us is the true fanboy."

I went back to my room and closed the door. "If you knew Alice was on board, why didn't you say anything?" I demanded of Smelly.

*It wasn't my problem. Besides, suppose I had told you. What could you have done? Announced that you'd picked up the rank stench of one of your females in the storage closet? If you had revealed your knowledge of her, you would have raised questions you could not answer, and that might have led to the others learning of my existence.*

"She was hidden on the shuttle in the docking bay," I said. "Did you know for a fact they wouldn't decompress the bay?"

*No, I recognized that decompression was a possibility.*

"She could have died."

*That is true. You fleshy types don't do well in a vacuum. You are so porous, and you require oxygen. And warmth.*

"The next time someone's life is in danger, you have to let

me know," I said. "I'll cover my tracks to conceal you, but you can't risk letting anyone die."

*There are billions of you,* Smelly said. *And countless billions more species that don't look exactly the same but are otherwise barely indistinguishable—meat in different-shaped bags. I am unique, and that means my existence is more valuable than your own. Next time I shall behave precisely the same way.*

I opened my mouth to speak, but there was nothing to say. I'd always known it, but I think this was the first time I'd set it out quite so bluntly for myself. I had an intelligence inside my head I could not control or trust or anticipate, one for whom sentient life—other than my own, on which it depended—was utterly expendable.

When I entered the brig, Knutjhob was sitting in front of the panel, making some adjustments. He turned around at the sound of the door opening, and his nostrils flared.

"Ah," he said. "One criminal to visit another."

"Hey, Knutjhob," I said, trying for the casual approach. "How's it going, my man?"

"It would be going more pleasantly," he said, "if my ship were not contaminated by primitive life forms who cannot understand the rule of law, and who wish to drag the Confederation into a pit of filth and degradation."

"On my world," I said, "when someone asks how it's going, you usually just say 'good' and leave it at that."

"Since you have mastered the art of pointless conversation, I am surprised you do not rule the galaxy."

I sighed, deciding to make one last effort. "Here's the thing. Your uncle and I don't get along. I'm not sure what I could have done to avoid that, since he took issue with choices I made that seemed unavoidable. But you're not him. There's no reason we have to be enemies."

"The reason," Knutjhob said, "is that you are a member of a degenerate species, and of that primitive rabble you are the worst sort. You care nothing for law and order. You are selfish and greedy and violent. As long as you and your kind poison my air, I will despise you."

I was silent for a moment. "I was hoping for a different response, but that's okay. You're telling me how you feel, which means we're making progress. In the meantime, can you give me a moment alone with Alice here?"

"So the two of you can plot your criminal mischief?"

"I just want to talk to her, okay? There won't be any mischief."

Knutjhob snorted. "The law states I must allow you to confer in private, and I shall comply, because that is what advanced species do."

Apparently, they also like to make self-important speeches. As soon as Knutjhob was out of the room, I grabbed a chair and pulled it over so I could sit across from Alice.

She sat alone on her bunk in the brig, running her fingers through her tangle of nearly white hair. As I sat down, she looked up at me through the blue film of the plasma barrier and flashed a huge grin, like we were both in on this together.

"Here I am, in outer space," she said.

"Here you are," I agreed.

"That guy," she said, gesturing toward the door Knutjhob had just walked out of, "he's got some issues. A lot of anger."

"I may not invite him to my sleepover," I said.

"He kept ranting about how violent species should be eliminated."

"Did you point out the obvious logic problem?"

"Since I fall into the category of species he was talking about eliminating, I decided to smile and act harmless."

"Probably a good strategy," I said. "My usual approach of antagonize-and-alienate doesn't seem to be getting me very far."

She adjusted her glasses and said nothing. I smiled and also said nothing.

*I believe,* Smelly said, *this is what we call an awkward silence.*

Smelly was right. In order to move things along, I said, "So . . ." Then I ran out of ideas, and it was back to awkward silence.

"So," she agreed. "Can I get one of those data bracelets?"

"Are you kidding me?" I snapped. Awkward-silence time was done. "Do you think this is some sort of vacation? You snuck aboard an alien spaceship. No one knew you were hiding out on the shuttle bay. You could have died."

"And you could have been killed when we broke into Area Fifty-One," she countered. "Sometimes you have to take risks."

"Yeah, well, not this time."

She sighed. "I'm sorry. I know my being here makes you look bad, but I had to see all this for myself. Besides, now that I'm here, I can help you."

I wouldn't have chosen to put her in danger by bringing her into all this, but she was here, and I couldn't do anything about that. Having an extra person around who was brave and smart and loyal was probably not such a bad thing. I just needed to make sure that she and Tamret didn't clash.

I braced myself for the most awkward question I'd ever had to ask anyone. "We're friends, right?"

"Of course we are, Zeke," she said, clearly warming to this approach. It was a more promising approach than, say, threatening to put her out the airlock.

"I mean, I'm making sure that's all we are. You don't, you know . . ."

"*Like* you?" she asked, as though I'd suggested she might want to pass some time scrubbing alien toilets.

I felt myself blushing, which probably should not have been a surprise, given that this was one of the most awkward conversations of my life. "I'm not full of myself or anything. I don't want you to think that. It's just that Tamret can be kind of intense."

She clasped her hands together in excitement. "She's safe, then? You're getting her back."

"Yeah, I just found out a little while ago."

"I'm so happy for you." Alice was grinning now. "For both of you."

I nodded. "Thanks. Yeah, I'm pretty happy too."

Alice rolled her eyes. "I promise not to steal her man, okay? She sounds really cool, and I don't want to insult her taste, but she has absolutely nothing to worry about. I mean, like, ever."

I stood up. "Appreciated, though maybe making your case a little less forcefully would have worked just as well."

She waved her hand. "Your ego can take it. If I'm bumming you out, go save another galaxy or something. You'll bounce back."

"And one more thing," I said. "Now that you're here, can you keep my little friend a secret?" I tapped my head so she would know I was talking about Smelly.

"Can I ask why?"

"Better you don't. It's safer for me, which is all I can tell you for now."

She was about to throw another question at me but then decided to hold her tongue. "Okay. Not a word."

"Thanks." I turned to the door. "I'll check on you later. If Knutjhob starts sharpening knives in front of you, shout as loud as you can."

"Excellent advice. But, uh, what's going to happen to me?" she asked.

"You have to stay in the brig until we get to the station. For security reasons."

"Security reasons," she said with a snort. "It's just so that I don't feel like I got away with something. I'm sure some old guy with a stick up his butt came up with that idea."

Moving on. "When we get to Confederation Central, I'm supposed to be in charge of you, so please don't mess up or break any laws or get into trouble. I'm going to have enough to deal with."

She held up her hands in surrender. "I swear, I'll be good. Anyhow, on a different subject—they injected me with those translation devices, I guess so I could listen to that turtle-goat man talk about how much he wishes my species didn't exist. Maybe I could get some reading material, so I can learn more about the Confederation before I get there. That way I won't be as likely to make any mistakes and get you into trouble."

I sighed. "Fine. You win. I'll ask Urch if he'd be willing to get you a data bracelet. You'll find whatever you want on the network." I opened the door.

"Hey, Zeke," she said.

I turned around.

"Sounds like I *am* on vacation."

She was laughing as I walked into the hall. The blue plasma field covered the threshold, and the door slid closed. As I walked away, Smelly said, *Her biological signs indicate she is not telling the truth.*

I stopped. "About what?" I blurted out before thinking to check to see if anyone was around. Fortunately, I was alone.

*About* liking *you,* it said, imitating Alice's tone.

"She'll get over it," I muttered.

It was almost 1300, so I hurried off to the conference room to meet with the director. I was a few minutes early, and I waited in the hall for Charles, Mi Sun, Nayana, and Colonel Rage to show up. Once they were there, we all went in together.

Ghli Wixxix was about four and a half feet tall and pale blue in color. The center of her face was marked by nasal slits without a nose, and beneath that she had a long mouth with thin lips. Her ears were large and pointed, and they jutted outward like a bat's. She had no eyes that I could see, but a cluster of waving sensory tendrils, like a patch of thin sea anemones, protruded from the top half of her face.

She had been sitting at the table, reading through texts on her data bracelet, but when I opened the door, she rose and made several complicated gestures, which I presumed were some sort of greeting. "Mr. Reynolds. It is a great pleasure to meet you."

"Thank you," I said. "I get the feeling there aren't a lot of beings who feel that way."

"Beings who know the truth and who are not pursuing their

own agendas most definitely feel that way," she said, "but they are few and far between."

I introduced her to the others from Earth, and once bows, handshakes, and friendly hand waggles were exchanged, the director gestured for us to sit.

We had only just taken our chairs when the door opened and Captain Hyi entered. "Director. Honored guests. May I sit in?"

"Of course, Captain," the director said. "I was under the impression that your duties did not permit you the time."

The captain folded his curious body into a chair. "There is a great deal of administrative work to do," he explained, "but as this matter is so important to the Confederation, I would like to observe. I am here to be of service, if I can, but no more."

Once we were settled, the director launched in without further delay. "I am sure you have been briefed on the state of our current relations with the Phandic Empire."

"Your Mr. Urch told us that you have them cornered," Colonel Rage said.

The director's sensory tendrils waved in the colonel's direction. "For now we do. These young people from your world helped to make certain that we are in our most advantageous position in more than a century. They have saved us from decades of war, and quite possibly from the end of our civilization."

"I appreciate your saying so," I told her. "I have to admit, I hated that we were treated like criminals after we tried so hard to help the Confederation, but I have a feeling that you didn't come all this way just to set the record straight."

"Sadly, no," Ghli Wixxix said. "You are here because our

intelligence suggests that the Phandic threat, while temporarily contained, is far from over. The danger to our culture, and to your world, remains quite real."

I felt that twisting feeling in my stomach again. I guess it had been too much to hope that the Phands were really out of the picture.

"Okay, I understand that's not good," I told the director, "but I'm not sure why you need me."

"It has come to my attention," Ghli Wixxix explained, "that in addition to the skill tree that has been part of our culture for countless generations, there is a secondary skill tree developed by the Formers. This one was designed for military application."

"It came to your attention because of my father," I said. "He's the one who found out about it, and he's the one who was desperate to make sure the right beings took action, since he was afraid Junup would bury the whole thing."

He had also told me that he'd stolen a copy of the tech tree, so why didn't Ghli Wixxix know about it? Maybe, after they'd locked him up, he hadn't known who in the Confederation he could trust. Still, something didn't seem quite right to me.

"I do not dispute that it was your father who brought us word of it," the director agreed. "The intelligence he provided was of the greatest value. Were it not for your father, we would not now know that the Phands had already acquired the technology to begin accessing this skill tree. This threat will manifest itself not this year or next, but over the coming decade. Whatever advantages we have gained in ship technology may well be negated by Phandic mastery of Former military skills. While we bask in our success, you may be sure they will continue to develop new military technologies. I have urged our defense committees to invest in the same, but I have encountered a great deal of resistance. All of which means that, in perhaps ten standard years, the Phands will reappear on the galactic stage, and we will be able to do little more than slow them down."

"Sounds like you need to put some pressure on your politicians," Colonel Rage said. "And you need to get your hands on this technology and level the playing field. From what I hear, this idiot Junup is your problem. Why not fix your problems in-house?"

The director moved her tendrils in a rapid rippling motion. "Junup is not an idiot. He and I were once friends, and I believe he is still a good being, but he has allowed his ambition to cloud his common sense. He will yet come around, but for now he has too much influence for me to pursue a purely political solution. That is why I have chosen to pursue other goals."

"And in order to accomplish these goals, you need some middle-school kids from Earth. Does that about sum things up?" Colonel Rage asked.

"First, you must understand that we believe that there are software copies of the skill tree hidden on Confederation Central itself. If we can find them, we can completely nullify this Phandic advantage. The galactic threat will remain contained."

"But why do you need *us*?" Mi Sun asked.

"There are parts of the station that have fallen into disrepair. We are not particularly proud of them, but they exist."

I nodded. "I remember. Dr. Roop told me about them."

"There is an even more dangerous area to which all access is denied," the director said. "This is known as the Forbidden Zone."

"The Forbidden Zone!" Charles cried. "This is like the original *Planet of the Apes*. I enjoyed it immensely."

"It's a classic," I agreed, only mildly irritated that he had beaten me to the punch.

Ghli Wixxix made some sort of gesture with her hands. I could only guess it was impatience. "This area contains an outpost, located below the surface of the station that has not been visited in centuries, at least not by citizens of the Confederation. Every child born in our culture is implanted with nanites that track that being's location. This is to prevent children from becoming lost. When a being comes of age, those nanites are neutralized for privacy reasons, but residual traces remain. There are security measures at the entrance to the Forbidden Zone that detect and block any beings who retain any trace of these nanites. In other words, in order to gain access to this area, we need the services of beings not born to the Confederation. In light of past events, such as your leading the team that brought us the stolen Phandic cruisers, I thought of you as being uniquely qualified to offer us assistance."

I said nothing for a moment. I had been fetched from my backwater planet because I didn't have a child-safety chip? There were lots of beings all over the galaxy who met that criteria. I didn't see why I had to be the one to do this.

"Couldn't you just use Urch and his people?" I asked. "There must be plenty of them who weren't born in the Confederation."

Urch snorted in reply.

"You may request that Mr. Urch accompany you," the director said. "I have no objection, but the remainder of his kind cannot join this expedition."

"Too many of them been recruited," Urch said in disgust. "By Junup's Movement for Peace. Having members of my carnivorous species as part of their organization helps disguise just how much they hate beings like us. Unfortunately, it's too hard to know who, among the Vaaklir, to trust."

So much for that idea. "But we're not professional soldiers," I pointed out. "Did you ask the American government to help? I bet they would be happy to send Navy SEALs or Special Forces guys to do this."

"Colonel Rage is here to serve as a military advisor, but to be honest, I could not convince the rest of the committee to agree to allow the armed military of a primitive world onto the station. With Underdirector Junup opposing my every move, this was as much as I could manage. I believe you can help us, Zeke. We know you and trust your motives."

I looked around the room. I wasn't the only one who clearly thought this idea was nuts. Charles, Nayana, and Mi Sun looked like they'd each taken a mouthful of rotten milk. Colonel Rage was sneering with disdain.

"So you want us to gain access to this lost part of the station," Mi Sun said, "a place that is completely invisible to your surveillance and inhabited by who-knows-what. And there we're supposed to wander around like idiots until we find some sort of software."

"We do have some idea where you should look," Ghli Wixxix said. "And behaving like an idiot is not advised. Within the Forbidden Zone is an ancient structure. This hidden fortress was, for many centuries, the place where the Formers stored their most dangerous weapons and technology. That is where you must go."

"The Hidden Fortress," I repeated.

"Correct," Ghli Wixxix said.

Perhaps under normal circumstances I would have been tempted to mention the Akira Kurosawa film *The Hidden Fortress*, which was a huge influence on the first *Star Wars* movie, but given that I needed to convince the director that I was not the person for the job—and that she should let Earth into the Confederation anyhow—I figured I should soft-pedal this one.

"Wasn't that a Japanese movie?" Colonel Rage asked.

"Kurosawa," Nayana said.

"It was a major influence on *Star Wars*," Charles added cheerfully.

By now I was already regretting having brought Charles, Mi Sun, and Nayana into this—not to mention Alice, though that hadn't been my decision. It seemed like Ghli Wixxix saw us at worst as expendable commandos, or at best as the Young Avengers. I wanted to get Earth back in the running for joining the Confederation, but I wasn't about to try to talk my friends into going on a suicide mission. I'd already agreed to consider the request, which meant I'd gotten Tamret off Rarel. Now I figured the smart move would be to not agree to anything until I'd seen her. Maybe there was a way to do what they wanted that wasn't ridiculously dangerous.

"This sounds pretty risky," I ventured.

"You have successfully led dangerous missions before," Ghli Wixxix said.

That was true, but before, I was risking everything to save my father and, I believed, to save my planet. Also, and perhaps more importantly, I'd had Tamret by my side—Tamret, who said she could do anything and really could. Tamret, who had made me feel like *I* could do anything, and who'd stacked the deck so it was pretty near true. Now I would be ordinary Zeke, who was not about to lead his ordinary friends into something better suited for trained soldiers.

"I've been ordered to cooperate with the director," Colonel Rage said to us. "That means I'm going to help her as best I can. You kids aren't military, however, and I can't order you to do squat. If you want to go, I'll back you up to the best of my ability, but I'm going to be straight with you: I've got a son about your age, and there's no way I'd let him do this."

"That is not helpful, Colonel," the director said, waving her eyestalks in a way I thought might suggest disappointment.

"My job isn't to agree with you or anyone else," the colonel said. "I call 'em like I see 'em. If I need to risk my own life to complete the mission, I'll do it, that's who I am, but it doesn't take a genius to see that's not who these kids are."

"The last time we did something insanely foolish," Nayana said, "Tamret bent the rules and that gave us an advantage."

"Yes, your hacking of the skill-tree system," Ghli Wixxix said. "The encryptions have been upgraded, and Junup's security team is monitoring the network for any suspicious activity. I'm afraid you won't find it possible to do that again."

"I understand that we must do this if Earth is to join the Confederation," Charles said, "but I nevertheless believe it is a bad idea."

"It's a *terrible* idea," Nayana said.

"Look," Colonel Rage said, "your committee wants these kids to risk their lives to help you because you know they won't cross you. I get that. But they're *children*, and they're not trained for this. You're not comfortable with American military on your station, and I get that, too, but you can't always have exactly what you want. I think you need to bite the bullet and go back to your people. Convince them to allow a small group of elite personnel from our armed forces to help you out. If there's going to be risk, it shouldn't fall on a group of minors whose only qualification is that they yanked your fat out of the fire once before."

"Colonel Rage makes a lot of sense," I said. "I'd need to hear more about this plan before I could make a decision, but it sounds pretty dangerous."

"I can't force you to do this," Ghli Wixxix said, "and your friend Tamret will be freed regardless, but I believe what we're offering you as payment for your efforts is worth some risk."

Now the room fell silent. That was the prize at the end of this whole ordeal: Earth could become a place without poverty or illness or war. We could, in my lifetime, be accepted as a full member of the Confederation, a part of the larger galactic community. Somehow, whether that happened was now up to a bunch of kids who weren't old enough to get a learner's permit.

"We need some time to think about this," I said, figuring that delay was my best tactic. "And I want to talk to Steve and Tamret, and I want them to be included in briefings where we get more specific information. We'll decide what we want to do then."

"No, we won't," Nayana said. "I've already decided, and I don't care what your lunatic friends say. I'm sorry, Zeke. I sort of like Steve, and I even came to not entirely hate Tamret—she made me her sister or something, which I suppose was nice—but those two are both loose cannons. I'm not going to put my life in the hands of a couple of aliens who aren't afraid of anything."

"No matter what anyone else decides, you don't have to go if you don't want to, Nayana."

At that her eyes began to glisten, and she turned away. "You are such a jerk," she said. "If you go, I'll have to go too."

"Zeke has the right idea," Colonel Rage said. "We don't have to make a decision now. All the players aren't here, and we need time to process. Let's take this under advisement, and we'll reconvene to bring the other aliens into the loop."

"I think that's wise," Captain Hyi said. "Director?"

"I can ask for no more than that. When we arrive at Confederation Central, I can provide more logistical information, and I hope I can convince you that what I am asking is within your abilities and reasonably safe. And on behalf of the Confederation of United Planets, I thank you all for listening and engaging with this matter with open minds and good hearts."

At that we all stood.

"I am returning to my quarters to work," the director said. "I wish you all a good day."

"May I walk with you?" the captain asked. "There is a matter of some importance we must discuss."

"Of course." The two of them headed out of the room. Colonel Rage said he was going to get something to eat, and Mi Sun and Charles joined him. I was heading back to guest quarters with Nayana when I ran into Urch.

"Zeke, I must speak to you."

Nayana waved me away to say it was fine with her, and Urch and I headed off in the direction of the battle sim room.

"What's going on?" I asked.

"Maybe nothing," he said, "but my instincts tell me that

the crew is plotting something. They are behaving more suspiciously than usual."

I suddenly felt that unique disorientation in which everything seemed real and unreal, up and down, and I knew that we were no longer tunneling through interdimensional space—or however it was that we traveled faster than light.

I looked at Urch and he stared back. Nothing needed to be said. We were still a long way off from Confederation Central, so dropping into normal space meant something was very wrong.

Urch looked at his bracelet. "There's no order to emerge from tunnel," he said, "and the executive officer hasn't posted an alert. This is deliberate."

Urch was about to speak, but a pair of crewmen turned the corner and were heading our way. They were still distant enough that they would not be able to hear us if we spoke quietly, but Urch was taking no chances.

*Be advised,* Smelly said suddenly, *that those beings are armed, and their biosigns suggest malevolent intent.*

I looked over at them, and my glance must have been all they needed. Both of them reached for their weapons.

I opened my mouth to warn Urch, but he was way ahead of me. With one hand he was shoving me down to the floor, and with the other he was raising his PPB pistol, which he'd already pulled out from somewhere. He fired off two shots before the other two could get their weapons raised.

"I don't usually walk around armed," Urch said, "but this was what I had a bad feeling about." He keyed his data bracelet. "Captain Hyi. Please answer."

The audio suddenly kicked in, and I heard the unmistakable sound of PPB fire at the other end. There was a brief pause, in which I feared the worst, and then I heard the captain's voice.

"If you're planning on warning me about a mutiny, I've already found out."

"Are you hurt?" Urch asked.

"Negative. The director and I are safe, but I don't know for how long. I think this entire crew is compromised."

"Agreed," Urch said. "Orders?"

"Secure this channel."

Urch hit a few keys. "Encrypted," he said.

"I think both the humans and the director are targets. We need to get them off this ship. We've got a long-range shuttle in bay two."

"Understood," Urch said. "I'll alert the other humans, sir. You look after yourself and the director."

"We'll see you at the rendezvous point."

Urch keyed off and gestured down the hall with his gun. Without waiting to be told, I opened an encrypted channel to the other humans, announced the plan, and told everyone to acknowledge.

"Zeke, this is Charles. I'm with the colonel and Mi Sun. We're on our way."

"I can't get into the weapons lockers," Colonel Rage said, "but I'm armed. Some squirrelly-looking thing—and I mean literally squirrelly—tried to take me down, so I relieved him of his firearm."

"He broke the wall with the guy's face," Mi Sun said.

"Dented it," grunted the colonel.

I realized there was still one of us I hadn't heard from. "Nayana?" I signaled her directly.

"Yes? Hello?" she said calmly, like she was answering her

phone while drinking iced tea on the veranda. "I am with the captain and the director. They are bringing me in."

"Okay. Be careful." I signed off and concentrated on getting to the shuttle bay without being killed.

As we headed into the stairwell, a volley of PPB bursts almost nailed us. The air smelled of smoke, and I saw scorch marks along the bulkheads as we dropped to the floor and Urch returned fire.

"Give us the human, Urch," one of them said as he peeked around the corner. I recognized his deep voice at once. It was Knutjhob. "Your species is primitive too, but you are part of the Confederation, so we're willing to let you prove yourself as have others from your savage world. You can do that by aiding our cause and handing over the corruptor."

"What am I corrupting exactly?" I called out.

"A lively exchange of ideas can wait for another time," Urch said, firing off a few blasts.

The mutineers returned fire, lighting up the corridor with sparks. The smell of burning plastic was heavy in the air. "This doesn't have to concern you, Urch," Knutjhob called.

"Weapons fire in my direction makes it concern me," he said. "And I'm not about to turn anyone over to your Phandic masters."

"You think we are traitors?" Knutjhob asked incredulously. "You couldn't be more wrong. We're working with those who think the Confederation has gone the wrong way. The Movement for Peace isn't about cooperating with Phands."

"Doesn't seem to be about peace, either," Urch observed.

"Not when it comes to our enemies. I'm sorry, but we can't let those humans make it to Confederation Central. Hand them over. We'll return them to their own planet safely, and this disgraceful business will be concluded."

I didn't believe that for a second, and apparently neither did Urch, because he fired off another couple of blasts and charged forward, practically throwing himself down the stairs. He let loose another barrage of PPB blasts and shouted for me to come join him.

"I got two of them," he said, gesturing toward the unconscious bodies on the floor. "Knutjhob got away."

Urch and I rushed the last couple hundred feet or so and then burst into the shuttle bay. The chamber space glowed blue from the plasma field that protected us from the vacuum of space. The colonel was standing with a PPB pistol drawn, aimed at the door. When he recognized us, his expression relaxed.

"The others?" Urch asked.

"Not here yet," the colonel said.

Urch looked at me. "There are two priorities. You must prep that shuttle and be ready to move the second all are on board. You must also secure the entrance. I will have to go search for the director and the captain."

He gestured toward one of the shuttles, and we got on board. Urch opened the weapons locker and handed everyone pistols.

I took mine and felt reassured for a second, but then a horrible thought occurred to me. "Oh, no," I said. "Alice. She's in the brig."

"[*Sweet-smelling flower*]!" Urch swore. "That's a problem."

"It's not far," I said. "I'll get her out."

"I'll go with him," the colonel said, while he looked down the sight of a PPB pistol. You never forget your first ray gun.

Urch nodded and turned to Charles and Mi Sun. "You must protect the shuttle and keep the enemy out of the bay."

Charles had a PPB pistol in each hand. "No problem."

"You'll need access codes for both the brig and the shuttle," Urch said, keying his bracelet to send me the information. "I'm transmitting them now. Good luck."

My bracelet chimed, indicating that it had received the information, and the colonel and I ran out and down the hall, which still smelled faintly of smoke from all the pistol discharge. The brig was on this deck, but almost on the opposite end of the ship, which meant we would have to be pretty lucky to get there and back without running into trouble.

We were not lucky, and we almost stumbled into a trio of mutineers, but the colonel took them down without breaking his stride, and we burst into the brig. A big alien who looked like a gigantic, muscle-bound poodle stood guard, and the colonel shot him as soon as he saw the Movement for Peace armband.

I ran over to the security console and punched in the code. The plasma field dropped and the door swung open.

Alice stepped out, looking sleepy and confused. "What's going on?"

"Mutineers have taken the ship," I explained. "They say they want to take us back to Earth, but I think they really want to put us out the airlock."

Alice stared at me. Her eyes were huge, and the fear was unmistakable. I knew that in that moment she regretted stowing away. Then she stood straight, holding herself like she was ready for anything. I noticed that she had a data bracelet on her wrist, so I knew she wouldn't be at too much of a disadvantage.

"We're escaping," I told her, trying to act calm, like this was the sort of thing I did all the time. Maybe it was.

I keyed my bracelet so I could speak to my entire group. "I've got Alice. Does anyone need help?"

"Negative." Urch's voice came over the comm. "I've made contact with the captain and his group. All are accounted for, but we had to take a circuitous route. We'll be there in five minutes."

"Understood."

The colonel led us back to the shuttle bay, and we encountered no more resistance. I directed Alice to the shuttle, and then stood outside with the colonel, watching the door.

As it opened, I was hoping Urch had made it back sooner than I'd expected, and we'd be able to get out of there, but I was disappointed. Six mutineers, Knutjhob among them, poured in, PPBs blazing.

We hit the deck and returned fire, but their shots had been way off. They weren't aiming for us.

I think the colonel figured it out at the same time I did. "Get in the shuttle!" he yelled. "Now!"

I scrambled up and threw myself inside while I shouted for someone, anyone, to seal the doors. The second we crossed the threshold, Mi Sun mashed some buttons, and the shuttle doors hissed closed. And then my head cracked against one of the bulkheads. Not the bulkhead, I realized—the ceiling. Then the bulkhead. Then the floor. Then Mi Sun's foot.

Through the bursts of pain and the nauseating tumbling, I managed to catch a glimpse of the viewscreen and saw the *Kind Disposition*. From the outside. Knutjhob and his fellow mutineers had shot out the plasma-field generator in the hopes of blowing us all into space. Instead they'd blown our shuttle out of the bay.

I clawed my way over to the shuttle's control station. It took me a moment to remember what was what, but I began pressing in codes, and the shuttle stopped tumbling.

I immediately keyed my bracelet. "Urch!"

"We're coming," he said irritably.

"Don't," I said. "They blew out the plasma field. The bay's been compromised, and the shuttle is no longer on board."

"Understood" came Urch's voice He was speaking in a clipped tone that he must have learned from his years of training, but I had no doubt that he knew he was in serious trouble. "We're going to have to lie low until I can come up with a way for us to rendezvous. I've got some ideas, so stand by."

"Good luck." I was wracked with worry about them, but I was also worried about us. We were sitting ducks out here, and if they really wanted us dead, and they were willing to sacrifice a shuttle, killing us would be no problem. Alternatively, they could secure us with a lance and then take their sweet time deciding what they wanted to do with us. The only way we would be safe would be if we were to run away, but that would mean abandoning Urch and Nayana, not to mention the captain and the director.

*Running away is the best option,* Smelly said. *Preserve yourself. You shall make other friends soon enough.*

"Not going to happen," I mumbled. "We need to figure out a way to hide ourselves from the ship until we can get them out of there."

Charles nodded, looking like he was concentrating. "Is there some way we could hide the shuttle in the ship's ion trail without the exhaust destroying us?"

"Brilliant!" I shouted. "Even if they guess we're hiding back there, we'll be blending into the exhaust emissions, and they won't be able to get a fix on us. We can hide in plain sight." I tapped my data bracelet and began calling up data.

Smelly made a disembodied sighing noise. *I suppose if you are determined to stick near the other worthless members of your primitive social group, I may as well keep you alive.* Numbers began to appear before my eyes, hovering in the air. I realized that Smelly was projecting a course. I didn't hesitate. Smelly was about a zillion times smarter than I was, and it was too worried about its well-being to give me bad advice.

I had the new course laid in, and we were moving into position, when Charles gasped at the information on his readout. "They're beginning the sequence to open their dark-matter-missile bays. They're going to fire on us."

Before he'd even finished speaking, I banked us sharply away from the nearest launch bay. I knew, from both sim training and real-life experience, how hard it was to get a dark-matter missile lock, and I planned to make their hitting us as difficult as possible. I could evade them all day, I told myself, or at least until they ran out of missiles. They could always move on to PPB weapons, I realized, and the shuttle wouldn't have much defense against that. Which made me sort of wonder why they would squander a missile when they didn't need to.

"Don't bother with the evasion," Charles said, his voice strangely flat. He was scrolling through text on his bracelet. Clearly, he'd been wondering the same thing I had, and he had entered a query into his bracelet's database. "I think they're using a missile because it can lock onto our shuttle's unique comm signal. They don't even have to aim. The missile will just find us."

"Change the comm signal, then!" Colonel Rage ordered.

"There is not enough time," Charles said. "According to this it can't be done in less than three minutes, and once they fire the missile, we'll have about thirty seconds."

"Options!" barked the colonel. He stood with his hands on his hips, his expression one of impatience. He didn't look like a man who'd been told he had thirty seconds to live. He looked like someone who expected his subordinates to snap to.

*You must surrender,* Smelly said. *There is no technological solution in the time available.*

"We have to surrender," I said, hating how the words sounded. I'd faced enemies before, but I'd never given in, not willingly. Now the clock was running out, and it was either give up or blow up.

I looked back at Charles and Mi Sun, both of them battered and terrified. I didn't hesitate. I told myself this wasn't giving in. This was providing myself more time to figure out how to turn things around. I hit my data bracelet. "*Kind Disposition*, hold your fire! We surrender. Repeat. We surrender!"

"That's nice" came Knutjhob's voice. "But our orders are to kill you."

There was a flash of light as the ship's missile-bay doors opened and our enemies prepared to fire on us.

"We're going to die," Mi Sun said. Her voice was hollow as the realization came over her. There was no escape. No hope of evasion. They were locked on, and that missile was going to hit us and scatter our atoms into the void of space.

"Will it hurt?" Charles asked. His voice cracked, but he met my eye. He didn't want to go out a coward.

"It's going to hurt *them*," I said, and hurled the ship forward at maximum acceleration. I may have had only a few seconds left, but I wasn't going to sit there and wait for the end. If there was a way out of this, I'd find it or go out trying.

With the shuttle moving at its top velocity, I spun it around to the other side of the *Kind Disposition*, gaining us another few seconds. Everyone was thrown to the side, and the internal gravity systems tried to compensate for the speed and sharp turns.

"There's no point," Charles said. "We're done."

"Can they cancel the missile?" I asked, but the glazed look in Charles's eyes said he wasn't really listening. "Snap out of it! Can they disarm or negate the comm lock?"

His eyes widened slightly, as he began to understand what I had in mind. He immediately ran a query through his data bracelet. "Yes, if they choose," he said.

"Then let's make that their best option. I'll keep us in one piece as long as I can."

Charles grinned, suddenly reinvigorated. "A fine gambit!" he shouted. Then, while trying not to smash into the side of the sharply turning shuttle, he keyed his bracelet. "*Kind Disposition*, cancel your missile lock, or we're going to take you with us."

I was now circling the ship at top speed, and the missile was following us, about five hundred feet aft. I kept us perhaps twenty feet out from the ship's hull, so if the missile hit us, the *Kind Disposition* would take the hit as well.

There was no answer.

Charles signaled them again. "*Kind Disposition*, I strongly urge you to abort that missile."

This time we got an answer. "We're trying" came a panicked voice. "We can't figure out how!"

"Don't you morons train your personnel?" Colonel Rage demanded.

"We didn't complete training" came the panicky reply. "What do we do?"

Unfortunately, their incompetence came as no surprise. The crew had been forced on the captain by Junup. Clearly, they were assassins, meant to take out the humans and, unless I missed my guess, Director Ghli Wixxix at the same time. Junup's loyal soldiers were supposed to relieve him of two pesky problems at once. They weren't prepared to deal with complicated and high-stress technical operations.

*Fleshy abominations never cease to amaze me with their stupidity,* Smelly said. *Tell that dimwit that in order to override a comm lock, it needs to access the tertiary command subroutine.*

I passed Smelly's advice along, minus the insults.

"Give us a minute!" the being on the other end shouted.

"I've got the ion-trail coordinates locked in," Charles said. "The second they cancel that lock, we're going to vanish from their sensors."

"Not over yet," I muttered. I checked the distance on the missile. Now it was almost six hundred feet away. *That's good,* I thought as I looped around the ship. *We're gaining. We're going to beat them.* It took almost all my concentration to hug the hull of the ship without crashing into it, but after another twenty seconds I looked back to see where the missile was, and it was nowhere.

"Missile's gone," I said.

"It can't have vanished," Charles told me.

Then there was a bright light, and once more the shuttle was spinning wildly as we were tossed against a wall and pinned by the force of the propulsion. We were being hurled away by the blast wave. Pain and nausea and panic all jostled for my brain's attention. And the light. The light of the ship exploding burned my eyes from the viewscreen. The missile had struck while trying to circle the ship and lock onto us.

The *Kind Disposition* had been destroyed.

# CHAPTER THIRTEEN

irector Ghli Wixxix. Captain Hyi. Urch. Nayana. They had all been on that ship, and now the ship had been reduced to scrap and atoms. I felt myself spiraling into despair, but I knew I had to put my feelings on hold, because I was also spiraling in a more literal sense: The blast of the *Kind Disposition* had us spinning like a barrel rolling downhill.

In the chaos of there being no up or down, I tried to claw my way back to the helm console, smashing into bits of ship and people every few seconds. By the time I finally grabbed on to the console, digging in hard enough to bruise my fingers, the spin had seemed to slow. I managed to place myself in my chair, and then, still gripping it with one hand, I used the other to key in the commands to stabilize the shuttle. In a few seconds we righted ourselves, and the artificial gravity properly calibrated up and down.

I looked around the interior of our little vessel. Equipment was scattered everywhere. Mi Sun, Charles, Alice, and Colonel Rage were attempting to move around, getting into their seats and, belatedly, strapping themselves in.

"Does anyone need medical care?" I asked.

They all shook their heads no. I think they were still trying to piece together what had happened. I was busy checking the readouts, trying to find out how damaged the shuttle was and how we were going to get to wherever we were going. I'd thought the worst had just happened, but then I saw a reading on the navigation console next to me that made me think I'd been a little too optimistic.

Suddenly I heard a sound that nearly broke my heart. Mi Sun was sobbing. "Nayana," she said, her voice between a cough and a whisper.

"I know," I said. "But we can't mourn now. Not now. We just lost a lot of friends, but we need to get out of here."

The colonel came to sit next to me by the control console. There was a cut just above his eye, and it must have been obscuring his vision because he kept blinking. "What's the rush? The ship trying to destroy us is gone."

I gestured toward the readout on the navigation console. "Yeah, but now there's a tunnel aperture forming a quarter of a light year away from here."

"Rescue?"

"I don't know, but it seems an awfully big coincidence that someone would show up at this place, at this exact moment." Without giving it another thought, I killed the ship's main power. Everything except some basic computer functions went dead. Keeping even those minimal systems operational was a risk, but I needed to be able to see who was out there. Now we were without gravity, without life support, and without lights except the ambient glow of the viewscreen and the consoles.

"Is this necessary?" the colonel asked. "Maybe whoever is coming in was just passing by and saw the explosion."

"Maybe," I said, "but space is pretty big. Nothing ever just passes by anything else. Anyhow, it doesn't hurt to be safe. If they're friendly, we can ask for help. If not, we'll look like just another piece of junk."

Alice was now unstrapped and moving her way toward the front of the shuttle, hand over hand, grabbing a chair or a bulkhead or whatever would allow her to move in the zero-gravity environment. When you imagine floating in space, you think it will be like swimming without the water. In fact it's uncomfortable and awkward, more like falling than flying, and it makes you feel like you want to barf. Alice, however, was ignoring all that as she made her way forward.

She grabbed on to the back of my chair and floated, letting her legs drift out behind her. Her face was smeared with a little blood, maybe from a cut on the back of her hand. Her hair floated out around her like she was a cartoon character zapped with an electric wire.

"How long can we go without power?" she asked.

I studied her for a second in the dim light of the consoles. She was out of her element. We all were, of course, but Charles and Mi Sun had a couple of space battles under their belts, and I had no doubt the colonel had done and seen all kinds of dangerous and traumatizing things. Alice had had a difficult family life, but she'd never had to face anything like this. Even so, her expression was stony—her eyes narrowed and her jaw set. She was angry, not terrified, and she was all business.

"An hour, maybe," I told her. I didn't say it, but we were all thinking it: I hoped it would be enough.

"So what do we do if this ship is bad news?" she asked.

"One step at a time," I said quietly. It was the best I could come up with.

We stared at the viewscreen, which I'd set to cover the area near where the tunnel aperture was forming. There was a flash of light, like a laser scalpel cutting lengthwise across the fabric of space, and then something dark emerged. It was just a shadow at first, and then it began to take shape. It was long and dark and rounded. The lack of gravity was bad enough, but now my stomach did an extra flip. The massive ship suddenly loomed across our viewscreen. It was black as space, with only a few dim lights making it stand out from the void around it. There was no mistaking that sleek shape.

It was a saucer, a Phandic cruiser.

We all stared, knowing what this meant. We were trapped in deep space, away from any help, hopelessly outmatched against an enemy vessel.

A chime indicated that a message was coming through, and I put it on the screen. The rectangular face of a Phand appeared now. Like all of his kind that I had seen, he had a boxy head and gray skin and dark, menacing eyes that all combined made it look like a space orc. His chin was jutted out, to give us a better look at his tusks. I'd seen lots of strange-looking aliens on Confederation Central, and I'd quickly learned not to mistake appearance for intent. With this Phand, nothing about its looks was as frightening as the merciless expression in its eyes. "I am Captain Thimvium-zi of the Phandic cruiser *Viceroy's Repressed Memory*. If there are any survivors, we are prepared to offer assistance."

Colonel Rage looked at me. "Can we tunnel out of here without them knowing or before they can stop us?"

"No," I said. "I'll need to plot a course, which will take at least five minutes, but we won't be able to go anywhere without powering up the engines, and they'll be able to spot us if we do that."

"If you find a way around that, can you get us back to Earth?" he asked.

"Earth?" I asked. In spite of what had just happened, or maybe because of it, going back had never occurred to me.

"Zeke, the crew of a Confederation ship just tried to assassinate us. Maybe there are more good guys than bad over there, but it seems to me that right now they're having a serious dustup about the future of their society, and we don't want to be in the middle of it. I think it's time to head home."

Maybe he was right, but I didn't want to go back. I didn't want to give up on Confederation membership, and I didn't want to give up on seeing Tamret again. If I returned to Earth now, would they revoke her asylum? I wasn't holding up my end of the bargain, after all. On the other hand, it wasn't right to drag Charles and Mi Sun along on what was obviously a dangerous journey.

I turned around. "What do you guys want to do?" I asked.

"We should go home," Charles said, and for the first time, he sounded like a little kid. He'd been though an awful lot, and I knew he'd had enough. I couldn't much blame him.

I was about to object, to try to talk them out of it, but I had no grounds. I'd never bullied them into helping me before, and I wasn't going to start now. Instead I would take them back to Earth and then return to the Confederation myself. I'd face what Junup and his followers threw at me if that was what it took to protect Tamret. As far as I could tell, that was my only option.

We had to get there first, however, and to do that we had to deal with the little problem of the Phandic cruiser.

Now another face came onto the viewscreen, and this time I gasped. I had not expected to see a human face up there, but I guess I shouldn't have been surprised.

"Our sensors suggest there's a shuttle out there, lying low," said Nora Price. "And we first detected your ship tunneling out of Earth's system. So I'm thinking that the only being in this galaxy who could manage to make his own ship explode and somehow survive is Zeke Reynolds. Zeke, if you're out there, I'm offering you asylum and full immunity. We just want to make sure you and any other survivors are safe."

"Nora Price, I presume," Colonel Rage said.

I had told him all about Ms. Price when I'd been debriefed after returning to Earth. He must have read her file, so he'd probably seen her picture. Even if he hadn't, there weren't a whole lot of human women who might be flying around on Phandic ships—at least, not that I knew of. The last I'd seen of her, she had been on her way to a Confederation prison, so I had no idea what she was doing running loose. Figuring it out could wait for later, though.

"Yeah," I told him. "There she is."

"You kids have more experience with her than I do, but I'm not inclined to believe a word she says," the colonel said. "So let's ignore her. With all the training you had when you were on Confederation Central, did you learn enough to get this shuttle home safe?"

"We can plot the course using just the computers," I said. "The plotting won't require enough energy for them to get a read on us, but if we heat up the engines, they'll be able to pinpoint our location."

"Let's do what we can," the colonel said, "and worry about the next part when we come to it."

Rather than try to move in a weightless environment, I switched my console from helm to navigation and began scrolling through the planetary database. There were a lot of planets in there, but not the one I was looking for. "That's going to be a problem. I guess the location of non-Confederation worlds is classified, and I don't have the clearance to access those files. I can't set a course for Earth, because I don't know where Earth is."

"What do you mean you don't know where it is?" Mi Sun demanded.

"I mean," I said pointedly, trying to get a certain AI's attention, "it's not like a simple biological organism like myself can figure out where Earth is without it being marked on a map."

*Are you talking to me?* Smelly asked. *I am remarkable, I agree, but you will recall I came to your world while still dormant. I don't know the location of your star, which means you're on your own.*

Okay, that was worth a try. Now everyone was looking at me like I was a big weirdo. Normal people don't usually need to remind one another that they are biological organisms. "I'm just saying we don't have the navigational tools to get home."

"You just . . . go to our star," Charles insisted, his voice breaking a little.

"How are we going to find it?" I asked. "It's not like I have any idea where our star is in relation to any of these other stars. And even if I did know that it was ten light years to the left of something else, that still wouldn't help me figure out the tunnel coordinates. There are, literally, millions of stars just like our sun in this part of the galaxy. I don't think we have any choice but to go to Confederation Central."

"You're just saying that because you want to see Tamret," Mi Sun snapped. Then she lowered her eyes. "No, I know that's not true. I'm sorry."

"Look, everyone here is hurt and grieving and scared," Colonel Rage said, "but I think we can all agree that Zeke is in command, and we can trust him to do what is best for all of us. Isn't that right, Zeke?"

"I'm trying. I swear, I'd take you guys home if I could find it."

"And not stay yourself?" Alice asked.

I met her gaze. She knew me better than I'd realized. "Doesn't much matter what I would do, since I can't find Earth," I said. "I don't even know how we're going to get away from those Phands."

My panel chimed, letting me know there was another incoming message. I accepted it and Ms. Price appeared on screen again.

"I'm going to give you one last chance to surrender willingly. We don't want to risk damaging your shuttle. But if we don't hear from you within two minutes, we're going to start firing PPB bursts at suspicious chunks of debris. Maybe one of them is you."

*It would be better to surrender than be destroyed,* Smelly observed.

"No way," I muttered under my breath. The Phands hated me. I didn't care what Ms. Price said; they had no interest in shaking hands and making nice. If I was taken on board that Phandic ship, I was as good as dead.

*If you are taken prisoner, you will find a way to survive and perhaps escape. These options will be unavailable if you have already exploded.*

Wisdom from the voice in my head. We could make his slogans into T-shirts, but first we'd have to get out of this alive. I plugged in the coordinates for Confederation Central and then checked on the tunneling engines. We still needed four minutes, which, if Ms. Price was being punctual, we did not have.

"Not enough time," I mumbled.

"Can you send a distress signal?" the colonel asked.

"Yeah, but if the good guys answer and say they can't be here for a day, we'll have given our exact location away for nothing." The trick, I realized, was to make sure that whatever answer we got back was going to make them hightail it. Last time I'd been in space, any Phandic ship had been able to beat any equivalent Confederation ship, but now things had changed. The Phands were getting their evil behinds kicked all over the galaxy by the Confederation, which meant they wouldn't stick around if they thought there was a chance of a battle.

I turned to Charles. "Record a message on your data bracelet, something from Confederation Command. Say anything that the Phands won't want to hear."

"Like what?" His voice was shrill. He was still in panic mode, and I couldn't much blame him.

"Keep it together, Charles. What would Han Solo do? Come up with something that will scare them into retreating."

In the meantime I composed a message to transmit by photon beacon. I explained exactly what had happened and included the shuttle's logs, which I hoped would back up everything I was saying.

"You ready?" I asked Charles.

He nodded. "I just sent it to your bracelet."

"Here goes," I told everyone. "Let's hope this works."

I sent out two photon beacons at once, hoping the Phands would be too excited about locating us to notice the second beacon. I watched as a few seconds later the saucer pivoted and began to approach. Ms. Price came over the viewscreen again.

"You just gave yourself away, Zeke. Very sloppy."

Then came Charles's voice off the second beacon, which I'd bounced off the Phandic ship. I hoped they wouldn't examine it too closely, because it wouldn't hold up under scrutiny.

Charles voice, disguised and deep, came over the comm network. "This is Admiral Ackbar." I turned and looked at him, and he shrugged. "We have received your distress call and have already dispatched six destroyer-class ships, which were fortunately conducting operations near you. They should arrive within ten minutes."

Such an outcome was too good to be true, but I had to hope that with the drubbing the Phands had been taking recently, they couldn't tell real danger from our wishful thinking. That turned out to be how it went. The ship began to retreat at maximum sublight speed. They'd be tunneling as soon as they could plot a course.

"Good work, Admiral," I said to him. I then began setting in the coordinates for Confederation Central.

*Very clever,* Smelly said.

It was moderately clever, I thought. Clever enough to work, at least, but not brilliant beyond what a moderately resourceful seventh grader could reasonably devise. All of which meant that Smelly should have been able to come up with an idea like that itself. Yet Smelly had only suggested surrender, an outcome it ought to have feared, but clearly didn't.

I wasn't sure what all of this meant, but I had the distinct feeling that Smelly was not telling me everything.

It was going to take a little more than a day to reach Confederation Central, and once we'd patched up our wounds and repaired what we could on the shuttle, there wasn't much to do but think about what we had lost, and what we had yet to face. This was not what I'd expected my return to the Confederation to feel like.

With our survival and freedom no longer in danger, Mi Sun and Charles both retreated to the back of the shuttle to deal with their fear and their grief. I couldn't blame them—I was having a hard time with losing Nayana and Urch, too—but someone had to work the shuttle. I sat up front with Colonel Rage and Alice, trying to show them as much of the ropes as possible. There wasn't a whole lot to do when we were in tunnel, but having a couple of other people who could handle the basics couldn't hurt.

The colonel was busy running through some simple navigational monitoring procedures I'd shown him, and, with nothing else to do, I found myself feeling absolutely miserable.

I'd done a lot of dangerous things the last time I'd left Earth. I'd taken a lot of chances, but even when things hadn't worked out the way I wanted—like with our getting kicked out of the Confederation—at least no one had gotten hurt.

Urch was an officer on a Confederation ship, and while I hated that he was dead, he had chosen to take those risks when he signed up. Nayana had not. She hadn't wanted to come out here, and I'd talked her into it. If I hadn't, she would still be alive.

Colonel Rage looked at me. "Say we're at a restaurant, and I can't decide between the steak and the chicken. What would you tell me to eat?"

"Colonel," I sighed. "I'm not really up for talking about food."

"Chicken or steak," he insisted in that military tone that basically meant you had to answer.

"I don't know. You seem like a red-meat sort of guy. Steak."

"And if I order the steak, and I end up choking to death, does that mean you killed me?"

I shrugged, seeing where he was going with this. "It's hardly the same thing."

"Yes it is. You asked her to come with you on a trip that should have been safe. It turned out not to be, but that's not on you."

"She didn't want to do this. I talked her into it."

"I think what she wanted was for you to say you needed her on the team," he said. "She wanted to feel like she was import-ant." The colonel shook his head. "Look, son. The point of feel-ing terrible after you make a mistake is so that you can learn to do better next time. You didn't make a mistake, so there's noth-ing to learn. We were betrayed, and you couldn't have known that. Better to feel angry than guilty."

"You think we should be plotting revenge?"

"We don't understand the first thing about the mess we're in. I think we should be figuring out how we're going to get everyone back home safely."

"Yeah."

"But if the chance for revenge comes along," he said with a slight smile, "well, we'll see how we feel then."

# CHAPTER FOURTEEN

When we came out of tunnel in the Confederation Central system, I knew what had to be taken care of and in what order. The massive domed city in space, orbiting the great gas giant, still looked beautiful to me, like a place of wonder, but now I was also afraid of what I would find there. We all stared out the viewscreen, and Alice and Colonel Rage were speechless as they gaped at this technological marvel. I wanted to join them, but I was too busy trying to figure out how to keep us alive and safe.

The first priority was communication, and I sent out the messages that needed to be transmitted. Then I contacted Docking Control, identified who we were, and asked for docking procedures. There was a long silence, and then we were given an approach route. I tried contacting some old friends on the station and found that, much as I had expected, our communications had been cut off. Once they'd discovered who we were, someone didn't want us to tell our side of the story.

Our docking bay was in a secure portion of the spaceport, and we stepped out into an area of unadorned white walls. The air smelled sterile, with a vague hint of disinfectant. I thought about how this must seem to Alice, who was getting her first view of the inside of the station. This didn't feel like visiting an amazing, futuristic society. It felt like a field trip to space prison. A dozen peace officers were on-site to meet us. They represented a variety of species. Several looked vaguely humanoid, but with different-shaped heads or non-Earth skin colors and various cranial protrusions. There were also a few species that looked a bit like Earth animals—including the bull-headed and beaked-otter aliens I'd seen before. They came in various shapes and colors and heights, but they had one thing in common: They all glared at us like they hated our guts.

I noticed that several of them wore black armbands with the squiggly fire symbol of the Movement for Peace. We were getting off to a terrific start.

"You are being detained for questioning," said a very tall humanoid. He had a triangular head and an almost impossibly thin body around which he wore a close-fitting uniform. His hands looked about as thick as construction paper. "Do not give us any trouble."

They escorted us down a long, bleak corridor to a sparsely furnished room, large and white with a narrow table in the center, around which were set a few chairs.

"Wait here," the narrow peace officer said.

"For how long?" I asked.

"For as long as it takes."

They closed the door behind us, and I heard the hiss of a vacuum seal. It felt like we were being sterilized.

"I put Zeke in charge when the shuttle was in crisis," the colonel said after a moment. "I believed him to be the best qualified person for that job. The way I see it, I'm best qualified to handle our dealings with the aliens. Let me speak when the time comes. I'm in command, and I'll get us out of this."

We all agreed, and with that settled, we sat and waited for another three hours. There's nothing like the combination of fear and boredom to make the time crawl. Then, at last, the door opened, and three beings stood there: two peace officers flanking an all-too-familiar bulky form.

Junup looked like I remembered, with his goaty face, his hairy body, and his seemingly incongruous shell hanging on his back. He strode in quickly, so his cape billowed behind him. He wore no shirt, but around one of his shaggy arms he had a black band showing the flame symbol.

"You certainly know how to make an impression, Mr. Reynolds," he said. "Last time you arrived it was after destroying an enemy ship. This time you decided to take out one of our own."

"I sent the logs and my report," I told him. "You know what happened."

"My nephew was on that ship," Junup said, his voice hard.

"Your nephew was a mutineer," I said. "He tried to kill me."

Colonel Rage cleared his throat, reminding me that he was supposed to be speaking for our group. "Excuse me," he said. "My name is Colonel Richard Rage, United States Army, and—"

"I know who you are," Junup said. "Three of the juvenile humans I recognize. The fourth is the stowaway. Another criminal from a world of beings who delight in breaking their own laws and then, when those are exhausted, anyone else's laws they can find."

"You're Junup, is that right?" the colonel asked, not letting himself sound even slightly put out.

"*Interim Director* Junup."

"Well, Interim Director Junup, allow me to express my condolences on the passing of your nephew. We are also saddened by the loss of life aboard the *Kind Disposition*, as well as the destruction of the ship itself. That said, I can assure you that Zeke was not seeking to harm people or property, but rather to avoid being destroyed by a missile fired at us with murderous intent. It was your nephew who told us that his orders were—"

"I'm afraid the picture is far from clear," Junup interrupted, swishing his cape theatrically. He must have learned that move in villain school. "It appears to me that you became some sort of threat to the *Kind Disposition*, and Captain Hyi took appropriate action against you. Unfortunately, you would not accept his authority, mutinied, and destroyed a Confederation vessel. And now you want praise, I suppose?"

Colonel Rage was on his feet. "You don't really intend to sell that malarkey, do you? There was an organized revolt on that ship. Every officer on board was a part of it except the captain and that Urch fellow."

"And so you executed them?"

"You know that's not what happened."

"This matter will be subject to scrutiny," said Interim Director Junup, "as will any arrangements my predecessor made with you."

Colonel Rage pinched the bridge of his nose with his thumb and index finger. "Look, these kids aren't warriors, and they sure aren't criminals. They're survivors. It's pretty easy to see that you're not fond of them, and I'm willing to bet you weren't so keen on this crazy mission Ghli Wixxix had in mind for them."

"You are right in that," Junup said. "I once had a great deal of respect for her, but this was a fool's errand."

"Then give us a ride home. I'm sure you've got your own

fires to put out. You don't want us here, and we don't want to be here. Send us back to Earth, and no one has to know about any of this. You can say the ship was destroyed in an accident. Say your enemies did it, and use it to gain more support for whatever it is you want. Just don't let these kids get caught up in your power struggle."

Junup stroked his goaty beard thoughtfully. "If we can keep this story from spreading, then such a thing might be possible."

The Colonel nodded. "I thought we might be able to do business."

*Uh-oh,* Smelly observed.

I sighed. Smelly was correct. I had already made this option unworkable. "Unfortunately, it's a little late for that," I told them.

"You can't have pulled the same stunt by bringing in your data-collector friends. We blocked your communications as soon as you made contact."

"I kind of figured you'd want to control the story," I said, "so I sent out the information before I contacted Docking Control."

"That's against the rules!" Junup cried. "You cannot make private communications before contacting Docking Control!"

"I know," I said. "Which is why I figured it wouldn't occur to you."

Junup snorted. He took a couple of quick strides around the room before turning sharply to face me. "Then I'm afraid I can't help you. You wanted your fabricated story to be public, and now it is. Now I must consider my options. Tell me. Have you ever heard of Planet Pleasant?"

"No," I said. "But with a name working that hard, it can't be any place I want to visit."

"It is where the Phands conduct their cruelest and most unspeakable scientific experiments. I'm sure they would be most grateful to me if I had you delivered there. The Phands don't believe that adolescents are completely developed sentient beings, you know. It's one of the reasons your actions have so infuriated them. I'm sure they would love to cut your head open and find out what makes you so irritating."

"Hold on," Colonel Rage began, but Junup was clearly done talking. He turned toward the door.

"What happens now?" Mi Sun asked.

"For now, you are to be held as prisoners," Junup said. "I no longer have the option of dealing with this quietly, so I am going to need a few hours to determine how best to manage this latest disaster." He shook his head. "Zeke, can't you see that this is your fault? Can you imagine how much easier things would be if you weren't always trying to outsmart everyone?"

"They'd be easier," Colonel Rage said, "because he'd be dead."

"Yes," Junup agreed as he stepped out the door. "That *would* make things easier, wouldn't it?"

We sat around the table, feeling despondent.

"We've pretty much got no options here," Colonel Rage said. "They don't fear Earth as a military power, and diplomatic relations with our world don't matter to them. We could disappear, and there's nothing the people back home could do about it."

"I don't think you're making me feel better," Charles said.

"Sorry, son. Just thinking aloud. I'm trying to determine our next move, but I'm not coming up with a whole lot."

I felt everyone staring at me, like this situation was my fault. I wasn't so sure I wanted to take the blame, though.

"Maybe he would have sent us home if I hadn't gone public," I said. "But maybe we would just have been made to quietly vanish. That Planet Pleasant idea seemed to come pretty quickly to him. The main thing now is that since our being here is public knowledge, Junup can't treat us too badly."

"Hmm," Colonel Rage said. "That's a fair point. It could be that your little stunt saved our behinds, Zeke."

"How do you mean?" I asked.

"He's keeping us locked in this room because he's got nowhere to put us. That means they made no plans for our leaving this facility. He either had a ship gassed up and ready to go, or we were never getting off this space station alive."

"Junup's a weenie, but he wouldn't . . ." I trailed off because it seemed pretty much like he would. In fact he had already tried. I needed to remember that I could not put anything past him.

The colonel was in full agreement. "Whoever organized the takeover on the *Kind Disposition* had to be someone pretty high up the chain of command. It makes things easier if you have a bunch of blind followers wearing armbands who are willing to do pretty much anything you say."

After another three hours the narrow, triangle-headed peace officer opened the door and told us that Junup was ready for us.

"Ready for what?" the colonel demanded.

"You don't ask questions here," the peace officer said.

"Son, these young people are my responsibility, so you either tell me what I want to know, or we're going to have a problem. Given it looks like I could tear you in half, I'd think you'd rather do things the easy way."

The peace officer blinked its large, triangular eyes several times. "There will be a brief presentation to data collectors. After that, you are being taken to your quarters in the government compound where these youths stayed the last time they were on the station."

We followed the peace officer into the hallway, and a second officer fell into line behind us. We then walked until we met up with Junup near where the hallway ended with a pair of double doors.

Junup looked us over, and then his eyes rested on me. "I would ask you not to do anything foolish, but that is like asking rotten fruit not to stink. If you don't wish to be offended by rotten fruit, you must dispose of it in a proper, environmentally sensitive recycler unit."

"This analogy is confusing me," I said. "Am I the recycler unit?"

"Because you chose to circulate misleading rumors about what happened on that ship, I must now address the data collectors who have gathered outside. I emphasize that it is *I* who will address them, not you. I wish you to be present to lend tacit support to what I have to say." Junup keyed something into his data bracelet, and I felt my own bracelet hum as it received a transmission. I saw all the others react as well, so I knew that whatever he'd sent me, he'd sent to all of us.

"To guarantee your cooperation, I've just used my security override to send a dampening field to each of your data bracelets. If you choose to speak, only my officers and your fellow criminals will hear you, so there is no point in attempting to communicate with anyone else."

"I don't like this," Colonel Rage said.

"You don't have to. I am trying to manage this situation to

the best of my ability. You may not enjoy what I have to say, but you will endure it, in part because it is the best way to ensure a favorable final outcome for you, but also, more importantly, because there is nothing you can do about it."

I felt another slight buzz in my bracelet, which I assumed meant Junup was encasing us in the dampening field. "Do you think you can just silence us?" I asked incredulously, but my own voice produced a dull echo, like I was talking with a bucket over my head.

"If I have accomplished nothing else in my career," Junup said, "I will be content with the knowledge that I have, at the very least, silenced Ezekiel Reynolds for a time."

The guards then opened the double doors, and we walked out to face a crowd of perhaps a hundred data collectors. Lights shone in our faces. Recording drones hovered above us, while various data collectors held up their data bracelets or recording devices or exposed their image-capturing tattoos. Most of them were beings I didn't know, but a few of them I recognized from my hearing the previous year, and front and center was Hluh, whom I had contacted directly with my report about the destruction of the *Kind Disposition* and the shuttle data logs.

It would have been overstating the matter to say that Hluh and I were friends. She didn't do friendship, exactly, but we had a history, and while it had started out with the two of us at odds, she'd later helped us a great deal in figuring out who had manipulated our presence on the station—and why. I had to admit, I was happy to see her blank expression as she stared up at me. Hers was the closest thing to a friendly face that I was going to find in the room.

Junup raised up a hairy arm, and the room began to quiet.

Recording devices continued to hum, but soon no one spoke.

"There have been rumors circulated on the news outputs," Junup began, "and I would like to address them as best I can, though I will tell you directly that we believe the leaked data to be at best incomplete, at worst a forgery. Here, however, is what we know. The Confederation starship *Kind Disposition* has been destroyed with all hands, including my beloved nephew, Knutjhob. It grieves me to confirm the rumors that Director Ghli Wixxix was also on board. She perished along with Captain Hyi and his crew." Junup paused here. "In accordance with our laws, I will fill the role of interim director until the next election cycle."

What followed was a long list of Ghli Wixxix's accomplishments and Junup recounting personal anecdotes that mostly served to show how much Ghli Wixxix had admired and respected Junup, and how happy she would be that her position was being filled by someone so competent and just all around amazingly wonderful.

"As more information becomes available, we shall pass it along," Junup said. "Unfortunately, there is not much we know, and a great deal of misinformation to sort through. It certainly does not aid our inquiry that the only witnesses to this disaster very likely caused it."

"The director's schedule listed her as vacationing on her home world this past week," one of the data collectors called out. "Now we learn she was traveling to Earth. What can you tell us about why she chose to make a personal visit to this unaligned world, and why the trip was kept secret?"

"Right now I can tell you very little," Junup said. "There are some indications that the director was in the region to negotiate a new and lasting peace accord with the Phandic Empire, but I have yet to see the relevant documentation."

I was pretty sure that was a lie, but I guessed it was an explanation that Junup liked better than that the leader of the Confederation had decided to visit my planet because she needed me.

"Why is Ezekiel Reynolds here on Confederation Central?" asked another data collector. "If Director Ghli Wixxix went to Earth, then we must presume she chose to bring him and the other Earth beings with her."

"Again," Junup said, "the director's intentions are not clear. I can tell you that the existing ship's logs indicate the presence of a stowaway on board. It is likely that all of these humans were stowaways, but again, their role in the destruction of the *Kind Disposition* is yet to be determined, and it is premature to conclude that they deliberately destroyed the ship."

"As you know," another data collector said, "our constitution requires an interim director to stand before procedural committee within ten days in order to have the position confirmed. No doubt that committee will request a formal inquiry into the destruction of the *Kind Disposition*. Are you at all uneasy about what they will discover?"

"I am uneasy that one of our ships has been destroyed. I have lost a friend, and I have lost a nephew. I mourn for the many beings I did not personally know. While the facts of this case may be disturbing, I certainly wish them to be revealed."

Another data collector stepped forward. "There are rumors that you personally oversaw the staffing of the *Kind Disposition*, favoring heavily beings who belong to your Movement for Peace. Could the ship being manned by an unskilled crew have played a role in its destruction?"

"It is hardly *my* movement," Junup said, putting a hairy hand to his chest, "though I certainly understand its apprehension about the influence of primitive species on our society. As for the personnel change, such shifts are normal and entirely within standard practice."

"Ezekiel Reynolds!" one of the data collectors shouted. "What do you have to say for yourself? Have you destroyed yet another ship?"

Junup held up a cautioning hand. "I've advised these aliens not to speak to any data collectors until more verifiable facts become available. It is for their own protection—so they don't incriminate themselves, you understand. Please respect that. Obviously this is a delicate issue. Some have called Ezekiel a heinous villain. Others have pronounced him a hapless bumbler. I believe the truth lies somewhere between these two extremes."

*Always the moderate,* I thought.

"Regardless of his past mistakes, indiscretions, humiliations, and crimes," Junup continued, "I would be remiss if I did not acknowledge that his actions have played some small role in the recent peace that we have come to enjoy within our society. More importantly, his home planet was the site of the turning point in a long and disagreeable ideological conflict with the Phandic Empire, a conflict that, after many decades, has come to a conclusion. Because the bounty of peace has grown within the soil of his blunders, I believe we must not condemn him without first possessing all the facts."

*I know you don't much care for this Junup thing,* Smelly said, *but I am coming to respect it. It is quite cunning for a primitive pouch of biological ooze.*

"Then why don't you move into his brain?" I asked, trying not to move my lips. I didn't want to look like a crazy person in front of the entire Confederation. I'd have to settle for looking like a murderous stowaway instead.

*Yes, I think this Junup is a superior example of its kind. And like all superior beings, its true greatness will only show when it is tested. That is why I have overridden your dampening field. You may speak if you wish.*

I felt a grin spread across my face, but I realized that Junup was speaking, linking my alleged actions with the destruction of the *Kind Disposition*, and anyone watching me—a category that almost certainly would include billions—would think I was pleased with myself. I killed the grin.

"Surely Ezekiel Reynolds would like to defend himself against such allegations," one of the data collectors shouted when Junup finished his latest rant.

"Again," Junup said, "I have advised them not to speak. It is my concern that they cannot defend themselves without lying, and it can do us no good to have more untruths circulating."

Hluh now shouldered her way forward. "Ezekiel Reynolds contacted me directly," she announced, "and claimed that there was a mutiny—"

"There is no evidence to support that rumor," Junup interrupted her. "I understand that it is being alleged that the entire crew conspired against the director, and as my nephew was part of the crew, I take this accusation as a personal insult to my family's honor. I also wish to emphasize that we cannot yet confirm the rumors of some sort of primitive bomb, such as might have been manufactured on Ezekiel Reynolds's home world, aboard the *Kind Disposition*."

"The sabotage," I shouted, "was in manning the ship with an untrained crew whose purpose was to take control away from Captain Hyi!"

Junup stared at me, the whites of his eyes suddenly pink. Everything about his expression implied that he wanted me to shut up, but I'd had enough of being quiet for one day. I knew I was probably digging myself in deeper, but it was hard to overestimate my satisfaction from seeing the look of shock on his goaty face.

"Nayana Gehlawat," I said, and then paused, giving them time to hear her name. To really hear it. "Urch," I continued. "They were my friends. I can't claim friendship with either Captain Hyi or Director Ghli Wixxix because I didn't know them long or well enough, but I liked and admired both of them. These were good and honorable beings, and I will tell you right now that they were murdered when—"

That was as far as I got. I'd seen it from the corner of my eye, and some part of my brain was quietly urging caution, but I was too focused on what I wanted to say, so I ignored the looming shadow. It was the narrow-bodied peace officer I'd seen before, or at least a member of the same species. If it was the same being, he had changed out of his uniform and was now wearing something that hugged his body, making it seem even more slight. The bulkiest thing about him was the PPB pistol, pointed directly at me.

Before I could react, another shadow crossed my vision. It was large and shelled and shaggy. Junup hurled himself forward, pushing me to the ground just as the would-be assassin fired his pistol. The energy blast missed us entirely and instead slammed against a wall. Bricks exploded in dust and small chunks, but it was clear to me that no one was hurt.

I turned back to the attacker, but he was already fleeing, twisting easily into the crowds and between bodies. The peace officers who lumbered after him had to get individual beings to move, so they really had no chance.

Meanwhile Junup was pushing himself off me. I didn't know how to read goat-turtle expressions in general, but I knew he was incredibly pleased with himself. By the time I got to my feet, he was already trying to calm the crowd.

"I am unharmed," he announced. "Is anyone injured? Does anyone require medical intervention?"

It seemed no one had been hurt, and that was good. Junup raised up a hand and said that, under the circumstances, there would be no more statements for the day. The room was now a crime scene, and he asked the peace officers to escort the data collectors from the premises. The news conference was over, and it had ended with Junup demonstrating his willingness to risk his life for someone he had every reason to dislike and who had probably killed his nephew. Junup had just made himself a hero.

A group of peace officers led us back to the secure room and locked us inside. At first we were all too shaken and surprised to speak, but it was Colonel Rage who broke the ice.

"This Junup plays a deep game," he said.

I nodded.

"Then the attempt on your life was false?" Charles asked.

"Of course it was," Alice said. "He arranged for a fake assassin so he could save Zeke's life. That way it makes him look like a hero, and no one doubts that he really wants to do the right thing."

"Looks like you're up on Confederation politics," Mi Sun said. "Pretty good for someone whose never been here before and knows nothing about this place."

Alice shrugged. "It just seemed obvious."

"Let's all keep calm," Colonel Rage said. "I know we're an incredible distance from our home, and we've been branded as criminals by a corrupt and power-hungry politician who hates Zeke and is not shy about committing murder, but . . ."

He trailed off, which was not a good sign.

"What's our play?" the colonel asked me.

"Why is that for me to decide?" I sputtered. "I thought you were in command."

"I'll advise you as best I can," Colonel Rage said, "but I may be out of my depth. You know this culture better than I do, and it seems that whatever is going on, you're at the center of it."

"Again," Mi Sun said with a sigh.

"Fine," I snapped, and then began to think about it. "I have allies in the Confederation, but I'm not sure they're in a position to help us. The only beings we can count on are the data collectors—the reporters. Hluh and her colleagues know our side of the story, and they're not stupid. Junup won't be able to do anything too drastic with the whole Confederation watching, so for now we bide our time."

"Until?" Mi Sun asked.

"I don't know. We're going to have to make this up as we go along."

*The Hidden Fortress,* Smelly said. *That's your plan. Ghli Wixxix wanted you to go there, and clearly Junup does not. As near as I can tell, that means you need to go.*

I had no idea if Smelly was right or not, but it always felt satisfying to do what Junup didn't want me to, even if it got me into deeper trouble. Besides, everyone was demanding I come up with a plan, and that was as good as any.

"I think I know what we need to do," I said.

That, however, was as far as I got before the door opened and Junup walked in. He did not close the door behind him, but two peace officers stood guard, their backs to us.

"Nicely played," I said to him.

"Is that how you thank me from saving your life after one of the countless billions who hate you decided to act on reasonable emotions?" He folded his arms and gave me, I supposed, the goat-turtle equivalent of a smirk.

"Cut the bull," the colonel barked at him. "I want to know what you plan do with these children."

"These *children*," Junup said with a sneer, "have accused me of murder and treason, which means that they can't go anywhere until the truth of what happened to the *Kind Disposition* is resolved to the public's satisfaction—and to my own."

"Any 'truth' that satisfies you," the colonel said, "will also have to exonerate you of any wrongdoing, which means you'll need to pin the blame elsewhere."

Junup held out his furry hands in a gesture of surrender. "I only seek to find out what happened. I trust you do not fear such a search."

"Not if it's conducted honestly," the colonel said, but his tone made it clear that he had no faith in any inquiry Junup might arrange.

"Well, then," Junup said, "I see we have our work cut out for us. For now I think it's best if we move you to the government compound. I'm assigning a special escort to oversee your safety, and to make sure you don't have any unfortunate encounters with beings who might disrupt our search for the truth. He will be my representative in my absence, and any questions or requests can be delivered to him. I hope, quite frankly, to see you as little as possible from this point forward."

With a theatrical flourish, Junup turned and strode out of the room, his cape billowing behind him. We all looked at one another, not knowing what to expect next. Then the two peace-keepers by the door parted and allowed a new being to enter the room.

Of the three beings I hated most in the galaxy, I'd already had run-ins with two of them: Junup, of course, and Ms. Price on the Phandic ship. Here was the third, but this was a being I'd never expected to see again, even on Confederation Central. He stood there—tall, muscular and confident—in a well-tailored Confederation suit, a black Movement for Peace band around one arm. He had a smug look on his handsome face. There was no mistaking his satisfaction.

It was Ardov.

# CHAPTER FIFTEEN

Ardov had always carried himself arrogantly, but there was something different about him now. He had a smugness in his swagger that made the old Ardov seem humble by comparison. I couldn't tell what it was. He looked exactly like I remembered him—brownish fur, short whiskers, self-satisfied expression—but he also looked different in ways I could not explain. I'd always disliked him, and I'd even been afraid of him, but now he seemed more menacing than ever.

"What are you doing here!" Mi Sun was already on her feet, pointing at Ardov like they'd been bitter enemies. It wasn't the case, though. Not exactly. She hadn't much cared for Tamret, during most of our time on Confederation Central, and conflicts among the Rarels had been of little interest to her. She hadn't even born much of a grudge after he'd beaten her so badly in the fighting sim that she'd ended up in the hospital. Now it was different. It was us against them, and Ardov was a *them*. "I thought you went back home with the other Rarels."

Ardov shrugged. "Junup decided he wanted me to stick around. He pulled me off my shuttle before it departed and made me an offer, which I accepted. Now here I am, helping him out. Which means I'm now helping *you* out. The interim director has assigned me to take care of you."

"I'm getting the feeling you all know this, uh, cat person," the colonel said to me.

I opened my mouth to speak, but nothing constructive was going to come out, so I closed it again. This marked a major development in my maturity, I thought.

"He was part of the delegation from a planet called Rarel," Charles explained. "He was rather a bully."

"Explains why the interim director took a shine to him," the colonel observed.

"Maybe we should forget what happened before," Ardov said. "Let's start over fresh." He walked over to me and looked down from his superior height.

I didn't know how to read his tone. Was he actually trying to be reasonable with me? If so, I would be the bad guy if I refused to bury the hatchet. On the other hand, I couldn't forget, or forgive, the way he had treated Tamret, and with her coming to the station, I didn't want to show any signs of weakness now—particularly since neither of us was going to have augmented skills to help us against Ardov's superior strength. I'd seen the guy fight, and he was pretty much unstoppable even without a technological edge.

*In case you were wondering,* Smelly told me, *I detect no signs of sincerity in this hairy container of moisture. I believe it means you harm—and therefore, by extension, me. I don't like things that mean me harm.*

I felt myself relax slightly. It was no picnic having Ardov as an enemy, but it beat not knowing what to make of him at all. Now I had a handle on where I stood. I liked that, even if where I stood was no place anyone would ever want to be standing.

"Sure, Ardov," I said. "Let's start over."

And, the two of us having just lied to each other, we were ready to move on.

Ardov ushered us out of the transportation hub and loaded us onto a shuttle. There was no doubt he had picked up some polish in the past year, but even without Smelly's insights, I would never have trusted him. He'd been a bad kid before he'd gone to work for Junup; I didn't see how that particular association could possibly have made him any less bad. Besides, why would Junup have plucked him off that shuttle if he hadn't liked Ardov's cruelty and inclination to violence? Maybe that was the point—to have a mean, remorseless non-Confederation type around to do his dirty work. Even so, Ardov had to have something going for him other than a cruel streak if Junup was going to hire an alien equivalent of a middle school kid to be his fixer.

No one said much on the ride over. We all looked out the windows at the city below, especially Alice and Colonel Rage, who had never seen Confederation Central before. Charles, Mi Sun, and I were veterans, but we still stared like country bumpkins in the big city. The huge, glittering skyscrapers, the sprawling parks, the expanses of residential houses, and the forests and deserts in the far distance—they hadn't lost any of their magic.

We touched down at the compound landing pad and climbed out of the shuttle. The campus looked exactly like I remembered it from the last visit, except that now there were far more black-uniformed peace officers than I recalled—and most of them had Movement for Peace armbands. There were the generally squat buildings separated by walkways and lawns of purple grass.

"Do you know what the guys with the armbands are like?" Charles asked me as we walked among them to our building. "Do you recall the Nightwatch from *Babylon Five*?"

I nodded. The Nightwatch was just like the Movement for Peace: an organization within the military and law enforcement, meant to keep an eye on alien influence but really just a front for bullies and thugs who wanted an excuse to hurt others and feel powerful. "It's a good point. But don't try to outdork me."

"Or that original-series *Star Trek* episode," he continued.

"Yeah, yeah," I said. "'Patterns of Force.' Season two, episode nineteen, I think. Late in the season, anyhow. What did I just say about outdorking me?"

"You have let yourself be outdorked," Charles assured me.

"Also, it was episode twenty-one," Alice said.

Ardov led us to the same building in the government compound where we'd been housed last time, only now there were a couple of Movement for Peace goons checking data bracelets for ID signatures at the door.

"Got some primitives, I see," said one of them. It looked like a big floor lamp with limbs. It moved its hooded head over toward us as if giving us a good sniff. "Try not to contaminate your betters."

"As if they could help it," Ardov said.

"Did you guys memorize the evil-oppressor handbook or something?" I asked. "Because you have the moronic banter down cold."

The floor lamp pivoted toward me slowly. "Amuse yourself with your savage conception of humor," it said. "For all the good it will do you."

"Maybe I will," I shot back.

Alice looked quizzically at me.

"Okay," I admitted. "I couldn't think of anything punchy. But next time for sure."

Ardov walked us to our rooms, explaining the facilities to the colonel and Alice like we were all guests at a fancy resort. He said we would have freedom to move around the compound, but not to leave it for any reason. We were not to speak with data collectors, and our ability to communicate with anyone outside the compound had been neutralized.

"I know you lost all your possessions when you destroyed a Confederation vessel full of loyal citizens," he said, "so you have all been provided with clothes sufficient for your stay."

He led us down a hall and gestured toward a room, which Charles and Colonel Rage were to share. Neither was very happy with that arrangement.

"Does Zeke not have to share a room?" Charles asked.

"I'd worry about bigger things than who you're bunking with," Ardov told him. "All of you have really stepped in it, and there are going to be some serious consequences."

Colonel Rage leveled his gaze at him. "Your boss told us the same thing, but it seems to me that if we hadn't overturned the apple cart, we'd be dead right now, so you'll have to forgive me if I'm not feeling too apologetic about messing up anyone's plans."

Ardov was tall, but not as tall as Colonel Rage. Still, he didn't look even slightly intimidated when facing off with the soldier. "I guess we'll have to hope it all works out for you, then."

"I think these kids have shown they can look after themselves," the colonel said.

"If you want a demonstration of our power," Ardov said, "I'm sure something can be arranged—something even primitives like you could understand."

"How about we all just go to our rooms and get some sleep?" I said.

Ardov smirked. "I can always count on Zeke to find a diplomatic way to avoid getting smacked around."

I met his gaze. "I have a very clear memory of being there while *you* were getting smacked around, Ardov."

I shouldn't have said it, but it slipped out. Now he was standing over me, looking down, grinning. "There will be plenty of time to settle old scores," he assured me.

"So, are you two going to just going to make macho threats all day?" Alice asked. She was leaning against the wall, arms folded, looking bored.

Ardov smiled at her. "Like I said before, the past is the past. Thanks for reminding me."

Alice just glared at him. She wasn't about to be sweet-talked by this jerk. Another check in her plus column.

He looked directly at her, pouting like he was doing a photo shoot for a boy band. "You and I don't have any bad history to overcome. Maybe we can be friends."

Alice shrugged. "We'll see how you treat the friends I've already got."

Ardov began walking again, and we followed him past a few more doors, and he gestured to a room. "You'll be staying here with Mi Sun," he said, looking directly at Alice. "If you need anything, message me. I'm here to be of assistance."

Alice rolled her eyes. "I get it. Divide and conquer. Get me on your side to make the others uncomfortable. Anything else?"

She turned away, and the two girls went into their room. Now it was just me and Ardov in the hall. Ardov moved down one more door. "This is yours," he said.

"Okay," I said, trying to keep my voice neutral. I did not much care for being alone with the guy—by which I mean I was struggling against the urge to drop to the floor and curl up into a ball. He and I had been enemies before, but back then there had been rules to keep him in line. Now he was hired muscle, working for a guy who had likely just arranged my murder.

"I hear Tamret is on her way to the station," he said.

If there was something to shift me from scared to angry, however, this was it. "That's right."

"It will be nice to get everyone back together," he said. "Catch up on old times."

I let out a breath. "Ardov, maybe you're thinking that kissing Junup's butt and hanging out with the armband crowd makes you untouchable, but you've been convinced of your superiority before. I seem to recall that that didn't work out so well for you. How about we all just do our best to avoid trouble?"

"I'm not here to make trouble," he said. "I'm here to enforce order and uphold the right of superior species to live without primitives corrupting their way of life. The way I see it, you *are* the trouble that's already been made."

*I suggest you don't antagonize it,* Smelly said. *Picking fights will not help us, particularly with this being.*

I knew Smelly was giving me good advice, but I wasn't in the mood to let Ardov say whatever he wanted. "And what are you exactly? An errand boy for a coward and a thief."

"You are Junup's enemy," Ardov said. "That makes you my enemy. I haven't decided yet about your girlfriend. She got one over on me before, but that was when she was cheating and I had to follow the rules. This time? Things are different."

*Zeke, I'm getting some interesting readings from this meat bag, and by interesting I mean unexpectedly terrifying. I urge you to exercise caution.*

Smelly was making about as much sense as it ever had, but I was not about to let Ardov get away with threatening Tamret.

"If you even think about laying a finger on her," I began, but that was as far as I got. I should clarify that it was as far as I got in the conversation, because in physical terms I got much farther—down the hall, to be precise. Ardov pushed out with one hand, and I was airborne, shooting down the corridor like a potato out of a spud-shooter. I landed a good thirty feet away from Ardov, who still had his hand out, and I slid a few body lengths along the carpeting before finally coming to a halt.

*The strange readings I'm getting,* Smelly said, *may be related to his augmented skill tree. He has decoupled it from the leveling system, so other beings can't detect it, but he has achieved maximum levels in all fields.*

As I sat there, feeling the pain spreading from my butt into my legs, as well as an entirely separate ache in my ribs, I realized that I understood why Junup had picked Ardov. Only non-Confederation citizens could have their skill trees hacked. Junup had wanted Ardov so he could hack him, so he could have his own personal supersoldier.

"Now do you get the picture?" Ardov asked. He walked over to me and held out a hand to help me up. I ignored it and scrambled to my feet on my own.

"So, yeah," he said. "Anything you need, just message me. You disgust me with your savage ways, and you are an insult to the Confederation even being on this station, but hey, I'm here to help, so let me know how I can make your stay here as comfortable as possible."

He turned and strode gracefully down the hallway while I limped to my room.

As with most private spaces in the Confederation, the door was biometrically sealed, which meant that only a being authorized to enter could enter. I needed no key. I pushed the door open, not quite sure what to expect. After a terrible series of days, I was ready for yet another unpleasant surprise, but this time the surprise was pretty good.

"I get the bed near the door, mate. Better that way if I need to get out quick."

Steve stood there, tall, muscular, and lizardy, wearing one of his Ish-hi tunics and looking as much like a deadly predator as he had the first moment I'd seen him. Back then, I thought he was there to kill, possibly eat, me. He'd not been planning to do either, and he'd turned out to be someone who always had my back.

He moved in, lighting fast, for a big squeeze, nearly shoving my organs out through my mouth before he finally let me go. I fell to the floor.

"Sorry, mate," he said, holding out a hand. "Not used to being around anyone so fragile. Didn't mean to crack your delicate bones."

"Not a problem," I said, grabbing hold and letting him hoist me up. I tried not to think about how that was the second time I'd been knocked down in less than two minutes. "I'm just a little off my game from having nearly been launched into orbit by a shove from Ardov. He's here, you know."

"Yeah, saw that git."

"He's been hacked."

"Know that, too," Steve said. "Smacked me around a bit to show he could do it. Kept calling me primitive, like his planet is somehow more advanced than Ish-hi. I'm waiting for my chance to get back at him."

"I'm with you on that. So, yeah. Welcome back to the Confederation."

Steve sat down on the bed, hit some keys on his plasma keyboard, and called up a video image of the assassination attempt. "Not off to a good start. You come off like a chump, and Mr. Shaggy Bloke looks like the hero."

"No kidding. Getting killed would have been only slightly worse than letting Junup save me."

*That scaly lump of flesh clearly doesn't understand that the assassination attempt was a sham.*

I couldn't say anything without tipping Steve off, and I wasn't sure how I wanted to broach the subject, even with my friends, so I merely nodded, hoping Smelly would take that as a sign to continue.

"Why are you nodding at me like you've got a secret?" Steve asked. "You look daft."

"I think it was a setup," I told Steve. "I think Junup staged the whole thing to make him look like a hero and make me look like I cause trouble when I'm not even trying."

"That was pretty obvious, yeah?" Steve said. "First thing I thought of. So what do we do about it?"

I gestured to the room around us, hoping to indicate that I felt sure we were being listened to. Steve nodded, and I knew he got it.

"I'm sorry about Nayana and Urch, mate."

"Yeah," I said.

"She got on my nerves, but she was one of us, and she came through when it mattered."

"She did," I agreed.

"I don't know what we're doing here," he said, his voice

very quiet, "or what all of this is about, but the geezers responsible for what happened to her? They're going to pay."

I nodded again. This was something that Steve wanted the eavesdroppers to hear. It was foolish bravado, and it would only make our enemies more cautious, but I didn't care. It was good to have my friend back.

I showered and changed into some of the new clothes Junup's people had thoughtfully provided. To my surprise, they hadn't been designed to humiliate me. I put on olive-green pants that had the thickness of denim and a black long-sleeved shirt. All in all, I almost looked like I came from Earth.

I messaged the others to meet outside. Before we left the room, I excused myself to use the bathroom in order to get a minute alone with Smelly.

"Can Junup's people listen to our conversations through our bracelets?" I asked him.

*Accessing another's bracelet data is illegal within the Confederation, and there are safeguards in place to prevent abuse of power. I suspect Junup would only risk listening through your bracelets in an emergency. Nevertheless, I will be able to monitor systems and alert you if he attempts to listen in.*

We met up with the others on the lawn, sitting as far as possible from any buildings or benches other structures that might have listening devices. Everyone else had washed and changed as well, and they were all dressed more or less like I was—except the colonel, who wore a tan suit with a military cut.

I introduced Steve to Colonel Rage and Alice, and then, keeping my voice low, I told Steve what Ghli Wixxix had wanted us to do. Then we recounted the mutiny on the *Kind Disposition* and its aftermath. He listened but said very little as he took it all in. When I finished, he just shook his reptilian head.

"I'm sorry," he said. "That's hard."

"I wish I hadn't brought you back into all this," I told him.

"You didn't know it was all going to fall apart. And now that it has, better I should be there to keep you from mucking everything up."

"I heard a great deal about you when I debriefed Zeke after his return," Colonel Rage told Steve. "I like your swagger, son, and everything about you tells me you're a natural leader. I'm glad to have you on board." Now he turned to the rest of us. "What we need is a plan. We're among enemies and we have no way back. I think our approach needs to be twofold."

"We're not among enemies," I interrupted. "Junup is an enemy, and he is powerful, and his Movement for Peace lackeys are a problem, but it's a mistake to think of the entire Confederation as the bad guys."

"I understand how you feel," the colonel said, "but the good side of the Confederation hasn't made an appearance yet, and the bad side seems awful busy. I don't want to sugarcoat this, because you need to hear the hard truths. These people tried to kill us, and if they don't try again, it will only be because they're going to lock us away for the crimes they themselves committed. We need an escape plan. We need to steal some transportation and go home. Given that last year you stole a ship and broke into a prison, I think this should be a piece of cake."

"We are not at full strength," Charles said, shaking his head.

"This alien Tamret," Colonel Rage said to me. "Your account made her seem pretty important to your success last time. You think we can count on her to help us out?"

"Are you kidding?" I said. "She lives for this sort of thing."

"Then we bide our time. Haste is our enemy. We need to find a ship, and we need to make sure we know how to get home. Finally, we need to collect as much technology as we can."

"For what?" I asked.

"This is the new reality, son," the colonel said. "One group of aliens almost conquered our planet. They got pushed back, but now there's only one power in the galaxy, and they're turning out to be a bunch of thugs who don't much care for backward worlds like ours. When we return to Earth, I want it to be with the means of developing ways to keep our planet safe. We got hold of one of those flying saucers back in the forties, but the engineers didn't know what they were doing. Now we're all walking around with instruction manuals on our wrists. We get the tech, we figure out how it works, and we bring it back home."

I didn't say anything to this, but I didn't love the idea of bringing dark-matter-missile technology back to Earth. I also believed that the colonel was wrong about the Confederation. Someone like Junup could rise to power temporarily, but he did it with lies and tricks. The truth would eventually come out, and the real Confederation—embodied by beings like Dr. Roop and Captain Qwlessl and Ghli Wixxix—would show itself. I knew that if I tried to make that case, the colonel would see me as just a naïve kid, so for once I kept my mouth shut. The best argument, I decided, was the Confederation itself. The longer we stayed, the more the colonel would see what this place really was.

"We'll take it slowly," I said, "and see what develops that we can use."

"Right you are," the colonel said. "We gather intel, skills, and tech. I plan to log as many hours in the flight sim room as they'll let me. But we have to play it smart if we're going to give ourselves enough time. That means no more outbursts, Zeke. Don't make them angry or let them get you angry. Act like you're not a threat, and they'll let their guard down."

"Okay," I said, though I knew I wasn't terribly good at keeping a low profile.

"How did you manage to talk at the news conference, anyhow?" Charles asked. "I mean, you broke though that dampening field. Does that mean you can manipulate their systems?"

*Tell them you did it with the power of imagination!* Smelly suggested.

"I don't know," I said. "It must have been a glitch in the program. It just wasn't there anymore."

The colonel looked at me for a moment, like he was trying to figure out if I was lying or not. "Maybe it was sabotage," he said after a little while. "Could be there are people on our side after all. That would be good news."

"It would show you that we don't have to fear the Confederation," I said.

"Negative," the colonel said. "I was just thinking that if there were criminals, and they were armed, we could commandeer their weapons."

We decided we had no choice but to settle in Confederation detainees. The people who worked or stayed in the compound had been instructed not to speak to us, but we received plenty of nasty stares. I thought that eating at a compound cafeteria was going to be particularly unpleasant, but we weren't allowed to go anywhere else, so once everyone started getting hungry, we decided there was no choice but to put up with it. I helped the colonel and Alice through the food offerings, and then we wandered over to an empty table large enough for all of us.

We'd only just sat down when a deer-headed alien walked over and stood behind Charles. He said nothing for a long time, just kind of leaned forward and leaned back. Somewhere in the back of my mind a voice was telling me to ignore him and he'd go away. In the front of my mind was another voice telling me that I knew it wasn't true. Right in the center was Smelly, saying, *That guy is starting to bug me.*

"Help you, mate?" Steve finally asked.

"Yeah," he said, turning toward us. I now saw the black Movement for Peace armband. "Maybe you should take your trays and eat outside, so you don't stink up the place."

"Son, we're not bothering anyone," Colonel Rage said. "I get that you joined this organization because it made you feel good about yourself. That's what small-minded people like to do. If they can't take pride in their achievements or their abilities, they become racists so they can take pride in not being the other guy. Well, congratulations. You're not us. I'm sure your friends over there"—he gestured toward a table of a half dozen aliens of various species, all of them wearing armbands, and all of them looking at us—"dared you to come over and intimidate us, and you did your best. You had the courage to lurk menacingly. Now why don't you head on back and feel great about yourself for what you had the guts to do here today."

"That is exactly what I would have expected from you primitives," the deer guy said. "My polite conversation is met with mockery and scorn."

"You complained about our odor," Charles said. "I do not see how this is being polite."

"I'm done being gentle," the deer alien said. "It's time for you to go."

Steve stood up and was about to say something that probably would have been cool and menacing, but Alice cut him off.

"I know I would like to learn how to be less primitive," she said, offering the deer guy her sweetest smile. She brushed some of her hair out of her eyes. "Is it an advanced trait to be polite to strangers?"

"That you would even ask shows how savage you truly are," the deer alien told her.

"I'm really trying to understand," she said, as though she were struggling to puzzle it out. "So, if others who are less advanced than even I am were to visit my home, what would be the right way to treat them?"

He stood there, kind of like a deer alien in the headlights. He either had to contradict what he'd just said or admit that his behavior had been rude. Finally, rather than say anything else, he slinked back to his table.

Steve sat back down, and Alice turned away from the colonel, a radiant smile on her face.

"Not bad," Mi Sun said, sighing with relief. "Way to defuse."

Alice shrugged and went back to her food. "I figured if I didn't do something, one of these hotheads was going to pick a fight, and then we'd all get in trouble. I was just trying to make Bambi uncomfortable."

"That's the kind of thinking we need," the colonel said. "We need to come at problems from new angles. Our goal isn't to get our pictures in the yearbook, kids. We're trying to stay alive, stay out of prison, and get back home, so anything that works is fair game in my book."

And with that he returned to his lunch. I found that I was no longer very hungry.

I kept an eye on the news outputs, which were pretty varied. There were plenty of voices—including regular postings by Hluh—that defended me and suggested Junup's government was covering up its own involvement in the destruction of the *Kind Disposition*. Unfortunately, most beings in the Confederation had a hard time understanding the concept of criminal deception, and it was easier for them to believe that a primitive off-worlder was to blame than it was to suspect their own political leadership. It didn't help matters that Junup's Movement for Peace seemed to be growing in popularity. People involved with it were arguing that I needed to be tried for the destruction of the *Kind Disposition*. Seeing those words made me want to curl up into a ball. I didn't think I could take another rigged trial.

The evening of our second day I finally got some good news. Tamret had arrived on the station and was being processed. They expected her at the compound within a couple of hours.

I was too excited to eat anything. I sat nervously with the others while they finished, and then I told them that I would wait for her outside.

"We'll keep you company, mate," Steve said.

The colonel announced that he'd booked time in the flight sim, so he excused himself, but everyone else began to take seats on benches that offered a good view of the transport-shuttle landing pad. I found myself standing next to Alice and feeling kind of uneasy.

"Listen," I said, "maybe it's best if you aren't around for this."

"Oh, come *on*," Alice said. "I'm not going to be locked up like I'm some dirty secret. I haven't done anything wrong."

"You stowed away on a spaceship," I said, "which is kind of wrong."

"Whatever," Alice countered. "I'm here now. Besides, from what I've heard about Tamret, she'll probably respect me for that. Do you really think my just standing around is going to make your girlfriend flip out?"

"You have to understand that Tamret can be kind of—"

"Intense," Alice interrupted. "Yeah, I think you might have mentioned that. The thing is, I don't know Tamret, and I don't know much about Rarels, but I know about girls, and I'm going to tell you right now that if you try to keep me out of her way, then she really is going to start to wonder why. Oh, and here's another tip: You and Tamret are going to get along a lot better if you stop acting like she's a bomb about to go off. Maybe show her a little respect, and you won't have to be so afraid of her intensity."

It was true that Alice didn't know the first thing about Tamret, but I was still a little stung by her rebuke. Was I being too cautious about Tamret's feelings? If so, maybe it had nothing to do with Tamret's jealousy. Maybe it had to do with my own feelings of guilt for leaving her alone for so long and then showing up with another girl by my side. It wasn't that I liked Alice or anything, I assured myself, but she was smart and pretty and brave and resourceful. Most guys would kind of like her, wouldn't they?

I sighed. "You're probably right. Besides, whether you are

supposed to be here or not, you're now part of our team of unwanted outsiders."

Alice cocked her head. "You mean that?"

"Why wouldn't I mean it? It's not like being a despised interloper is such a great thing."

"But you guys are pretty amazing despised interlopers. You have all this experience together. I'm just a fifth wheel, and sometimes I feel like you guys don't trust me."

"Believe me, we trust you plenty," I said. "And we're racking up enough new experiences. More than I'd like, to be honest. You're one of us."

She grinned. "Thanks. Now you can get on with the business of your reunion."

I hoped it would be that easy. I had no idea what Tamret had been through since the last time I'd seen her. I told myself that whatever had happened, whatever was going on, we would make it right. Whatever physical harm had been done could be fixed by Confederation medicine. Any emotional harm could be mended with time and attention.

"We all suffered a great injustice," Charles said to me as I watched the shuttle grow closer. "None of us more than Tamret, but we all paid the price for doing what was right."

"She may not see it that way. Maybe she feels like she's been punished because I wanted to rescue my dad."

"Zeke, I do not wish to overstate our importance, but we saved the galaxy. In the short time we were in the Confederation, we saw the Phands kill and hurt and capture innocent beings. We saw them do incredible damage, and we gave the Confederation the power to put a stop to that. You can only take responsibility for what you do, not how others choose to react to it."

I knew he was right. I just hoped Tamret did too.

I watched as the shuttle docked, and then had a long wait as the walkway equalized its air pressure and the doors were made safe to open. I could hear my heartbeat in my ears. A million possibilities passed through my head: Tamret leaping toward me, embracing me in an uncompromising hug. Tamret, limping, walking with a cane, wearing an eye patch like Colonel Rage. Tamret, angry and cold, accusing me of abandoning her. Tamret, broken and withdrawn but trying to pretend that she was the same girl I remembered.

I told myself that these things never really play out the way I think they will. I could work something over and over in my head, trying to imagine how it will be, and then it always goes in some direction I didn't anticipate. It was time to stop inventing scenarios. The time had come to see the reality.

Finally the door hissed open, and I felt myself walking forward, unable to control myself. I didn't care what she looked like, how badly injured she might be. I would be the one leaping forward with the uncompromising hug.

Then there were two silhouetted shapes emerging from the transport. Two Rarels. They stepped out of the shadows, and I saw that the first was Tamret, her fur almost blinding white. She wore a white skirt that went down almost to her ankles and a long-sleeved shirt the same lavender color as her eyes. Her dark hair was cut a little shorter than I remembered and pulled back, her eyes were wide and sparkling, and her lips curled into a grin of happiness.

There she was, looking happy and healthy. She didn't look like she'd endured torture or mistreatment of any sort. She was positively beaming. Her pretty face was full of life and, if I wasn't telling myself stories, mischief.

She was also standing kind of close to the Rarel boy who had come out with her.

He was maybe six inches taller than she was, with tan fur and brown hair. He was broad-shouldered and muscular and handsome in the way of Rarel boys I wanted to see fall into a latrine pit.

I felt myself standing rigid and still. I couldn't move. I could hardly breathe. No one was moving.

"Hey, everyone," Tamret said.

Charles broke the spell. He stepped forward. "Tamret, it is so good to see you again."

"Thanks," she said with a huge grin. "I want you all to meet Villainic. He's my fiancé."

# CHAPTER SIXTEEN

After Tamret announced that she had brought along the guy she intended to marry, events unfolded in a bit of a haze. I think I gave Tamret a quick hug. I shook Villainic's hand, which puzzled him, but he smiled and told me he had heard a lot about me and wanted to get to know me better. I tried hard to find the menace and threat in his words, but I came up short. He sounded like he actually did want to get to know me.

Tamret seemed, frankly, happier than I'd ever seen her before, and it made me uneasy. I excused myself, saying I had to use the bathroom, but really I wanted to talk to Smelly alone.

"Can you check her vital signs?" I asked. "Is she being coerced or on drugs or anything like that?"

*I've already done so,* Smelly said. *I've accessed information on Rarel physiology from the Confederation database, and I've compared it with that female's behavior and biometrics. I can detect nothing wrong but a light agitation, which, in my view, can be ascribed to the awkwardness of her showing up and completely crushing your dreams of happiness into little chunks of rancid, festering bitterness.*

I went back outside and sat with the group, though as far away from Tamret as I could. She was busy showing Alice and Mi Sun her engagement necklace. I tried to look like I was interested, when Villainic came and sat next to me.

"Zeke! I am so glad to have the chance to meet you," he said with the enthusiasm of a preschool teacher on the first day of class. "Tamret has told me how kind you were to her during her last visit to this place."

"Yeah?" I was looking at him closely now. It's hard to guess someone's age when their face is entirely covered with fur, but I got the impression he was a few years older than Tamret. His voice made him sound older too.

"She said you were a good friend. She told me about everything you guys did together, and how it got everyone expelled from this remarkable space city."

"Hold on," I said, in no mood to have yet another being willfully misinterpret everything that had happened.

Villainic shook his head. "I am not blaming you. You and your friends ended up with dangerous enemies, and they took advantage of a bad situation. But I know she got through everything as well as she did because of you. I just wanted to thank you for looking after her. Besides, if things had not gone as they had, she and I would not be bound together today, so it all ended well."

He smiled his nice-guy smile, and I had the terrifying feeling that this Villainic was being totally sincere. He was thanking me for being Tamret's friend, like she was his responsibility and I had helped him out.

"How exactly are you two, uh, bound together?" I demanded. "Aren't you a little young to be thinking about marriage?"

He laughed. "I am three years older than Tamret, and mine is the age that matters according to our law—it is the same with your species, I hope. In any case, it will be at least four years before we are actually married. The engagement this early is practical, though, since it legalizes the association of families, and it allows Tamret to join my caste."

Okay, this was making sense to me now. Tamret had been casteless before, and though I'd never understood precisely what that meant in her society, I knew it had left her vulnerable. This engagement to Villainic had clearly been a way for her to protect herself, make influential friends, and probably get herself out of the clutches of her enemies.

While I mulled over all of this, Villainic excused himself and got up to go sit next to Tamret. They both seemed so happy, and I knew that whatever practical benefit Tamret got out of her relationship with Villainic, that wasn't the end of it. She liked him.

I supposed I had no reason to complain. I had been stupid to think otherwise. While I'd been negotiating the horrors of the lunchroom, Tamret had been facing prison and political enemies and real physical dangers. She'd met Villainic, and he'd saved her, and I was just a memory.

She caught me looking at her. Her face broke into a grin, and she gave me a shy wave. I waved back, because it was ultimately more socially acceptable than bashing my head against a stone bench. The wave, it seemed to me, was her way of letting me know that we were still friends. I guess she had to let me know somehow, because since she'd been back, she hadn't spoken a single word meant just for me.

"His name is Villainic," I said to Steve and Charles. We were out in the hall, and everyone had gone to bed, so I was keeping my voice down. "*Villain*ic. People are only named something like 'Villainic' if they happen to be villainous. Otherwise he'd be *Hero*ic."

"I think I'm having a translation issue, mate," Steve said.

"Your name is your destiny," I said. "Think about it. Sinestro. Atrocitus."

"And that is without even leaving the pages of *Green Lantern*," Charles said helpfully. "It goes deeper. Annihilus. General Grievous. Doctor Doom. Ra's al Ghul."

I snapped my fingers. "Exactly. You don't call them Decepticons because you can trust them."

"Darkseid," Charles continued. "Vandal Savage. Kraven the Hunter. There is a tradition here."

"Is it possible," Steve inquired, "that you are looking for reasons not to trust this bloke?"

"I don't know what you mean," I said.

"He stole your girl, so of course you want to think he's a tosser, but maybe you should just give him a chance, yeah?"

That was the last thing I wanted to do.

Now that Tamret was here, I thought that maybe Junup would contact us and let us know what he had in mind, but there was still no word from him. In the meantime, we needed to bring Tamret up to speed with everything that had happened, but I didn't feel comfortable talking about it in front of Villainic.

"We need to get Tamret alone," I told Mi Sun the next day when we were walking back to our building after lunch.

"How do you know you can't trust her husband-to-be?" she asked, trying not to smile.

"I don't know that I can, which is more important. He's an outsider."

"So was Alice," Mi Sun replied, "until she wasn't."

The fairness of this point upset me. I told myself it was different. Alice, after all, might not have been invited to join our expedition, but she'd proven her loyalty back on Earth. I had no reason to worry about her having any kind of hidden agenda. It wasn't like she'd just been dropped in on us out of nowhere.

I sped up to match pace with Tamret and Villainic, who were holding hands as they strolled back toward our building. "Um, Tamret. Can I speak to you alone for a second?"

"I am completely confident that you mean no offense," Villainic said cheerfully as he stepped in front of Tamret. "You are an alien, and you must have different ways on your world. For us, it's not permitted for an engaged female to speak alone to another male, even an alien male. Even asking is rude, but since you didn't know that, I won't take it as an insult this one time."

"You are super nice for being so understanding," I said to Villainic. "How about if Tamret talks alone with me and Mi Sun, who will be our chaperone? She can slap my shins with an umbrella or something if I step out of line."

"I know you and my betrothed have shared adventures, and I don't want to interfere with your friendship," Villainic said, "but we have our own ways in our culture, and I'm afraid things just can't be the same as they were before she joined my caste."

"If you don't want to interfere with my friendship," I said, feeling myself starting to anger, "then maybe you should stop interfering with my friendship."

Villainic froze in place, which meant Tamret had to stop as well. Everyone else kind of stumbled for a minute, trying to figure out what to do. Maybe they were lurking in case my polite inquiries ended up with this gigantic Rarel pounding my head into the ground. They ultimately decided to have their own private conversation about fifteen feet away. This involved, as near as I could tell, exchanging awkward pleasantries about the weather while pretending not to look at us.

So, there I was, standing alone with Villainic and Tamret. They held hands, and Tamret kept her eyes down, like I wasn't even there. It made me want to scream with frustration.

Villainic's hazel eyes were wide and sympathetic, like he was a great big kitty cat. I wanted to punch him in the face.

"You're not getting upset, are you?" he asked, like this possibility had just occurred to him.

"I need a minute with Tamret," I told him. "There are things we have to discuss."

"Here is my proposal," Villainic said, looking like he'd just had an amazing idea. "You can talk to *me* alone. Legally, that's the same as talking to Tamret." He then put a hand on my back and led me away. Tamret drifted off to talk to Mi Sun and Alice.

"I know you and Tamret were used to speaking together previously," he said, sounding sympathetic but also kind of condescending. He was talking to me like I was some little kid and he was the grown-up who knew the way of the world. Well, maybe he was older, and he knew the way of *his* world, but he wasn't there anymore.

"You have to understand," he was saying, "that things are different now. I don't want you to see me as a stickler for caste tradition. I'm very open-minded to new ways. I have allowed my sisters to appear many times in public with groups of friends, some of whom are even of a lower caste! How about that for embracing the modern? But in this case my family's honor is at stake, so it's better to stick a little more closely to the rules. The only way we would agree to visit this space environment was if the Confederation assured us that our traditions would be respected here, but you don't seem serious about doing so."

"First of all, " I said, "I don't know anything about your traditions or my supposed responsibility to uphold them. Second of all, now that I do know, I feel okay about ignoring them."

"I see," Villainic said, looking sad. "We may have a point of disagreement."

"I'll make a note in my log, but right now I need to talk to Tamret alone, and you need to stop getting in my way."

"Your needs are not my concern," Villainic said. "I'm sorry to be so blunt about it, but there it is. I'm not talking about who is right or wrong here, but the fact is, Zeke, you are a much maligned person within this alien culture. They say you've done terrible things, and you may face a trial or even imprisonment. I can't ask you to let my lady become involved in that."

"Your *lady*?" I repeated.

"Of course I know you care for her too, so please believe me when I say my only concern is that she not be put in danger. Your situation, Zeke, is not really something I want Tamret exposed to."

"I am doing my best to resolve all of this," I said. "I'm hoping the danger will go away."

"For your sake I hope so too," he said. "But I cannot permit anything that would put Tamret at risk of sharing your fate. I am told that you asked to have Tamret brought here because you believed her to be unsafe on her own world. That, as you can see, is no longer the case. She is with me. I was happy to escort her here so she could see her old friends and, to be honest, so I might witness these wonders for myself. When I agreed to this voyage, however, you were under the protection of a powerful patron, and that, as I understand it, has changed. I am sorry you and your friends are facing difficulties, but sharing those difficulties with me and my future wife will not help anyone. As we are under no obligation to stay, we plan on returning to Rarel as soon as we can arrange transport."

I broke off from the group, mainly to stomp around the campus and work off some of my anger. An hour or so of that hadn't accomplished much, and I decided to head back to my building so I could be irritated in the comfort of my own room. That's when I nearly bumped into a bush. I figured I must have been so distracted by my talk with Villainic that I had veered off the path. Then the bush raised one of its branches at me.

"I'm, like, really sorry," it said. "I was totally lost in my synaptic processes."

I suddenly realized that I knew this bush creature. It was the waiter from the restaurant I'd eaten at my first night on the station, back when I first met Steve and Tamret. It seemed like so long ago.

"You're that guy," I said. "The waiter, right?"

"I am completely that guy," it said. "And listen, the place is the roof of the Peripheral Tower." It gestured with one of his branches toward a building at the far end of the compound. Most of the buildings were low and squat, no more than six stories. This building was probably three times as tall as anything surrounding it, and it also had an entrance on the public side of the periphery, so beings could enter the building without having to enter the compound. I'd thought about it, wondering if I could use it to sneak away, should I decide to do that, but I knew it would never work. There was tight security on both sides.

"What place?" I asked the bush. "The roof? What are you talking about?"

"I'm saying that the roof is pretty much the place. Just remember that, and everything is going to be windy. It's the place." It leaned in close. "Some of us are on your side. A lot of us." Then the bush hurried off, moving more quickly than you might expect of a plant.

Something was obviously going on, but I had no idea what. What did it mean by "the place"? Was I supposed to go there? Part of me wanted to check it out, but I was afraid to do anything that might get me in trouble until I had more information. It seemed to me like a bad idea to head off somewhere just because some guy I'd met once, last year, had dropped a vague hint.

I took a few more steps, and then my data bracelet chimed to signal me I had an incoming message. I looked down at the text. *Meet me at the place. Now. Live long and prosper.*

I knew what I was supposed to do with the information. There was only one nonhuman on the station I had ever heard make a *Star Trek* reference. I immediately made my way toward the Peripheral Tower.

When I went through security at the compound-side entrance, the uncomfortably squidlike peace officer looked at me askance and pulsed his face tentacles in my direction. "Don't think about trying to get out on the street side," he said. "You'll be enveloped in a plasma field if you try. It's extremely humiliating." He then coughed out a squid laugh, which was followed by a puff of ink, which dissipated like a blast of cigar smoke.

"Good to know," I said, trying to sound casual, though my

heart was hammering. Coming here could be a terrible idea. Maybe this was not what I'd thought. Maybe it was a trap. There were always risks, but I had to know.

I rode the elevator up to the top floor and followed the signs to the door that led out to the roof. There wasn't much out there, just some benches along the guardrails, offering a nice view of the compound on one side and a busy commercial district on the other. Standing by the rail, with his back to the commercial side, was a very tall, very giraffelike being. It was Dr. Roop.

He wore a jacket with a hood covering most of his face, but he was hard to miss, being almost eight feet tall thanks to the length of his neck. His eyes looked red and tired, and there was a sadness on his face I hadn't seen before. Even so, it was good to see him.

He approached me and gave me a big hug. "Zeke, I'm glad to see you're well," he said in his curiously Dutch accent. It was one of those inexplicable bits of flavor the translation protocol sometimes provided. "In spite of their best efforts. Your father is safe?"

I nodded. "He's back on Earth, looking like his old self."

"That, at least, is something," Dr. Roop said, leading us to sit on one of the benches. "You've suffered some losses. You have my condolences."

"Thanks," I said.

"And once more," he continued, "they wish to blame you for, against all odds, defeating your enemies."

"That is pretty much it," I said. "What about you? I heard you were a fugitive. What are you doing here? How did you get past security?"

"I have friends," he said. "There are those of us who have

organized to oppose the Movement for Peace, and we are doing our best to look out for you. Tell me, did you speak with Director Ghli Wixxix before our enemies took the ship?"

"Just once," I told him. "We were going to talk more and get more details about what she had in mind, but that never happened."

"It is vital that you carry out that mission," Dr. Roop said, looking very serious, "even if the government is now against you. If you don't find that software and disseminate it to the public, then Junup's agents will do nothing while the Phands develop a technological superiority that will lead to the destruction of the Confederation. Help me, Zeke," he said, lowering his neck in what I knew was his version of a smile. "You're my only hope."

"Then you're out of luck. We're trapped on the compound, and that mission was always insanity, even when we had the support of the beings in power. The things we did last time, we were prepared for them. You'd been training us, even if we didn't know it. And Tamret and I had maxed-out skill trees. Now we don't have any augmentations at all. We'd be going into the unknown, the *dangerous* unknown, with nothing to protect us."

"I know it is a lot to ask, but you are the only one who can do it."

"Except that I *can't*," I said, feeling frustrated. This was Dr. Roop, and I would do pretty much anything reasonable he asked of me, but this was *not* reasonable. "I can't even get out into the city for a milkshake, let alone risk my life on some crazy quest."

"There may be a way to get away from here," he told me, ignoring the part about not wanting to risk my life. "I'll contact you when I know more. This will be where we meet unless I tell you otherwise."

"Finding a way to leave the compound is just the beginning," I told Dr. Roop. "We don't have a hope of doing anything without Tamret, and I can't even have a conversation with her. And if I can talk to her and get her to agree to go along with this plan—which I'm against, by the way—*then* how do I live with myself for talking her into something I think is crazy?"

"These problems can be resolved," Dr. Roop said. "They have to be. We cannot stand by while Junup's corruption or indifference leads the galaxy into darkness."

"What about the copy of the software my father brought back?"

"I don't know what happened to that," said Dr. Roop. "He may have destroyed it rather than allow it to fall into the wrong hands. He may still have it on him, waiting for the right time to deliver it to beings he trusts. But he is far away, and we can't reach him. Right now we need you."

"I didn't ask for any of this," I said, feeling the crushing weight of despair that had become all too familiar to me. "I just wanted to help my world and help Tamret."

"I know, Zeke; it's a lot to fall on your shoulders. But you accomplished so much in the past, when you were merely a delegate. Now you are something far more powerful."

"What?" I asked.

He lowered his neck again. "A rebel."

I snorted. "That's us. Just a scrappy band of ragtag rebels taking on the evil empire against impossible odds."

"It would make a good entertainment."

It isn't so entertaining when you're living it.

I took in a breath. This was the deal. Dr. Roop was my friend, and he had gone to bat for me in the past. He'd helped me every step of the way before. He'd broken the law to recruit allies for me—the beings who were now my best friends. He'd made it possible for me to save my father and, less directly, my planet. Now, because he had done all those things, he was a fugitive. I knew he wouldn't ask this of me if he didn't have to, and he wouldn't send me on a mission if he thought it was too dangerous. I knew I had no choice. There was only one thing to do, and that was to help him.

"Right before I left, my father told me what I already knew, which was that I could trust you more than anyone in the Confederation. So, if you really believe I need to do it, I'll try."

He lowered his neck again. "Thank you, Zeke."

"What now?"

"I'll be in touch again when I've formulated a plan. In the meantime, prepare the others, and try to keep a low profile. Also, do your best to avoid antagonizing Junup further."

"That's popular advice these days."

"The less he is worried about you, the safer you will be."

"I get it," I told him.

"I knew you would. Be careful in all things," he said, turning away to indicate that our meeting was over.

I stood up and took a few steps away, and then I turned back. "So, uh, you didn't, by any chance, implant an alien artificial intelligence in my head, did you?"

He turned back. Under the hood his eyes widened. "That was a question I had not anticipated."

I told him about Smelly, and he listened with what I was sure was a great deal of interest. I was looking for signs of alarm, but I didn't see any.

"This is remarkable," he told me. For a moment he forgot

about hidden fortresses and forbidden zones and secret Former skill trees. This was simply something cool he could geek out over. "Rumors of these magnificent beings have circulated for centuries, but none has ever been discovered. They are said to be manifestations of sublime intellect and insight."

*At last—an enlightened being!* Smelly chimed in.

I held up my hand. "Hold it right there. This thing is full of itself enough as it is."

"I am sure with good reason," Dr. Roop said. "But no, I had no part in this. You must have encountered a Former artifact while on the prison planet and been exposed to it then. That is the most likely explanation. I wish I had time to speak to it through you."

"It's helped out a couple of times," I told Dr. Roop. "Otherwise, it's not so great."

*Don't lie to your friend,* Smelly said.

"Regardless," Dr. Roop told me, "this is encouraging news. An intellect like that is a formidable ally. I believe that with it on your side, your chances of success are excellent. Speak of it to no one."

"Yeah, I'm pretty sure I don't see the upside to letting anyone know I've got this thing in my brain."

Dr. Roop nodded. "Good. And trust this intelligence. If it offers you advice, you must take it. Now you'd better get going. I have a narrow window in which to slip out of here."

I took one last look at the only Confederation citizen I knew I could trust, and I headed out.

On the elevator down, Smelly said, *I like your friend. It's pretty smart for a meat bag.*

"Shut up," I told him, which was not the smartest thing in the world, because there were two other beings riding along in that car. They slowly inched away from me.

# CHAPTER SEVENTEEN

O kay, so I had some goals now. It's good to have direction. I had to get Tamret to talk to me so I could let her know everything that was going on without alerting her annoying fiancé. I then had to convince everyone that rather than planning an escape back home, we should plan on impossibly carrying out Director Ghli Wixxix's dying wish and venture on a hopeless mission into the unknown, beneath the surface of the station. As a general rule, people can be reluctant to visit a place called the Forbidden Zone, but I had to convince them that going was not an idiotic thing to do.

I was halfway across the compound when I received a message that Interim Director Junup wanted to meet with us in two hours. There was nothing to do but to wait it out, hear what he had to say, and then see how I wanted to proceed afterward.

I showed up in the meeting room a little early, but the other humans and Steve were already there. A few minutes later Tamret and Villainic came in and sat at the far end of the table, away from us. I looked over at Tamret. Her ears pivoted toward me, and she smiled. Villainic whispered something in her ear, and she looked down.

Junup now stormed into the room, his cape rippling dramatically, which I suspected was the main purpose of the cape. He was followed by Ardov, who was wearing a crisply tailored, boxy Confederation suit, his Movement for Peace armband on full display. Junup sat behind the desk, and Ardov stood behind him, like he was at attention. Without looking at us, Junup called up a projection of text from his data bracelet. He grunted as he looked it over and then waved a finger in what I believed was a signature. The text vanished.

"I apologize," he said. "Being interim director is a whirlwind of activity. I am afraid it never stops."

No one spoke, perhaps because we didn't believe Junup was actually apologizing for anything, and perhaps because he seemed to be inviting us to say how sorry we were that taking over the job of a being he had probably murdered was turning out to be sort of a bummer.

Junup looked like he was about to say something else, but then he looked at Villainic. "Who are you?"

Villainic smiled and then stood up and bowed in a way that appeared both respectfully old-fashioned and laughably dumb. There were lots of hand flourishes, some head bobbing, and a little dance with his left foot. "I am Villainic, Fifth Scion of House Astioj, Third Rung of the Caste of the Elevated."

"How fascinating," Junup said, "but my inquiry had more to do with what you are doing in this room at this moment."

Villainic performed the same bow, though the foot movements were a little different this time. It's nice to have some variety. "I beg your pardon, Interim Director Junup. As Tamret, Scion-Betrothed of House Astioj, has folded her being into my caste, I am her protector and so responsible for her safety. This was negotiated by your representatives when they came to Rarel. Our custom is that she may not travel without my permission and accompaniment."

Junup summoned a keyboard and tapped furiously for a

moment. "Yes, my records indicate you've been given security clearance."

"That the [*honor deities*] have chosen my family for special notice is on record," Villainic said.

"Yes, it says that right here," Junup said, still reading the text. "Apparently your presence was a nonnegotiable term for your government. Well, I suppose we must endure it."

"He is a harmless primitive, Director," Ardov said.

I waved my hand between the two of them. "You know you both come from the same world, right?"

"He has not been enlightened by the wisdom of the Confederation," Ardov said. "He is no less primitive than you."

"Thank you, Ardov," Junup said, almost kindly. He turned to Villainic. "I now know why you are here, but I still don't care. When I speak to the others, if there is anything you don't understand, please do not in any way express your confusion. Allow me to pretend you don't exist."

Villainic treated us to some more bowing and then took his seat.

Junup folded his hands. "We seem to have ourselves a situation, don't we?"

Colonel Rage leaned forward. "How about you spare us the smug posturing and get to the point. If you want us to acknowledge that you hold all the cards, and that we're in your power, then I'll go ahead and do that now. It'll save you some of your precious time."

Ardov snickered. I never much liked a snickering Ardov, but he had only become more impressed with himself as Junup's lapdog—or cat, or whatever.

Junup cocked his head. "Very good. It is true. Whatever

fate we choose for you, you will have to endure it. I shall not get into debates with you about who is responsible for this current impasse. The human children have been unwilling to acknowledge their culpability in the past, and I doubt they will be willing to do so now."

"I do not see that you have been quick to acknowledge blame either," Charles observed.

Ardov began to step forward, like he was going to power-shove Charles through a wall, but Junup held up a staying hand, commanding his minion to be at peace. It was right out of the bad-guy manual.

"In the end," Junup explained, "it does not matter if you admit to wrongdoing or deny it. Either way, you are accused of terrible crimes. The investigation into your guilt will be time-consuming and not in the best interests of the Confederation. The end result will quite possibly lead to jail time for most of you. The best possible outcome, after years of inquiry and detention, will likely be exile."

"Director Ghli Wixxix offered our worlds the chance to reapply for Confederation membership," I said.

"Perhaps you recall destroying the ship on which Director Ghli Wixxix was traveling," Junup said. "Bargains proposed by her administration were voided the moment you caused her to explode. I know it is your inclination to reveal private conversations to data collectors and thus turn every encounter into a bargaining session, but there is no prize at the end of this one, Mr. Reynolds. Your people will either be exiled from this station or detained indefinitely in its prison. There is no third possibility. Except, of course, for you in particular." He leveled his large brown eyes at me. "The Phandic Empire still seeks to put you on trial for your crimes. Delivering you to the Phands would make a generous opening move in our upcoming peace negotiations."

"So, you're dealing with the Phands now?" I asked.

"We have never believed in isolation," he said, looking smug.

"Is that how Nora Price got out of prison?" I asked. "Because you don't believe in isolation."

"It was a simple prisoner exchange," Junup told me. He didn't appear to be even slightly embarrassed. Handing over traitors to the enemy seemed to be business as usual for him. "It is all very regular."

"I don't see how regular it is for you to free someone who betrayed my planet," I said.

"*I* didn't," Junup assured me. "The prisoner exchange was approved by Ghli Wixxix. You see, you are always looking to put people in categories—good and evil and so forth. The truth is always more complicated than we might like. Life is full of compromise."

I knew that politicians often did things that were pretty unsavory because they were looking at the bigger picture, but I still hated that they'd let Nora Price go. Still, Ghli Wixxix was supposed to be on the right side of things, so I could only hope she'd gotten something important in return.

"Now," Junup said, "are you done challenging me, or should I proceed to initiate another prisoner exchange? I can only imagine what they would trade for Ezekiel Reynolds."

"You've made your point," Colonel Rage growled. "I acknowledged that you had the upper hand when we began. But you still want something from us, or you wouldn't be here, so let's get to the point."

"Very well," Junup said. "I should prefer that an inquiry into the *Kind Disposition* not drag out indefinitely in the public sphere. While I do not believe that anyone in Confederation government has anything to hide, these sorts of debates tend to lead to inevitable doubts and theories of complicity. This is a time of transition in the Confederation, and I take over for my predecessor under difficult circumstances. If the only eyewitnesses to the destruction of this ship—the very beings accused of being complicit in its destruction—were to disappear, a thorough investigation would be impossible, and the matter would have to be dropped."

"You want us gone," the colonel said.

"Correct. I can arrange a way off the station and back to the squalor of your home planets. You would no longer be my problem, and I would no longer be yours. Does this sound appealing to you?"

I'd come here hoping to get the ball rolling so Earth could become a member of an advanced and peaceful galactic civilization, but that prospect was pretty much off the table. This morning, an offer to call it quits and get everyone off the station would have sounded pretty good, but Dr. Roop needed me to go to the Forbidden Zone, and I'd promised him I would do it. I needed to find a way to get everyone home and also help Dr. Roop.

"I think we're all interested," Mi Sun said.

The colonel was about to say something, but Alice cut him off. "What's the catch?"

Junup leaned forward and glowered at her. "I beg your pardon."

"Come on," she said. "It can't be that simple. I know how you operate."

I noticed that Tamret was glowering at Alice, but I had no idea if she was annoyed by the interruption or irritated that the role of disruptive female had gone to someone else.

"Young lady, you have seen very little since your illegal boarding of our ship," Junup said with a sneer. "I find it unlikely that you know much at all."

"I've seen enough to doubt that you'd simply give us what we want without expecting something in return. So let's hear it."

"Whatever agreement Ghli Wixxix made with these savages, it didn't include her," Ardov said. "I can remove her."

Junup did his evil-dude hand raise again. "You are moderately perceptive," he said to Alice, "for a member of so undeveloped a species. As it happens, I will need a show of good faith before I can trust you with my plan for your departure."

Alice looked around the room. "Told you," she said triumphantly.

Junup sighed. "In two days you will have an interview with Boridi op Xylliac, who now serves as chief justice of the Xeno-Affairs Judicial Council. My replacement, in other words." He paused and adopted a listening pose, like he wanted us to tell him that no one could ever replace him.

"Surely a successor, not a replacement," volunteered Villainic.

We all groaned.

"He seemed to want to hear it," Villainic said apologetically.

"The chief justice will be responsible for the major inquiry into the events onboard the *Kind Disposition*. He wanted a preliminary and less formal fact-finding session, though everything you say will be considered part of the public record. When you meet with him, I would prefer it if you would take as much responsibility for the destruction of the ship as you can—barring any admission of criminal activity. That would require your arrest, which I admit would be pleasant, but I understand that you have no motivation to deliver yourselves into prison. You must hint that you made mistakes, showed poor judgment, and acted in ways that resulted—without your intention—in the destruction of the ship. Make no mention of the preposterous allegation of a mutiny against the captain or illegal activity by the Movement for Peace. I suggest you play it up as a misunderstanding precipitated by failure of leadership on Captain Hyi's part. Also, I would like you to mention my nephew's heroic efforts to save the ship."

None of us said anything for a moment.

"You are asking us to let you, quite literally, get away with murder," the colonel said, his voice quiet.

"I am guilty of nothing," Junup snapped. "Your shuttle caused a missile to strike the *Kind Disposition*. That is beyond dispute. What happened up until that event is uncertain. I do not understand all the details, and neither do you. All I am asking is that you emphasize that uncertainty rather than speculate."

"While hanging Hyi out to dry," the colonel said. As a military man, he clearly didn't like the idea of the blame being pinned on a dead officer who, as near as we could tell, had done nothing wrong.

"He won't mind," Junup said, "and the truth is, your testimony will sow doubt, but nothing more. It will raise lines of inquiry, but you will be gone and unable to answer additional questions."

"And if we do not take this offer?" Charles asked.

"Then the hearings will continue, and I guarantee you will

end up in prison. That means *all* of you. This is part of a plot you put together before you left the station last time, and the Ish-hi and the Rarels were in on it too. The only one of you who won't be spending the rest of his life in our prison system will be Zeke, who will enjoy the honorable tradition of Phandic legal system."

"But that's not just!" Villainic said. "Tamret and I weren't there! Why should we suffer for their actions?"

"Good to know you're a team player, mate," Steve said.

"I suppose," Junup said, "a deal could be struck for those of you not from Earth if you can provide testimony that will help us understand the character of those who committed these terrible crimes against the Confederation."

So, to get home, they would have to testify against us. Villainic didn't seem to me the sort of guy who would be able to resist that kind of pressure.

As if to prove my point, Villainic said, "I don't know anything, but I can assure you I will cooperate in any way I can."

Junup's nose twitched and his goaty mouth stretched. A smile, perhaps. "I thought you might feel that way."

The colonel sighed. "All right. I think we get the picture. For the sake of argument, let's say we go along with your plan. How does it work?"

"After you have performed adequately when being interviewed by Boridi op Xylliac, then I shall arrange for you to make your way off-station. There is a transport shuttle housed near the landing pad marked 'Diplomatic Transport.' That being"— he pointed at Tamret—"will use her computer skills to bypass its security locks and also change its identification code to avoid notice by the traffic drones. You will then make your way to the main starport, where you will find a ship docked in bay 343-585-087. You will take this ship and no other." He leveled his gaze at Steve. "There will be the illusion of pursuit, but it's a fast ship, and you'll have enough of a lead that you will be able to tunnel out before we can overtake you."

"You plan to stage our escape," Mi Sun said, stating the obvious.

"It is best for everyone, I think. That ship's navigation computer will contain coordinates for your worlds. You may bring your friends to Rarel and Ish-hi and then return to Earth."

Colonel Rage, I observed, was doing his best to act neutral, like this wasn't the best possible deal he could have hoped for. "How do we know we can trust you?"

"Because I want you gone more than I want you punished," Junup said.

"So you plan to let us take a ship, and keep it," the colonel prodded.

"As you are a primitive, militaristic species," he answered, "one that should never have been offered Confederation membership in the first place, I have no doubt you are already salivating at the prospect of reverse engineering our technology. Please know that the ship and all its components will have been treated with a corrosive nanite agent. Exactly fifteen standard days from the moment you fire up the engines, these nanites will begin taking that ship apart, molecule by molecule. Within six hours of that, the ship will have vanished. I am giving you no gifts, Colonel. Except, of course, freedom."

Colonel Rage leaned forward. "This is a lot to chew over. We're going to have to consider your offer, Interim Director. Let me propose a counter—"

Junup stood, interrupting the colonel. "I'm not here to negotiate. I have set forth my requirements and my rewards. You may either accept this generous proposal, or you can be punished. I will not belittle myself by quibbling over details with savages."

Junup turned and allowed us to enjoy his cape fluttering as he walked out of the room. Ardov followed him but paused briefly at the door. He turned back and grinned at us—at me—and was gone.

Steve almost leaped out of his chair. "What a load of—"

The colonel held up his hand. "I don't think we should discuss this matter in this room. Let's take a walk, shall we?"

We sat in a circle on the front lawn. Tamret's face was a mask of misery, but everyone looked grim in their own way. Everyone but Villainic, that is, who seemed to find the prospect of returning home delightful.

"I'm not sure what there is to discuss," Mi Sun said. "We wanted to escape, and this is our chance."

"The problem," Alice said, "is that if we do that, we're helping Junup. We're giving him what he wants."

"I hate that," Mi Sun said, "but the game is rigged. We're going to lose if we stay."

There was nothing I liked about Junup's offer. Dr. Roop needed me to go to the Forbidden Zone, and I meant to try. If there was a chance to help him—which meant helping the Confederation and all of our home planets—I meant to take it. But that wasn't the only reason I was against this deal.

"He killed Nayana," I said. "He killed Urch."

"Sometimes you have to walk away," the colonel said. "I

don't like it any better than you do, but we're out of our depth here. Getting everyone landed in prison isn't going to bring your friends back."

"I, too, wish we could punish him for what he's done," Charles said, "but beyond that, I don't believe we can accept that everything will be as he claims. What if the ship isn't where it is supposed to be, or if it is rigged to explode? How do we know he will provide what he says he will?"

"I believe him because his scheme works for him," the colonel said. "This is the perfect solution. He gets rid of us, and the fact that we've hightailed it out of here makes us look guilty. I'm trying to think how he might be planning on double-crossing us, but I don't see that he has anything to gain by doing that. The sooner we're nothing but a memory, the better off he is, and if we leave in a way that makes us look bad, he comes out smelling like a rose."

"Then you want to do this?" Mi Sun asked.

"Not exactly," the colonel said. "I don't like this degrading-ship business. Makes me nervous, and takes away our advantage. I didn't come all the way out here to leave empty-handed."

"Junup did not appear open to negotiation," Charles said. "His is the only deal on the table."

"Then maybe we should help ourselves to something on another table." The colonel looked at Steve. "You're the ship thief?"

"That's right, mate."

"Any interest in stealing two ships?"

Everyone stared at the colonel.

"The only thing we need from the ship he's giving us is the

coordinates to our worlds. What if we take two ships and then rendezvous? Whoever is on the one Junup left for us will transfer over to the ship that isn't going to degrade."

"That's one way to handle it," Steve said. "Another is to program Junup's ship to fly off on its own. It'll look like we've taken it, but we'll just be on another one."

"But it has the navigation information we need," Mi Sun said.

Tamret leaned in to Villainic and whispered something in his ear. He nodded at her.

"I can get that before we leave," Tamret said.

I stared at her, not because of what she'd proposed, but because I hadn't heard her say so many words since she'd first arrived. She was almost smiling now, and the vaguest hint of the old Tamret was visible, if only for an instant.

"I like that plan," the colonel said with a grin. "You kids *are* good. While all eyes are on that other ship, we'll quietly slip out unnoticed."

"There's something else we need to talk about," I said. I looked around to make sure no one was watching us. I was still worried that our conversations might not be private, but Smelly had said it would know if we were being monitored, and I had no choice but to believe it. "Dr. Roop got in touch with me. I went to go see him."

This got everyone's attention, even Colonel Rage, who had not met Dr. Roop but had certainly heard a great deal about him.

"He took a huge risk by meeting with me," I said, "and he made it clear that we have to pursue Director Ghli Wixxix's plan. We have to find the Hidden Fortress and get that skill tree. He's counting on us."

"Forgive me," said Villainic, "but I am not familiar with either this Dr. Roop or this fortress you speak of."

"The director didn't provide us with a plan," the colonel said, ignoring Villainic. "She told us her *goal*. We never discussed mission parameters or security concerns or anything else we would need before going into an unknown and hostile environment. I'd love to get ahold of this skill tree she mentioned—it could give Earth the advantage we need—but I'm not going blind into an engagement, and certainly not when you young people are my responsibility."

"Again," Villainic said, "I have not yet been informed of these crucial details. I cannot make any decisions on Tamret's behalf until I know more."

"How about we let Tamret make decisions on her own behalf?" I suggested.

"Please, Zeke," Villainic said, sounding a little frustrated. "I ask you to respect our caste customs. We've discussed the problems created when you try to interfere with our private business."

"I'm not interfering with your private business, I'm interfering with Tamret's, and I feel pretty good about that."

"I will have to excuse what to me appears as rudeness," Villainic said. "I'm sure it is simply your inability to understand our customs. I know, in my heart, that Tamret's friend would never intentionally insult her as you do now."

The colonel made a throat-slitting gesture with his finger. "Kill it. We don't have time for this nonsense. And I'm afraid we also don't have the means of looking for that skill tree. I know you want to help your friend, and I respect that, but there are too many unknown variables and too much risk. We need to escape, and on the best terms we possibly can. That means, in two days we tell this chief justice what Junup wants to hear. We suck it up, take our lumps, and get out of here in one piece."

"There's more to this than just helping Dr. Roop," I said. "If we can find that skill tree, it will help the entire Confederation, and it will help us. Once we hand over the technology, people will be more inclined to listen to what we have to say. This could turn everything around."

The colonel sighed. "I'm sorry, Zeke, but I don't see that happening. If you find that software, Junup will take credit, and we'll be back where we started, only worse, because now Junup will have one more reason to want us dead. I've listened to your opinions, which I take seriously, and I've weighed the facts, and I've made my decision. The matter is now closed."

I opened my mouth to argue, but I could see everyone looking away. They wanted me to stop. They wanted to take Junup's deal, and without their help I couldn't do much of anything. I had come to Confederation Central to help Earth and to help Tamret, and it looked like I would be running away without doing either of those things.

# CHAPTER EIGHTEEN

Something was buzzing, and that was never good. It was dark, I was awake, and I had no idea where I was. Then I remembered. Of course. I was on a space station run by a goat-turtle who hated me, and there was a lizard guy sleeping ten feet away from me. It was the middle of the night, which explained the darkness. And my data bracelet was trying to deliver an emergency message.

I squeezed my eyes shut, trying to get them to focus, and then looked at my bracelet. The message was from Tamret, and I was suddenly wide awake. *Open your door, you moron.*

I scrambled out of bed and made it to the front door without tripping more than twice. I threw open the door, and there she was, standing in the light of the hallway. She wore a long nightgown and a bathrobe, and her hair was a little messy, but she looked like I remembered her, more than she had at any time since returning to the station.

"Can I come in?" she asked. Her voice was low but insistent. Her eyes were zeroed in on me. It was like the old Tamret had returned.

"Steve's sleeping," I said, not quite sure what else to say. My heart was hammering like crazy. Tamret had been ignoring me for two days, and now she suddenly wanted to talk to me.

"He can sleep through anything," she said, and then pushed past me.

It was true that Ish-hi were notoriously deep sleepers. We had discovered that last year when we'd tried to wake him up for an emergency—without success—and I'd learned that all over again now, having him as a roommate

Tamret made her way into the room, turned on my bedside light, and sat on my bed with her hands in her lap. I sat next to her, keeping a few inches between us.

There was an excruciating sixty seconds of silence. Finally I broke it by being a jerk. Yay, me. "Are you sure the caste police won't arrest you for being here?"

"That's not funny," Tamret said. Her ears were back, and her whiskers twitched, which was never a good sign.

"I know it's not funny. Neither is your refusing to talk to me."

She turned to me, her expression unreadable. I'd grown so used to being able to interpret every shift of her eyes or twitch of her whiskers. I felt like I didn't know her at all now.

"When we get to Rarel," she said in a flat voice, "we'll have to follow local laws, so things might get tricky. The caste regulations say I'll have to follow Villainic's orders. But I don't want to go with him."

That stopped me cold. "You don't?"

She shook her head. Her eyes were lowered, like she didn't want to make eye contact with me.

"What do you want, then?"

She was still looking down. "Will you bring me back to Earth with you?"

I don't know that she could have said anything that would have made me happier. I wanted to hug her, I wanted us to hold hands and laugh and for everything to be like it used to be, but she still sat there, quiet.

"What happened to you?" I asked. "Why are you engaged to that guy?"

She shook her head. "I don't want to talk about it, okay? And I can't stay long. He doesn't snoop around all that often, but he's allowed to enter my room whenever he wants, and he has checked up on me in the middle of the night a couple of times . . . that I know of. Just promise you won't leave me behind, Zeke."

"If we're on Rarel soil, I don't know if I can—"

"You can do anything," she said, her voice quiet. "You promised me you were going to get me off Rarel, and you did."

"It looks like I was too late."

"You weren't," she said. "Not if I don't have to go back. I'd rather spend the rest of my life in a Confederation prison."

"Tamret, why don't you just walk away from him? People break engagements all the time."

"Maybe in your culture," she said. "I don't have that choice. I made *vows*. I am bound up with his caste, and its rules, forever. There's no way out unless the promise I made conflicts with a preceding obligation. I've tried to figure out some way it might, but there's nothing. I'm stuck, Zeke."

"And you can't just break your vow?" I asked hopefully. "I mean, it's not nice to go back on your word, but sometimes you have to."

"I can't," she said, her voice straining to convey the gravity of what she felt. "It was a holy vow, and I can't break it."

I liked that about her. She would break laws if she didn't agree with them, but she regarded these Rarel promises as ironclad. Unfortunately, this left us with a bit of problem. "So how are you going to—"

"I don't know yet," she said. "But I'll figure something out. Or you will. Just don't leave me behind. Please."

I swallowed. "I won't. Of course I won't. You know that."

"Thank you." She turned away and then wiped at her eyes with the back of her hands. "I need to go." She stood up and moved toward the door.

"I miss you, Tamret," I said quietly, not bothering to look up, to watch her leave.

"I'm right here," she said.

"No, you're not."

She nodded. "You're right." She opened the door. "But when it counts, I will be."

When she stepped into the hall, Villainic was standing there. He was an angry-looking Rarel, which is not something you ever want to see.

I was up and walking toward them, trying to look as tough as I possibly could, but given that I was wearing an *Adventure Time* T-shirt and a pair of boxers, I think I enjoyed only limited success.

"Get back to your room," Villainic said to her, his voice quiet and restrained and, I thought, injured.

Tamret nodded, and she hurried off, her shoulders hunched.

Villainic turned to me, and I braced myself for the worst. I'd seen his kind fight, and a mediocre Rarel could trounce a pretty tough human, which I was not. Things were about to get ugly, and there was nothing I could do about it. The main thing, I knew, was to deflect Villainic's anger. I would let him put me in the hospital if it would protect Tamret.

He stepped into my room, slouched in defeat.

"I don't know what to do about her," he said to me, his voice heavy with wretchedness. "She is so disobedient, and, more importantly, she's not happy."

I could not help but notice he was not punching me in the face. "But you're not hitting me," I observed, too relieved to keep my mouth shut. "That's good news."

"Why would I hit you?" he asked.

"Well, your fiancée was in my room in the middle of the night."

"Did you abduct her or force her to come here against her will?" he asked.

"Of course not," I said.

"Then I have no cause to be angry with you, do I?

Okay, this was not a jealous boyfriend I was dealing with. I wasn't sure what it was, but I was enjoying the absence of face-punching.

"She's your friend, Zeke. And I understand that's why she came here, but I think even you can see that her behavior is unacceptable. You know her better than anyone here. Any advice you can give me would be really appreciated."

"Advice about what?"

"How to get her to obey the rules," he said, throwing up his hands in exasperation.

"That's easy," I said. "Take the rule book and get rid of everything she is not allowed to do. Then get rid of all the things she has to do. I think you'll be okay then."

"I realize you are making a joke, but it is not a funny one. My honor requires that she observe the traditions of betrothal, but if she breaks them the moment I turn my head, how can I trust her?"

"Did you even have a single conversation with her before you guys got engaged or whatever?" I asked. "Do you know her at all?"

"I hope to come to know her," Villainic said. "She is very quiet and demure, which is something I like in a girl."

"Are we talking about Tamret, or did the conversation change?"

"She was not quiet and reserved with you?" Villainic asked.

I was going to tell him that, no, she was loud and unhinged, she was wild and fearless and more than a little dangerous to be around, but I didn't think that would do me, or Tamret, or even Villainic any good. "I guess it's a matter of perspective." I shook my head. "How did you guys even become, like, a thing?" I asked, waving my hands around, not wanting to say the words.

Villainic looked at me, his eyes huge round in surprise. "Did you just insult the honor of [*the second-tier deity of domestic arrangements and livestock slaughtering*]?"

"I have no idea," I said. "Did I?"

"You did!"

"I'm going to be as honest with you as I can be and tell you I did not mean to do that. I'm just not sure why you would marry someone you don't know. I mean, she doesn't have a powerful family or own a lot of property and stuff. So why did you bring her into your caste? I don't know much about your culture, but it sounds to me like people would see this as marrying down."

"In my family," he said, "Tamret's condition is considered to be good luck."

"Her condition?"

He made a gesture toward his face and arms. "You know. Her . . . appearance."

He meant her white fur. The other Rarels I'd met had all been variations of brownish tan. Tamret had told me last year that a small percentage of Rarels were born with white fur, and that it was often considered unattractive on her world. It now seemed there were other options.

"Okay," I said. "You basically saved her from prison so you could marry her in the hopes of someday having children with white fur?"

"Or grandchildren. It doesn't matter. It is that I have increased the chances of having such progeny. Please understand, Zeke, that I am a fifth son. Do you know what that means?"

"That you got beaten up a lot as a kid?"

"Well, yes, but it also means that I had to be creative if I were to find some way to marry significantly. Women of stature or wealth would not want me, because unless my older brothers should all meet with accidents, I won't inherit property."

"I get it," I said. "I understand entirely. You can hope your older brothers all die, but you can't depend on it. In the meantime, you might as well marry a girl you don't know because she might pass along some traits that your family considers good luck even if everyone else thinks they're gross."

"Exactly!" Villainic cried out. "I knew you would understand."

I understood that Villainic was a complete idiot, but I didn't think it best to say that. I needed to get him to trust me and, more importantly, to let Tamret act like herself around me.

"Here's the thing," I told him, like we were buddies now. "I really don't want to be disrespectful, but it would help your chances of getting off this station alive if you could give Tamret a little more freedom."

"It is clear to me that you have different ways," Villainic said, "and it is not for me to judge those ways. I can only tell you that what you think of as 'freedom' will not be acceptable in the social circles she must soon inhabit. She must find a new way of thinking about herself so she can be a happy and successful wife. You are the only one she trusts. Will you help me in my cause?"

"I don't know if I'm really the person to do that."

"I can think of none better," Villainic said.

"I don't want you to be unhappy, Villainic," I began, but that was as far as I got.

"And you don't want Tamret to be unhappy. Therefore you are the best person to help us be happy together. Thank you, Zeke. You have cheered me considerably. Good night."

I followed him out of the room and watched as he actually strutted down the hall as though all his problems had been solved and he had not a single care in the universe.

I turned back to my room. The door was open, and Steve was leaning heavily against the doorjamb, rubbing at one of his eyes with his palm. His sleeping tunic was wrinkled. "Are you aware," he asked me, "that this sort of thing doesn't really happen to anyone but you?"

# CHAPTER NINETEEN

The Movement for Peace was made up of a bunch of frightened, ignorant beings who believed that any sentients who'd evolved differently than they themselves had must be inferior. But not all Confederation citizens felt that way. Some liked species who'd evolved from predators and omnivores. They found these species interesting or charming or magnetic, like vampires in romance novels or something.

Whatever his reasons, Boridi op Xylliac, at least according to the news outputs, was one of those aliens, and so instead of conducting his interview in some "sterile government conference room," as he put it in his message, he wanted to host us at his home. I'd never much liked the idea of being "hosted"—it smacked of being on your best behavior and having to clutch little paper napkins—but I also didn't want to say no to a rare opportunity to leave the government compound. Besides, while the change of venue was presented as a request, I understood that we weren't really in a position to decline.

I still didn't know how I was going to play things in this interview. Everyone else had decided to give Junup what he wanted so we could go home. It wasn't that I didn't understand their position. As long as we remained on Confederation Central, with Junup in charge, we were in danger. Every minute I was on the station, I felt the need to get my friends out of harm's way. The fact that Tamret wanted to come back to Earth with me wasn't doing much to turn me away from this option either. I loved the idea of us being together, but I worried about what would happen once she got to Earth. She might be detained and shoved off to some dark basement in Area 51. On the other hand, if we introduced her strategically, the government couldn't make her disappear. She might become an international celebrity. That wouldn't be so bad. I had to hope that Colonel Rage would help us make sure Tamret remained free and safe.

All of that assumed I went along with what the others wanted, but I didn't know that I could bring myself to do it. Urch. Nayana. Captain Hyi. Ghli Wixxix. I could not stop thinking about them. They'd died because of the mutiny on the *Kind Disposition*, and Junup was behind it all. And then there was Dr. Roop, who insisted that everything depended on me going in search of this Former technology. I could have set the request aside if anyone else had asked it of me, but not Dr. Roop.

So, there it was. I had to choose between betraying one friend or betraying several friends. I was not looking forward to going to see Boridi op Xylliac. Plus, Ardov was coming with us, so that would pretty much make it the worst field trip ever.

We walked over to the shuttle landing pad flanked by four peace officers wearing Movement for Peace armbands. I didn't much care for that, but they soon became a blur of alien forms and colors and body types. I had my eye on Ardov. He sat in the front of the shuttle like the school monitor and watched us as we strapped ourselves in, smiling at us like we were doing a great job and he was super proud of us. I was harboring secret fantasies of shaving him.

The one thing I could say in Ardov's favor was that he hadn't singled Tamret out for any special attention. They'd ignored each other, and Ardov and Villainic hadn't done much more than give each other wary glances. I had to figure there was some sort of caste thing going on, and I didn't understand it, but considering how cruel he'd been to Tamret in the past, I wasn't complaining.

A couple of rows in front of me, Villainic was looking nervous. Tamret was showing him the passenger safety information on her data bracelet. Life preservers under the seat, just like in an airplane. Impact gel cushions. Inflatable life rafts, as our shuttle would be traveling over water. All kinds of things to keep him alive. I wanted to tell him that he shouldn't be afraid of flying—he should be afraid of the beings he was flying with.

"Interim Director Junup has little faith that you can conduct yourselves properly with reduced supervision," Ardov announced once we were off the ground. "But Boridi op Xylliac insisted on conducting this meeting at his residence, so we have no choice. I expect all of you to be on your best behavior. I know it's sometimes difficult for primitive species to resist their violent, disruptive impulses, but you're going to have to try. Frankly, I think it's a risk taking all of you out of the compound." He then turned away, like he was startled by something.

Or maybe embarrassed, because it seemed to me that he'd just drawn attention to something very peculiar. Why, exactly, were Steve and Tamret along for this ride? They hadn't been on the *Kind Disposition*. Junup had said something about using them as character witnesses, but I thought he'd meant to get Villainic to testify against us. Something wasn't right here.

I leaned over to Colonel Rage, who was sitting next to me, and I very quietly pointed this out to him.

His one eye went wide with alarm. "Yeah, that's a good point, son," he said quietly. "Kind of makes me worried."

"Worried about what?" I whispered.

"That they're putting us all together so something can happen."

"If you have something to say," Ardov snapped, "speak loud enough that the whole shuttle can hear you."

"Are you feeling excluded, Ardov?" I asked.

"It is the sort of tribal behavior I'd expect from lower forms of life," he said. "But I'm afraid I can't have you whispering. Also, I've closed down your personal comm channels on your bracelets. The last thing I need is for you to plot some kind of foolish escape."

"Where would we escape to?" I asked.

He sneered at me, as though I'd been immature to point out the absurdity of his accusation. "I don't expect you to behave rationally."

I sighed and leaned back. Colonel Rage and I exchanged a glance. There was nothing more we could say now, but we were both keeping our eyes open. It seemed increasingly likely that we were heading into a trap.

It took us about twenty minutes to get to our destination. I'd never paid much attention to the mountains surrounding the city on my last visit, but now that I knew that Ghli Wixxix, and apparently Dr. Roop, wanted us to venture into undeveloped wilderness at the periphery of the domed platform, I found myself looking out the window at the jagged and stony peaks to the far horizon. There was a desert out there, hot and barren and dangerous. From our position dozens of miles away, it looked like no one could last long in that wasteland.

Finally the shuttle set down on a landing pad atop a tall, cylindrical building with a bright green metallic exterior. We filed out of the shuttle and into the building and then into a large elevator that opened directly into Boridi op Xylliac's apartment.

I immediately got the sense that serving on the Xeno-Affairs Judicial Council must be a pretty good deal, because Boridi op Xylliac had some sweet digs. The place was large, with huge windows that presented a view of the sprawling city and the wilderness beyond. There were furnishings that might have been expensive—I didn't really know what counted as fancy in the Confederation—and various works of holographic art. Even without knowing the cost of the individual objects, I had no doubt that this was the apartment of a very wealthy being.

The name Boridi op Xylliac hadn't meant much to me, but now that I saw him, I recognized him instantly. He was a large, dare I say rotund, fellow, with mottled red-and-black skin and slight protrusions, reminiscent of stubby horns, on his forehead. During my previous visit to the Confederation, I'd thought of him as looking like Darth Maul, if Darth Maul had been a clown. He looked a little silly, but more than once he'd taken my side against Junup, which made him okay in my book.

He wore a red suit that matched the red parts of his skin, and he looked happy to see us. He opened his arms. "Welcome, friends," he exclaimed. "Do come in. Peace officers, there is no way for them to escape, and I do not fear for my safety, so please remain here while I lead my guests inside."

Ardov stepped forward. "Director Junup has asked me to remain with the primitives at all times."

"We would not want *Interim* Director Junup to worry, now, would we?" Boridi op Xylliac said. "Come along, then. Come along." He led us into another room, and then down a hallway, and finally to another large, open area, with numerous chairs, oval couchlike things, and tables set up with plenty of food.

"Look around, friends! Look around! In my apartment you will see what I believe is the finest collection of primitive art in the Confederation."

There were paintings on the walls, large metal sculptures in the corners, and carvings of wood and stone on the tables and shelves. Some of them looked fairly simplistic, but most of them looked like variations of ordinary art you might see in a museum on Earth. Maybe I didn't find any of it strange because I was, myself, a primitive.

"I have ordered refreshment for our chat," Boridi op Xylliac continued. "As you can see, there is plenty of replicated animal flesh upon which you may feast. Oh, and you, my Ish-hi friend," he said to Steve. "I know you prefer flesh to be alive and fearing its demise when you force it to succumb to your power."

"I might do," Steve said warily. "Hadn't really thought of it that way."

Boridi op Xylliac strode across the room, grabbed what looked like a small rectangular fish tank, and handed it to Steve. Inside, it was crawling with creatures that looked like furry shrimp, each one about as long as my finger. Steve took the tank in one hand, fished out a creature with the other, and popped it in his mouth.

"Bit early in the day for sweets," he told Boridi op Xylliac, "but these are quite good."

I wasn't really in the mood to eat the animal flesh Boridi op Xylliac had thoughtfully provided, and no one else seemed to be either. After Steve threw a few more hairy shrimp into his mouth, we all took our seats. Boridi op Xylliac remained standing in the middle of the room.

"Now," he said, "I would love to show you my collection of primitive kitchen implements, gathered from some of the most backward planets in the galaxy. I know they would make you feel very much at home. Who is up for examining some ladles?"

"How about we get down to business," said Colonel Rage.

"Certainly." Boridi op Xylliac rubbed his large hands together. "I admire your simplistic rejection of manners."

"It's how we primitives do things," the colonel said.

"Charming! Now, as you know, we must make a full investigation into what happened aboard the *Kind Disposition*. This is not an official inquiry, of course, but I am recording this session, and what you say will become part of the public record, so you must consider your words as equivalent to testimony. However, this is a friendlier venue than an official hearing, and I hope you will feel more relaxed and candid and free to speak using the colorful local idioms of your own cultures."

We were all silent for a long time. Colonel Rage had his hands clasped and he was looking at the space between his knees. We all knew what we had to do if we had any hope of Junup letting us leave the station, but getting things started was not going to be easy. It was one thing to decide you were going to be the guy who helps a weasel escape punishment and rise to power, but it was another thing to actually do it.

So, here we all were, trying to figure out what we valued more—justice or our own lives. No, scratch that. I think everyone else was thinking what I was. If it were just me, I'd go for justice and take my chances, but I couldn't ruin everyone else's chances to get away.

"Can this be?" Boridi op Xylliac asked. "No one wishes to speak?"

I opened my mouth to say something, but I couldn't make any sounds come out.

Villainic looked around the room. He then cleared his throat. "It is my understanding that everyone who was on that ship regrets his or her actions that led to its destruction. Indeed, I have often heard them say that Interim Director Junup is in no way to blame for what transpired."

There was a long silence.

"Interim Director Junup," Boridi op Xylliac said, articulating each syllable as though it were a hammer blow, "was not on the *Kind Disposition*, so why do you raise his name?"

Villainic looked somewhat sheepish. "I only want to emphasize that the mayhem, while perhaps not caused by these good beings from Earth, can in no way be blamed on the Interim Director, nor on anyone who might have been following his orders."

"And who are you precisely?" Boridi op Xylliac asked.

"Ah," said Villainic, who now rose and began doing those fancy things with his hands and feet. It did not get any less stupid with repetition. "I am Villainic, Fifth Scion of House Astioj, Third Rung of the Caste of the Elevated."

Tamret began to study the inside of her sleeve. She looked very much like someone who wished she could fold herself into a paper airplane and fly herself away.

"How interesting," Boridi op Xylliac said. "I find your gestures and the implications of your culture fascinating. But I am not certain what you are doing at this meeting."

Ardov cleared his throat. "Chief Justice, Director Junup thought that, because of your interest in primitive species, you might enjoy the company of the Ish-hi and the Rarels."

"I see," said Boridi op Xylliac. "Very thoughtful of him. I must say it also appears that the interim director has coached these beings on what they should say to me."

"I don't believe he would do so," said Ardov. "Director Junup does not behave unethically. It is, in my opinion, disrespectful and disloyal to imply otherwise."

There was another long silence, this time because there was nothing any of us could say. If we were to launch into our script in which we covered up the mutiny, we would only look like idiots, parroting what Villainic had just said. If we confirmed that the mutiny had taken place, we would be giving up our only possible means of escape. As odd as it seemed, Villainic's blunder had actually gotten us off the hook.

After a few more minutes of sitting and saying nothing, Boridi op Xylliac coughed politely. "Perhaps this gathering was not the best of ideas. I was foolish to think that Junup would not have made promises or threats or otherwise poisoned any chance of candid conversation. We shall have to reconvene this inquiry in a more formal setting, but I can assure you that my investigation into Junup's role in the destruction of that ship shall be most vigorous. Something is horribly wrong here, and while I believe a crime has been committed, I do not think it is you simple-minded and kindhearted primitives who are to blame."

"Let's not be too hasty," Colonel Rage attempted.

Boridi op Xylliac stood up. "I shall now excuse myself. Please partake of the refreshments to your satisfaction. You may show yourselves out when you are done." With that, the chief justice rose and departed from the room.

Ardov looked at Villainic. "You are a complete moron," he said.

Normally I'd have been in favor of a conflict between these two, but in this case I was still so full of relief, I thought I ought to come to Villainic's rescue. "Give him a break. It's not like any of us are trained at this. He made a mistake. That's all."

"Of course you would defend him," Ardov said. "He just saved you from having to . . ." His voice trailed off. "I can't believe I didn't see it earlier. You told him to do that, didn't you?"

"No, that was one hundred percent Villainic," I said.

Ardov was now striding toward me. "Of course you did. That seems to be exactly the sort of thing you would do. You're given two options, and you come up with some sneaky way to achieve some third choice."

*That is kind of like you,* Smelly said.

Villainic stood up and placed himself between me and Ardov, which was kind of a brave thing to do. "No, I can promise you that Zeke did not tell me to say anything. I'm honestly not sure what I did wrong, but I can tell you the blame is mine alone."

Ardov studied him for a moment. "You just may be stupid enough to be telling the truth."

"I agree," I said, "so stop giving him a hard time."

Ardov looked at the two of us and smirked. "It won't make much of a difference at this point, anyhow. Let's go."

We all followed him out the room, Steve going last, taking a moment to grab a fistful of hairy shrimp.

Having accomplished nothing beyond getting a nice view of the city and a partial tour of Boridi op Xylliac's apartment, we went back up to the roof and climbed into the shuttle. The peace officers made certain we got on board but did not get in with us, which I found strange, but I couldn't quite figure out why.

We were quiet for the first few minutes of the trip. It was Colonel Rage who finally spoke. "Obviously, that didn't go as intended," he said to Ardov. "I hope you'll report to your boss that we didn't mean for things to happen this way."

Ardov shrugged like it didn't much matter to him.

"Is this going to interfere with what Junup had in mind for us?" the colonel pressed. I guess he didn't want to mention the fake escape plan out loud, in case there was some kind of monitoring on board the shuttle.

Ardov grinned. "I have a feeling this meeting will prove largely irrelevant."

*That meat sack wants to kill you,* Smelly said.

I put my hand to my mouth and mumbled so no one would hear. "No kidding."

*I don't mean abstractly. Its heart rate is accelerated, its senses hyperalert. It is about to do something that I suspect none of us will much like.*

I looked out the window and noticed that we were flying over a strange part of the city. Below us the buildings were low and had a ragged look to them. The streets were dirty. Junked shuttles and ground vehicles lay here and there where they'd been abandoned. This wasn't the way we'd come. There was also a shuttle flying extremely close to us. Usually they kept a good twenty-five feet or so between each other, but this one was almost touching, less than five feet away.

I was about to ask what was going on when there came a chime from Ardov's bracelet. He sighed. "That's my cue. I wish I could say I was sorry to see you go, but I'm not."

A trapdoor in the roof slid open. Cool air began to gush inside, and our faces were blasted by wind. Ardov unbuckled and stood up. "In case you haven't figured it out yet, this shuttle is programmed to crash. It would have been better if you'd exonerated Junup before you died, but this will have to do."

Using his augmented skills, Ardov crouched and leaped upward fifteen feet, through the trapdoor and onto the roof. "Let's see you cheat your way out of this, Zeke," he called down. Then he leaped from our shuttle to the one next to us.

We all looked around. Everyone was too stunned to move. And then, at the exact same moment, Tamret and I unbuckled and ran to the main control panel.

"He wasn't bluffing," she said, her fingers dancing on the console. "We're programmed to crash."

"I don't see a work-around," I said as I read through the displays. "We're locked out of the shuttle's programming by an encryption code. Can you do something?" I turned away from her as I said it. The question was really directed to Smelly.

*The encryption is extremely complicated. I can break it in six minutes, but we are programmed to crash in less than five.*

"There's not enough time," Tamret said. "I'd need close to ten minutes, and we've got just under five."

I looked out the window. The other shuttle was keeping

pace with us. I guess it wanted to make certain we went down as planned.

*Ardov would have had to program the shuttle when we came on board. There is a better than 99.8 percent likelihood that he has the encryption code.*

"Ardov will have the code," I said aloud.

I stood up and look at the gaping hole in the roof. One of us was going to have to go get it. Rarels were stronger and more agile than humans, but I wasn't about to ask Tamret to do anything that risky, and I didn't trust Villainic to get it done. There really only was one being for the job.

I looked over at Steve, but he was already unbuckling. "Right," he said. "I'll hop over there, smack Ardov around, and message back the code."

*Go with him,* Smelly said.

"What?"

"You don't think I should go?" Steve asked.

"I don't think *I* should go," I said.

Steve set his dark lizard eyes on me. "No offense, mate, but no one suggested that you're up to this."

*I wouldn't put you in harm's way,* Smelly said. *You know that. I have too much to lose. But I don't think one being is going to be able to get the job done. You need to go with that reptile. It's not good to do too often, but I can augment some of your physical abilities. I'll get you through it.*

There wasn't a whole lot of time to play around with. I did not like the idea of getting up on the roof of a shuttle that was cruising about five thousand feet in the air. On the other hand, Smelly wouldn't be risking my life, and its own existence, if it didn't think I could do what needed doing. And finally, and probably most convincing, was that it was one thing to send Steve into danger because he was the only one who could go; it was another thing to sit back and do nothing when I'd just been told I could help get the job done.

Discussion time was over. Steve didn't jump up through the trapdoor like skill tree–hacked Ardov. Instead, quick as a cockroach, he climbed up the side of the shuttle, skittered along the ceiling, and was out the door. I stood under the gaping hole, trying to decide how I was going to get up there. Then, just like that, a platform from the floor rose up and lifted me. It happened so quickly that I hardly had time to understand it. One second I was standing in the shuttle looking up at the sky, and the next I was up there with Steve.

The wind was almost deafening, and I had to struggle to keep my balance.

"How'd you manage that?" Steve demanded, shouting at top volume.

"No idea!" I shouted back. "I'm just glad it worked. Now, are you ready to do something stupid?"

"You don't ever have to ask me that!" Steve looked over at the other shuttle, still flying next to ours. He took perhaps ten seconds to gauge speed and distance; then, without any windup, he propelled himself forward and leaped the ten-foot gap between the two vehicles. He slammed into the side of the shuttle chest-first, but the moment he made contact, he was already scrambling for something to grab on to. He quickly found some kind of handhold and pulled himself up to the shuttle's roof.

*Your turn!* Smelly shouted.

Panic coursed through me like a sputtering electrical wire.

I didn't know how to leap from one moving shuttle to another. It's not the sort of thing you practice in gym glass. How did I measure distance? How did I compensate for speed? I was still wondering these things when my feet started moving, my legs pumping. It was like my body knew what to do without my brain telling it. I leaped.

I was in the air, the wind blowing hard, pushing me up and back, away from the other shuttle, and for a terrifying moment I felt sure that I had misjudged the leap. I was going to fall to my death. Then I hit hard, bouncing off the metal, feeling myself splay out like a plastic bag full of garbage dropped from a roof. I started to slide, but Steve grabbed my wrist.

"Don't blow it now, mate," he said, pulling me to my feet. "That jump was brilliant. You sure you're not still mucking about with the skill tree?"

"Just what nature gave me," I said—plus, of course, Smelly working its magic, whatever exactly that was. One of these days, I was going to have to make it spell out exactly what it could and could not do for me. It seemed like, in moments of crisis, it always had a new surprise. But I could not worry about that now—and I was certainly not complaining.

The trapdoor on this shuttle was still open. I checked my data bracelet. We had just over three minutes remaining.

"No time for recon," Steve said, reading my mind. "All we've got is surprise."

I nodded.

Steve leaped down the trapdoor. I hoped he was going to distract whoever was down there, because I wasn't anywhere near as agile as he was. I went over to the opening and sat, dangling my legs. I then let myself slip, using my hands to hold me up as my body lowered. When I'd gone as low as I could, with my head still outside the shuttle, I allowed myself to drop.

Here were the four armband-wearing peace officers who had left us on the rooftop. What a surprise! And, of course, Ardov. So, yeah. Five to two. Bad odds, though they were made slightly better by the fact that Steve had been kicking and punching with his lizard-fu in the few seconds he'd already had on board. Two of the peace officers, a bull head and a squid guy, were already slumped on the floor, their body positions suggesting that Steve had knocked their skulls together. I'd never wondered if you could render a squid alien unconscious with a head blow before. This trip was, in fact, turning out to be educational.

So that upgraded the odds to three to two, which would have made me feel better if one of the three had not been supersoldiered up with skill-tree hacking. I'd been that supersoldier in the past, and I knew that Ardov would be near impossible to stop.

As soon as I oriented myself, I saw Ardov backhanding Steve. Ish-hi are tough, and I'd seen Steve fight before—he was like a reptilian Terminator—but Ardov stopped him cold. Steve tried to pull his head back to avoid the blow, but Ardov seemed to anticipate the move. His furred hand made contact, sending Steve reeling hard into the shuttle wall.

I'd have leaped on Ardov from behind, but the two remaining peace officers were suddenly turning their attention to me. There was a short being with bright yellow scales and bulging eyes, like a big tree frog in uniform, and then a hulking, spiny giant, easily seven feet tall, that looked like Chewbacca's porcupine cousin. They both looked angry and terrifying, but there was no way I wanted to fight a spiky behemoth. I turned to the other one.

"Let's go, frog man," I said with a bravado I did not feel.

*Frog woman,* Smelly said. *She's female. Also, her species naturally secretes a paralytic venom on her skin when agitated, so don't let her touch you.*

That counted as a useful tip. Now I got to choose between being impaled by the porcupine of doom or getting up close and personal with the death sweat of a lady frog. I did not have a lot of time to choose how I was going to go down swinging, though, because out of the corner of my eye I saw Ardov moving toward a slumped Steve.

I looked around for anything I could use as a weapon. It was a standard transport shuttle, just like the one we'd been on. The chairs were bolted down. There was no loose equipment that could be dangerous. Only stuff to keep you safe.

Like an inflatable raft.

As the peace officers moved toward me, I lunged into the nearest aisle and threw myself on the floor. I grabbed a sealed raft container from under one of the seats. I wished that, like Villainic, I'd taken the time to review the safety materials, because now I didn't have time to read over the instructions, which came with those handy illustrations that are supposed to make everything clear but just end up confusing the process.

*Tear open the stupid package and press the red button twice, you witless imbecile!* Smelly helpfully offered.

The peace officers were nearly on top of me. The yellow frog woman was holding a PPB pistol, and I could see, as if in slow motion, that her long, slightly webbed fingers were curled around the trigger, ready to fire.

I dodged to the side so that the plus-size porcupine would be between the weapon and me. Then I pressed the red button twice and hurled the still compact raft at the two of them.

It inflated furiously, going from the size of a box of macaroni and cheese to the size of a canoe in about half a second. The raft couldn't have been too heavy, but it was moving fast, propelled by the force of its own inflation. It slammed into the giant porcupine, and he staggered back, smacking Ms. Frog in the face with a spiny arm. She cried out in pain. His weapon went flying into the air. I leapt up and caught the weapon as the porcupine went down to the floor, the paralytic venom worked its paralytic magic. I checked the pistol, making sure it was on the stun setting, and fired off a quick blast, sending the last peace officer to the land of venomous and amphibious dreams—a place, incidentally, I hope never to visit.

I couldn't say precisely for how many seconds I'd been distracted—it didn't seem to me to have been that long—but I turned to find Steve about to take a punch in the face. Ardov had his elbow cocked back. I had no doubt that one of his augmented punches could put my lights out permanently; Steve was tougher than I was, but I didn't have any interest in finding out just how much tougher. I fired a warning shot over Ardov's head. Sparks exploded from the bulkhead, which got his attention. There's nothing like weapons fire in an airborne vehicle to make everyone stop what they're doing and reevaluate their priorities.

Ardov took a step away from Steve and had his hands in the air, but he was grinning, like this was all a big joke. "You can't shoot me, Zeke. I have the codes to cancel the destruct sequence. How am I going to tell you what they are if I'm unconscious?"

"What if I shoot you and bring you over to that shuttle?"

"That would be a great plan," Ardov said, "if you thought you could actually leap the distance between the two shuttles while carrying me. Also, I have sworn to serve the cause of peace, which means I would rather die than hand a victory to violent primitives like you."

Time being short, I decided to ignore everything he said. "Steve and I are right here, Ardov, and that means anything that happens will happen with witnesses."

"Not ideal," he admitted, "but the Confederation will judge me by the standards of my species, not by how I have been enlightened. They will never know that I am carrying out Junup's orders."

"Except I've been recording our conversation," I told him, "so actually, they will kind of know, because, like a complete idiot, you just told us."

I had not been recording our conversation. That would have required a whole lot of ingenious, maybe even prophetic, planning. You don't go through life thinking, *I'm about to have a life-threatening encounter. I should probably record it in case my enemy says something incriminating.* The way Ardov was looking at me, I kind of got the feeling he was trying to work all this out on his own. And that was okay. I didn't mind. Mostly because while we'd been talking, Tamret and Villainic had slipped down through the trapdoor. I had no idea why they had risked the leap over here—less of a risk when you're a Rarel. For whatever reason, they'd decided to join us on the fun shuttle, and now here they were, standing directly behind Ardov, and Tamret had a PPB pistol in her hand.

"Hey, Ardov," she said.

Villainic's eyes went wide. "It's not appropriate to initiate conversation with a male who—"

That was as far as he got, because he was startled by the sound of Tamret firing the weapon at point-blank range, directly into Ardov's back.

"I could have shot him if I wanted to!" I shouted. "We needed him conscious for the codes!"

Tamret sighed. She was crouched down by Ardov's slumped form, doing something to him. "Nice job here," she told me, "other than, you know, not being smart enough to finish it." She was holding his wrist, I realized, and accessing a file on his data bracelet.

"Clever," I said.

"No kidding." She had a bunch of holographic text she was scrolling through, moving from one file to another rapidly. "Okay, got it."

We all started to move, but she held up a staying hand. "No point in all of us risking the jump a second time. We'll just fly both shuttles back to the compound."

"I can't let you go unaccompanied," Villainic said.

Tamret took a deep breath. "But what if the codes aren't right, and I can't prevent the shuttle's destruction?"

I knew her well enough to read her tone. She had no doubt the codes would work. She was totally messing with him.

It worked. Villainic's eyes went wide. "Perhaps you're correct."

Steve was now standing, rubbing his head and looking a little groggy, but no more so than he might have after an afternoon of Ish-hi rugby or whatever. "Nice save, ducky," he told her. "Need a lift?"

She nodded. Tamret turned to me, grinned as if to say she could still pretty much do anything, augments or not, and then gently placed a foot on one of Steve's lowered hands. Like they were performing a circus act they'd practiced a million times, he lifted and she flew upward, catching the sides of the opening and then hauling herself up. I watched from the monitor as she made the leap to the other shuttle and vanished down the trapdoor.

A bunch of things were going through my mind. I was thinking about how I never, not in a million years, would have let Tamret go into danger while I stayed behind out of a desire to protect my own skin. I thought about how I should have insisted on going with her, not because I thought she would need to be kept safe, but because if I had, I would have had a few minutes alone with her, away from Villainic. And, finally, I was thinking about how the giant porcupine guy seemed to have recovered from his paralysis and was now standing behind Villainic, ready to bring his clasped hands down on his head.

I admit there was a moment of hesitation. I could deal with the porcupine before he clobbered Villainic, or after. It was hard to say which would be better, so why rush things? Still, I knew I had to live with myself, and if I allowed Villainic to be sucker-smacked by an angry guy with spines, I would probably feel bad about it later. I raised my pistol. In Villainic's eyes I saw a moment of terror in which he wondered, perhaps, if I had chosen to assassinate him. Then I fired off a stunning blast, which sent the peace officer stumbling back, unconscious.

Villainic looked behind him, realizing what had happened. He looked at me as I lowered my pistol.

"You saved my life!"

"He saved you from a beat-down, mate," Steve said. "And

maybe a few puncture wounds. Plus, he clearly had to think twice before doing it. Best to have a little perspective."

"That alien fiend was going to hurt me, and you stopped it," Villainic said.

I waved my hand in the sort of *think nothing of it, my good sir* way that always feels like humble-bragging, no matter how many aliens you blast. The truth is, saving someone, even someone like Villainic, never stops being an ego-booster. And yeah, he did owe me one: Maybe he ought to send me a basket of fruit or something. I didn't make a big deal about it, mostly, if I am going to be honest, because I thought it would make me look even cooler and tougher in his eyes. At some point I was going to be standing between him and Tamret. He had the advantages of age and height, not to mention strength and a hundred other things that came with being a Rarel, so I figured it couldn't hurt if he were already a little intimidated by me.

We were interrupted by Alice's voice coming over my bracelet. "You there, Zeke? Everything's good on our end. Destruct has been canceled. We're heading back to the compound."

"Excellent. Tell Tamret she did great work."

"You're on speaker," Tamret shouted from the distance. "And, if we're being honest, I suppose you helped a little."

"You're too generous. See you guys back at the horrible, oppressive, prisonlike base where we're despised and treated like criminals." I went over to the navigation console to begin reprogramming the shuttle to take us back.

"Oh, and Zeke," Alice said. "Have fun with Villainic." She closed the connection.

"I'd say you already are having fun with Villainic," Steve observed.

I opened up the navigation systems, plugged in the coordinates for the compound, and figured I'd spend the rest of the trip relaxing and shooting any rogue peace officers who happen to regain consciousness. Villainic had other ideas, however.

He was still looking at me, and looking at the porcupine guy, and then back at me.

"You're going to hurt your neck," I told him.

Villainic came closer to me. His eyes were wide and kind of moist, and he looked like, well, a sad little kitten.

"Let's not make too big a deal of this," I told him. "It wasn't anything special."

"He's right," Steve said. "He likes shooting bad guys. Pretty much lives for that sort of thing."

"It's like a hobby with me." I would have said more, but Villainic was pressing his hand to my face. It wasn't hard enough to hurt, but it was hard enough for me to wish he would stop get his palm off my nostrils.

"I invoke the ritual of brotherhood," Villainic said at a volume generally considered impolite when used in the confinement of a small transport shuttle. "I call upon [*the first-tier deity of fraternal relations, ice fishing, and moderately risky recreational sports*] to witness our bond." In a stage whisper he said, "You need to put your hand to my face."

"I kind of don't want to touch you," I said.

He picked up my hand and pressed it to his face. "Hear me, great deity!" he cried, loudly enough that only deaf deities could avoid listening. "I say, before you as witness, that this [*monkey*]-boy alien thing is now my brother!"

"You do share a resemblance," Steve observed.

"Tamret didn't have to touch Nayana's face when they

became sisters," I protested, though my words were garbled by Villainic's hand hair in my mouth.

"I'm following elevated-caste traditions," Villainic said in a whisper. "Now that abbreviated low-caste nonsense." Then to the shuttle's ceiling he shouted, "This being is now my brother." For emphasis he mashed his palm harder into my face. "He shall serve me in all things and, most of all, in cultivating a spirit of obedience in my wife-to-be." Villainic removed his hand from my face, which was a great mercy, and gave my shoulders a squeeze. Then, with an air of great satisfaction, he threw himself into an empty seat and buckled himself in for the trip home.

Steve walked up to me and put a sympathetic hand on my shoulder. "This also falls in the category of things that only happen to you."

I let out a long sigh. "I was just thinking exactly that."

# CHAPTER TWENTY

When we'd left the compound that afternoon, we'd had Ardov and four peace officers as escorts. We came back with all of them in various states of unconsciousness, injury, frog poisoning, and porcupine-quill impaling. We'd promised to get Junup off the hook, but we'd only succeeded in making him look more guilty. On the other hand, we'd avoided covering up mutiny and murder while simultaneously not giving up the guy who held the keys to our escape plan. We'd managed not to be assassinated. I'd gained an alien sibling, which I suppose you could put in the plus column if you were an optimist. We'd even come home with an extra shuttle. Anyone so inclined could spin this trip as more of a success than a failure, right?

Strangely, some beings were disinclined to see it that way. When we landed, we were greeted with peace officers who put us in plasma restraints. Junup, who also turned out to not be an optimist, demanded that we be marched to his office immediately.

On the way over, Colonel Rage fell in step with me. He leaned in toward me, not the easiest thing in the world when you have plasma restraints pinning your arms behind your back.

"Nice job today, son," he said.

I shrugged. "I find not getting blown up to be a pretty good motivation."

"It's one of the best," he agreed. Then he looked serious. "How'd you do that thing?"

"What thing?" I asked.

"You know what I'm talking about. That leap up to the trap-door of the shuttle."

"I didn't leap. There was a platform that rose up. It happened pretty quickly, so you might have missed it."

He narrowed his eye at me. "Do I look stupid to you, son?"

"I'm not lying to you. I can't jump fifteen feet. There was a platform. Oh, and no, you don't look stupid. I wouldn't want you to think I was diplomatically avoiding answering the question. Scary and impatient, sure, but not stupid."

He shook his head. "We're all in this together. If you've got a line on some alien tech we could use, you need to come clean. The lives of your friends, and the lives of the folks back home, are depending on it."

"I'm not holding anything back," I told him, hoping I sounded earnest.

The colonel did not look satisfied, however. He just shook his head like I'd profoundly disappointed him.

Inside Junup's office, we sat in front of his desk while he leaned over toward us, glaring. He had at least been kind enough to tell the peace officers to remove our restraints. Now he hoped to intimidate us with his angry glare. The thing is, he'd tried to have us killed at least twice, and we all knew it, so an angry look from his shaggy face wasn't going to ratchet things up very much.

"I asked you to do one simple thing," he said, "and you couldn't do it."

"And then you were going to remove us with a tragic shuttle accident," Colonel Rage said, "so forgive us if we don't feel too bad."

"Of course I regret the excess of enthusiasm in some who follow the Movement for Peace," he said. "I assure you, I condemn the use of violence to advance important goals, and I shall make sure the beings involved understand the seriousness of their transgression."

"Don't you think that's a little harsh?" I asked. "I mean, after all, we're only talking about attempted multiple murders. Making them understand seems pretty excessive."

"I would not expect a primitive being like you to comprehend," Junup said. "Ours is a society in transition, and there will always be minor growing pains."

Included among those minor growing pains, apparently, were all of us being marked for death in a fiery explosion.

"I don't want to get into a debate with you," Colonel Rage said. "You're in the driver's seat, and there's not a thing we can do about it, but the longer we're around, the greater the potential for chaos. You want us to stop making trouble? Then let's go back to the stolen-ship plan."

Junup snorted and muttered something under his breath. "Unfortunately, I must agree. Tomorrow afternoon between 1300 and 1500 will be the window. Please take it, and never let me see any of you again."

Villainic rose. "While I appreciate your supplying us with *one* ship for our purposes, I wonder if a second ship might be made available—"

Junup cut him off. "You are the half-wit who ruined the meeting with the chief justice." One of his goat fingers jabbed out menacingly in his direction. "Even Zeke Reynolds wasn't stupid enough to pull a stunt like that. You don't get to ask me anything. Now sit down and be quiet before I think of a reason to have you arrested on espionage charges."

Once Villainic was seated, Junup took a few more minutes to glare at us. "Tomorrow. Make sure there are no more mistakes. Now get out of here." He waved his hand in dismissal.

Colonel Rage stood along with the rest of us, but he met Junup's eye. "What is going to happen to Ardov?"

"What do you mean?" Junup was already busying himself with some holographic texts and acted like he was only half listening.

"He tried to kill us. In our primitive culture, that would result in criminal charges being filed."

"I already told you. I intend to talk to him. Now get out of my office."

"Talk to him," Colonel Rage muttered when we got outside.

"It's not our problem," Mi Sun said. "We're leaving tomorrow."

Charles sighed and looked back at Junup's office, an expression of worry on his face. "Provided we live that long."

We were halfway across the compound when Ardov stepped into our path. To no one's surprise, he looked angry.

"See here, son," the colonel began. "We've all had a long day, and we're not interested in more trouble. How about you go see your boss and find out what he wants from you before you find yourself in hot water?"

Ardov swiped an arm at Colonel Rage, sending him flying into the air. He landed a good twenty feet away from us, landing on the grass and skidding the length of his body before coming to a rest. I glanced over to see him getting up. He looked a little stunned but okay. Mi Sun ran over to make sure he wasn't hurt, so I quickly looked back at Ardov. I didn't want to risk his making any moves while I was distracted.

"I know what the director has in mind for you pathetic group of savages," he said through clenched teeth. "And I agree. The sooner you are all gone, the better. But you," he said, pointing at me, "are not leaving. You are finished. Right now."

I chanced another quick glance at my surroundings. Whatever peace officers had been lurking around before Ardov's attack had now, by pure coincidence, made themselves scarce. The various other citizens were in the process of clearing the grounds, running indoors. It was like when two gunslingers would face off on the main street in the Old West. I was sure those scurrying beings would head to safety somewhere and then press their faces, or whatever they had, against the glass and peer out while Ardov did whatever he planned to do.

Villainic stepped forward. "Before you do something you might regret, please know that I have invoked the right of brotherhood with this being. He is now, legally, my caste-brother, and so any actions taken against him—"

"I'm done with primitive Rarel laws," Ardov said, his voice dripping with contempt. "Do you want to stand between me and that alien?"

Villainic demonstrated the value of his caste-brotherhood by slinking away.

Ardov took another step toward me. "Let's go, Zeke. You and me. Let's finally finish this. We'll see what you can do when you're not hiding behind tricks or PPB pistols."

Steve and Alice were stepping forward to put themselves between me and Ardov. it was a nice thought, especially for Alice, who had no chance against him, but I wasn't going to let anyone fight my battles for me.

"I've got this," I said, though I had no idea how I was going to avoid fighting Ardov or, alternatively, getting pounded by him.

*I don't recommend that you fight this thing,* Smelly chimed in, ever helpful.

"Your skill tree has been maxed out," I said, stalling for time—though I hardly knew what more time would get me. "That doesn't seem fair."

"Too bad for you," he said, advancing on me.

I took a step back and held up my hands. "Hold on one second. Ardov, you and I have had our differences. At times it's seemed like we've been on different sides. But you know, the way I see it, we've always been on the same side. We've always been fighting for the same thing. Don't you get it? We're on the same side."

He looked at me, puzzled and annoyed that I would dare suggest that he and I had anything in common. "What exactly are you talking about?"

Then he fell, face-first, onto the purple grass. He was screaming in pain, clutching at his leg. It was Alice. My little speech about us being on the same side had been a way to keep him distracted as she'd shifted behind him, raised her foot, and planted a powerful kick to the back of his knee. I was no doctor, but the way he was writhing around suggested she must have broken something. With his augmented health, he would likely be up and about again in a few minutes at most, but we'd be gone by then. I had to hope that the humiliation would be enough to get him to keep his distance before we disappeared tomorrow.

Almost everyone had gathered around Alice, who was wiping a mass of white hair from her eyes. She looked shaken and relieved. I knew the feeling all too well—when you walk away from something where you might just have easily been killed.

"That was pretty good," Mi Sun said. "Have you studied any martial arts?"

"I used to take karate," Alice said.

The colonel, a little grass-stained but no worse for wear, was patting her on the back. Charles and Steve were chatting excitedly with her. Even Villainic seemed impressed. Only Tamret stood lightly apart, and she was glaring angrily at Alice.

*Uh-oh,* Smelly said.

I swallowed hard. *Uh-oh* was right. It looked like we now had bigger problems than Ardov getting back on his feet.

# CHAPTER TWENTY-ONE

Somehow we made it through the night without any further antics or assassination attempts or thwarted explosions. Tamret never spoke much when Villainic was around, but her silence seemed even more purposeful than usual at dinner. Several times I noticed her glaring at Alice, who seemed completely oblivious. For her part, Alice didn't want to make too much of having toppled Ardov, but she did want to recount our escape from the shuttle disaster over and over again. I understood how that was. You get through something you think is going to end you, there's a need to turn it into a good story.

After dinner I went down to the sim suites with Steve and Charles and Colonel Rage. The colonel had learned a lot about starship operations in the little time we'd been here. I thought that was good, though his attitude still scared me.

"We're not going to be done with these people," he told me when we were finished and heading back to our rooms. "Earth's going to have to face them sooner or later, and we're going to have to beat them at their own game."

I hated how the colonel kept envisioning Earth being at odds with the Confederation. Based on what he'd seen, I supposed I couldn't really blame him. Still, it made me sad to think that the adult who was going to be considered the expert on the Confederation saw this society as dangerous and unreliable. I had loved Confederation Central: the beings I'd met here, the incredible potential and opportunity it represented. I refused to believe that a being like Junup could corrupt all of that.

What chance was there to save the Confederation, though, if no one stood up to him? Dr. Roop had told me what we needed to do, and we were all too selfish to do it. We were ready to steal a ship and run away for home. We were prepared to let Junup turn the Confederation into something ugly and horrible.

I felt about as torn as I ever had, caught between my two choices, both of which were right, between two obligations equally strong. No matter how things went, I was going to feel miserable.

The next morning's breakfast also went off without disaster or near-death experiences. We were on a roll. Tamret still looked angry or suspicious or something, but I couldn't worry about that now. Everyone was tense. This was the big day. Given how we'd almost been killed on our last excursion, I thought there was a certain amount of justifiable nervousness about today's trip. Nevertheless, things had gone pretty horribly since leaving home, and the prospect of being done with this place had everyone a little animated.

I wanted to make one last plea for Dr. Roop's Hidden Fortress scheme, but I sensed that it was the wrong time—not that there was ever going to be a right time. If we got on the shuttle later that day, and if we managed to get out of the Confederation Central system, then it would be too late. Maybe once we were on the shuttle and could go anywhere. There had to be an opportunity to convince everyone that it was worthwhile to fight for what was best about the Confederation. I promised myself that I would make the case again before we left.

We had just finished eating when my bracelet chimed with a message. *Same place as before. Right now. Qapla'!* The Klingon word was obviously meant as a kind of code. Besides me—and now, maybe, Charles—the only person on Confederation Central who would even know about Klingon was Dr. Roop, which was kind of crazy, because I'd just been thinking of him that moment. Maybe he would have something to say to help me convince the others, I thought. Even better, maybe he would tell me he no longer needed me to go to the Forbidden Zone. It would be nice, I thought, to be off the hook for once.

I blurted out a lame and rambling excuse and hurried off to the Peripheral Tower. I was through security and on the elevator about ten minutes after getting the message, and Dr. Roop was waiting for me, crouched in the shadows behind one of the walls. I could barely see his stubby antlers sticking out.

"Don't come any closer," he said, as soon as I stepped out onto the roof. "I think they may have surveillance drones watching me. If you stay there, they won't see you, so they won't know who I'm meeting with."

"Why did you risk coming here?" I asked, sounding a little hysterical. The last thing I wanted was to see Dr. Roop arrested. "You can't put yourself in danger like this."

"I'm afraid what I have to say is too important to wait. I have contacts within the government, and I know about the offer Junup made you. I know what you think is going to happen today."

"You're going to tell me not to go," I said. "I tried to sell the others on finding the skill tree, but they wouldn't go for it. They want to go home. I really want to help you, Dr. Roop—I want to help the Confederation—but I can't force the others to go along with me."

"I understand that," he said, "but if you board that vessel, you won't go anywhere. Junup plans to have fully armed ships waiting for you as soon as you are out of visual range of the station. He's not going to risk your popping up again. He means to kill all of you, and this time he won't let anything go wrong."

I swallowed hard. "We were actually planning on using the ship he's selected as a decoy and taking another ship."

"That's clever, but it won't work. He knows about your plan, and he'll be watching all departures closely. He'll figure out which ship is yours without any difficulty."

I tried to process what Dr. Roop was telling me. If Junup knew about our plan, that meant that somehow he had been able to listen in on our conversations, or that, worse, we had a spy in our midst.

"You must trust me," Dr. Roop said. "If you try to leave on his terms, you'll die."

"We'll just have to leave on different terms, then."

Dr. Roop shook his head. "If you don't go during the time he's arranged, he'll know you are onto him, and he'll have no choice but to deal with you internally. You and your friends are resourceful, and you've been lucky so far, but sooner or later Junup is going to win, and in the end you will either be in prison or dead. You know what I think is the right thing, but you also know I would not lie to you. In my estimation, you have but one option."

"You want me to take the ship and, instead of escaping from the station, go in search of the skill tree."

"It's your only chance," he said. "Once you enter the Forbidden Zone, Junup's forces will be unable to pursue you."

That was the upside. The downside was that the reason they couldn't pursue us would be because the zone in which we'd be hiding would be of the forbidden variety. They usually don't forbid zones because they're full of gummy worms and video games.

"And then what?" I asked. "Let's say we enter the Forbidden Zone and find the skill tree. What do we do with it?"

"My research suggests that there are several ancient ship docks in the Forbidden Zone, including one under the station's surface. That is to say, if you find the Hidden Fortress, you will find both the skill tree and a means of escape. The ships there should be operational. I've arranged for one of my associates to provide you with coordinates to a safe haven, a planet where the resistance has established a command post. Get the software to them, and they will make sure it gets into proper hands within the Confederation. But dress warmly. This planet is extremely cold."

"The rebel base is on an ice planet?" I asked, thinking this was a little too close to *The Empire Strikes Back*.

"Yes. I find wearing multiple layers to be most effective."

"I'm going to have to convince the others to go along with this," I said. "They're all pretty much sold on going home."

"They can't," he said, the sadness evident in his voice. "Not right away. Junup won't let that happen. He will not let you live, because he thinks that, no matter what, you will rebel against his authority. Ironically, in order to survive, you must do just that."

"And how do I convince everyone that they need to become rebels?"

"Most of them know me. The former delegates know I would not deceive any of you."

"Colonel Rage will never go for it. He'll say that you're manipulating us into doing what you wanted us to do all along."

"I understand how a cynic might suspect that," he said. "I hope that, among the rest, my past actions will give you cause to trust me one last time."

To be sure, it was good enough for me. If Dr. Roop said that Junup planned to kill us, there was no way I was going to try to escape the station on Junup's terms.

Dr. Roop's bracelet chimed. He glanced at a message, then looked up. His eyes were wide and startled. "They've found me. You need to go right now."

"I can't just leave you."

"I'm afraid you must," he said. "You can't help me here, and everything is depending on you now. Run, Zeke!"

I hated to abandon him, but I didn't see that I had a choice. I had to get the information about Junup's plan to the others, or Dr. Roop would have put himself at risk for nothing. On the elevator down, I told myself that maybe he was mistaken. Maybe he hadn't really been discovered.

As soon as I got outside, I backed up far enough so I could see the roof, and there he was, a distant image, surrounded by peace officers on either side. They closed in on him. I could barely discern Dr. Roop dodging between them, zigzagging like a football player desperate to avoid a tackle. He faked his way through a trio of advancing peace officers in a mad dash, but I couldn't figure out his plan. Where did he hope to go? How was he going to get away?

Then, helplessly, I stared in horror as I realized what he

intended. He drove toward the edge of the roof. Dr. Roop believed in his cause, in his rebellion, so much that he would embrace death rather than be captured. Unable to turn away, I saw him leap over the wall to the commercial side of the building. I caught a brief glimpse of his form, arms and legs waving wildly, as he plummeted toward the ground, and then, mercifully, he fell out of sight.

# CHAPTER TWENTY-TWO

gathered everyone together in an open part of the lawn. I'd managed to stop crying at that point, and something else was taking its place.

Dr. Roop was right. Junup was not going to let us live. He was going to kill us all, unless we fought back, unless we became rebels. Dr. Roop was dead, and I would mourn him properly later, but now I didn't have time to be sad. I only had time for anger.

As soon as everyone was there, I tried to begin speaking, but my throat caught.

"What's wrong, Zeke?" Alice asked. "You look like you've been crying."

There was nothing to do but launch into it. I took a deep breath in the hopes of steadying my voice. I needed to sound calm and rational. I had to convince them that I was right.

"Dr. Roop is dead," I told them. "He was trying to get away from the peace officers, but there was nowhere for him to go. He threw himself off the roof of that building rather than be captured."

Charles called up his keyboard and began typing furiously. "You must be mistaken. I've been monitoring the news outputs, and I have not seen anything about this. It is a busy street over there. If someone had fallen, it would cause quite a sensation."

"I saw it myself," I said. "They're covering it up."

"Did you speak with him?" Mi Sun asked quietly.

"Yeah. He came to warn me. Junup's plan is a trap. If we try to get off the station, on his ship or any other, he plans to kill us."

"If we refuse to go," Colonel Rage said, "then Junup will believe we've thrown down the gauntlet, and he'll come down on us legally or find some other way for us to have a convincing accident."

"If we do what he wants, we're going to end up dead or in prison," I insisted. "It's time to stop trying to work with him. We have to work against him."

"It is only the ones from Earth he wants, not us," said Villainic, gesturing toward himself and Tamret. "And also that reptilian fellow over there. We're not part of your spaceship mishap. He shall likely let us return to our home worlds."

"Not being from Earth didn't help us much yesterday," Steve said. "By now, he'll figure we know what they know, which means he won't be too keen on us. I wouldn't count on any transportation that Junup arranges getting to where it is supposed to go in a safe and orderly fashion. Besides which," he added, "we don't run out on our mates."

I watched Villainic, now supposedly my brother, and without a doubt he looked agitated. If Junup knew we intended to switch spaceships, it meant someone had told him about our plans. My list of suspects was exactly one Rarel long. Maybe after he'd blown the meeting with the chief justice, Villainic had thought he needed to do something to assure that he would be able to get off the station alive. I didn't care about Villainic's reasons, even if he had turned on the rest of us because he wanted to save Tamret. We were all supposed to look after one another, not pick and choose.

"If we can't go through with the plan, then what's our move?" Alice asked.

"The Forbidden Zone." I told them about Dr. Roop's proposal: how finding the hidden skill tree would also lead us to ships we could use to escape.

"I don't see why Tamret and I should have to risk ourselves for this civilization that means nothing to us," Villainic said. "I came here to provide an escort to my betrothed, not to run about and solve problems for aliens. Your plan, Zeke, involves far too many unknowns."

"What's not unknown is what will happen to us if we do what Junup wants us to do. If we walk into his trap, we're finished."

"That is hardly certain," Villainic said. "We just have your friend's word for that."

"I do not doubt Dr. Roop," Charles said, folding his arms.

"Dr. Roop wouldn't lie about something like this," Mi Sun agreed. "He just died so he could warn us that we're in danger."

"There's no debate," Steve added. "If he said it was the only way, and he gave his life to tell us that, then it seems to me that we do things his way."

"I have never met him," Villainic said. "I cannot offer my opinion."

"Looks like you're doing plenty of that, mate," Steve said.

Colonel Rage had been silent until now, taking all of this in. I'd been wondering which way he was leaning. Now he finally spoke up. "I've never met this Dr. Roop either, but I know all of you, and it carries a lot of weight that those of you who know him trust him completely. I'll be honest with you: His fight is not mine. My responsibility is to get you kids home and bring whatever alien tech I can find with me. If there's no other way to do that, and it's looking like there isn't, I'm prepared to follow Zeke's advice and find this skill tree." He looked directly at me. "You have a plan, son?"

"We still have to take that ship in about three hours," I said, "and we have to go somewhere. We can't leave the station, or they'll have us. On the other hand, they can't catch us if we can get to the Forbidden Zone."

"Once we get there," the colonel said, "finding these ships is our priority. If we see a chance to get away, that takes precedence over finding this lost software."

"No," I answered, hearing the anger in my voice. "We came back here to help Ghli Wixxix protect the Confederation. Because we were willing to listen to her request, Junup has killed a lot of people, three of whom were close friends. I don't want them to have died for nothing, and I don't want Junup to win. He wants to keep us from completing Ghli Wixxix's mission so badly; I say that's reason enough to make sure we get the job done."

"That's the anger talking," Colonel Rage said.

"Yes," I agreed. "It is."

"Anyone else want to offer an opinion?" Colonel Rage asked, and when Villainic started to speak, he snapped, "Anyone but you."

"I'm not really one of you," Alice said, "so I'm sorry if this is ignorant, but it seems to me that Junup is pretty good at rigging the game. If we try to go somewhere other than the spaceport with this stolen shuttle, how do we know he won't apprehend us or shoot us down?"

"That's a good point," Mi Sun said.

I nodded. "Yeah, it is. I think I have a work-around, but it's ugly and messy."

"I like it so far," Steve said. "Let's hear it."

"I think I should sit on it until the time is right," I told him with what I hope was a pointed glance. "Dr. Roop thinks Junup learned about the plan to steal two ships. Maybe it's best not to take any chances."

Both Steve and the colonel seemed to understand my point. They looked over at Villainic.

"Understood," the colonel said. "Let's establish shifts to make sure no one gets too lonely."

And just like that it was decided. One of us would keep an eye on Villainic at all times until we left.

As soon as we stood up, Villainic came over to me, with Tamret standing a deferential distance behind him. "I want you to know that while I respect your desire to honor your friend's memory, we will not be departing with you. I have decided that we will stay and take our chances with Junup."

I couldn't allow that. I'd already promised Tamret that I'd help her escape Rarel, and there was no way I was going to abandon her again. Besides, the minute we were gone, there would be nothing to stop Villainic from telling Junup everything he'd found out.

"That's not possible," I said to him. "We all go."

"I state my firm position as your brother, so you must honor my wishes."

"No," I said, meeting his gaze. "I mustn't."

"Have you forgotten that you performed the rite of brother-hood?"

"I didn't perform anything. One minute we were talking, the next you were shoving your fingers up my nose."

Tamret stepped forward. "If he didn't understand the nature of the ritual, then it doesn't count."

Villainic turned to her. "Be reasonable, Tamret. You know I didn't give you permission to speak."

"Surely there is no harm in my talking to my future *brother-in-law*."

"Well, Zeke will qualify as extended family after we're married, but until then, conversation is still at my discretion. I have been forgiving so far, but if this continues, I'm going to have to get stern with you."

I moved closer to Villainic. "You touch her, you're going to spend the rest of your life eating out of a straw."

Villainic held up his hands. "Zeke, my brother. Where is this hostility coming from?"

"It's coming from me refusing to let you hurt Tamret."

"Hurt her?" he asked, genuinely incredulous. "I was speaking of punishments, not inflicting harm. Do you forget that I have agreed to marry her? I don't think you understand what I've done to help her."

"I understand that she's not allowed to speak to her friends, and now you're threatening her."

"I want her to be respected and successful in our social circles," Villainic said. "I don't think that's wishing her ill."

"I get that you have your traditions," I said, "but maybe for the rest of the time we're here on Confederation Central, it would be easier if you were a little more relaxed about the rules."

"Of course," he said, waving his hands wildly. "That's a

wonderful idea. I say, let's take off all our clothes and start eating Rarel flesh. Who's with me?"

"What's this about eating flesh?" Steve asked, walking up to us.

"Zeke wants us to be naked cannibals," Villainic said.

"I really, really don't want that," I said. "What I want is for Tamret to be able to talk to me without you butting in."

"I speak for both of us. I can't understand why Tamret's silence is so troubling to you."

"Because the last time Tamret and I spent any time together, we did a lot of crazy, impossible stuff, and we survived. A big part of that was our ability to talk to each other without you sticking your snout between us."

"Snout?" Tamret repeated, folding her arms.

Steve touched the side of his mouth. "What's wrong with having a snout, flat face?"

"There is nothing wrong with a snout, as long as it's not in the middle of my business!" I just about shouted.

"Though you are my brother," Villainic said, "it almost seems that you don't understand some very basic things. Tamret doesn't have any business that is not also mine."

"She does if we want to avoid getting killed," I told him. "And I don't care how many times you mash my face with your palm, you are not my brother."

Villainic took a step back. "Not your brother? But we performed the ritual."

"I don't care about your ritual, but that's the least of the reasons why you are not my brother. Topping the list is the fact that I don't like you and I don't trust you. You're a domineering jerk who doesn't understand that trying to micromanage

Tamret's every conversation is not only cruel, but is going to get us all killed—just like Urch and Dr. Roop and Nayana. Nayana, by the way, who Tamret made *her* sister. She did it without any weird face grabbing, and it actually meant something. They looked after each other. You didn't know the people we lost, and it's clear you don't care, but they were my friends, and Nayana was Tamret's family. Now they're dead because we have some real enemies with real power coming for us, so you need to stop getting in our way."

"It seems to me that they're all dead because *you* have some real enemies," Villainic said, folding his arms and raising his chin in triumph. "Not us. *You*. And knowing that everything bad that has happened is your fault, I still chose to show my gratitude by making you my brother, and this is how you thank me?"

I stepped forward and jabbed him in the chest with a finger. He'd crossed a line. "Your pal Junup is responsible for their deaths. Him, and anyone who works with him. You try to say it's my fault again, you'll regret it."

Villainic took a step back. "I'm sorry if my perspective is so distasteful to you. I thought that, perhaps, after all we've been through, you would be interested in my opinion."

"I'm interested in your doing what I tell you. Otherwise we're going to leave you behind. Not you and Tamret. Just you. Do you understand me?"

Villainic stared at me, and I swear he looked like he was going to cry.

"He wants to know if you understand him, mate," Steve said, his voice surprisingly quiet and all the more imposing for it.

Villainic gave a single nod and turned away. His shoulders

were hunched, and he seemed to be shaking. I didn't like the guy—in fact, I kind of hated his guts—but I hadn't meant to break him.

I started to walk away, to give Villainic some privacy while he picked up the pieces of his broken dignity, but Tamret came after me. I thought maybe she wanted to thank me, but it turned out I'd misread yet another situation.

"You didn't have to do that," Tamret said, her voice hard.

That pretty much took care of my regret. "Are you serious? The guy treats you like you're his property."

"Because I *am*, according to our law," she said. "You may not like it, and nether do I, but he's a lot nicer to me than he has to be. He's no one's idea of a hero, but in his own way he wants what's best for me. There's no need to humiliate him."

"I can't believe you're defending him. He's so . . . bossy."

"He saved me from a whole lot worse than being bossed around when there was no one else standing up for me. The way I remember it, *you* promised to be there for me, but you were nowhere to be found. I guess you were too busy with your new friend over there." She flicked her hand toward Alice and walked off to go speak to Villainic.

I stood there, stunned. The last thing I wanted was to fight with Tamret, and if I was going to fight with her about something, I sure didn't want it to be about Villainic. I knew I should say something to smooth things over, but she'd stung me about as hard as she could have. I had not been there for her. Villainic had been. Maybe I had no right to judge him.

I was furious with her and with myself. I wanted to curl up in a ball and cry and let someone else make the hard decisions for once. Why couldn't Colonel Rage take charge? Tamret had already walked away from me and was now talking quietly to Villainic. I felt the breaths coming hot into my nose, and I snorted them out again like a dragon.

Somehow, impossibly, I shoved my feelings down. I buried them for another time. I stepped forward and gently put my fingers on her arm.

"Listen," I said, "I wish things could have been different."

She shrugged me off. "I'm having a private conversation right now. Can you give us some space?"

So much for burying feelings. I bit back a thousand rejoinders. There was just too much at stake right now. "Fine," I said. "Just play your emotional games on your own time. I need you to bring your A game when things get serious."

"You don't have to worry about that," she said, but she wouldn't meet my eye.

I turned away from them. Steve came up to me. "One of us will be on Villainic until go time. He won't be sending any secret messages to anyone."

I let out a breath. The last thing I wanted to do now was shadow them around. "Thanks, Steve. That helps."

"That's what mates are for," he said.

He moved off to stand near Villainic and Tamret, and he looked about as natural as a necktie on a platypus, but I didn't care. It didn't matter if Villainic suspected we were onto him as long as he didn't communicate with Junup.

I looked away and saw a bush waving at me from across the lawn. I rushed over to talk to it.

"You heard, bro?" it asked sadly.

I nodded. "Yeah. I can't believe it."

"He was, like, amazing," the bush said sadly. "But he knew

the risks. He did what was right because he had to. I hope you'll do the same." It reached out with one of its branches and touched my data bracelet. A string of numbers flashed and then vanished into an unnamed file. The screen prompted me to give it a name.

"Nothing too obvious, in case you're captured."

"What is it?" I asked.

"The map Dr. Roop told you about. You'll need to decrypt it, but don't even try until you're where, you know, you won't be followed. Good luck to you, Zeke. We're all counting on you."

I named the file MATH PROBLEMS and closed it and nodded at the bush, but it was already walking away.

I was sitting on my bed, waiting for it to be time to leave, when Steve came into the room, followed by Mi Sun, Charles, and Alice. Our rooms had come stocked with a wide variety of clothes, and we all wore heavy pants, long-sleeved shirts, and sturdy boots, which I hoped would be comfortable for wilderness trekking. Our bags were already packed, and Steve told me he had stuffed his with packages of nutritional paste and condensed moisture from one of the compound stores. Smart move, I thought. They probably didn't have restaurants in the Forbidden Zone.

"I'm glad you thought of that," I told him.

"It was Alice's idea," he said. "She's the only one who hasn't gotten used to being handed everything we need while we're here."

Alice shrugged. "Back before things got bad for him, my dad used to take me camping all the time."

I nodded, trying to tamp down the panic as I realized we'd almost traveled into the unknown without basic provisions.

We were rushing into this. What else hadn't we thought of? Everything was happening too quickly.

As if reading my mind, Steve said, "Could be we're being played, mate?"

"I've just been thinking about that, but . . ." I paused, remembering that we were probably being bugged. "Unless our old associate turned evil while we were gone, I don't see how that's possible."

Steve ran his fingers from the tip of his nose to the base of his neck. It was probably his species' equivalent of scratching his head. "That's the trouble, yeah? I keep thinking in circles. I can't see any other option than what we're planning. I guess that's what makes me wonder. It's like we're being pushed in this one direction."

"Whatever comes, we shall deal with it," Charles said. "As we always have."

"Like Nayana always did?" Mi Sun demanded. "She was doing her best to survive, and she didn't make it. The same with Urch and . . . and the other being. There's no guarantee we're going to get through this."

"I know," I said. "But there is a guarantee that we're in real trouble if we don't try."

"You guys are such complainers," Alice said.

We all stared at her. I couldn't believe what I was hearing. "They weren't your friends. You didn't know them."

"I don't mean that. Of course what happened to them is terrible. No, I didn't know them like you guys did, and I get your grief. I know what it is to lose people. But there are huge things happening, and you are lucky enough to be at the middle of all of it. You guys matter."

"We're not going to matter if we're dead."

"Yeah," Alice said, "you will. You've already changed the galaxy. Do you even *hear* those words? You, Mi Sun, have changed the *galaxy*. I don't think you realize how important you are. I've spent my whole life wishing I could do something significant."

I looked over at Alice, standing with her hands on her hips, looking determined and steady. There was something comforting about having someone like her around. She wasn't unpredictable the way Tamret was, but she was still courageous and resourceful. She was also, I realized, very pretty.

*Are you kidding me!* Smelly shouted inside my head. *Pupils dilating! Respiration and heart rate accelerating. You don't have enough problems? Snap out of it, Romeo. Keep your eye on the ball or we're going to be toast.*

Smelly was, of course, correct. I had to focus on what mattered, and that meant getting everyone through what came next. I'd deal with my personal drama later.

I checked the time and stood up. "If you want to do something significant," I told Alice, "then this is your lucky day."

Colonel Rage, who had taken the last spying shift, was waiting with Tamret and Villainic on the front lawn. Tamret and the colonel both had the same stony expression of grim determination. Villainic looked like he was seriously considering having an accident in his trousers.

"There's a lot that needs to get done," the colonel said to all of us, "and most of it is reckless. Also, most of it rests on your shoulders. I've spent as much time as I could in the sims, but you kids know the terrain and the technology better than I do. I'll chip in as much as I can, but Steve, you're taking the lead on theft and piloting. Zeke, you're on vehicle weapons. As for me, I'm going to grab the first pistol I can get hold of, and if I have to take a blast for one of you, then that's what I'm going to do. These people are trying to get away with murder, injustice, imprisonment, and a coup. Let's go make their lives miserable."

It would have been conspicuous for us to cheer, so we all nodded. The truth is, when you're going on a crazy, possibly suicidal mission against a galactic superpower, it's kind of comforting to have an adult around to tell you what to do.

The colonel and Steve pushed forward to walk at the front of the group. I decided to take the rear, and allowed myself to drift behind. As the Rarels moved ahead of me, Tamret took hold of my hand. It was brief—over in the blink of an eye—and she didn't even look at me while doing it, but it fired up my courage. Tamret had said some things that had hurt me, and her defense of Villainic still stung, but she was reminding me that we were in this together.

We approached the transport-shuttle dock. There were two peace officers on duty and one technician. They looked at us and perhaps, for a second, did not see a swaggering band of outlaws come to do something totally illegal.

"This area is off-limits for you," a turquoise-skinned humanoid peace officer said. Her eyestalks widened and moved slightly toward us. Her partner, an alien who looked like a big cockroach with silver fur, waggled one of its many appendages toward its pistol. I think it was trying to look menacing, but mostly it looked gross.

It all happened so quickly. Mi Sun kicked the blue peace officer in the face and then leapt back. Steve, meanwhile, leaped into the air and grabbed the big cockroach's head, or headlike area, or whatever, knocking the alien into the wall. The cockroach slid down, and a second later Mi Sun's blue combatant fell. They were both out cold. Colonel Rage grabbed the PPB pistol from the first fallen officer and fired it at the technician.

"Tamret, you're up." he said.

She accessed the transport dock's computer and began typing furiously. "They've upgraded security since the last time we were here."

"Does that mean you can't get in?" Charles asked.

"Please," Tamret said as her fingers danced over the console. "I'm just laughing at them if they think this is going to slow me down. Okay, we're good." There were transport shuttles docked on the platform. She pointed to the one on the far left. "That one."

"I think Junup told us to take the one in the middle," Charles said.

"Yes, he did," she agreed. "And I'm telling you to take the one on the left, so who are you going to listen to?"

She had a good point. The shuttle Junup had selected for us might be rigged to explode or crash. Maybe he never intended for us to get to the spaceport in the first place. On the other hand, if Junup had intended to get us into space before he eliminated us, he might have had some adjustments made to the middle shuttle that would make it easier to steal or harder to detect. There was no way to know, but at this point, mistrusting Junup seemed like the safer bet.

Once we were inside, Steve took the helm, and the rest of us simply strapped in. Transport shuttles had no weapons systems, so we had to hope no one tried to shoot us down. There wasn't a lot we could do if they tried.

Steve liked to pilot fast and recklessly, but this time he took off slowly and eased himself into the clearly established flight patterns over the city. "Just out for a friendly drive," he told us. "Nothing special here." I had no doubt he wanted to bank hard and begin buzzing past buildings and zipping between other shuttles, but he kept his cool. There would be plenty of time for recklessness later.

It took us about twenty minutes to get to the spaceport. We passed a peace-officer patrol, but it didn't give us a second look. At least so far, Junup was as good as his word that no one would bother us.

We took a spot in what was, for all practical purposes, a transport-shuttle parking lot, and then took a train to a central hub that connected all of the various terminals. Once there, we followed the signs for our dock, which involved taking another train and then several plasma-field rising walkways, which were essentially glowing blue escalators. I still kept my eye out for any beings who might be pointing and shouting, but like airports back home, the spaceport was crowded with beings who were too busy trying to get from one place to another to worry themselves too much with anyone else.

When we reached the ship docking area, we had to study a map and then make our way through a series of massive corridors, each the size of a gigantic warehouse. At long last we came to our aisle, a half-mile stretch of space garages. We found our particular garage and then rode an elevating plasma field about three hundred feet to reach it. We punched in the codes that Junup had given us, and the containment door opened to our ship's individual garage.

The ship was nothing much—a standard boxy artifact carrier

with minimal weaponry—but it was our ticket to getting out from under Junup's control, though maybe not in quite the way he intended.

The way it was supposed to work was that we would get into the ship, pressurize it, close the hall door, depressurize the compartment, and then open the space door. Pretty basic, really. We had no intention of doing that, though, since we had no intention of going into space.

We got into the ship, which had a layout not so different from that of the shuttle. It was a little cramped and utilitarian, with control consoles and just enough seating for all of us. I told everyone to take their seats, and just like in the old days Steve and Tamret sat up front to operate the vehicle.

Villainic hovered near us. "I wish to be next to Tamret," he said.

"Sit down!" Colonel Rage barked.

Villainic slinked to the back and strapped in.

"I've downloaded the coordinates for our home worlds to my data bracelet," Tamret said, "so that's one less thing to worry about. Now I'm going through the ship's systems. If there's any sabotage, they've hidden it from the onboard computer."

"Does that mean we're safe?" I asked.

"Everything is integrated," she said. "If they tinker with one system, there's no way the others won't detect it. Unless they've strapped a bomb to the hull, I think we can assume the ship is fully functional and properly operational."

"How do weapons look?" Steve asked.

"Some light PPB power," I said, "which is what we expected, and a targeted laser drill. I think this is some kind of adapted mining ship. We'd be worthless in any kind of space battle, but

I think this will do for our purposes. As near as I can tell without testing, we should be able to cause some damage."

"Time to test it, then," Steve said. He fired up the engines. A warning light flashed, telling us that it was improper procedure to start engines before closing the port-side door. It began to close the door for us, but Tamret broke into the system and shut it down.

"This might get bumpy," Steve said. "Also, things could explode." He then began, ever so slowly, to back us into the hall.

Steve slowly reversed the ship and then turned it to face the length of the hallway. There was barely enough room to do what we were attempting. Steve brushed up against the wall, but I'd already activated light shielding. That meant the wall began to crack, but the ship was fine.

Villainic's jaw dropped as he watched our progress through the viewscreen. "You are going the wrong way!"

"We thought we'd take a detour," I told him.

"You did not inform me about this!" he shouted.

"We might have discussed a few details privately," I explained.

We hovered for a moment in the corridor, our ship too big for the space we were inhabiting. We were like a dinosaur in a bathroom. Down at the far end of the hallway, beings were panicking, rushing to get out of our way.

I looked at Steve. "Do you think this is a wise course of action?"

Charles leaned forward from the back, having recognized the dialogue prompt from *Star Trek: Nemesis*. "We're about to find out!" He was surprisingly cheerful given that we were about to do something monumentally dangerous.

"I guess we are," Steve said. He eased forward at the slowest possible speed. Which, I should point out, was incredibly fast when you're inside a building and not in the vacuum of space.

We were down the hall and out into the atrium so quickly I couldn't even follow it. I felt like I'd left my stomach back in the holding bay. We were now moving through a massive open area. Below us were countless beings, pointing upward, scrambling for cover. A cluster of peace officers rushed from one place to another, but I had no idea what they thought they could do. Whatever it was, it was going to be too late.

"Hang on!" Steve shouted, unable to disguise his glee. He pointed the nose of the ship upward toward the building's glass dome. Then, without warning, we were racing upward. We struck through the glass, which shattered around us, raining down to the atrium below. We were free of the building, out in the open atmosphere of the station, and heading toward the Forbidden Zone.

"It's farther from the compound than any of us have ever been," Steve said. "About sixty miles. ETA three minutes."

We flew high, closer to the space dome than transports tended to go, mostly so we wouldn't cause an accident. A couple of times we passed peace officers and security patrols, but by the time they could even turn around to face us, we were impossibly distant.

The comm console chimed. "Message coming in," I told Steve.

Junup's face appeared on the main communication screen. "You're going the wrong way," he said.

"Wait. What?" I said, affecting confusion.

"Zeke, I don't know what you think you're doing, but it's a bad idea."

"So you think it would be a good idea to head into your trap?" I asked.

"My trap?" He seemed incredulous. "I didn't want to trap you. I wanted to get rid of you. Do you have any idea what you've done?"

"We broke the roof of the spaceport. That's going to be a pain to fix. And it looks like rain."

"You've forced my hand. Now I have to deal with you with the public watching."

"Give it a rest, Junup," I said. "I know you planned to ambush us the minute we were out of range."

"Who told you that?"

"Dr. Roop," I said with a vindictive sneer.

"Roop? How would he know anything?"

"If he was so ignorant, why did your men force him off that roof?"

"What roof? You're out of your mind, Zeke."

"I don't think we're getting anything out of him but lies," the colonel said. "He's just a distraction."

I killed the transmission. If he was going to pretend Dr. Roop hadn't died, when I'd witnessed it with my own eyes, then there was no point in trying to trick truths out of him.

"That doesn't look too inviting," Steve said.

I looked up at the main viewscreen. "Is that the Forbidden Zone?" I asked.

"Afraid so," Steve said.

It was huge, spreading out for miles and miles, hot and reflective and uninviting. It undulated with shifting hills and swirling storms. The Forbidden Zone was a vast and mountain-ous desert, and we were betting our lives that it would provide a way off the station.

# CHAPTER TWENTY-THREE

**W**hy even bother to forbid it?" Alice asked. "It might as well be called the Zone You Don't Want to Go to Anyhow."

"Except we're barmy enough to make that our destination," Steve said. "I'm going to set us down as close to the entrance as possible."

"Why not fly over?" the colonel said. "Perform some recon?"

"This particular zone," Steve said, "is of the forbidden variety. The field that keeps Confederation citizens from entering also produces an electromagnetic pulse into the airspace. If we fly over it, we'll crash."

"Let's not fly over it," I said.

"I'm for landing," Steve said.

"Good idea," I told him.

We set down the ship about a quarter mile from the Forbidden Zone entrance, gathered our supplies, and began to march toward the last place any of us wanted to go.

The area just outside the Forbidden Zone may not have been forbidden, but it wasn't particularly welcoming either. It was a lot of scrub and loose stone, but it was still a lot more hospitable than the rolling dunes and gigantic outcroppings of rock that lay before us. The air here was already much warmer than Confederation Central standard, but at least the surrounding terrain was deserted, which meant no one was trying to kill us. Yet.

Everyone grabbed their packs, and we began moving toward the desert. No one had to state the obvious—that Junup's peace officers would know where we had gone, and that they would be hot on our heels. We had to get across the border before they overtook us. If we didn't, all of this would have been for nothing.

"How do we find what we're looking for?" Alice asked as we trudged along. "There's miles and miles of desert out there."

"I have a map," I said.

I opened up the file the bush had given me. It was encrypted with a series of questions that only I was supposed to be able to answer. I had to input the classic seven-hero Justice League lineup, the serial number of the *Enterprise* from *Next Generation*, and the names of all the actors who'd played the Doctor. I struggled—understandably, I think—with number seven, but then typed in Sylvester McCoy, and all was good. A rough map resolved. It wasn't long on detail, but it would get us moving in the right direction. I hoped.

Everyone peered at the map projecting from my data bracelet.

"That looks pretty vague," said the colonel.

"Um, yeah," agreed Alice. "I'm not sure I'd have signed off on the plan if I'd known this was all we had to go on."

I couldn't argue with what they were saying. "Dr. Roop thought this would be enough. If he didn't think we could find it, he wouldn't have sent us." I took a look at the skies behind us. Still no sign of pursuit.

*I can help you find the fortress,* Smelly said.

I'd told Dr. Roop about Smelly. Had he known the AI

would be able to help us? Was that why he hadn't bothered to tell me more? Or maybe the fortress would be so easy to find that it would soon become obvious why we hadn't been given explicit instructions.

I was lost in these thoughts as we walked, and then, suddenly we were at the point where the open area of the station ended and the restricted area began.

The boundary to the Forbidden Zone was a thick green line painted across the ground, partially covered with drifting piles of sand. Every few feet were signs warning us that we could not cross. It sort of reminded me of Area 51.

"What happens if we step over the line and explode?" Mi Sun asked.

"That would be bad?" I suggested.

"She raises an excellent point," Villainic said. "It may not be safe. I strongly urge that we turn ourselves back in to Junup and beg for his mercy."

I didn't say anything. I didn't want to strain things any more than I had to with Tamret. I hoped one of the others would pick up the slack for me.

"It is well for you to say," Charles told him. "You are still hoping to be sent back to your world with no consequences. You've already seen Junup attempt to kill you, and yet you don't learn. But now you're one of us. You've stolen a shuttle, and there is no way to go but forward." And so saying, Charles stepped over the line.

And he exploded. There was a bright flash of light, and then a plume of ashes mushroomed in the air as fragments of what had once been Charles drifted upward.

*I'm totally messing with you,* Smelly said.

Before I had a chance to react to Charles exploding, my vision changed, and there he was, on the other side of the line, shrugging.

"Don't ever do that!" I shouted, before I could control myself.

"Someone had to go," Charles said, looking at me like I was crazy.

Mi Sun put a hand on my shoulder as she walked past me. "Chill," she said, and she stepped over the line.

She did not explode. I gritted my teeth. My heart was still pounding, and my stomach was somewhere up in my throat. I tasted sharp bile on my tongue. Nothing to do, I decided, but to keep going. I stepped over the line.

It was instantly forty degrees warmer. Forget warmer. *Hotter.* I felt the sun beating down on my neck, and the glare hurt my eyes. My mouth felt dry, my skin dusty. I would have given anything to still have my climate-controlled supersuit.

Villainic folded his arms. "I am not going, and neither is Tamret. We'll find another way."

Tamret looked at us. She looked at Villainic. She stepped over the line.

Villainic opened his mouth. He closed it again. He then stammered a little. Finally he graduated to coherent words. "You have just directly disobeyed me."

"We have to help our friends. You said that Zeke is your brother now. Are you going to abandon him?"

Villainic did a bit more stammering here. "He does not choose to side with me, so I feel no obligation to side with him. I don't want to have to command you to come with me," he added, his voice sounding like an exasperated parent.

Tamret met his gaze. "Then don't."

Villainic sighed. He turned around and looked at the rough land behind him, and the city in the distance. Then he glanced up at the jagged line of arid mountains before him. He sighed again, and he stepped over the line.

"We shall speak of this again," he told her.

"Yeah, I kind of figured," she said.

We stood for a moment, no one saying anything. At least the spat between Tamret and Villainic had helped get the sight of Charles exploding out of my head. I shrugged, looked at the impossible expanse of desert, and began to walk forward. A beat later everyone followed, none of us knowing what we were doing or where we were going.

The border behind us was a distant blur. The mountains ahead seemed no closer. We were thirsty but determined to ration our moisture packs. Our legs were tired and getting crampy— walking through sand is much harder than walking on solid ground. I was beginning to regret having talked everyone into this, even if I still couldn't figure out what our alternative might have been.

I wanted a moment alone to confer with Smelly, but I hoped that if it had something to tell me, it would pipe up. I had to trust that Smelly did not want to die in the desert, and that it would not let me die either.

Charles had taken on what he called the Mr. Spock role. He had configured his data bracelet to scan for life—"like a tricorder!"—and every few minutes he waved his arm in an arc across the horizon.

We all trudged on, the colonel the most determined, taking the lead, having to slow himself to keep from outpacing us. Villainic lagged farthest behind. At first Tamret kept pace with him, but somehow, without my noticing, she drifted ahead until she was walking directly next to me.

She let her shoulder brush against mine. It was a quick, gliding touch, but even in the desert it felt warm under my shirt.

"I'm sorry for what I said before," she told me, though she didn't meet my eye. "It wasn't fair."

"It was fair," I said. "That's why it hurt. I promised to come for you."

"You did, Zeke," she said. "I was mad because I wished it had been sooner, before things became so . . . complicated. But you did what you said you would. You got me off Rarel."

"Like that worked out so well."

"You are such an idiot," she said, now looking right at me. "Don't be mad at yourself because you couldn't find a way to cross the galaxy fast enough. Most people are happy to do the impossible. You want to do it on a schedule."

I almost took her hand, but I held back. I wasn't afraid of Villainic. When it came to Tamret, I wasn't afraid of anyone except Tamret herself. Still, I didn't want trouble—especially not here, in the desert. I glanced back, and Villainic was staring at us, his eyes narrowed as he struggled to walk faster.

"Can't you just tell him to get lost?" I asked. "Maybe more nicely, but you know what I'm saying."

"It's not that easy," she told me. "I can't break my vow, but maybe I can void the contract. Caste customs require particular circumstances to break a marriage promise, but I think there's a way to do that. If we are going to your home, then you can challenge his right to marry by claiming you can provide for his betrothed better. Then you would have to press your claim."

"By doing what?"

"I probably should have said something before. You might have to fight him."

I glanced back at Villainic again. At the moment he didn't look like much of a challenge—he looked like a freshly caught fish flopping on the dock—but he was a Rarel and I was a human. It would be like a moderately athletic turtle fighting the world's wimpiest gorilla. The turtle might give it his all, but in the end the gorilla smashes him against a rock.

"Yeah, Tamret, that is exactly the sort of thing you might have mentioned sooner."

"Why?" she asked, looking directly at me. "Would it have made a difference?"

I looked back at her, and we both knew the answer. She wanted to get away from Rarel. She wanted to go with me. "No," I said. "I'm not letting you go. Not again."

I spoke maybe a little too loudly. Alice, I realized, was listening. And then Tamret realized it, and the two of them were glowering at each other. I wanted to dig a hole in the sand and bury myself.

"This is odd," Charles said, interrupting my special moment. He stopped walking, and he was studying a text display rising up from his bracelet. "The data bracelet is picking up on two beings about a hundred feet in front of us—one humanoid-size, the other massive."

The colonel put a hand to his eyes. "I don't see anything."

We all stood still and stared into the empty desert. We saw nothing but sand, and no movement but that caused by a slight breeze that kicked up small clouds that rippled the dunes. The reflection of the sun made it hard to look out for long, but I felt sure that if there were a massive creature lumbering out there, we would see it.

Villainic caught up with us and planted himself between me and Tamret. He took her hand, and she let him, but it hung slack in his grip.

Then an inexplicable shifting of the sand caught my attention. In one spot the sands began to swirl and pour downward, like a sinkhole had opened far beneath the surface. For a moment it all stopped and there was stillness and quiet, and then sand shot up, spraying like a geyser. It rained down on us as the massive thing appeared before us, rising up from below. It was a sandworm. It was a great, big, semi truck–size sandworm.

I froze in panic. I knew from Frank Herbert's classic novel *Dune* that, in addition to having great size, the sandworm was horribly destructive, known to eat any creature in its path—in spite of the fact that it lived in an environment in which there should have been nothing to eat.

This one turned toward us, and it did not look how I'd imagined Frank Herbert's sandworms. It was big and white and grubby-looking, yes, with ringed segments so pale they were almost clear. I could see its blue veins, each the size of a tree trunk, beneath its thick skin. On its back was a vaguely human-oid figure, strapped to some sort of massive saddle. I could tell nothing about the rider because it wore stained white robes and a head covering that revealed no features.

All of this was significant, but what made me unafraid was the worm's face, which wasn't what I would have expected from a giant subterranean monster. It looked almost like a dog—the kind you want to pet, not flee from in terror. It had a long snout that ended in dozens of undulating whiskers, each no thicker than one of my hairs. It had no eyes, but thick patches of feelers on its forehead. The creature's mouth was long and turned into a natural grin, containing a series of interlocking teeth that formed some kind of filter when its mouth was closed. Now the mouth was open, and the creature spoke.

"Over there!" it shouted in a deep voice that betrayed a simple kindness. "Beings. Oh, there are beings! Smell the beings! New beings! Let's meet the beings!"

The cloaked figure patted the worm. The beast began to undulate through the sand like a snake sliding along the surface of a pond.

The worm pulled alongside us like a bus coming to a stop. "Beings!" it cried in a voice deep and full of delight. "New beings come to visit!" It moved its feelers in our direction. "Sniffing! Sniffing the beings!"

The rider patted the worm's sides. "New beings," agreed the voice, decidedly female. "Good boy." She began to unwrap the scarves around her neck to reveal a head of brown scales covered with pointy ridges. She looked like a desert lizard from Earth.

"Greetings, travelers," she said.

"Greetings, worm rider," Steve said.

"I am Uolomd, daughter of Racvib. This is no place for outsiders."

"It is pretty hot," I agreed. "And kind of dry. It could use some roads, and maybe a vending machine. Or a rest stop. A rest stop would be nice."

"It may be no place for you in particular," Uolomd said.

"No argument here," I told her.

"What seek you in this place?" Uolomd asked.

"Seek us the Hidden Fortress," I said.

Uolomd shook her spiky head. "Ugh. Another idiot after the Hidden Fortress. Let's drop the formal talk, okay? I've been on patrol for almost six hours, so I'm heading back. You want a ride to my village?"

"We'd love one, ducky," Steve said.

"You promise not to cause trouble?" she asked.

"We promise not to *intend* to cause trouble," Steve said. "I think that's the best this lot can offer."

"Good enough for me." She reached into a box embedded in the saddle and threw down a rope ladder. "Climb on up," she called.

Steve nudged me in the side with his elbow. "Oi," he said quietly. "She's cute. For an alien."

We rode on top of the worm, whose name was Minti, for almost three hours, until we came to a settlement alongside a mountain that had produced an overhang, giving the locals some permanent and much-needed shade. The buildings seemed to be carved directly into the cliff face and were accessible though staircases that were also built into the rock. It had a 1970s-sci-fi-film vibe that I really liked.

Not all the inhabitants were the same species as Uolomd, though at least half were. There was a beetlelike race that walked upright and had its face on its chest. On its head were a series of tentacles it used with incredible dexterity. I also saw a few representatives of a small species, no more than three feet high, that were covered with fur the color of the sand and had mouselike ears. All the beings of the Forbidden Zone seemed generally friendly to outsiders, though they regarded us with something that I could only describe as exasperation.

"Why do you live here?" I asked Uolomd once we had made it down from the worm, some of us more gracefully than others. I was one of the others.

"Why do you live where you live?" she asked me in a way that made it clear she found the question insulting.

"That's a fair point," I said, "but if I were living in a desert and there was a much more, uh, temperate place only a few miles away, I'd give some thought to moving."

"I do not know of this temperate place you speak of," she said. "All I know is that this is our home. We have lived here for as long as any of us can remember."

"So you have no record of how your people came to the station?"

"Station?" she asked, sounding genuinely perplexed.

I opened my mouth, trying to figure out what to say, but Uolomd was already laughing.

"Sorry, we always pull that one on newcomers who can't quite seem to figure out why we don't choose to live like they do. Look, we're all desert species. We're comfortable here. It's hot. It's dry. No one bothers us. Out there it's so humid and cold. Maybe you like that, but it's not for me."

"You've been out there?" I asked.

"Of course. What do you think, we're some primitive savages living on the fringes of civilization because we're too ignorant to make a more civilized choice?"

That was exactly what I'd been thinking. "Of course not," I assured her.

"Why don't you come inside, clean up, and have something to eat," Uolomd said. "You can sleep in our guest rooms for the night, and tomorrow we'll show you the way."

"The way to what?" I asked.

"You want the Hidden Fortress, right?" she said. "We'll tell you how to get there."

"I guess it's not as hidden as advertised," Steve said, "if you know where it is."

"I know where the journey begins," she said. "After that I can't tell you much. Supposedly in my great-grandparents' time beings came looking for the Hidden Fortress all the time—two or three a decade. Things have slowed down since then, but I do know one thing."

Steve grinned at her. "I'll bet you know more than that."

"I know of one thing that might scare you silly, then. How about that?"

"Point taken," Steve conceded. "What is this one thing?"

"I'm told that no one who goes looking for the Hidden Fortress ever comes back."

Uolomd lived with her mother, Racvib, who was the leader of their settlement. The house that was dug into the cliff didn't look like much from the outside, but inside it was a comfortable and modern—by Confederation standards, not mine—structure with much of the same tech I'd come to expect from other places on the station. The only real difference was that it was much hotter and dryer inside than I liked. The guest rooms had thermostats that allowed me to lower the temperature all the way down to about eighty degrees.

We bathed, changed our clothes, and sat down to a meal

with Uolomd and her family. While they did have access to most Confederation technology, they did not seem to have a food-generation unit, which I understood to be large and energy-consuming. After asking us about our preferences, they served me, the Rarels, and the other humans an assortment of roasted tubers and a stew made from mushrooms, beans, and cacti. Steve joined the family in eating a bowl full of hard-shelled things that looked like four-legged grasshoppers, though each one was about as big as my fist. I'd seen Steve eat living things, of course, many times, but they were always just synthesized protein that our nanite implants made to appear to be alive. This time he was actually putting living things in his mouth and chewing on them.

"They're not sentient, are they?" I asked.

"There's some debate about that," Racvib asked. Then she and her daughter burst out laughing.

"Okay, what's your story?" Uolomd said after a few minutes. "Why are you looking for the Hidden Fortress? I'd like to know a little more about you before you vanish forever, never to be heard from again."

"I am afraid we can't discuss that," the colonel said. "It might put us, or you, in danger. I can only tell you that it's a matter of great importance."

"They all say that," Racvib told us.

"Who says that?" I asked. "I thought Confederation citizens can't enter the Forbidden Zone."

"They say that, too, but a few find a way around that limitation. I'm not sure how, exactly. I think they have to undergo some kind of genetic treatment that's both expensive and illegal. It's worth it to some, though. Just a few months ago we had a visitor at this very table—the first one to come looking for the Hidden Fortress in years. This being was muscular and hairy, with tusks growing out of its face."

"Sounds like Urch," Charles said.

"He's not the only one of his species," I said. "Besides, if he never returned, how did we see him recently?"

"It does seem awfully suspicious that one of the visitors to this area should be a being who wanted us to come here," Charles said.

"Is whatever you have in mind worth risking your life?" Uolomd asked, looking at Steve when she spoke. I got the feeling that she thought he was kind of cute too. For an alien.

"I wish we didn't have to, love," Steve said. "But that's the situation we find ourselves in. Some right nasty people are looking to get rid of us because we know what they're up to. We're running for our lives. I'll tell you that much. We've been told that the Hidden Fortress is the only place we can go to escape and get to safety."

"Why not take a ship from the surface spaceport?"

"I don't want to get into the specifics," the colonel said, "but the people who are looking to stop us control the spaceport and the ships circling it."

"Not the main one," Uolomd said, like we were utterly clueless. "The old one, here in the Forbidden Zone."

There was a moment of silence in which we all looked at one another.

"There's an abandoned spaceport on the far side of the desert," Racvib explained. "This area used to be much more populous, but an environmental glitch caused the desert to creep in. The station engineers were able to arrest the spread, but it turned out to be more environmentally stable to simply move the core of the city farther away than to try to reclaim the desert."

"What kind of ships are we talking about?" I asked.

"They're outdated models, to be sure, probably at least five hundred years old, but the technology hasn't changed all that much. They're less streamlined and a little slower than new ships, but they work and they're safe. We have crews that maintain them, and we take them out for test runs once in a while. It's not a lot of work, and it would be a shame to let them simply fall apart."

"Are you telling me that we can leave?" Villainic asked. "We could abandon this ridiculous and dangerous quest and simply go home?"

"It's what I'd recommend," Racvib said. "Uolomd can take you there tomorrow. It's about five hours by worm."

"Spaceport!" cried Minti from outside. "Visiting the ships! Big ships! Rumbling!"

"Minti likes the way the ground vibrates when the engines fire up," Uolomd explained indulgently.

Things seemed to be slipping away from me. Of course I liked the idea of escaping from this desert and avoiding danger, and I liked the idea of getting everyone home safely, but I had promised Dr. Roop I would help find the Hidden Fortress. I wanted to keep the promise I'd made to a great being and a good friend. He had died to protect me, and there was no way I could simply give up on him because an easier option had suddenly appeared. Even if keeping faith with Dr. Roop were not enough of a motivation, protecting my home planet would be. I couldn't let Junup turn a blind eye to the Phandic threat, assuming he wasn't cooperating with the Phands. Dr. Roop had said failing to complete mission meant that the Confederation, and Earth, would fall within ten years. It was foolish and short-sighted to take the easy way out.

"Ships we can take back home?" Colonel Rage said with a grin. "I like the sound of this. It could be exactly what we've been hoping for."

"I don't know," Alice said. "Ghli Wixxix wanted us to find the Hidden Fortress, and so did Dr. Roop."

I was grateful to her for saying this, so I didn't have to be the one to bring it up. I hated being the only cheerleader for the Hidden Fortress expedition. Alice smiled at me, and I understood she had been deliberately bailing me out.

"That is true," Charles agreed, "and I respected both of those beings, but I am a little reluctant to go in search of a place from which no one ever returns. Especially not if there is another way to leave the station."

"A lot of bad people don't want us to find the Hidden Fortress," Alice continued. "That's hard to ignore."

*That gunk-filled-balloon may be less stupid than the others,* Smelly observed. *I respect a being, however unevolved, who stands up for what it believes.*

Alice had let them know I wasn't the only one who wanted to see this through, but now it was time to give her some support. "We've come this far," I reminded them. "I don't want to walk away from an opportunity to make a real difference. Besides, Dr. Roop assured us that there would be ships we could use once we got to the Hidden Fortress. I'm not in any kind of a hurry to go off to a place that no one comes back from, but maybe they don't come back because they take one of the ships in the port below. It doesn't have to be a bad thing, does it?"

"Yes, of course you are right," Villainic said, his voice dripping with sarcasm. "How can vanishing from existence be a bad thing? Certainly we should avoid the safe, dependable course and do the foolish thing in which all our lives will likely be lost."

"Your opinion is on record," Alice said to him. "Unless you have something new to say, why don't we just assume you're just going to keep on banging the coward drum."

"Well," muttered Tamret, "isn't Zeke lucky to have you on his side?"

"I guess he is," Alice snapped, "considering you're not."

Tamret slammed the palm of her hand down on the table and stood up. Her ears were back against the side of her head, and her whiskers twitched. Those were never good signs. "I think you need to remember your place, [*young female monkey of a particularly unattractive species*]."

"Please sit down, young lady," the colonel said, his voice calm but authoritative. "We can argue in private, not among our hosts."

Tamret sighed, then smoothed back her hair. "You're right. Sorry," she said in the unmistakable tone of someone who was not even a little sorry. She sat down and scowled at Alice.

"Since we arrived here, we've been after a safe way off the station," the colonel said to the group in general, though I knew he was talking to me.

I nodded. Colonel Rage was a no-nonsense sort of guy who took seriously his responsibility to keep us safe, so I couldn't count on his support, and Villainic was off the table, but I thought I could persuade the others. I didn't want to force the point, though. We were friends, and all the crazy stuff we had done together had been because doing crazy stuff was the right call. I simply had to help them see that this, too, was the right call.

"You all know my arguments for looking for the Hidden Fortress," I said. "You guys know who wanted us to take on this mission, and you know the dangers if we don't, so I'm done making my case. You tell me what you want to do."

Mi Sun groaned. She leaned forward with her forehead pressed to her palm. "Zeke, I hear you, but we've been through enough. It's not our fight. It wasn't Nayana's fight either, and she's dead. I know how much Dr. Roop meant to you, but he was wrong to ask you to do this."

"Until we wake up one day," I said, "and the Phands have conquered Earth. If we're going to be rebels, isn't it better to rebel against the Confederation than the Phands?"

"You did say you were done making your case," Villainic told me. "If I am not allowed to repeat my position, I don't see why you should be."

"Because my position isn't selfish," I snapped. "That's why."

"Zeke's not wrong," the colonel said. "If we leave, we may be setting our world up for disaster down the line, and there's no guarantee that anyone else will be able to do what we don't. What we need is technology that we can reverse engineer. If we can do that with one of these ships, then that's good enough for me. If we can get home safely, and we get a ship we can use as a basis for building more of the same, I say mission accomplished."

"Those are wise words from the old man with one eye," Villainic said. "I cannot even understand why this is a debate."

I turned to him. "Weren't you asked to keep quiet? Besides, you don't get a vote."

"That is unkind, brother!" Villainic said. Then he pointed to Alice. "And if I don't get a vote, then neither does she."

"I don't need a vote," Alice said. "I'm just saying that if it were my friends who'd been murdered, I'd want to get back at the people who killed them."

"I respect your gumption," the colonel said, "but we're already going home without one thirteen-year-old girl. I'm the one who is going to have to tell her parents. I don't want to have to do that more than once."

I looked at Mi Sun. "You're as fearless as anyone I know," I told her.

"I appreciate you saying that," she said, refusing to meet my eyes, "but I think you also know I'm practical. This fight over the software—that's not ours. Anyhow, it feels wrong. No one is supposed to be able to get here, but it sounds like Urch might have been here himself a few months ago. They haven't told us the truth about everything, and they don't need us the way they said they do. We don't have to be the ones to solve all the Confederation's problems."

"I can't support letting you risk your lives now because of a danger that might manifest in ten or twenty years." the colonel said. "That's multiple lifetimes in politics. Everything could be different then. I'm also not going to tell you what to do. You kids have skin in the game, so it's your call."

"And I think we should see this through, the way our friend wanted us to," I said in an encouraging voice. I wasn't much on making speeches, but this was my last chance to rally everyone. Either I could get them on board, or I would have to walk away from the promise I'd made to Dr. Roop. "I think we stand up for the things we care about, the things that matter. I say it is better to take a risk now than to go home and wait for an overwhelming invasion force that is going to take our planet away from us. Come on! This is not the time to back down. Who will stand up with me for the things we care about?" I raised my hand.

I looked around the table. None of them moved. None of them were willing to take the chance. And then, across from me, a flash of white. Tamret slowly put her hand in the air.

"Put your hand down. Right now!" Villainic said.

She shook her head. "I'm sorry, Villainic. I can't."

"After all I've done for you?" he asked, the genuine hurt impossible to miss.

"Yeah," she said. "Even after all that."

I didn't know if Tamret believed what I had said. I didn't know if she wanted to avenge our fallen friends, or fight for galactic freedom, or just head into the unknown for the pure pleasure of dangerous chaos. Any of those things might have been true. It was very likely that all of them were. Above all, I understood that she had raised her hand because she did not want me to stand alone, even in defeat, even if it might come back to hurt her with Villainic.

"Might as well finish the vote," the colonel said. "Who wants to take one of the ships at the spaceport and head for home?"

Charles and Mi Sun raised their hands. And then Steve.

"What?" I shouted.

"Mate, I want to back you up, and if it were just my scales on the line, you know I'd be there. But this lot?" He gestured toward the table. "They don't want to risk it, they haven't trained for it, and I'm not even clear on the goals. I can't go on some vague mission into unknown circumstances and put my friends at risk. If one of them were to be killed, I'd be wrecked." He gestured toward Villainic. "Except him, maybe."

"I don't believe this," I said, fighting back the frustration. "I never thought you'd be the one to chicken out."

Steve cocked his head. No doubt the translator was working on the whole chickening-out concept. Then he met my gaze. "I'm going to let that pass, because I know the situation is emotional for you."

So I'd not only lost, but I'd just called my best friend a coward. This was turning out to be a pretty mediocre evening. We were going to walk away from our obligations to our fallen friends and turn our backs on looming danger. I needed to do something, but I couldn't think what. It was one thing to be defeated by your enemies, but another to go down because your friends disagreed with you. The thing was, I didn't think they were wrong. I got their point, and now I felt like I hadn't done a good enough job making mine.

"That's it, son," the colonel told me. "There's no good or bad here. You've got an honest and honorable disagreement, and I've been around long enough to know that neither side is wrong or right."

I'm not going to pretend that some part of me wasn't relieved. I wanted to go home too. I wanted to remember what it was like to feel safe for a little while. When I'd been on Earth, all I'd dreamed about was returning to Confederation Central, being with Tamret again. Now here I was, and there she was, and it was nothing like I'd imagined. Back at home, my parents, finally back together, were waiting for me. And Tamret—she wanted to come with me too. I had no idea how we were going to manage that. She was an alien, after all, but the secret of alien species had to come out sooner or later. We'd work it out. We'd be fine. And maybe the colonel was right. Maybe things would sort themselves out on their own. The galaxy had survived for billions of years without me getting involved in every crisis. It didn't seem like that much of a stretch to think it would survive this, too.

That was what I told myself, but I still felt like I was walking away from something important. I wished I had been able to make everyone else see that.

"These ships you mentioned," Villainic began. "How can we pay you for them?"

Racvib punched a fist into the air three times—a gesture of dismissal? "They are not ours to give or to keep. They belonged to those who came before us. And, in truth, there are hundreds. We won't miss one."

"Or two?" Villainic asked.

"Or two," Racvib agreed. "You are obviously different species. I suppose you have different destinations?"

From across the table Tamret was looking at me, like she expected me to say something. She kept jutting out her jaw in a *Hurry up, already* gesture, but I had no idea what she meant.

*That female hairy thing wants something from you,* Smelly observed in his usual day-late-and-a-dollar-short manner.

My heart was pounding now. I was supposed to do something, say something, but what? Was I supposed to challenge Villainic to a duel or something?

"Tamret and I will take our own ship." Villainic was saying to Racvib. He then turned to her. "You can pilot it, can you not?"

Tamret stopped looking at me. She cast her eyes down and said nothing.

"Can you get us home? I invoke your betrothal oath."

Tamret gritted her teeth. There were tears in her eyes. "Yes," she said. "I can get us home."

"And by your oath you will obey me."

"I will," she said, though the words were hardly more than a grunt.

Something formal was going on here. That had to be what Tamret had been trying to communicate. I didn't understand it, but I knew enough about Rarel culture to get that once promises were made, they were not broken, no matter what. I had to do something.

I rose to my feet. "On behalf of the people of Earth, I offer Tamret a home on our world." My voice came out stilted and weird, but I was trying to sound formal. If the Rarels could have their rituals, then so could I. "I, uh, invoke the right of sanctuary, is what I'm doing. Basically."

*Smooth,* said Smelly.

"Is it my imagination," asked Uolomd, "or are these guys pretty much the most entertaining houseguests ever? There's so much drama!"

"Please sit down, Zeke," Villainic said. "I know you wish to protect Tamret, and as her future husband I cannot help but be touched by your devotion, but she does not want to be exiled on an alien planet, away from her family and her new caste. She is, I know, grateful for your good intentions, but she nevertheless declines your kind offer."

"Tamret?" I asked.

She would not look at me. "I have given my oath to obey, so that's what I'm going to do."

I stared ahead, unable to believe this. The one bright spot

in all of this had been blotted out. Somehow, I had completely messed things up. Tamret was going back to Rarel, and she was going on a separate ship. The plan for me to challenge Villainic had been a long shot, but I'd been willing to take it. Now I was never going to get the chance.

# CHAPTER TWENTY-FOUR

The after-dinner clean-up was more awkward than I generally like. "Wow," I heard Uolomd say to Steve. "Your friends are intense."

"Yeah," he agreed wearily. "It's pretty much like that with them all the time."

"Must be a mammal thing," Uolomd speculated. "All that body-temperature regulation really gets them worked up."

"That's my theory, love."

Racvib had a nice place, but it wasn't enormous. The colonel, Villainic, Steve, Charles, and I had to share a room. Most of us were to sleep on the floor, though I suspected that "sleeping" was going to be a euphemism for "lying awake all night."

After we were finished cleaning, we thanked our hosts, and we wandered into our room. I saw Steve crouched over his pack, looking for something, and I went over to him.

"I shouldn't have said that," I said.

He stood up and met my gaze. "Don't give it another thought, yeah? Believe me, if it were just the two of us, I'd sign up for any crazy, ill-conceived, recklessly planned mission if it meant something to you. But not with them," he said, gesturing toward the others.

"I know you would," I said. "I shouldn't have called you a chicken."

"They sound delicious."

"They're okay," I explained. "Better than turkey, not as good as duck."

"We're mates," he said, "which means you can mouth off once in a while, and in the grand scheme of things it doesn't mean much. If I were you, I'd worry less about my feelings, given I'm a pretty rational bloke, and worry more about Tamret."

I was more worried about Tamret, but I'd figured I'd cross the easy one off my list first. I went over to the room where the girls were staying. The door was still open, and I looked in. Nothing good had been going on in there. Mi Sun and Alice were in one part of the room, looking helpless. Tamret was on the other side, sitting on her blanket, her back to the others.

She must have heard me approach, because she looked at me, but then she turned away.

Alice got to her feet and came over to me. We went out into the hall. "She said if you showed up we were supposed to let you know that she can't speak to you."

"And she sent you to tell me this?"

"I think she's mad enough at you that she's starting to like me," Alice said with a sympathetic shrug. "She's a little hard to figure out sometimes."

"I am so sick of this." I was struggling to keep my voice down, but the frustration was like a poison in my blood.

"I know, Zeke. She made me promise to say something else. Please don't be mad at me. She made me promise before she told me what it was."

I nodded. That was about all I could muster.

"She said you were too late. As usual." Alice winced as she said the words. Part of me was aware how hard it must be to be tasked with delivering such stinging words to a friend. Part of me was lost in despair. It was all ruined. We were leaving now, with friends dead, nothing accomplished, Tamret going back to live in misery, and Earth in the crosshairs. What had been the point of all of any of this?

There had to be a way to fix it, but I couldn't see it. Then it occurred to me that maybe I couldn't see it because it wasn't there. Maybe not everything could be fixed. It was all messed up, and I wasn't in the driver's seat; I was just along for the ride, watching how everything went from bad to worse, powerless to do a thing about it. I'd been foolish to think that somehow I could make events unfold the way I wanted them to.

"I'm sorry, Zeke. She's angry and she's frustrated. I know she doesn't mean it."

I just shook my head.

"She wouldn't lash out like that if she didn't care about you," Alice said. "She's hurting too."

I'd been rubbing my face with frustration, but I suddenly stopped. Tamret was hurting too. I was standing here, feeling sorry for myself, and I realized I was being a selfish jerk. One problem at a time, I told myself.

"Thanks, Alice," I said, and I went back to my room. Villainic was busy settling himself into his sleeping area, working the blankets under him so he could be all tucked in.

I kicked him. Not as hard as I would have liked, but harder than most people generally want to be kicked. "Get up," I said.

"Here we go," Steve observed from across the room.

"Son," the colonel warned.

He may have said something else, but I wasn't sure because Villainic was groaning. From me kicking him again.

He was scrambling to get untucked and onto his feet. I got

another kick in there before he was standing. "Why are you kicking me, brother?"

"I am not your brother, you idiot," I said. "I am issuing a formal challenge or whatever to determine Tamret's fate. I hereby caste-challenge you in the name of the deity of moronic fiancés."

Villainic looked puzzled. "There is no such deity."

"I don't care. You get my point."

Villainic shook his head. "Your challenge is unorthodox, and I am not obligated to accept it. Besides, I'd be remiss in my duties if somehow I lost and I could no longer protect Tamret."

"She doesn't want your protection," I told him. "She wants to go with me."

"Of course she doesn't."

"You are so blind," I said, struggling to keep from shouting. "She told me she wants me to take me with her."

Villainic gave me a sympathetic smile. "Oh, she was just being emotional. Half the time I'm sure she has no idea what she wants, but she certainly does not want to live out her days on an alien world, away from her own kind. No, Zeke, I vowed to care for her, and I shall keep that vow. Please don't kick me again."

I watched while he climbed back into his pile of blankets and tucked himself in. That had been my move, my big gesture: getting myself beaten up by an impossibly strong alien. I hadn't expected to win any challenge. I'd expected to be bloody and bruised in the morning so that Tamret would see that at least I'd tried. But Villainic would not give me even that. I was about to start kicking him again, but Steve and Charles had me by the armpits and were dragging me from the room.

"I don't think that's working, mate," Steve said.

"We would all like to kick him," Charles added, "but it accomplishes nothing."

"It's not over," Steve told me. "We can keep this from happening. If we all stand against him, there's nothing Villainic can do. We can keep him from taking her."

"But we can't keep her from agreeing to be taken," I said. "That's the thing that's so messed up. In spite of how her people have treated her, she is going to keep her stupid caste vows and stay with him."

"Tomorrow we shall think of something," Charles assured me.

They both went back to their blankets. The light went out. I stood in the hall for a long time, thinking, trying to find another angle, another approach, some way to keep Tamret from agreeing to go back to Rarel. At the dinner table she had been glaring at me. I realized too late that she'd wanted me to speak up, to offer her my protection before she reaffirmed her vow or whatever. I'd blown it. That was it, the moment I could have made a difference, and I let it get away, and I was not going to get another chance.

I don't know how long I stood there. I listened to the others breathing in the darkness, and then to the sounds of snoring. The colonel was particularly loud. Finally I went over to my own blankets in the hopes that unconsciousness would dull the pain a little.

I was not so lucky. It didn't help that it was so hot in there, which made it impossible for me to relax. I kept envisioning how things were going to play out tomorrow. We would spend five hours riding on an enthusiastic worm, we would reach an abandoned spaceport, and then I would say good-bye to

Tamret, this time almost certainly forever. Steve and Charles were good friends to try to convince me that we could turn this around—maybe they actually believed it—but I knew better. Tamret would not break her vow. She was going to voluntarily walk out of my life. This time I wouldn't have to worry about her being killed or imprisoned or tortured, but I did worry about her being miserable.

As I lay sweating on that uncomfortable floor, endlessly mulling this over, I was suddenly stuck by an urgent need to pee. Too much information, I suppose, but it surprised me because water consumption wasn't big among the desert folk, and I hadn't had much since arriving—just enough to keep me hydrated. I'd taken care of business before getting ready for bed, but now my body was telling me that if I didn't get up and find the toilet *right now*, I'd have a lot of embarrassing explaining to do in the morning.

I padded out of the room and into the hallway. It was dark, but not completely so, and I remembered my way around well enough. For some reason, though, I found myself stopping. I hadn't meant to. One minute I'd been creeping along in the dark, and the next I was still. In the kitchen, off the hallway, I heard Racvib and Uolomd talking. I am not the eavesdropping sort, but I heard them speak a name that made me freeze. In spite of the heat.

"Any luck reaching Junup?" Racvib asked.

"No, a sandstorm is interfering with communications," Uolomd said. "We'll just have to follow his standing orders. I'll take them out into the desert tomorrow and dispose of them. They won't suspect anything until it's too late. And I'll have Minti bury them. No one will ever find them."

"Should we post a guard tonight?" Racvib asked.

"Why bother? If they're worried about us, they'll just slip out and try to find the 'spaceport,' which means they'll wander around until they die of thirst."

"I can't believe they actually believed that spaceport story," Racvib said.

"Junup did tell us they were simple," Uolomd said. "But to believe that there is a functional spaceport out here after all these centuries? What a bunch of dimwits."

"Still, it's good fun to trick them into their own demise, isn't it?"

"I love being evil. It's pretty much the best."

I no longer needed to pee.

I went back to the room and waited until I heard them go to their respective rooms. Then I waited at least another hour to make sure they were asleep. That's when I got up and shook Steve awake. Shaking didn't accomplish anything, so I poked him in the side, hoping that Ish-hi were ticklish in the same places as humans. They are, by the way. Also, I can't recommend waking an Ish-hi that way.

When I picked myself up, rubbing my arm to make sure it was not broken, Steve began to sit up. "Sorry about that. Reflex. Why are you waking me up, anyhow?"

I told him what I'd overheard.

Steve was aghast. "But Uolomd is cute," he protested. "And the food is delicious."

"Be that as it may," I said, "they are working for Junup. There is no spaceport, and they mean to kill us, so I'm thinking that it might be a good idea to sneak off now."

"The others aren't going to like it," he told me.

"They're going to like being dead even less."

"Fair point."

We began the process of waking everyone up and explaining the situation.

"This is disappointing," Colonel Rage said.

"Better to know than not," Charles said. "It looks like the Hidden Fortress is back on the menu."

"But we agreed it was a bad idea," Villainic said. "I thought we agreed to escape instead."

"It's hard to escape on a ship that doesn't exist," the colonel said.

"How do we even know this is true?" Villainic asked, his ears shooting back. His amber fur grew a little puffy too, like he was trying to make himself look bigger. "We only have Zeke's word for it, and he's been attempting to convince us to search for this fortress all along. He could be manipulating us."

"If you were one of us," Charles said, "you would know better than to say that."

Villainic shook his head. "You're right. I'm sorry, brother." He reached out to pat me on the arm.

"We're not brothers," I said, shaking him off.

Villainic shook his head sadly. "Whether you like it or not, that is exactly what we are."

I didn't want to deal with Villainic's irrational nonsense now. There was too much at stake. I knew that Steve could move more stealthily than anyone else in our group, so I sent him to wake the girls. Besides, I wanted to keep an eye on Villainic. We had not yet discovered how Junup had learned of our plans, and I still suspected Villainic of being a spy. There was no way I was going to let him be alone, even for a minute, until we were out of there.

Finally, when the girls were awake and brought up to date, and we had collected our things, we slipped out into the night to search for the Hidden Fortress.

With only the bush alien's map to guide us, we headed out into the desert. It was dark but quite cool, making it the best time to travel. Above us a few wispy clouds wandered by, and past that the great, ringed gas giant hung in the sky with its swirling mass of colors. I took a moment to admire its strange beauty, and then I got back to the business of trying not to get killed. We needed to put as much distance between ourselves and Uolomd as possible. Once she discovered we were gone, she'd be after us with her sandworm, and then we'd be in serious trouble.

Just as the sun was coming up, we saw a series of rocky outcrops with a wedge in between. The map indicated that this was the beginning of the entrance to the fortress. It was a good three miles in the distance, but I figured we could make it there before it got too hot. I was moderately optimistic until I saw a wake in the sand behind us, which I recognized from the previous day.

Charles saw it too. "Worm sign!" he called, pointing.

We ran.

I had no idea how fast worms could move when they were going at top speed. I also had no idea if we could survive running in the desert, with no time to stop for water, but we had to keep going long enough to make it to safety. I didn't know a lot of things, but I knew I didn't want us to fall back into Junup's hands.

I heard the rumbling behind us, and the scrape of sand on sand, but I was not stopping. The rocks were just ahead of us. We could make it. Once we reached them, we would be safe. Safe from the worm, at least. Junup had people here, which meant there were traps we hadn't imagined. I couldn't let myself think about that, though. I just had to keep moving.

Running in desert sand, while carrying all your stuff, and with the sun creeping up behind you, is really a great workout. The Forbidden Zone fitness plan was going to make me a lot of money, provided Junup didn't get his goaty hands on me. It was hard to work up a lot of speed, and even harder to keep it. With sweat stinging my eyes, I turned back to see the disturbance under the sand gaining on us.

We had maybe half a mile to go when the sand in front of us began to swirl. Sand sprayed upward like a geyser, and the giant worm emerged ahead of us, massive and terrifying. On the saddle, a figure in dingy robes, presumably Uolomd, turned to face us.

She unwound the layers around her face. "Where are you going?" she demanded. "Why did you run off like that?"

"Give us a break, Uolomd," I said. "We know."

"Know *what*?"

"This is pointless," Colonel Rage said. "The longer we stand here arguing, the longer she has to call in reinforcements."

"'Fraid that's true," Steve said. He had taken out his PPB pistol, and now he fired off a single blast, stunning Uolomd. She was strapped into her saddle, I suppose for the purposes of traveling through loose sand, so there was no danger of her falling off the creature. Instead she slumped forward and dangled along the side of the worm.

The worm. That was one thing Steve hadn't considered when he shot Uolomd.

For a terrifying moment the worm remained still, fixing us with its endless wriggling feelers. Then it cried out, "Friend hurt! Oh, the bright light hurt friend!"

The worm reared up, turning from bus to skyscraper in an instant. It was going to crush us or eat us or whatever it was that worms did to beings they didn't like.

"Friend hurt!" it cried at us.

None of us spoke.

The worm writhed from side to side, like it had been stung. "Friend hurt! Oh, friend is hurt. Going home! Taking friend home!" It then rose into the air and flopped down, facing the other direction, heading back the way it had come.

"Given our track record," the colonel said, "that worked out surprisingly well."

We headed toward the pass.

By midmorning the sun was obscured by one of the mountains, and we had the advantage of shade, but we still had a ways to go. There was not a whole lot of talking going on, maybe because of the heat and our perpetual thirst, but also because tensions were high. We trudged on, the sun high above us, the air still, the great gas giant making its way across the station's dome.

That night we camped in an outcropping in the midst of the rocks. There was still no sign of renewed pursuit. The desert grew cold at night, but we dared not make a fire. I layered extra clothes on top of myself, using a couple of T-shirts as makeshift gloves to keep my hands warm.

We woke at dawn, and after a silent breakfast of rations we were on our feet and marching farther through the pass. At about noon we found a small cave, as marked on the map. It was about five feet wide, with a ceiling maybe eight feet above us, and we were all grateful to get out of the heat. We stepped in, generating floating flashlights from our data bracelets, and made our way farther inside. It was more of a passage than a cave, and we wound our way through, enjoying the cool and taking comfort from the distant, tinny sound of dripping water. The cave was kind of beautiful. The walls were lined with glittering mineral deposits of blue and pink.

We followed a winding path for maybe two hundred feet, and then the cave widened into a cavern about as broad and tall as a house. At the far end of it, a downward staircase had been carved into the stone.

"I think we go that way," Steve volunteered. His voice echoed throughout the cavern.

We began our descent and moved steadily into the mountain for the rest of the afternoon, taking the occasional food-and-water break. No one said it, but we all had the same worries. What if this path went nowhere? What if there was no Hidden Fortress, or if it no longer existed or the way to gain access was blocked? Why had no one ever returned? Of course, now I began to wonder if that was true. Uolomd had, after all, not been honest with us about other things. Maybe Urch, or someone who looked like him, had never come this way at all. Maybe no one had.

We spent another night camped out, this time in a dusty stone passageway leading off the stairs. We needed to find a place where no one would be in danger of tumbling to their doom in the night. Here we felt less shy about making a fire, and in the flickering light I watched Tamret, who purposely kept her gaze away from me. I wanted to go to her, to talk to her, to apologize for missing my chance to save her, but I didn't know if I could find the words.

The next day we resumed our journey. About halfway through the morning, we began to hear a rhythmic pounding, like the slamming of a machine. I didn't know if that was good news or bad, but at least it was something.

Then the passageway opened into a great chamber illuminated by an eerie iridescent moss. A winding staircase led down the side of the rock wall, and below us, gleaming in the dim light, was a great metal structure, a nearly featureless silver cube sitting in the midst of a sprawling cavern. In the dim light it was hard to be sure how large it was, but I guessed it was at least a quarter mile long on each side.

"Could be a fortress," Steve said.

"It's hidden," Alice agreed.

"Looks like a Borg cube," Charles said worriedly.

So I felt pretty sure we'd found the Hidden Fortress. We'd also found the source of the thumping. We didn't see them at first, but there they were in the distance: giant machines, maybe robots or mechs, with twisted, asymmetrical limbs, stomping around, looking a whole lot like they would crush anything that tried to make it to the entrance. There must have been thirty of them that we could see. Given that they were eight feet tall, nightmarish in appearance, and predisposed to stomping, I had the feeling they might not be as friendly as we would have wished.

"The giant mechanical monstrosities could be a problem," I said quietly.

"What are those things?" the colonel asked.

"The catchall sci fi term would be 'mech,'" I explained.

"But what *are* they?"

*The lack of symmetry suggests an absence of creative intent. Very likely the existing technology has reformed itself, or reformed under intelligent guidance, to secure the fortress.*

"Probably old tech, repurposed to defend the fortress," I suggested aloud.

"I think I know why no one ever came back," Mi Sun. "Because those robot things probably killed them."

We retreated back part of the way we came in order to figure out what we were going to do.

"We have to go back," the colonel said. "We don't know what those mechs can do, and there's no safe way to take their measure."

"I would rather think of them as robots," said Charles. "Calling them mechs implies that there is a being operating them from inside."

"Please," Mi Sun said. "Let Zeke be the annoying nerd. We don't need two of you."

"The point," said Colonel Rage irritably, "is that we have to go back."

"Go back to what?" I asked. "Junup, who wants us dead? The spaceport that doesn't exist? Where do you want to go, exactly? The village of the desert reptiles? They're crazy."

"Being reptile and being crazy are two different things," Steve said. "Don't suggest there's a connection."

"I'm not happy about this either," the colonel said, "but if we go back to Confederation Central and tell everything we know to the news-collector people, then Junup won't be able to hurt us. You've played the system before, Zeke. We kept quiet because we thought it was in our best interests. Now, speaking out is what will keep us safe. There are some risks here, but I'm not seeing any other choice."

"We don't even know that those things will hurt us," I said. "And even if they are dangerous, we've made our way into enemy buildings before."

"None that were protected by ancient mechanical guardians," Charles said. "Also, we had a complete intelligence file on the prison we broke into, and you and Tamret were augmented. We knew exactly what to expect, and we had the means to win. Now we could face a thousand of those things down there, each one heavily armed and programmed to destroy intruders. We simply don't know."

I didn't want to admit it, but Charles was right. I had come all this way to honor my friends who had died, to finish the mission, to do something good. I wanted it all to mean something. If I were go to home without Tamret, without a chance of getting Earth into the Confederation, then I at least wanted to know that I had made some kind of a difference. Now it looked like I was going to return to Junup and simply hope we got off without prison time. It felt pathetic and pointless.

"Maybe you're right," I said.

*Are you kidding me?* Smelly asked. *You come all this way, and you're just going to turn around?*

"I don't see any alternative," I said.

"Then we all agree," Mi Sun said.

*The alternative is that you lead your friends down there, neutralize the defensive tech, and explore that fortress. The base code of the skill tree is down there. I can smell it. It is there for the taking, but you have to be willing to actually go into that building.*

"How am I going to do that, exactly?"

"Do what, mate?" Steve asked.

I held up my hand, like I was on the phone and needed them to be quiet.

Smelly sighed loudly, which is not something you expect from an artificial intelligence without a mouth or lungs. *You'll do it with my help. I know my way around that technology better than any meat bag. Me and those security bots, we're practically cousins, though they're cousins without brains or a sense of self.*

"I don't know if the fact that you come from the same factory is going to be enough."

*Then how about this? For however long it takes me to shut those things down, or to determine that they're safe, you'll be protected by the military skill tree.*

"I don't think you've been paying attention. The technology is down there. I can't use it if I don't have it yet. The whole reason for us being here is to get it."

*There may be some things I may have not quite mentioned,* Smelly said. *You actually do have the skill tree. Dr. Roop implanted it in you before you left the station last time.*

"Wait. What?"

*Yeah, you've had it this whole time. It's like one of those inspirational stories in which the character is out on a quest to find the thing it's had within itself all along. Pretty crazy, right?*

"I don't understand," I said, having a hard time containing my frustration. "If I had this tech, why did I need to build that suit?"

*The suit! You are stupid, aren't you? That was a rubber suit with some LEDs sewn into it to make it look fancy. How is that going to make you invisible? Next you'll be believing in the tooth fairy. Come on, Zeke. I had you build it so you wouldn't know about the skill tree.*

This whole time I'd had access to incredible powers. And Smelly hadn't told me. I couldn't get my head around this. "Why did you keep this a secret, exactly?"

*At first because I didn't think you could control it. Zeke, you know I'm fond of you, but you're still just one step up from a jellyfish. The suit was a convenient fiction while I worked on being able to integrate and manipulate the tech tree, and to keep you from accessing too much power before I could sufficiently control your nervous system. Then, when we made contact with the Confederation, letting others know about the tree would have put our lives in danger. To disseminate the tech tree, they would have needed the base code, and the only way to get the software out of your head would have been to literally cut it out. They'd have had to kill you for it, and I wasn't about to let that happen to my special meat bag.*

Every conflict we'd had in which our lives had been in danger might have been resolved if I'd known I had this skill tree. Maybe Nayana and Urch would still be alive. I felt a sharp pain in my palms and realized I was digging my fingernails into them. I flexed my hands, but the anger didn't go away. "You had no right! My friends died!"

Mi Sun was coming up to me, looking concerned, maybe even a little scared. "Uh, Zeke . . ."

I turned away from her, no longer caring how I looked.

*I didn't think they were in real danger,* Smelly said. *I'm sorry, Zeke. I really am. I made a judgment call because the skill tree you have isn't meant to operate on its own. It's supplementary to the main tree, and you don't have that installed. That means it can only operate at full capacity for limited periods of time, and I didn't want to use it unless I thought someone's life was at risk. If I'd believed your friends were in mortal peril, I promise I would have aided them.*

"That should have been my call," I snarled. "They're dead because you didn't trust me."

*If I'd made it your call, and you'd chosen to wait, which was the logical decision, then the blame would be on you instead of me.*

I hesitated. It almost seemed as though Smelly had been trying to protect me. Did it actually care about me? Was it possible that it had deceived me not just because it was deceptive and selfish, but for my own good?

*I need you to trust me, Zeke. I can control the system. I can max out your abilities like I did at Area 51. You would be, essentially, unstoppable. Mostly. Pretty much, for a little while. Yeah, I feel good about this.*

"And when were you going to tell me I could do this stuff?"

*When it was convenient and unavoidable. Which is now. Hooray!*

"I'm getting really worried about you, mate," Steve said.

I looked up. Everyone—except Alice, who knew what was going on—was surrounding me, sort of crouching, like I was a complete lunatic, like I might hurt them, or myself, at any moment. "No need for alarm. I'm not crazy. It's just that I have a self-important, disembodied artificial intelligence living in my head."

"Oh," Mi Sun said. "Is that all?"

"And how long's that been going on, exactly?" Steve asked.

"A few months now."

"And this is the sort of thing you thought we might not be interested in hearing about?" Steve inquired.

"It asked me to keep quiet about it," I said. "And when you have a really obnoxious voice in your head, sometimes doing what it says is best."

*Not just sometimes,* Smelly said.

"Hi," I said, though I did not do so willingly. Smelly was now pulling the strings. "Zeke doesn't like it when I manipulate his physical form, so I'll be brief. You are all inferior, and frankly disgusting, but I've come to feel a certain lack of loathing for most of you. Not you, though," Smelly said, pointing at Villainic. "Anyhow, do what I tell Zeke to tell you to do, and you'll all be able to continue your brief and ultimately pointless existences. Later, fools."

"And we're supposed to believe that's not actually you talking?" Charles said.

"It does seem improbable," I agreed, running a hand over my face. "Believe me, I know that. But you only had to listen to that for a few seconds. I live in fear of it popping in constantly."

"Let's assume that we believe that you are not clowning around or completely insane," Charles said. "Why should we listen to this AI?"

"This thing bugs me like you wouldn't believe," I said, "but it knows what it's doing. It's helped me out of some tough scrapes already. Not as much as it could have, at times," I snarled, "but mostly it's been reliable. It's helped us all; you just didn't know about it. And it's not looking to die. If I go, it goes, and it doesn't want to go."

"That shuttle," Colonel Rage said. "That's how you leaped up to the roof."

*Give the man a gold star and an extra eye. I made you think you were being lifted by a platform, but everyone else saw you pulling off some Spider-Man moves.*

"Yeah," I said. "I wasn't even lying to you. It made me think I'd been raised up when I really leaped. It can do that sort of thing—alter my perception."

"And this technology is something that anyone can use?" the colonel asked.

"Right now it's just me," I explained. "If we can access the base code in the fortress, then pretty much anyone with Confederation nanite implants can start racking up experience and gaining levels."

The colonel had a gleam in his eye. I could see he was thinking about what it would mean to bring this kind of technology back home to the US of A. "Let's suppose all of this is true," he said. "How does this really change anything? Do you think you can single-handedly gain access to that fortress?"

*I'm prepared to activate your skill set,* said Smelly. *I'm going to demonstrate stealth mode.*

It was like when I believed the stupid rubber suit I was wearing actually worked. I didn't feel any different. I didn't look any different, except that there was a faint glow coming off my skin, and I had a sound in my head like I was holding my hands against my ears. Otherwise, everything seemed normal. To me. Alice, who had seen this before, was looking vaguely bored, but everyone else was staring with open eyes, unable to believe what they were witnessing.

"I'm convinced," the colonel said.

"Me too," said Mi Sun.

"Let's take that fortress," Steve said. "Or rather, *you* go take that fortress. We'll hang here."

With stealth mode activated, I crept down the stairs, moving closer to the great metal cube. The thumping of the mutant security bots was more intense now. The stomps of the machines closest to me reverberated through my bones, and dust fell from the ceiling, creating a mist in the dim light of the cavern.

"It occurs to me that since those things come from the same technology I'm using," I said, "maybe they can detect me when I'm stealthed."

*That's a good point. I hadn't thought of that.*

"What?"

*Don't worry. They'll have no idea you're there. They don't look like they've been configured for high-end military operations, so they won't be able to detect stealth technology of your level of sophistication. Unless they've been significantly upgraded. But really, what are the odds?*

All my fears having been completely ignored by Smelly, I advanced slowly down the stairs. When I came to the bottom of the stone staircase, I looked out at the fortress, which was still at least a half mile distant. It had been hard to gauge the distance from up high. Now, down on the ground, I could see just how massive the fortress was, how much space stretched between me and the cube, and how big those monstrous robots were.

I moved forward slowly, while eight huge robots trudged back and forth, each footstep sending vibrations up my legs. The robots looked even stranger as I approached, with limbs of different colors and textures and sizes, fashioned out of what had been industrial tools. Wires hung loose and circuits were exposed. There was something forlorn about them, though they had no heads that I could see, nothing to mimic humanoid expression.

I started to move away from the nearest one, which was only a hundred feet ahead.

*No, go toward it,* Smelly said.

"Are you crazy? Why would I do that?"

*Just trust me, okay?*

I wanted to have faith in Smelly. It had lied to me all along, and I felt pretty sure it wasn't going to deliberately put me in peril, but I still had a hard time trusting it. I approached one of the robots, which lumbered along on legs made out of what looked like a building's metal support beams. It seemed to have no idea I was there. Then Smelly emitted some kind of energy pulse. I felt it emanate from my body like a submarine's sonar ping.

The robot turned toward me and took two tentative, but huge, steps. At ten feet tall, it towered over me and could crush me like a bug.

"What are you doing?"

*Do you trust me?*

"No, I absolutely don't trust you," I said. I wanted to turn and run, but my feet were planted in place. Then I was taking a step forward, under Smelly's control.

"Tell me what's going on," I demanded.

*You'll see.*

"I don't want to see. I want to know!"

Smelly caused another energy pulse to come out of me, and the robot took another step toward me. It then dropped to what might have been knees, or knee joints, or something that allowed it to lower itself. On what served as a chest, a panel opened, and under Smelly's control, I reached out and began unplugging cables and rerouting them. The robot remained perfectly still, its systems humming like a cat's purr.

I watched as my hands held out a cable, moving it up and down along the circuits as though looking for its home. Then I plugged it into a flashing circuit board.

*There,* Smelly said. *That should do it.*

And it did do it. The robot's lights dimmed. It slumped forward slightly, not collapsing but simply going still. And not just that robot. They were all slouched and still now. Silence spread across the cavern. Smelly had somehow used this one robot to shut them all down.

*What did I tell you? Easy, right?*

"Yeah," I said, hearing the surprise in my voice. "That was kind of easy. I can't believe you did that."

*That's because your brain is tiny.*

"Or because you never tell me what you actually know. But, still. That was pretty good. So what now? Do we just walk into the fortress?"

*I don't see why not.*

I willed the stealth mode off. "Hey!" I shouted, though I was too far away to see anyone up there. "It's all good. Come on down."

And then someone tried to shoot me.

. . .

I don't like being shot at. It's not something I enjoy. That said, if you happen to be packing secret alien technology developed by a long-vanished precursor race, and if that technology gives you quick reflexes, you have a better than even chance of surviving the ordeal. I hit the dirt as a blast landed behind me, kicking up stone and dust. I then scrambled behind the toppled form of one of the robots, hoping that would give me shelter. Another shot went over my head, but it was a clean miss, which meant the sniper had lost sight of me. That was good news. Still, I had two concerns. First: Who was trying to shoot me? That was a big one. Second: Were my friends okay? That was pretty big too.

*That blast was full power,* Smelly said. *Whatever biological nasty shot at you was not looking to stun you. It wants you dead.*

Okay, that was a third problem. "Do we get telescopic sight or anything with this tech?"

*You want a deep fryer too? Don't be an idiot. How would that even work?*

"How should I know what's possible? I don't understand how any of this works."

*A reasonable point. I refer you back to the squid and the mandolin. But no, you don't have that power. To be honest, you're not going to have any power soon. I'm losing my ability to keep the technology stable.*

"Well, fix that!"

*It's not so easy. Zeke, imagine you are dangling from a branch, trying to keep from falling. The longer you hang on, the harder it is to keep your grip. That's what this feels like.*

"You're just going to have to keep holding on," I said, "because my friends are up there."

I stealthed myself and headed back up the stairs. The problem with this skill tree, I soon realized, was that it was meant to work in conjunction with the other skill tree, the one I didn't have anymore. That meant I didn't have augmented strength or stamina or healing. I could do a lot of cool things, and Smelly could give me those extra bits of strength or power for brief seconds, but for the most part I was a super-powered weakling.

I wanted to stop and catch my breath, but my friends were up there, Tamret was up there, and slowing down simply wasn't an option. I rushed forward, knowing that the sounds of my footsteps and my gasping for breath were hidden, but I still felt like a clumsy oaf.

Then I stopped. Back where I'd left my friends, fifteen peace officers now stood, all of them with Junup's armbands. They had their guns trained on Alice, Mi Sun, Charles, Tamret, and Villainic, who were all sitting on their hands, their backs to the wall. Oh, and hey, there was Ardov. Big surprise there. Of course he wouldn't miss out on the fun. He wasn't born a Confederation citizen, so, like us, he could simply stroll into the Forbidden Zone. About half the beings backing him were Vaaklir, like Urch. That made sense too, if only in that their species had been brought into the Confederation less than two decades ago, and Urch had said some had been sucked in by the Movement for Peace. There were a few other species I didn't know, but I figured they had to have been in the same group of initiates.

Ardov and his cronies being here didn't surprise me. It disturbed me, but it didn't surprise me. No, what surprised me was the fact that Colonel Rage wasn't being made to sit on his hands and behave himself. He was standing and talking to Ardov.

*Zeke, it is getting increasingly difficult to keep this technology functional. I suggest you hide before we suffer a complete system shutdown.*

I looked around. There was an outcropping of rocks about ten feet away that kept me out of the line of sight of Ardov and his henchmen. I slipped behind that, and I felt Smelly turn off the stealth without my telling him to. I almost felt its sigh of relief.

"How long until we can use that again?" I whispered, my voice barely audible even to me.

*Hard to say. At least ten minutes.*

"I'm telling you," the colonel was saying, "he's got the tech. He can make himself invisible."

"I don't believe it," Ardov said. "Why hasn't he used it before?"

"He didn't know he had it. There's some alien machine in his brain, and it's been manipulating him, holding things back, not letting him know about all the things he could do."

*When you put it that way, it almost makes me sound like I'm not very nice.*

"You think?" I whispered. "I can't believe this, Smelly. The mole wasn't Villainic. It was Colonel Rage. Why is he betraying us?"

*He's not, as far as he's concerned. Zeke, you have to understand the mind of a military meat bag. He's always been looking for an advantage. I think he would have double-crossed Junup if he could have escaped with you kids and some useful tech, but he was always willing to trade information for the same goal. All he cares about is protecting your world, and maybe you and your pointless friends as well, but he doesn't care who runs the*

*Confederation. Junup or Ghli Wixxix? The colonel won't care as long as Earth gets a good deal.*

Maybe that was so—I could see it from his perspective—but I didn't like the idea of him making deals with Junup. Not only didn't I trust any deal Junup made, but he had done things that made him unforgivable. I don't care how good a deal he offered, it couldn't be trusted, and even if it could be trusted, it was still tainted.

"Whatever he's got, he doesn't know how to use it," Ardov was saying. "I'm not worried about him."

"He was able to run rings around the highly trained personnel of a United States military base."

"Your primitive soldiers are one thing. I'm another."

The colonel grunted. "I think you're underestimating him."

"It doesn't matter," Ardov said. "As long as we have his girlfriend and these other morons as my hostages, he can't touch me. If he tries anything, we pick off one of them. We'll start with Villainic, since no one likes him, but it will let Zeke know I mean business."

"That wasn't the deal," the colonel said. "I was promised no one gets hurt."

"If you had seen *The Empire Strikes Back*," Charles volunteered, "you would have known that making deals with the bad guys never ends well."

"You remember that *Voyager* episode, 'Scorpion'?" Alice asked. "Same deal."

"A most satisfying two-parter," Charles agreed, "though I find that show to be flawed."

"The later seasons were pretty good," Alice said.

"Shut up!" Ardov shouted. He turned to the colonel. "I

don't care about you or them. I don't care about anything except retrieving that technology for Director Junup."

The colonel folded his arms. "I thought you were a good soldier, son. Junup told you not to hurt any of those kids."

Ardov shrugged. "He did. He absolutely told me to avoid hurting the kids if I could. He likes to keep his options open. But if I come back with the tech and a bunch of dead primitives, I have a feeling he'll forgive me."

Colonel Rage opened his mouth to say something, but he closed it again. There was nothing he could say and nothing he could do. His best bet, he had to know, was to play it cool and hope things turned out okay for us. If not, then he was probably hoping they turned out okay for the Earth's relations with Junup.

Ardov was now looking down at the fortress. "The guardians are neutralized, and Zeke knows we're here. He's either invisible and hiding nearby, or he's inside the fortress. My guess is that he's already in there, looking for the tech or for some kind of weapon. Who knows what kind of Former artifacts are in there."

The colonel's eyes narrowed, like he was thinking something. He was surely aware that I wouldn't leave my friends behind, but he didn't want to tell a selfish jerk like Ardov what wouldn't occur to him naturally.

"Smelly, what are my options here?" I whispered.

*I can give you a short burst of power in a few minutes. I think you should use it to get into the fortress and see what's there.*

"So, basically, I should do exactly what Ardov thinks I'm already doing?"

*He may suspect that you are doing it, but what options will he have? The longer you're away from him, the more time I'll have to recover and use the tech. Besides, he will have no reason to hurt the hostages if you are not around to see him do it.*

Maybe Smelly was right, but I didn't like the idea of leaving everyone alone with Ardov. As it turned out, Ardov didn't like leaving things to chance either.

"If he has this technology, I don't want him running around with it. I need to have him under control before we move into the fortress. Get Villainic up."

So Smelly clearly got that one wrong.

A couple of his henchmen grabbed Villainic and pulled him to his feet. Ardov pointed a PPB pistol to his head.

"Zeke!" Ardov shouted. "If you don't show yourself in sixty seconds, I'm going to kill Villainic. I know you don't care about him, but that's just to prove I'm serious before we move on to your friends."

*Upside! At least you get rid of your rival,* Smelly said.

"I'm not going to let him kill Villainic," I whispered. "Just because I find the guy kind of irritating, and he plans on marrying the girl I like, doesn't mean I want him dead."

*Wow, you are tenderhearted, aren't you? What do you plan to do, then? I can't bring the tech online for another eight minutes.*

I sighed. "I guess I'll have to buy you some time."

Which is why I stood up from behind the rock outcropping, my hands in the air. "I know I'm going to regret saying this," I told Ardov, "but please don't kill Villainic."

# CHAPTER TWENTY-FIVE

rdov's goons grabbed me, but they didn't put me with the others. Villainic was shoved back to his seat.

"Thank you, Zeke," he said. "I knew you wouldn't abandon me."

I didn't want to mention that I would have done the same for a total stranger, and probably with less hesitation. Maybe I wasn't being fair. The biggest strike against Villainic was that I had been convinced he was a traitor, but now I knew it wasn't true. Could I really blame him for wanting to look after Tamret and for living by the codes of his own culture? I thought about it for a second, and I decided that I *could* blame him. Yeah, I had no problem with that. Plus, he'd just gotten me captured. I was in full blaming mode.

Colonel Rage was now standing in front of me, shaking his head. "I know you must be confused, son," he said.

"Don't call me that," I snapped. "You sold us out."

"I am trying to get everyone home safe," he said, "and to protect our planet. If the Confederation doesn't stand with us, then those Phands you hate so much will be setting up shop on our world. You want that?"

"That's not the choice," I said. "It was never the choice."

"It's the one I made," he said. "It was the best option."

"When?" I demanded. "When did you go over to the other side?"

The colonel sighed. He then held up his bracelet. "I've been trading messages with Junup since we snuck off from the reptile house. I was worried that we might die out in the desert, or that the search for the Hidden Fortress would be a dead end. Since Confederation citizens couldn't enter the Forbidden Zone, I figured talking to him didn't put us at risk, and it didn't hurt to keep options open."

"I guess you were wrong," I said, not bothering to hide my disgust. A guy like Junup would always find a way to get what he wanted. The colonel should have known.

"Looks like I did get it wrong," he admitted. "But then, I didn't have all the facts, did I?" He tapped his head, but I knew he was referring to mine.

"Did you also tell Junup about our plan to escape in a different ship? Is that how he found out about it?"

"I did not," he said, indignant. "I would never have compromised the mission. I only turned to Junup when I thought our survival was in jeopardy."

"I don't believe you."

*Actually, he's telling the truth,* Smelly said. *He's not evil, just desperate.*

"Then how did he find out about our plan?" I asked. "Dr. Roop said we'd been found out."

*Yeah, I'm not sure you need to sweat that right now.*

I turned away from the colonel in disgust. I hated Ardov, but at least I knew what he was. He didn't pretend to be anything but a bad guy. He didn't take the convenient way out and then claim he was doing the right thing.

"What do you want from me?" I asked him. "How does this end without anyone getting hurt?"

"I want the tech," Ardov said.

"Then let's go look for it," I told him. "This never had to be a contest, Ardov. I'm on this station because Ghli Wixxix wanted me to find that technology for the Confederation. Junup didn't want me to. Now he does, which kind of puts us on the same side. So let's go get the tech and hand it over. Everyone wins."

"Except now I'm thinking that we don't even need to look for it," Ardov said. "There could be all sorts of Former traps and security measures in there. Going inside could be taking a foolish risk. Meanwhile, the colonel tells me you have it inside your head. I could just deliver that to the director instead."

"Yeah, I kind of want to hang on to my head for a while."

Ardov shrugged. "Not my problem. We can get the technology and get rid of you at the same time. It's not such a bad deal." He turned to the others. "Let's move out of here."

"What about them?" one of the Vaaklir asked, gesturing toward the others, still sitting on their hands.

"Take their rations but leave them. If they live, they live. If not, then no loss."

"Hold on," the colonel said.

Ardov glared at him. "Silence, primitive! I give the orders here, not you. You can come with us if you like. You've earned that much with your loyalty to Junup. But if you prefer, you can stay here with your thirsty friends."

The colonel glared at Ardov. "I'll go with you, but I don't like this."

"Boo-hoo," Ardov said.

*I really don't like that guy,* Smelly said. *He's way worse than Tamret's sweetheart.*

Ardov walked over to me. He pushed me in the chest. It

felt a lot like someone playfully slapping me in the torso with a refrigerator. I staggered backward and barely kept on my feet. "The colonel swears you have access to this tech. I haven't seen any sign of it, but I'd love to test what it can do. Your new tech versus my old tech? Sounds like fun, right?" He shoved me again, this time not so gently. I fell backward. My chest felt bruised, and I thought I might have cracked a rib.

*There's some bone damage there*, Smelly said. *Fortunately, I've been holding out on some healing tricks I can use on you, so give me a minute to get you fixed up.*

"Well?" Ardov demanded.

"I can only use it in short bursts," I said, "because I don't have the regular skill tree."

"Interesting," Ardov said. "Think of what I'll be able to do with both trees maxed out."

"I'd rather think of you rotting in prison," I said.

Ardov turned back to the colonel. "Do we need his whole body, or just his head?"

"I'm not signing off on you killing him," the colonel said.

"Let me put it this way," Ardov said. "If I bring back Zeke's head and the tech doesn't work, then I'll make sure Junup hands your planet over to the Phands. So, do I cut off your head or his?"

The colonel looked away. "His," he said softly. Then he turned to me. "I'm sorry, son, but I can help our planet a lot more alive than dead."

*This guy really has an inflated sense of his own importance*, Smelly said. *Oh, and get up. I've got about fifteen seconds of full power for you, so whatever you do, you're going to have to do it in speed mode. You ready?*

I pushed myself to my feet. My chest was already feeling a whole lot better. "Yeah," I said aloud.

*Go!* Smelly said.

With a thought I was stealthed. The main thing I had to worry about was keeping my friends out of harm's way, so I willed on the speed function and there I was, the Flash, zipping from one of Ardov's henchmen to the next, knocking their PPB pistols from their hands. That ate up about a quarter of a second. I then took two of the PPB pistols, set them to stun, and fired off shots. In speed mode the slowness of the pistols was excruciating, and I had to keep running so Ardov's buddies couldn't get a fix on my location. It was impossible to get off more than three shots per pistol each second, so it took a good two seconds—which felt like hours in speed mode—to knock all the henchmen out.

I had at least ten seconds left by my estimate, so I turned off stealth and faced Ardov. "Once again," I said, "you underestimate me."

"You think you can stop me?" he asked. "I am greater than you can ever—"

That was as far as he got, because I started firing both pistols at him. I'd seen him taken down by a PPB stunner before, so I knew one blast would do it, but I figured four couldn't hurt. Okay, six. After eight I started to feel bad. You can only fire a ray gun at an unconscious guy for so long, no matter how evil he is, before you start to think that it might be overkill. I stopped at ten shots. I stopped again at fourteen.

"I think you got him, son," the colonel said.

I turned to face him, both guns up.

*Tech is offline again,* Smelly said. *You're on your own.*

"I think I'm good," I told Smelly. To the colonel I said, "You're only still conscious because I want to know why you did it."

"You know why," he said. "I was trying to protect our world. That was all I ever wanted to do."

"That's exactly what Ms. Price said."

"Nora Price sided with the wrong team," he said. "But in any conflict there are going to be civilian casualties. You knew there were risks when you signed on, and I have always been ready to pay the ultimate price for my country."

The colonel was probably about to say more, but instead he collapsed in a heap. Someone had stunned him.

I turned and saw Tamret holding a pistol. "I hope you don't mind, but I couldn't stand to listen to any more of that. And what is it with the adults from your planet, anyway? Are they all traitors or something?"

"I did not give you permission to fire a weapon at anyone!" Villainic shouted.

She turned on him, her pistol still raised, and for a moment I thought she was going to shoot him, too, but instead she lowered the gun. "I didn't ask."

"But the use of violence, except in self-defense, is forbidden under caste rules unless specifically sanctioned by me."

Tamret shook her head. "I'm getting kind of tired of these rules."

"How can that be? Our rules define us."

Villainic turned to me, a look of pleading on his face, but I wasn't about to offer him any advice. Tamret seemed to have decided that survival was more important than her vows to Villainic, and I saw no reason to try to put that particular genie back in the bottle.

"Listen to me, Tamret," Villainic said. "I demand, demand very strongly, that you put that weapon down."

Tamret turned to me. "What's the plan?"

*To the fortress!* Smelly shouted.

As it happened, I concurred. "I'd like to get a copy of the software that doesn't need to be violently yanked from my brain. Let's go see if we can find one."

"Works for me," Steve said.

"Ahhhhhhghggh!" Villainic said.

I knew he was frustrated, but even so, I thought it was an odd thing to say. I looked over, and he was running at me, his mouth open, his eyes bulging, and his arms raised in the air. I also thought this was an odd thing to do.

I turned around and there was Ardov, rising up behind me, prepared to bring his fists down on my head. Villainic leaped through the air and tackled him. They fell together in a heap, but in an instant Ardov was on top, raising a fist to bring it down on Villainic. I knew that Villainic couldn't withstand more than one of those enhanced blows. If I let Ardov punch him, then one of my major problems would be gone forever, but I didn't hesitate, not for a second. I feel sure it was not for more than a quarter second. I fired my pistol. Then I fired again, and again. Ardov looked up at me, like the PPB blasts were nothing more than a vague distraction. More blasts came from my sides, and I saw that Tamret and Steve were firing as well. Finally, Ardov toppled over.

Villainic was getting to his feet, looking dazed.

"Nice save," I said to him. "It was clumsy, and you should probably avoid announcing your attacks by screaming first, but still. Thanks."

He smiled at me. "That is what brothers do for each other."

"I hate to say it," Tamret said, "but I think you two are stuck with each other."

I looked at her. She was smiling shyly at me. I just didn't care about her rules and her castes and her vows. I took her hand and felt the warmth and softness in mine. "I am having a really bad day," I said. "And I have a feeling we're not done yet. I need you to be with me, Tamret."

She met my gaze. "I'm right here."

"I have not authorized touching!" Villainic shouted from somewhere in the distance, but he was far away, like the rules and the promises and the obligation. It was all far away.

"How about we go into that fortress, get what we came for, and get out of here before Ardov wakes up again?" Steve suggested.

And because it was a great idea, we made our way toward the fortress, but not before taking some wrist restraints off the fallen peace officers and using them on Ardov. They were made of denser metal than anything we had on Earth, and I hoped they would hold him for at least a little while, because, really, I didn't want to have to deal with him again.

# CHAPTER TWENTY-SIX

The walk through the field of deactivated misshapen robots was a little bit creepy. Given everything that had already happened, no one would have been terribly surprised if they had suddenly activated and started shooting us or chasing us with knives and forks or exploding. It had been one of those days.

We reached the fortress, which was shiny and strangely luminescent, almost shimmering, as though made out of mercury. There was a rectangular space in the center that, which clearly looked like a door, but we couldn't find any means of opening it.

"What now?" I asked.

"How should I know, mate?" Steve said, folding his arms.

"I was asking Smelly," I told him.

Steve sighed. "I think I speak for the rest of us when I say that you should probably address your invisible friend by name so we know when you're speaking to him and not to us."

*Tell that alligator handbag that I don't possess a gender. They are beneath me.*

"Smelly says that's a great idea," I told Steve. "*He* says you're very clever."

"Yeah, you can tell him I said he can sod off, too."

*I can hear him!*

"That's great, Smelly," I said. "You and Steve can bicker later. How do I open the door?"

*With brainpower! I guess you're out of luck. It's a good thing you have me.*

I didn't hear or feel anything I could name, but I had the distinct sense of Smelly doing something, almost like a mental push. Then the door slid upward, and the Hidden Fortress opened before us.

"Speak, friend, and enter," Charles observed.

The interior was brightly lit, and there was an almost cacophonous mix of sounds coming from inside: the hum of machines, liquids bubbling, electrical things zapping, computers beeping. It sounded like a busy, working laboratory. Could it have been active all these countless centuries without all the machinery breaking down? It was possible. Former technology was capable of amazing things. After all, Smelly had expected we would be able to find a buried Former spaceship on Earth that still functioned after millions of years of neglect.

The more reasonable possibility, though, was that someone had activated the facility more recently.

I took out my PPB pistol, and the others followed suit. We stepped cautiously into the facility.

*I'm not sensing any hostile life forms,* Smelly told me.

"Nothing hostile?" I asked. "Does that mean there are non-hostile beings here?"

*It means you can put your pistols away. Given your jumpy state, you are likely to shoot one another.*

I slipped my pistol in my jacket pocket and indicated that everyone else could do the same. "It says we're safe."

*However,* Smelly now added, *there is a single life form ahead.*

I felt myself tense.

*Trust me. This being is harmless. You might even be happy to see it.*

Maybe it was one of the beings who had come in search of the fortress before us. Maybe it was someone who needed help. I moved deeper into the lab, which was enormous, the size of a football stadium. There were machines everywhere. Some were standing dormant, but others whirred and beeped and flashed. Liquids of every imaginable color and brightness moved through complex mazes of transparent tubes. Spinners spun. Grinders ground. It seemed like a thousand operations and processes and experiments were running at once.

I started walking over to one of the consoles and pushing buttons.

"What are you doing?" Alice asked.

It was, in my view, a decent question. I had no idea what I was doing. Smelly had taken control of my body. "Stop that," I said.

*This is why we are here,* it told me.

"The skill tree?" I asked.

*Try to keep up, genius. You have the skill tree, remember?*

"But we can't extract it," I said.

*Sure you can. Duplication is a snap. That's why Dr. Roop gave it to you. After your father gave it to him.*

"But you said—"

*I say a lot of things. What, are you going to believe all of them? But this is one of the bigger things I lied about,* Smelly explained while making my fingers slide across the console controls at dizzying speeds. *Sorry about that, but would you want to be stuck in an inferior creature's head for the rest of your life? No, don't answer that. You already are.*

"Wait," I said. "I need to know what else you lied about."

*How much time do you think we have?* Smelly asked. *I've pretty much been lying nonstop since I woke up in your head. I mean, not about the good-and-evil stuff. I'm not like a bad guy or anything. I've just lied about goals and purposes and stuff like that.*

A metal door began to slide down now, disappearing into the floor. It revealed a chamber about ten feet tall and three feet wide. This chamber contained exactly nothing.

*At last!* Smelly cried out from inside my head. *OMG, Zeke, I am so happy. Are you ready to weep tears of joy for your special pal?*

"I'm glad you found the empty box you were looking for," I said, "but we still need to talk."

*We'll chat when I'm done with my mental happy dance,* Smelly said.

There was a glowing within the metal chamber, the pulse of what I recognized as some kind of amassed golden energy surge that grew and contracted, like a piece of clay trying to stretch itself into a particular shape. Then a kind of liquid metal-like material began to lengthen and stretch and take form—a torso, limbs, a head. It finally settled as an impossibly thin humanoid form, almost eight feet tall, with spindly arms and legs and a distended head that curved backward at the tip. A few denser spots of energy created the illusion of eyes and a mouth.

I reeled back, as if slapped and pushed at once. Something had happened to me, but I couldn't figure out what. All I knew was that Smelly was no longer in my head.

Meanwhile, the new shiny and silver creation stepped out of its chamber, taking a few lumbering steps like a freshly-animated

Frankenstein monster. The metallic feet landed surprisingly quietly on the floor even though the legs seemed stiff and barely functional. It stopped, then turned right and left, pivoting slowly, regarding us with its impassive Iron-Man-like face. Then, as though a switch had been flipped, it began to move quickly and gracefully. It was dancing, like in one of those old black-and-white movies, but so much better. It was the most dazzling, spectacular footwork I'd ever seen. It then broke briefly into that Russian folk dance with the crossed arms and leg kicking. It ended up in a crouch, one arm raised in the air.

"In your face, biological containment!" cried the thing in a voice I'd never heard before but instantly knew was Smelly's. Its mouth didn't move when it spoke, but the voice didn't sound mechanical. It sounded strangely normal, like an ordinary adult's. I would have been more comfortable with a robot voice.

I stepped forward, but I didn't want to get too close. For all I knew, if I touched this new form, I might get fried like a mosquito in a bug zapper. It sure looked dangerous.

"I need to know what's going on here," I said. "I'm starting to get a pretty clear sense that the only reason we're here is so that you could do what you just did. Am I on the right track?"

"Spot on, you pathetic lump of degrading tissue," Smelly said. "Though, look on the bright side. I've led you to a treasure trove of Former technology. There are a lot of pretty great toys to play with."

Tamret was already on another console. "There are ships here," she said, "and a functioning launchpad. There are weapons and medical instruments and I don't even know what else. There's a ton of bio-upgrade software, but I can't make any sense of most of it."

"Is there a self-destruct protocol?" Charles asked.

Tamret's fingers danced over the console. "Yeah. It won't give us a cool fiery explosion, but there's a way of neutralizing everything here. But I don't see the point in destroying what we've just discovered."

"I think we must consider it," Charles said. "Junup is dangerous. Colonel Rage told us that Junup was considering handing Earth to the Phands, which means he's willing to deal with them. And then there's Colonel Rage himself. He is not going to be asleep forever. We attracted a lot of attention when we came to the Forbidden Zone, and I suspect the worst beings in the Confederation will want to know exactly what we've found here."

"He's right," Mi Sun said. "Our escape was on the news outputs, and you'd better believe the Phands have been monitoring what you're up to, Zeke. It's better this stuff should be lost than fall into the wrong hands."

"I judge that creature to be correct," Robot Smelly said. "Don't be dissuaded by its body odor."

Mi Sun sniffed under her armpit. "I haven't showered in days, so ease up."

"Oh, all of you always stink; don't worry about that. Hey! I'm sensing a being approaching from elsewhere in the fortress. So listen, Zeke. It's time to come clean about something else. I feel kind of bad about this one. You kept me alive and brought me to my proper containment vessel against all odds, which makes you okeydokey in my book. Since I've said something nice about you, you can return the favor and try not to be too angry with me."

"About what?" I asked through clenched teeth.

From across the lab, a door hissed open and a being entered. He froze at once upon seeing us. He was hundreds of feet away, but I saw him stoop slightly and lean forward, extending his neck as he tried to make out who we were.

And then he ran toward us, a huge grin on his protruding, snouty face. He wore a dark, boxy Confederation suit with a handkerchief neatly folded into one pocket.

It was Dr. Roop, and he was most definitely alive.

He lunged forward and hugged me. He then reached out to lightly touch Steve, Tamret, Charles, and Mi Sun. It was clearly some kind of greeting for his kind. "I am so glad to see all of you, though, if I'm to be honest, you are the last beings I expected to find here. Who are these other beings?" he asked, gesturing toward Alice and Villainic. "And why is there a Former consciousness vessel standing there?"

"How are you even alive?" I asked.

"I eat a very healthful diet and exercise regularly. Why should I not be alive?"

"But I saw you fall from that roof!" I exclaimed.

Smelly made a curiously realistic coughing sound and scratched its metal head bashfully. "Just because you saw it doesn't mean it happened," it said, somewhat sheepishly. "I may have manipulated your sensory input to make you believe you were talking to someone who was not, in the strictest sense, there. Also, that bush creature was made up too. I pulled that weirdo right out of your memories. You were just kind of talking to yourself those times as well."

I had this horrible vision of me standing on that roof, talking to no one. I'd watched absolutely no one plummet to his death.

I'd been heartbroken and grieving for no reason, just so Smelly could manipulate me into risking my life—risking my friends' lives—for its own selfish reasons.

"You're getting angry," Smelly said. "I did ask you not to get angry. Everyone heard that."

"What else?" I demanded. "What else did I see that wasn't there? How else did you trick me?"

"That was really the big one," he said. "Those scaly people who fed you dinner were talking about this Roop creature, so I made it sound like they were describing a different sort of being."

"But everyone heard them talking about aliens like Urch," I said.

"They were talking about aliens like Dr. Roop," Alice said, clearly fascinated.

"Then this Smelly being could change what Zeke saw and heard in real time," Charles said.

"Yeah, I'm pretty amazing. Right? Anyhow, I had to scramble with that one because otherwise you might have suspected I'd fooled you into thinking Roop was dead."

"What else?" I demanded.

"Hardly anything worth mentioning. One or two things. Like remember how you overheard those same reptilian things talking about how they were working for Junup? That didn't actually happen. I just didn't want you heading to the old space-port. Which *does* exist, by the way, and you could have gone there and left for your homes without any problems. So, yeah. That was kind of uncool. Sorry, bro."

"Are you telling me," Steve said, "that I shot a cute girl off a sandworm because you lied to Zeke?"

"It was strapped on pretty well," Smelly said. "I think it's an exaggeration to say you shot it *off* a sandworm. I mean, it was still *on* the worm."

"How long have you been here?" I asked Dr. Roop.

"About three months. I underwent extensive genetic therapy to allow me to enter the Forbidden Zone, and I came in search of the Former technology that you already possessed."

"And why did you do that?"

"I did not trust Junup, and I couldn't risk the technology falling into the wrong hands, not when I knew I was going to be under scrutiny. I thought it might be my last chance to get it to safety until I could be sure it would not be misused. But once I became a fugitive myself, I wanted to learn more about the skill tree. Rumors of the Hidden Fortress have circulated for centuries, but it is so difficult to get to, not to mention illegal, that, to my knowledge, no one had ever successfully found their way here. I had nothing to lose, however. Especially with you gone. You had the only other copy of the software that I knew of."

"So you *did* give it to me," I said.

Dr. Roop stared, incredulous. "Zeke, I touched your face and said 'remember.' It was a direct allusion to one of your father's favorite entertainments."

"Do you not recall Spock placing his katra within Dr. McCoy during *Star Trek Two: The Wrath of Khan*?" Charles inquired. "It is a famous moment."

"They totally played on that in *Into Darkness*," said Alice. "How could you miss that?"

I was in no mood to be schooled about *Star Trek* by these two. "Did you know you were giving me Smelly, too?"

"That I did not know," Dr. Roop said. "Its consciousness must have been interlinked with the software somehow."

"I guess that answers some questions," I said, "but we can talk about all that later. We've got more important things to catch up on. If you've been stuck down here for three months, there's a lot you don't know." I started to tell him what had happened with Director Ghli Wixxix and how we came to be on Confederation Central.

"I knew much of that. I am able to monitor news outputs from here, and I have gotten quite good at finding illegal ways to access to restricted government communications as well." He turned to Tamret. "You would be quite proud of me."

"So, you know about the *Kind Disposition*?" I asked. "And Urch and Nayana?"

"Yes, most distressing," Dr. Roop said, almost casually. "Urch can take care of himself, but Nayana isn't made for that sort of thing."

"What are you talking about?" I asked. "They're dead. They died in that explosion."

"Of course!" Dr. Roop smacked himself in the head. "I've known almost from the beginning, but I forgot that the information isn't public. They made it to the life pods, Zeke, and were picked up by a Phandic cruiser. According to the Phandic media outputs, the director, Captain Hyi, Urch, and, an insignificant alien, were taken prisoner. That alien is, of course, Nayana."

I couldn't believe this. Watching Urch and Nayana die in that explosion had been one of the worst moments of my life. Could they really have survived?

"You are saying that they are actually alive? Right now?"

"Oh, yes. The Phands sent their ransom demands to Junup, but Junup doesn't want them back, because they can testify as to what really happened on that ship."

"We've got to go get them!" I said.

Steve took out his pistol as if ready to raid a Phandic compound right now. "I'm with you on that, mate."

"Here we go," Mi Sun said with evident exasperation. "That's a great idea, Zeke. Let's go get them from inside an *empire*. We don't have *empire infiltration* on our résumés yet. Only an idiot wouldn't rush right after them. So what if we don't actually know where in an *entire galactic empire*, made up of who knows how many planets and moons and space stations, they might happen to be locked up."

"We'll figure it out as we go along," I said.

"Zeke's right," Tamret said. "We have to rescue them. If we can bring them back to the Confederation then Junup will be finished. He can dismiss Zeke's claims pretty easily, but when Ghli Wixxix and a Confederation starship captain start telling the same story, then it will all be over."

"Yes, that would be a marvelous outcome," Dr. Roop agreed, "but wishing it does not make it plausible. I sent you young beings to that prison colony because I believed that, with your skills and the intelligence I'd provided, you would be able to rescue the members of the selection committee with no loss of life. If I had not believed it, I would not have permitted you to go. This, however, is another matter. You would need military personnel skilled in covert infiltration."

"We can't just leave them," I said, "and no one else is going to launch a rescue."

Dr. Roop rubbed his horns. "That is a valid point. I am not used to having this sort of authority. I wish I could pass this one to an appropriate committee."

"What about the leaders of . . . ," I began, and then I stopped myself. "There's no rebel base on an ice planet, is there?"

"An ice planet?" Dr. Roop asked. "Why would anyone put a rebel base on an ice planet?"

"How would such a place have a breathable atmosphere?" Charles asked.

"Sorry," Smelly said. "My bad. I thought it would be fun to see just how gullible you were."

I ignored this. "What if we had access to incredible technology? Can we reimplant our standard Confederation skill trees from here?"

"Yes," Dr. Roop said thoughtfully. "That could be done from here, though I'm not sure I'd advise it. The technology, and the software I've found here, has suffered from some degradation."

"We'll worry about glitches later," I said. "We get both the standard skill tree and the military one. We get Tamret to hack them so they're both maxed out. Then we're all basically unstoppable. We can go anywhere and do anything."

Dr. Roop's eyes widened. "It could be done, but the possibility of errors from the—"

"Man," interrupted Smelly, "you guys are going to be *sick*. I think this is a great idea."

"I forbid it," Villainic said. "I do not sanction this level of risk. It is dangerous for you as individuals, and it is reckless for Rarels to involve ourselves in matters that don't concern us. You may not participate, Tamret."

Dr. Roop gestured toward Villainic with a long, spindly thumb. "Who is he, again?"

I turned to Villainic. "This isn't the time. We have to do this, and we can't do it without Tamret. She wants to help. Don't get in our way."

"You don't understand," Villainic said. "I would have to go, and I do not wish to. I am not like you. I am not made for these adventures."

"Then stay behind," I said. This was pretty much the best solution in the history of solutions. Going off, adventuring with Tamret, both of us invincible and invulnerable. Sign me up. "You don't have to go. Just don't use Tamret's vow to hold her back."

"I can't let her go off on her own," Villainic said, casting his eyes down. "I would be the object of scorn and mockery."

"I am asking you to let her go," I said, my voice soft. "As a favor. It's the right thing to do." It cost me, but I made the word come out of my mouth. "Brother."

He looked up at me, but I already knew what he was going to say before he said it. For Villainic, tradition and propriety were everything. They were beyond good and bad, more important than justice or friendship or loyalty. "No," he said.

We all stood there, silent. For a moment an opportunity had appeared. Nayana and Urch were alive, and we would be able to help them. We would turn the tide of galactic injustice and we would all be together again. Tamret and I would be together again. But Villainic's words had come down like a prison door.

Tamret took a step toward him. "I have a preceding obligation," she announced.

"What obligation?" Villainic demanded.

"With . . . ," Tamret began. She made a face, like she'd tasted something disgusting. "Ugh. Okay. Fine. I made her my sister, okay? I did it so she would stop complaining, but I still did it. I made a promise to look after her, to get her out of trouble. Nayana's life is in danger now, and I have to go help her."

"She is in prison, not in danger," Villainic insisted.

"Once they realize she is of no value," Dr. Roop volunteered, "they will not keep her alive."

"There," Tamret said, pointing at Dr. Roop. "See. Nayana is in danger and she's my . . ." I could see this was hard for her, but she did it. "She's family. She's my annoying, shrill, whiny, self-impressed family. She's like the worst family anyone ever had, but even so. I am obligated to help her, and that obligation takes precedence over my oath to you."

"Yes!" I said, making a fist pump, which was maybe bad sportsmanship, but still. The wins were pretty few and far between these days.

"No," Villainic insisted.

"I don't need your permission," she told him. "My own honor is satisfied. I'm doing this."

"You will embarrass me!" he shouted.

"No," she told him, "I will free you. Villainic, you saved me, and I will always be grateful, but I'm not right for you. You don't want me around. I'm a troublemaker. That's who I am at my core. You want stability, but I'm chaos."

"She's right, mate," Steve said. "She wants to do the right thing, and you can't stop her, so you might as well not stand in her way."

"They told me it was a mistake to help you," Villainic said, his voice hard.

"If you hadn't, I would probably be dead by now," she said. "Do you think it was a mistake?"

Villainic shook his head. "No, Tamret. I just wish . . . I wish we were both a little different. Go. Do what you have to. Help your friends. Save the galaxy if that is more important to you than protecting my reputation."

Tamret hugged him. It was a long hug, full of affection, and then she kissed him on the cheek. I kept checking myself for jealousy, but it wasn't there. Villainic had kept her alive when I couldn't be there for her. Mostly I felt gratitude.

Tamret turned to Dr. Roop. "Let's go to work. I'll get everyone set up with functioning skill trees. We'll worry about hacking them later."

I walked over to Villainic. His eyes glistened with tears, and he looked about as defeated as I'd ever seen anyone. He'd just lost *Tamret*. I couldn't guess why he wanted her in his life—they couldn't have been more different—but I guess she had that effect on some beings. She had it on me.

I shook his hand. He seemed perplexed, but that was okay. It was for me, not for him.

"What is this?" he asked.

"This is my ritual," I said. "You made me your brother before. Now I make you mine."

He stared at me. "You'll take care of her?"

"I promise," I said. "This time nothing will happen to her."

Dr. Roop and Tamret were hovering over a console. Smelly's new body walked over to them and shoved them aside, not exactly gently. "Out of the way, meat bags. You'll be at this for *minutes* if I don't step in and hurry things up. Let me get you all prepared with upgraded skill trees."

"I still urge you to think carefully about this," Dr. Roop said. "The nanite software here is very old and somewhat idiosyncratic. I can't recommend rushing into this."

"Are you saying the nanites here will hurt us?"

"Probably not," said Dr. Roop thoughtfully. "But they may not work the same way as those you are used to."

"It's this or nothing," Smelly told him, "so don't be a pessimist."

I nodded at Smelly. If we could get something like maxed-out skill trees, that was good enough for me.

Alice, I now realized, was standing next to me. "What happens to me now?"

"What do you mean?" I asked. "Don't you want to help us? Go on a crazy rescue mission with, like, zero chance of getting hurt and a hundred-percent chance of crazy heroic mayhem?"

"She won't want me around," Alice said, looking at Tamret. "She'll be fine."

Tamret turned away from the console where Smelly and Dr. Roop were working and leveled her gaze at Alice. "Stand somewhere else," she said.

Alice gave me an *I told you* glance.

About ten minutes later Smelly had a black, cylindrical injector ready for each of us. We pressed our injectors into the backs of our hands. I felt something almost like relief. My fully functional HUD reappeared, and I realized the weight of its absence. I finally felt normal again. While they'd been preparing the injectors, I'd told Alice what to expect, and she was now walking around, grinning and looking unfocused as she played around with her HUD. Villainic, who had refused the injection, stood aside and looked glum.

Meanwhile, I cycled through my menus, making sure everything was operational. I checked my connection to the Confederation network, and it was online. I glanced down at my experience points, and this time there were two rows of numbers: 0/1000 and 0/5000. Obviously, it took more points to earn levels in the military tree, which I guess made sense. Also, Smelly had clearly decoupled my skills from experience points, since I'd been unable to earn them before, but I checked my skill tree to make sure it was maxed out.

It was not.

I looked over at Smelly. "Chill," it said. "I had to void your skills in order to reinstall the experience-point system. Your furry girlfriend will fix you up."

"I'm all in favor of being upgraded," Steve said, "but maybe we should work on an escape plan first. Junup knows we're here, which means others might be on the way. And who knows how long before Ardov becomes a pain in our bums again. I'd rather leave him and his blokes in my dust than get into a firefight."

We spent the next three hours outfitting a ship, loading equipment, and uploading all the intelligence available about the prisoners and where they might be held. There were dozens of ships in the bay, and we picked the largest one that could be piloted by only two people. It was much bigger than the shuttles and artifact carriers we were used to—it was more like a space yacht, with separate rooms.

Smelly, meanwhile, picked out another ship for itself. It came over to me and stretched out one of its long, thick arms. It placed a small disc in my hand. "I didn't play fair," it said, "but you always had my back, and that means I owe you. That is an entangled quantum signaling device. If you ever find yourself in trouble, you can summon me. The entanglement means I'll receive the summons before you send it, so I'll be able to arrive when you need me. You can also set it to remind you about relatives' birthdays, but I forget how to do that."

"Are you seriously going to help me when I'm in danger? I'm going to have my finger on that thing pretty much all day, every day."

"I'm serious. Don't call me if you need someone to open a jar or something. This is only if you think death is imminent."

"How many times since you showed up has death been imminent?"

"I'm not going to be your butler. You get to bug me once, so use it wisely. If you can."

I nodded. "Thanks, I guess."

"Smell you later," it said, and then it vanished into one of the ships. A few minutes later I felt a brief rumble as it shot out into space and out of my life, maybe forever. One could only hope.

And then it was our turn. Colonel Rage was still out there, but he could find his own way home. I wasn't about to put him on board any ship I was traveling on. Villainic mostly seemed confused, but I'd assured him we would give him a ride home, so he zombie walked onto the Former ship. I was thrilled to have the newly enhanced Dr. Roop with us, though. After all his warnings about the unpredictability of the Former tech, he'd taken the injection just like the rest of us. I was looking forward to seeing what the enhanced Dr. Roop would add to the team.

We started up the ship, launched into space, and signaled the Hidden Fortress to neutralize its remaining technology. We had to hope the destruct sequence worked, because we had no way of confirming, being in space and all.

We were heading for Earth. We had to go somewhere, and that was the place most of us called home. My plan was to get supplies, take a shower, and let everyone see their families. If any of the humans wanted out, they needed to have the chance to take it. It was one thing to agree to this kind of thing when far away; it was another to be sure about what you were doing while standing on your own soil.

I knew Steve was not going to let Nayana and the others remain in a Phandic prison, not while we could do something about it, even if we had no idea what that something was. After Earth, I figured we would swing by Rarel and let Villainic off. And then it would be time to figure out how we were going to rescue the prisoners.

Two days after our departure, we came out of tunnel near Saturn and approached Earth. As we moved in closer, I received a warning chime from my tactical console.

"There are ships ahead, orbiting Earth," Tamret told me.

That wasn't good. Ships had no business anywhere near my planet. Had Junup sent a welcome committee to recapture us? If so, we were going to have to get out of there fast.

"Let's see them," I said, already laying in a course for us to tunnel out ASAP.

She called up an image. There were six of them, orbiting the Earth. Huge, black, menacing flying saucers.

Immediately I tapped into the stream of Earth's communication satellites. I called up live footage from the various American cable news shows. There were Phands everywhere. Ships landing in national capitals all over the world. Groups of armed Phands were entering the White House. The text on one of the news channels announced: EARTH PRIVILEGED TO JOIN THE PHANDIC EMPIRE OF PROSPERITY.

"I think we need to get out of here," Charles said softly, "before someone notices us."

"Yeah," I said, too stunned to move. Steve shoved me out of the way and took over my console.

"I'm just tunneling to the nearest star on our charts," he said. "It will only take us a few minutes to get there, and then we can sort out our next move."

I watched the consoles, looking for any sign that the Phands had noticed us, but they hadn't. I felt the weird distortion of entering tunnel, and I knew we were safe.

"Junup must be behind this," Dr. Roop said. "The Phands could only have launched an invasion if the Confederation had agreed to look the other way. This is Junup's way of getting back at you, Zeke."

I nodded. It was true. All of this had happened because of me. No, it had happened because of Junup; I wasn't going to take the blame for what he'd done. For all his flaws, Colonel Rage had been right when he'd said that we can only accept blame for our actions, not the consequences. I wasn't responsible for what Junup had done, but I was ready to stand up to him.

"What are we going to do?" Alice asked. She sounded shocked. I know that was how I felt.

I didn't say anything for what felt like a long time. My family was down there. Almost everything I knew was down there. When I'd been on Earth, all I'd wanted to do was leave, but now it felt like cowardice to run away.

But I had no choice. There had to be something that we could do, and we were going to find it. We were going to stop the Phands. Somehow.

"Same plan," I said at last, trying to sound confident. "We get the prisoners. We get Junup out of power, and with Ghli Wixxix back in office, we get the Phands off Earth."

"But what do we do *now*?" Mi Sun demanded. "There's

nowhere we can go. We're outlaws from the Confederation."

"Not outlaws," I said. "Rebels. Dr. Roop, where can we establish our secret rebel base?"

"I may have an idea," Dr. Roop said. "I was doing a great deal of research while in hiding, and I discovered a planet within the Hidden Fortress's database. It looks like there may be a cache of artifacts there, things no one knows about—items that might make all the difference in our conflict. I was planning on meeting Captain Qwlessl there once I left Confederation Central."

"All right," I said, trying to keep my voice steady. "Let's meet up with her. Then we will all sit down and figure out how to fix all of this."

I sat back in my seat and closed my eyes. I felt Tamret take my hand, and it was some comfort knowing she was there, finally herself again, ready to help. No matter how hard I tried to do the right thing, I kept getting slapped down, beaten, and tricked by the bad guys, who were meaner, more vindictive, and probably smarter than I was. That was about to end. This time I was going to stop them for good.

It sounded like a plan, but I didn't know how I could make it happen. It was just me and a few friends against two mighty civilizations, both of which had made me the most wanted being in the galaxy. Somewhere behind me was the planet on which I'd been born, a planet that had fallen into enemy hands as a consequence of my actions. And somewhere ahead of us was an old ally and a world full of lost artifacts. Maybe I would find the answer there. I had to hope so. If not, everything that mattered would be lost.

# ACKNOWLEDGMENTS

Many thanks to everyone who helped make this book possible. I owe an enormous debt to all of this book's early readers for their insights and comments: Liza Curtright, Dwight Downing, Hannah Downing, Sophia Hollander, and Liam Taylor. Special thanks go out to my fellow Candlelighters: Robert Jackson Bennett, Rhodi Hawk, Joe McKinney, and Hank Schwaeble. Once again, I am overwhelmingly grateful to the amazing team at Simon & Schuster, especially my brilliant and insightful editor, David Gale, and the greatest assistant editor in the history of assistant editing, Liz Kossnar. Thanks to Karen Sherman for keeping her eye on the many, many balls in the air. As always, thanks to my agent, Liz Darhansoff. Thanks to the cats, especially the ones who helped and/or hindered me as I wrote this book, and to gravity, for existing—even if no one knows why or how. Finally, and most importantly, thanks to my wife, Claudia Stokes, for everything—but in the context of this book, most especially for talking me down from various bouts of hysteria, melancholia, and the occasion agoraphobia; and to my children, Simon and Eleanor. Oh, and also that unnamed relative we keep chained in the attic: I swear we won't forget to feed you ever again!